THE REDEMPTION MURDERS

Charles Dickens Investigations
Book Six

J. C. Briggs

SAPERE
BOOKS

THE REDEMPTION
MURDERS

Published by Sapere Books.

20 Windermere Drive, Leeds, England, LS17 7UZ,
United Kingdom

saperebooks.com

ISBN: 978-1-913518-73-8

For Tom Lomax Briggs who told me all about the sea and ships, and who had the bright blue eyes of Tom Lomax, his namesake in this story.

It is a still night ... when the moon shines very brilliantly ... where it mingles with the ever-heaving sea; a still night on the deep, and on the shore where the watcher stands to see the ship with her spread wings cross the path of light...
Charles Dickens, *Bleak House*

It is entered on the ship's log, and that's the truest book a man can write.
Captain Cuttle in *Dombey and Son*

CHARACTERS IN THE SERIES

Charles Dickens
Catherine, his wife
Superintendent Sam Jones of Bow Street
Elizabeth Jones, his wife
Eleanor and Tom Brim, their adopted children
Sergeant Alf Rogers of Bow Street
Mollie, his wife, (formerly Spoon) who runs the stationery shop for Eleanor and Tom Brim, whose father is dead
Scrap, shop assistant, messenger boy, and amateur detective
Constables Stemp and Feak of Bow Street
Fikey Chubb, known fence and criminal

IN THIS NOVEL:
ON *THE REDEMPTION*
Captain Louis Valentine
Pilgrim, his servant
Mark Wilkes, midshipman
George Gammon
Long Jodd
Ben Potter
Ned Carver
Albert Tooth
Tempest Slinger
The Reverend and Mrs Harvey, passengers

ON THE ISLAND OF ST LUCIA
Adam Valentine, plantation owner
Marcus, his son

Peter Best, his agent in London
Raoul Corneille, deceased
Jeremie, his son, in London
Gaspard L'Estrange, in London
Sir Napier Moss, in London

AT ERITH ON THE THAMES
Mrs Grace Fox, fiancée of Captain Valentine
Posthumous, her son
Mrs Pink
Faith and Hope Darling, servants
Shakespeare Tabor, a friend
Tar, the cat

AT LIMEHOUSE
Kit Penney, childhood friend of Dickens
Mrs Penney, his mother
Jam, Kit's dog
Mrs Jennie Slinger, a friend
Percy, her son
Rosanna Chibb
Sampson Meteyard, a butcher
Joe Bean, his assistant
Amelia Meteyard, his wife
Henry Meteyard, his son, barrister of Lincoln's Inn
Mug, the dog
Nick Barley, landlord of The Ship Aground
Mealy, potboy at The Anchor
Silas and Lavender Cly, lodging house keepers
Captain Pye
William Lambert, living on the Isle of Dogs
A farmer and his dog, neighbours of William Lambert

Lilian Twigg, lodging housekeeper
Ada Pitt, her niece
Lizzie Snook, shop assistant
Mary Betts, her landlady
The Reverend George Sax of St Anne's Church

AT BOW LANE
Mrs Judith Black, ship owner
Mrs Skillett, her housekeeper
Joan Speck, a servant

THE RIVER POLICE
Inspector Bold
Constable John Gaunt, godson of Superintendent Jones
Constable Perry
Constable Jack Straw
Sergeant Lorn
Sergeant Cox

AT RED LION SQUARE
Mr Justice Tallis
Mrs Madeleine Tallis, nee Valentine

AT RICHMOND
Mrs Robinson, Jeremie Corneille's aunt
Mrs Landless, her housekeeper
Stephen Winter, Jeremie Corneille's childhood friend
Mrs Pinn, Winter's housekeeper

AT BEVIS MARKS
A boy with a stone for sale
Simic Kaprillian, an Armenian merchant

Mr Riddle, his clerk

ALSO:
Dr Allan Woodhall of King's College Hospital
Mr Ernest Lovelock, solicitor of Symond's Inn
Tom Lomax, his nephew
Daniel Stagg, landlord of The Old Ship
Pips, his pot boy
Marie-Louise, hostess at Kellner's Café
Henry Wills, sub-editor of *Household Words*

PROLOGUE

A man with murder in his heart. A man in a sailor's peacoat. A man on the edge of the river, watching.

He felt the cold. The damp of the cobbled street seeped through his boots, the icy wind seeming to work its way into the very seams of his clothes. He watched the people, their grey faces, their stunted, grimy figures, and he listened to their shouts, their jeers, their crazed laughter. He watched for the face he wanted.

Swarms of men filled the streets, the lodging houses, the taverns where they'd break into coarse, raucous song, drinking until they were well-nigh senseless. In a moment a mood of rollicking geniality would change: song into wild shouting, dancing into brawling, ale into blood, and the filthy, tattered women with their bared, shameless breasts would scrap amongst themselves, tearing out clumps of hair and scratching faces with dirty claws, the men jeering them on then turning on each other. But they hadn't murder in their hearts. It was in the gin, in the rum, in the fists, in the knives they carried, in the broken bottle, in the lump of stone snatched up, in the heat of their mad recklessness.

Murder in the heart. Colder. A calculating thing. The consequences measured and weighed, and found light, the scales dipping in favour of the gains: money, safety, freedom, satisfaction of revenge — that dish best served cold.

The water drew him. He watched the dark vapours of the river rising and the dark tide running strong below him, and the lights of the moored ships reflected crookedly in the water like the eyes of drowned men winking up at him. He heard the slap of the water on the slimy causeway which led to the quay. The bitter wind blew squalls of sleet, rattling in the shrouds of the ships as though even they shivered. Rags of paper blew about his feet — dirty wet notices offering rewards for information about those found drowned.

He thought of a body plunging into the murky depths and never coming up again. But, no, he might come up again. It wasn't easy to drown. You fought for your life — your life, not another's — as he had, once. Take him in an alley? Who would notice? Not those roaring fighting beasts. They'd trample over him to get to their drink. Take him where he lay? Where he slept, perhaps, deep in dreams of far-off lands. A sailor's knife? Quick and silent, sliding through soft flesh. It was nothing.

Whatever he chose, his victim's end would be the same. He would go down into the dark as a man might go down into this black water. And never come up again.

PART I: WRITTEN ON THE WATER

1: THE SEA

Extracts from the Captain's Log of *The Redemption*

28th October. 6.00 a.m.
Set sail from Bombay in calm weather. Fresh north east trades. South across the Arabian Sea.

3rd November. 14° 26'N; 68°47'E
Dense lurid atmosphere, very peculiar appearance at sunset. Dark appearance to north-westward. Wind increasing and drawing to the eastward with thick weather, but always fine when going south. Kept her south. Midnight, from 10 knots ran into a dead calm. Benjamin Potter, deck hand, disappeared during night of calm. Spoke to watch — nothing heard or seen. Spoke to Enoch Jodd who came on board with him. Claimed he knew nothing. Clergyman, Mr Harvey, died in the night. Burial at sea.

28th November. 34° 59'S; 20° 42'E
Evening, southern tip of Africa, Sturis Baai, Cape of Good Hope sighted on starboard quarter. Fair SE winds round the Cape. Picked up Benguelas current. Good speed.

Captain Louis Valentine glanced over the entries he had made in the ship's log over the past month and then looked back up at the view in front of him. The great sails like piled-up white clouds bellied out before the brisk wind. The sea shone under the winter sunlight. Ninety-two days from Bombay with a rich cargo of ivory, indigo, cotton, silks and spices.

Home soon. And Captain Valentine would be glad of it. Three days. They were approaching the English Channel and the weather was fair. Now he looked up from his position on the quarterdeck, watching the sails, feeling the wind. They would be at Portsmouth soon, where most of the passengers would disembark.

The outward voyage had been a good, fast one — eighty-two days to Bombay and nothing to note in the log but fair weather. Captain Valentine loved his ship, a Blackwall frigate, built of English oak and imperishable Malabar teak. He knew her every pitch and roll, the creak and groan of her timbers as if she spoke to him.

He had an uncanny skill for finding fair winds; he was wise to every squall and changing current, every shift of the breeze. His crew trusted him, and he was careful of his midshipmen, the young gentlemen whose careers were to be made, as his had been, at sea. He had been fortunate to begin under a captain who had served the East India Company, a fair man who educated his young gentlemen in navigation and in sea nature. Captain Westlake took dredge and trawl nets to sea and preserved and classified his specimens as carefully as the scientist in his laboratory.

And there were classes in using a palm and needle for splicing and knotting: the Carrick knot to join hawsers; the midshipman's knot — the best if a man was overboard; the Blackwall hitch; the sheepshank to shorten a line, one of the oldest knots — mentioned by Captain John Smith of Virginia in 1627. And the knots for life and death: the surgeon's knot which, pulled tight into a loop, becomes the hangman's knot. And these things he taught his own midshipmen, including the young Mark Wilkes, son of a sailor friend from the early days who had died too soon. And the sailors taught them, too, especially relishing the hangman's knot and telling dreadful tales of men hanged by their own ropes.

But, there was to be no favouritism — discipline was smart. It had to be at sea. All orders were carried out to the tune of the bosun's whistle. The crew had their regular stations and regular drill so that whether the flying jib, or the spanker or a royal or a staysail had to be handed, there was no confusion. The midshipman on the bell was never allowed to leave the lee side of the poop — and when Mark Wilkes had thus offended, he was punished, son of an old friend or no.

But, this return voyage had been hard, heavy with storms and two dead. Valentine was not a superstitious man, but even he had felt the sense of something brooding in the dark skies and rough waters. There had been St Elmo's fire on the top sails. Most sailors were a superstitious lot, believing that the corposant, the pale fire, was created by the souls of drowned sailors trying to board the ship. A sign, they said, a warning. Even Pilgrim, his black servant, had been afraid, despite his captain's reassurances — but Pilgrim had felt, he said, that something was wrong on this their last voyage.

And, out on the Indian Ocean, Valentine, too, had felt dread in the ominous calm that came. Away on the horizon to windward, heavy cloud spread until it became a great swathe of smoking black, as if a vast cauldron were brewing. There were sudden sparks of lightning like sparks from a flint and steel, then blades of lightning slashing the blanket of dark. And he had seen the clouds rent asunder and the waterspout appear. But a fresh wind came, and they sailed on in front of the storm, *The Redemption* tossing and bucking like a frightened horse. But he stilled her, soothed her, his hands on the wheel, taking her south into the calmer straits of the Mozambique Channel.

A lucky escape, but it had been in the ensuing dead calm that Mrs Harvey's husband had died. In Bombay, Captain Valentine had seen that the man was ill — a cadaverous face with a nose as thin as a blade and dark eyes filled with pain. The ship's surgeon had warned him that Harvey would not last the voyage. Valentine knew it, but for the sake of the man's child and his wife, he had taken them.

And a boy overboard — not during that storm-tossed flight from the waterspout, but in that dead calm of the same night. It was inexplicable. Even the boy's closest companion, Enoch Jodd, had been unable to explain — or unwilling.

Long Jodd whom he had taken on, the ship being short of a hand. One of the great cases of spices had swung and knocked George Gammon off his feet. The man had fallen awkwardly, crashing against another crate and broken his leg. So Long Jodd, one of those who hung around the quay at Bombay, looking for a passage home, had volunteered. He'd been about when George Gammon had fallen — tried to push him away from the swinging crate by all accounts. Despite this, Valentine hadn't taken to him. But the lad with him, a poor raggedy thing, had looked so pathetic that Valentine had taken them both. That, Valentine reflected now, had been the beginning of a return voyage somehow uneasy and troubled.

The lad had been a puzzle — supposedly Long Jodd's nephew, who, that hard-faced fellow had explained, had been left in his care by a dying mother, his own sister. Jodd did all the talking. The boy said nothing, but looked at the older man as if his life depended on him. Perhaps it had. Perhaps his death had depended on Jodd, but no one was talking. Only Pilgrim who had told Valentine that he suspected that the boy had been treated cruelly by his so-called uncle. Then he was gone — fallen, jumped, or pushed, perhaps.

Valentine had questioned Jodd. Jodd knew nothing — accident, that's all. But, Valentine had seen the anger in Jodd's eyes when he had told him that there would be an enquiry when they reached London. And he worried about Mark Wilkes's best version of the hangman's knot — of which he had been so proud — which had disappeared in that same dead night.

And there was the matter of the pipes of Madeira wine. It was the custom to stop at Madeira on the outward passage to take up fifty or so pipes of wine to ship out east, reserving a third for home. The long voyages allowed the wine to mature. And there never had been any thieving by his crews. 'Tapping the admiral', the old sailors called it — a hole bored into a pipe and the contents sucked out through a goose quill. There'd been none of that on the voyage out, but it had happened on the return.

Home. Erith by the Thames and a tall house with bow windows. And at one of those windows, Grace would be sitting watching for him. Valentine had been married once; Alice had died while he was at sea on the ship which he had loved better than his wife. That would not happen again. He must give it up.

He had married Alice, the daughter of the shipyard owner, William Black, whose yard was on the river at Blackwall. He hadn't known that he didn't love her until it was too late. She was beautiful — and spoilt, but he had managed, simply because he had been away at sea so often. Black's son, James, he had liked, but he was dead, and the old man. The yard was run by James's widow, Judith, but Valentine had inherited his wife's shares. Judith wanted him to be her partner — in business and more, he knew. But he was going to marry Grace. The little that had passed between him and Judith was over.

They could still be business partners — he hoped, but he wondered, remembering her tight lips and furious eyes from the night before he sailed.

'Let go.' The order to strike the top-maul to release the chain and let the anchor fall. 'Let go.'

2: THE SHORE

Adam Valentine had thought life to be a matter of gain — what you could get for yourself. It was a lesson learnt early, the first time he had grabbed a dirty heel of stale bread from a boy smaller than himself. And that was how he had lived. Take what you want. Any way you want.

But now, near the end, he understood that life was about losing. You counted the losses, not the gains.

He was standing on the shore on the West Indies island of St. Lucia staring out over the glittering sea, deeper blue than the glass dome of the sky. Sparks glinted out there — *jewels*, he thought, the treasure that legend said was buried deep down on the wreck of a Spanish ship. He watched the silver-topped waves roll in, silver scattering silver and pale gold droplets like coins as if some hand were heaving up the treasure. Riches. Well, he'd had those. Ill-gotten gains.

He that is greedy of gain troubleth his own house; but he that hateth gifts shall live — hmm, some mildewed parson, he remembered. Bertram Civil, his name was. Dead of a fever. He remembered the man, yellow as a plant rotting in a cellar, but earnest and civil as his name said. Meant well, but Adam Valentine had merely smiled, looking round the mahogany table shining in the candlelight where the silver and crystal winked, and at his own beautiful wife whom he had loved but to whom he had lied. Well, she was dead, too, of the same fever, and the baby daughter she had given him. Losses. And his house was troubled now — Civil had been right.

The death sentence. 'An enlarged heart,' the doctor had said. He had been surprised at that. He had thought his heart would have shrunk.

The doctor had looked at him impassively. They had never been friends. He'd wanted to ask about the pain, but he hadn't. He was not afraid. There was nothing to hope for. He looked back at his fine house with its veranda where he should be sitting now, enjoying the cool shade, but he didn't want to go in. He didn't want to face the man who was his son. A son who hated him.

He looked back at the glittering water and away to the dark blue line of the horizon where sea met sky. He narrowed his eyes as if for a sign. He thought about a ship sailing from the east to London. A ship called *The Redemption*. Redemption. Did he want that? Not really. Too late. But there were things to be put right. Not for him, but for the woman to whom he had lied.

Marcus Valentine watched his father gazing out to sea. The old bastard. And it wasn't just a figure of speech, he thought. Who knew where his father had come from? He knew only that his father had been brought as a boy from London to St Lucia, adopted by the owner of the *Belle Regarde* Plantation of which Adam Valentine was now the owner, despite the fact that Robert Valentine had had a son of his own. There had been double-dealing — had to have been, for Marcus Valentine knew his father.

Marcus watched his father on the seashore. He knew well what he was up to. He had seen the glint in his father's eye when Marcus had told him that he knew what the doctor had said. But his father would be dead — all his schemes come to nothing, and Marcus would be free.

He thought back over the years to when he'd been a child and his mother was still alive. Not that he could remember much about her. She hadn't cared much for him, it had seemed to him. His father hadn't cared for either of them. He remembered a darkened room where the shutters were always closed and where his mother sat alone, unspeaking, with her hand over her eyes. He remembered nights when he woke and heard screaming and a woman's voice soothing. Once he had stood at the top of the stairs. He'd seen Mrs Etienne Valentine speaking to his father, her hand on his arm, his hand over hers. And then his mother had gone. No one spoke of her again. It was as if that shadow woman, dressed in her white gowns, had never existed, as if she had been extinguished like a candle flame — nothing left but the faint scent of lavender like smoke in the air. And Etienne Valentine had shot himself. A year later, Mrs Etienne had married Adam Valentine, who favoured her two children over the son of the forgotten woman whose dark face still haunted his dreams.

Marcus watched his father raise his hand to shade his eyes. He was looking out to sea, but there was nothing to be seen. Yet, there had been a ship, *The Endeavour*. Marcus had watched her sail out of the harbour, bound for London. And he knew that there was a package for his stepbrother, Captain Louis Valentine, to be delivered by his father's messenger, Peter Best.

Marcus Valentine looked out to the sea. So, *The Endeavour* was sailing to London. Well, so was *The Pursuit* — apt name — carrying his own man, the man who needed his favour — the man who wanted what he believed Adam Valentine had stolen from him.

In London, *The Redemption* sails into the great, wide estuary of the Thames: Queen's Channel; Five-Fathom Channel; flood tide; round by the Norelight; Shoeburyness; Sheerness; The Isle of Grain. Now the estuary narrows: Canvey Island; into Sea Reach; Lower Hope Reach; Gravesend; Tilbury; Greenhithe; Erith. In sight of a house with a bow window and a woman and a boy watching.

'It is. It is!' cries the small boy with a spyglass too heavy for his thin arms.

Grace Fox takes it gently from him and looks for herself. 'It is.' She smiles. 'He is home.'

At last, thought Grace, at last, and never again would she have to wait for endless months. Louis Valentine had said that he would not sail again. He knew that she fretted for him, afraid of wild seas, crashing storms, of pirates, of treacherous coasts, of fever and the thousand natural shocks that flesh is heir to. Her first husband had died; she could not stand to lose him, too, and he loved her enough to let go. And he loved the little boy who stood now with his hand over his forehead, watching, watching, until the ship disappeared, its masts glinting in the evening light. A glorious sunset, the sky barred with crimson and violet, and the river afire with glittering gold. And this shall be a sign. She would sleep tonight.

Judith Black was watching for *The Redemption*, too. Soon Louis would be back, and she meant to deal with him, to make him face the truth.

Judith Black had been brought up in the port of King's Lynn. Her mother, Mary Jane Clarke, owned two ships and was the managing owner in charge of all the shore-based business and accounts. And Mary Jane had taught her daughter everything. Judith was to inherit half of everything with her brother, John — half-brother. But Judith wanted more than half.

Mary Jane had understood. She knew her high tempered daughter and had given Judith the money. Judith would make her own way — beauty and money were advantages enough. 'Go to London,' Mary Jane had said. 'You'll do well there. Marry into business. Marry money.'

So Judith had gone to London to live with an aunt, the widow of an East India Company commander. Judith met the Blacks, who owned and built ships. Old Mr Black admired Judith Clarke, and not only for her beauty; he knew her history and it was his delight to engineer her meetings with his son. James Black was never well. What he needed, his father determined, was a strong wife who could manage him and his business affairs. He looked at glowing Judith. They'd have children, a sturdy son who would have his mother's brains and inherit the ships and the yard.

But old Mr Black died before there was any son. As did James Black. Judith gave evidence of his wasting sickness, his melancholia, his despair. Doctor Stephens, their neighbour, gave his medical evidence, and the coroner had looked at the beautiful grieving widow and directed the jury. Suicide.

Judith thought about her dead sister-in-law, Alice. Judith had raged at her own childlessness when Alice was pregnant. James Black was no husband. James Black could not do her bidding in their bed. God knows, she had tried, and she had been humiliated.

But Alice and the child died, too. So many deaths and not one she regretted. For more than ten years she had run this business. She understood it all. She was, although a woman, a ship's husband, the term used for the ships' managing owners.

The accounts, the insurance, the shareholders, the cargoes, the customs — all at her fingertips.

She did not love Louis Valentine, but she had planned to marry him. A son must inherit. And then Louis Valentine had announced his intended marriage to Grace Fox, who already had a son. She had wept — not that she meant it. She knew his tender heart. He had comforted her. But, he had pledged himself to Grace. Well, he must be made to change his mind.

PART II: WRITTEN ON THE HEART

3: BLACKWALL REACH

The Redemption lay at anchor in Blackwall Reach under the black sky. Her sails were furled — great wings folded. The thick, oily water lapped against the ship's side and there was the faint ringing of metal chains, and sometimes the timbers creaked as if she breathed in her sleep.

On board, Constable Perry of the Thames River Police took a white-faced boy and a sailor on crutches to another cabin, leaving Inspector James Bold and Constable John Gaunt to contemplate the body of the ship's captain, Louis Valentine. He lay where he had fallen, stabbed in the soft part of the neck. Surprise attack? It would have been quick, thought John Gaunt. But, it was odd — no sign of robbery. That's what you'd expect. There were all sorts of thieves on the river.

Inspector Bold was looking round the cabin. He saw the open boxes, the clothes ready to be packed stacked neatly on the bunk, a parcel neatly tied with string. He went over to look. One box had books in it, another some nautical instruments which he recognised, and beneath them a leather pouch in which there were a pair of compasses, a bodkin and a sailor's folding knife which he opened. No sign of blood. A seaman's knife in a leather sheath, but clean, and a dagger with an ebony handle. The killer had, no doubt, taken his weapon with him. All sailors carried knives — and they were often used in the number of brawls on shore, usually involving drink or women, or both. *The murder weapon could be at the bottom of the river by now*, he thought gloomily, or in some lodging house, or in someone else's pocket. Tidy man, the captain, everything well-kept and neatly stowed.

'Nothing disturbed. The lad'll have to come back when he's ready. I need to know if there was any money — a cash box, a pocketbook or something which might have been taken. There's money in the captain's pocket. Why didn't they take that?'

'Could there be some other motive? After all, the ship had been unloaded. There were no pickings —'

'But there are the tier-rangers. Get aboard an unloaded ship in the middle of the night, knowing that there'll be hardly anyone aboard, pick up the valuables from the captain's cabin and any other loose, portable items, watches, rings from other cabins and get off, quiet as you like. Rat catchers, bumboatmen, light horsemen — any of 'em could sneak aboard.'

'But they don't usually murder, and the captain's watch and money are still on him.'

'True. You're thinking someone intended to murder him for reasons we don't yet know.' Inspector Bold looked back at the body. 'Well, we need to find out who didn't like him — and that usually means somebody in the crew. We'll question George Gammon about that. Let's do it next door.'

John Gaunt turned to go. Then he noticed something odd, something out of place in that otherwise tidy cabin where the captain lay dead and where his clothes were neatly folded, ready to be packed into the sea chest.

'Inspector — the book. That's odd.' He pointed to where a book had been flung to lie face down, its pages open, its spine cracked. He went over to look at it. He recognised the green cloth binding and the gilt lettering. He had one just like it.

The Inspector glanced at the book. 'Leave it now. Let's go and ask our questions.'

Mark Wilkes, the midshipman who had found the captain's body, and George Gammon were waiting. Gaunt felt sorry for the boy whose face was white as paper and whose eyes were red from weeping.

Inspector Bold didn't mince his words. 'I need to know about the crew — who might have wanted to harm the captain? Did anything happen on your voyage home that might have led to this? Mr Gammon?'

Gammon told him about the storm, the night of dead calm, the deaths of the clergyman and of the boy, Ben Potter, and Jodd's resentment of the captain because the captain had said the boy's death must be reported to the ship's owner in London. 'An' Jodd thought the cap'n was suggestin' 'e'd been up ter somethin'. Anyway, Jodd kept tellin' anyone who'd listen that the cap'n oughter keep 'is mouth shut, an' Pilgrim —' He stopped suddenly, as if he had remembered something important.

'Go on, man — who's this Pilgrim?'

'Well, that's it, sir, I've only just thought — Pilgrim should be 'ere, on board. 'E'd not 'ave been gone all night. Why, 'e'd not 'ave been gone at all. I can't understand it.'

'But who is Pilgrim?'

'Sorry, sir — Pilgrim's the cap'n's servant. Been with 'im ferever — came from St. Lucia where the cap'n came from.'

'Black?' George Gammon nodded. 'And he's missing.'

Something in the Inspector's tone reached Mark Wilkes, who spoke suddenly. 'No, sir, it wouldn't be Pilgrim. He was devoted to the Captain. We all were.' The boy wept again.

Somebody wasn't, thought John Gaunt, but he didn't say anything.

'Let's get this straight, Mr Gammon — Long Jodd possibly had reason to harm the captain, and the missing man, Pilgrim, knew something about Jodd and this boy, Potter.'

'Pilgrim told me that 'e thought the lad was frightened of Jodd, but the lad wouldn't say anythin'. So, it was jest suspicion. Nothin' ter be proved, an' then the lad vanished in the night — overboard an' no one saw anythin' — leastways no one said anythin'.'

'You don't think this Pilgrim saw?'

'No, sir, 'e'd 'ave said — ter the captain — no reason not ter.'

'No idea where Pilgrim might be?'

'No, sir.'

'And you, Mr Wilkes?'

'I don't. Pilgrim stayed with the captain — always when they were ashore.'

'And where would that be?'

'At Erith, Vernon House — 'is lady lives there,' Gammon put in.

'And, Mr Gammon, where am I likely to find Long Jodd and any other of your crew?'

'Some'll be likely at 'ome — I knows where some of 'em lives. Some'll get lodgin's — could be anywheres round the docks. Some might still be drinkin'.'

Needle in a haystack, thought Bold. 'This Long Jodd — what about him?'

'Dunno, sir, but pally with Ned Carver. Might be with 'im. Carver's brother-in-law keeps a tavern, The Ship Aground, at the end of Blackwall Causeway, not far from the Old Dock. Some o' the others might be there. Albert Tooth an' them as wot were in with Long Jodd.'

Bold knew Nick Barley — Old Nick, they called him — a devil when roused, but decent enough. Not known for anything beyond the usual rough stuff — brawls, whores, some shady dealing, but nothing really criminal, and he had pointed them in the way of a brute who'd murdered his whore. He could handle himself could Old Nick, and he wouldn't stand for murder. If Long Jodd were to be found, Old Nick Barley would give them information, brother-in-law or no brother-in-law.

'I know it,' Bold said. 'And where do I find you if I want you again?'

'My brother's comin' ter fetch me. I'll be at 'ome in Cottage Row, 'ouse next ter the chapel — my wife's there an' the kids.'

'And, Mr Wilkes, what about you?'

The boy's eyes filled. 'The captain was to take me to the train this afternoon to go home — I'm going home to Rochester to my mother.' The tears spilled over.

'Right. Is there anyone else you can stay with for the time being? I'll need to speak to you again.'

'Mrs Tallis — that's the captain's sister. She lives in Red Lion Square. I know her. I could go there.'

'I'll take you. I'll need to see Mrs Tallis. She'll have to be told about her brother. Now, you two, just wait here while my constable and I see to a few things. Gaunt, next door.'

They went back into the captain's cabin. Gaunt stepped over to where the book lay. He picked it up. He was curious and he felt pity for the man who had been quietly reading while someone came into the cabin — he must have heard and stood. Perhaps to greet someone he knew — Long Jodd? The missing Pilgrim?

Bold was speaking. 'I'll have to take the lad and see the sister, Mrs Tallis — break the news. In the meantime — Gaunt, are you listening?'

'Yes, Sir, sorry, Sir, it's just that —'

'Never mind the damned book. Listen to what I want you to do. Perry's sorting out the removal of the body and bringing the surgeon. I want you to wait until he comes back. I want that boy off the ship before the business with the body. While you're waiting, get some addresses off George Gammon. Then I want you to get over to that tavern with some more constables and I want you to find this Long Jodd and Ned Carver and keep 'em there until I come. If Long Jodd isn't there, then find out from Nick Barley whether he might be with Carver. After we've got those two, you can go to find some of the others. Don't forget the black man, Pilgrim. You got all that?' He was impatient. What the devil was Gaunt about with that book?

'Yes, Sir, but, the book, Sir, it's odd, it isn't the captain's.'

'What? Whose is it?'

'There's an inscription. It's written to someone called Kit and the signature is that of Charles Dickens.'

Gaunt looked at the open page and read the words: '*To Kit, the original. For all that we were. Yours very affectionately, Charles Dickens.*'

'What does it mean "the original"?'

'Well, Kit is the name of one of the characters in the book. It's *The Old Curiosity Shop*. Kit must be a friend of Charles Dickens. It says "For all that we were" — he must have known him a long time. Why would it be here? You'd not give away a book from Charles Dickens. I wouldn't. I've got the same book signed by him. Superintendent Jones, my godfather, gave it to me. I wouldn't part with it.'

'So, what's it doing here? This Kit — knew the captain, maybe? And, was he here tonight? We'll need to find him.'

'It's strange, though, Sir. I mean, if he was here, why's the book thrown down like that?'

'Quarrel?'

'Could be. The murderer maybe grabbed it and threw it down, or —'

'No use speculating. If he was here, he has questions to answer. We'll ask Gammon and the boy if they know who he is. Get them back in. I want them to have another look and to ask about any cash box.'

John Gaunt brought them back. Bold had covered the body with a sheet and stood in front of it so that the boy would not see too much. He showed them the inscription, but neither knew anything of a friend called Kit.

'And no one came on board before you all turned in. No visitors?'

Neither Gammon nor Mark Wilkes had seen or heard anyone on board before midnight. Mark Wilkes and the captain had dined at a tavern nearby. Pilgrim and George Gammon had stayed on board — too much trouble to leave the ship — his leg, he explained, and he was adamant that he had seen no one.

'I want to know if the captain had a cash box — any large sums of money that could have been taken.'

George Gammon answered. 'The men was paid after we unloaded, an' yesterday the captain went ter the bank with the rest. I do know that.'

'Sir.' Mark Wilkes sounded anxious.

'What is it?'

'The boxes, sir, they're open — and his clothes on the bunk. Captain Valentine had already packed — he told me to do the same. He wouldn't have left it till the morning. He wanted everything to be ready.'

''E's right, sir,' George Gammon put in. ''E told me the same. "All packed up for the last time" — that's what 'e said.'

'The last time?' Bold asked.

'Swallowin' the anchor.'

'Giving up the sea?' Bold knew the term.

'Aye — gettin' wed ter the lady at Erith.'

'You're both absolutely sure that everything was packed?'

They had no doubt. The boxes had been closed. It was quite clear that someone had been in — someone looking for something. That raised a whole lot of questions for Bold: who wanted something so badly that he would kill? And what was it, if it wasn't money? And had he found it?

'Did he have anything valuable — other than money, I mean?' Bold asked.

Mark Wilkes and George Gammon looked blank. *They wouldn't know if anything was missing*, Bold thought. Louis Valentine was the captain — his possessions were private.

Gaunt took them back to the other cabin to wait. When he came back, Inspector Bold was looking at the open boxes.

'A tidy thief,' he said. 'I don't understand it. Everything neatly put back in the boxes, apart from the clothes. And including the captain's knives. What was he looking for?'

'Papers? Whoever did it had his own weapon? Long Jodd, maybe — something written down that implicated him in the death of that lad they told us about.'

'Captain's logbook — check if it's there.'

Gaunt looked in the box of books. 'Here.'

'Right, let's see what it says about Jodd.' Inspector Bold looked through the logbook. 'Gammon said they were still out in the Indian Ocean, so that takes us back some time. Let's see.' He turned the pages quickly and then read aloud: '*3rd November — dense lurid atmosphere, very peculiar appearance at sunset. Dark appearance to north-westward. Wind increasing and drawing to the eastward with thick weather, but always fine when going south. Kept her south. Midnight, from 10 knots ran into a dead calm* — just as Gammon said — now, this is what we want — *Benjamin Potter, deck hand, disappeared during night of calm. Spoke to watch — nothing heard or seen. Spoke to Enoch Jodd, who came on board with him. Claimed he knew nothing. Clergyman, Mr Harvey, died in the night. Burial at sea.*'

'Nothing there to provoke murder, surely — the captain doesn't make any accusation. What about the clergyman? Anything odd there?'

Bold turned the page. 'There's something written here: *This is to certify that the undermentioned passenger embarked from Bombay in the ship "The Redemption" under Captain Valentine, died on the voyage. Percival Harvey died 24th October at sea — consumption.* The surgeon has signed this. Nothing suspicious there, I shouldn't think. So, what was our murderer looking for?'

'Perhaps Captain Valentine wrote in more detail in private papers — something about Jodd and the boy,' Gaunt wondered.

'Whatever it was, it was important — important enough for our murderer to go very carefully through all the captain's possessions. He knew what he was looking for, and that tells us it wasn't someone who came on board on the off-chance, which makes it easier for us in the sense that we'll not be combing the wharves for a gang of water rats.'

'It was someone who knew him — knew about him, knew that he was here.'

'Which brings us to Long Jodd, the missing Black man, and to our Mr Kit.'

'I could go to see Mr Dickens — I've met him with Superintendent Jones.'

'All right — when you go back to the station, get Sergeant Lorn to organise the searches for Jodd and Carver then get off to see Mr Dickens. I'd like to find this Kit.'

'Would it be all right if I asked Superintendent Jones to come with me — he knows Mr Dickens very well and —'

'Smooth your path, eh? All right — you can tell the superintendent all about it if you want. I shan't mind. Now, let's get on.'

4: DARK WATER

When troubles come, they come not single spies — but in battalions, so Charles Dickens thought. Not that he had much sympathy with Claudius, the murderer of his brother, old Hamlet. Nevertheless, troubles came too many just now. Little Dora, his baby girl, so delicate, and with that ill-omened name — *Dora*, David Copperfield's wife whom he had killed. And Catherine so unwell with her headaches and dizziness — what was he to do for her? And then there was the worry of finding another house. The lease on Devonshire Terrace would end soon — Devonshire Terrace had been his home since 1839 — and he had been happy here. The years of his success. He had a kind of foreboding that leaving it would herald some change — and not for the better.

And Fred, his brother, continued to rasp his heart with demands for money to pay his debts. He had already sent £150 to Mr Widger to pay for Fred's furniture and now, it seemed, more money was needed if Mr Widger were to be prevented from harrying Fred at his office at the treasury. Why couldn't he live within his means? He had warned Fred when he married that what would follow would be a drudging life with butchers, bakers, landlords, tax gatherers, debt collectors of every kind coming round as regularly as stars in the sky. Fred ought to have known from their own experience as children — strangers on the steps, in the hall, at the windows, all wanting the money that their father owed — and where did it end? In the Marshalsea Prison. But then Fred knew that his brother would not let that come to pass. *Pay up then*, he told himself. But he looked out at the gloomy January afternoon.

Escape, that's what he wanted. Escape from himself and from London — a vile place with its great heavy canopy lowering on the housetops. Paris, perhaps? That might do it. Anything to escape. He felt feeble and guilty somehow. He knew he ought to be innocently merry, and happy, especially with his wife and children. Why was he always looking out at the back windows of life? And he was ashamed of his causeless rages and demoniacal gloom. A blight on his house, he was. Get to work. Pen to paper.

But the door to his office in Wellington Street opened and there was Superintendent Sam Jones, and behind him, someone else he knew. John Gaunt.

'Sam, this is a surprise, and, as I live and breathe, Johnno Gaunt. Come in, come in.'

John Gaunt laughed — Mr Dickens always called him Johnno after John of Gaunt whose palace had been on the Strand, barely a step from Wellington Street. His father had taken him there once to look at the old palace walls which were still standing. Perhaps, his father had said, their Gaunts were descendants of the great Duke who had ruled England as regent when Richard II was just a child. John had believed it. Not now.

'Not disturbing you, I hope,' Jones said.

'No, no, I was just brooding on my ills, and here you are to take me out of myself —' Dickens stopped, seeing Jones's serious expression — 'but, by your face, this is not good news.'

'A sea captain has been murdered on his ship, *The Redemption*—'

'Louis Valentine!'

'You knew him?' Jones asked.

'Slightly — I met him once — but what has this to do with me?'

'This was found in the cabin where he was killed — thrown on the floor. John Gaunt offered the book to Dickens, who looked at him questioningly. 'It is inscribed to someone called Kit and signed by you.'

Dickens looked at Jones and then at John Gaunt. 'And?'

'I wondered why the book would be in the captain's cabin, and who is Kit? And was he on the ship last night?'

'I'll tell you who he is, but before I say anything more — Kit Penney cannot be the murderer. He cannot. He is one of my oldest friends.'

'Charles —'

'No, Sam, no —' Dickens was fired up — 'I won't hear of it.'

'Charles, no one is saying that your old friend has anything to do with it, but John needs to know who Kit is and his relationship to Captain Valentine. He needs to know about the captain and if your friend can tell us anything about last night.'

Jones's tone was firm. Dickens heard it. Jones never jumped to conclusions, but he was a policeman. Their partnership was so close that Dickens sometimes forgot that Jones had a professional life that went on beyond their friendship and joint investigations. He looked at him and saw that steady gaze and firmness of purpose on which he had so often relied.

'Sorry Sam, and Johnno — forgive my hastiness. You'll understand when I tell you about Kit. Sit down, both of you. A drink? I've some brandy here.'

John Gaunt looked at Jones. No time for drinks.

'I'm sorry, Charles, but we need your friend's address. John just wants to find out about Louis Valentine and whether Kit had been there last night. If you would —'

'I see.' Johnno looked uncomfortable. 'No, Johnno, I do see. It is murder and you must interview the victim's friend — Kit was Captain Valentine's friend. I will stress that. Might I come with you?'

Jones made the decision. 'We'll all go, and you can tell us about Kit on the way. Where will we find him?'

'At his shop in Limehouse — Gun lane. Kit makes and repairs nautical instruments.'

'Right. John has a police galley waiting at Waterloo Bridge to take him to Limehouse.'

The four-oared Thames Police galley waited at the steps of Waterloo pier, rising and falling on the dark water. Two River Police constables waited, hunched up in their thick peacoats. The river was swollen and the tide running fast so that their journey to Limehouse would be speedy. John Gaunt tucked himself in beside one of the constables and took an oar from him. Dickens and Jones huddled together on the seat in the stern facing the wind. They could talk there.

There was something like dread in his heart, Dickens felt, as the galley pulled off. Perhaps it was the east wind, carrying its stinging particles from marsh and moor and fen, or just the blackness. In this late afternoon, every colour but black seemed to be departing from the world. The river was thick black. The heavy barges coming against the tide were slow as a funeral procession and the rushing, gurgling sound of the water seemed to carry suggestions of drowning. But Captain Valentine had not drowned, it seemed, and Kit might have been on board. He shivered.

'Cold?' asked Jones.

'Not especially. Just thinking of the captain. How did he die?'

'Stabbed in the neck. He had fallen to the floor. From the way he fell, Bold believes he was standing when he was attacked. Heard someone come in, most likely.'

'Then it can't be Kit Penney.'

'Why?'

'He wasn't strong enough. Good heavens, stab a man as tall as the captain and as strong. Never! I'll tell you about him, then you'll know.'

'I want to know, but, first, what about you?'

'Back there? Sorry, Sam — just an accumulation of worries. Our little girl, Dora, is not well. I don't know — she seems so fragile, so different from all those chopping boys clattering about the house. And Catherine...'

Jones waited. Dickens didn't speak much of his wife. Jones had met her. He had thought she was a sweet woman, with a pretty round face and ringlets. She had seemed good-natured if rather quiet, but then who wouldn't be with Charles Dickens as her husband? It couldn't be easy for her. But, there was something. Elizabeth, his wife, thought so, too. Their own relationship was so close, so loving that they couldn't help but sense that there was something wanting in Dickens, something missing somewhere.

But Dickens said no more about her, observing with a grin, 'Though I can bear a great deal, I am not a camel, if I know my own self.'

'A dromedary neither,' said Jones. That was Dickens. He'd change the mood, become one of his own characters, conceal himself behind a mask. He could be Mrs Gamp, Sam Weller, now Susan Nipper and her camel. But who was Charles Dickens? They were friends, but there was much hidden, Jones guessed — knew. No matter. Charles Dickens needed him to be Sam Jones whom he could trust to listen to his account of his friend. 'Tell me about Kit Penney.'

'I've known him for years. As a child I used to visit my godfather, Christopher Huffam, who was a rigger for the Navy and a ship's chandler. He lived in Church Row and had his shop and works in Garford Street. He was kind to me — a godfather who knew his duty and did it — to the tune of half a crown on many occasions. I loved going there with my father, roaming about the wharves, looking in the shop windows, peering in at the ropeyards and watching the great ships go out. Kit and I were friends — his father knew Christopher Huffam and had his own marine store which Kit now runs. He lives above the shop with his dog. Kit would have loved to go to sea, but he was a little lad with a club foot — he couldn't have dealt with that hard life. And he's small still, Sam, a little, open-faced, generous, loyal man who would not, physically *could not*, kill a man — let alone a man who was his friend.'

'And when John sees for himself, he will know, as I do —' Jones touched Dickens's arm — 'that the man you are describing is not the murderer of his friend. But, we shall need to see him to find out about the captain. What do you know of him?'

'Not much — I met Louis Valentine just the once last year. I'd gone to see Kit in March. We always went to eat whitebait at the Brunswick Tavern. Kit brought the captain. An appealing man, thirty-five or so in age, I thought, and a gentleman. He had been born in St Lucia, but had come to school in England as a boy and then went to sea. Loved it, and his ship, but, you know, there was something melancholy about him, as if there were some sadness in his past. I don't know — just an impression. He lived, or lodged rather, at a house in Erith where the young woman he was to marry lived. Oh, this is dreadful — murdered. What else did Johnno tell you?'

'It seems that a young midshipman found him this morning. The ship was to be towed to a yard in Blackwall for repairs.

The crew, bar the captain, the midshipman and a sailor with a broken leg, are dispersed. John's Inspector Bold is pursuing them, of course. The murder took place between midnight when the midshipman went to his cabin and six in the morning.'

'You don't know if Kit was on board?'

'Not before midnight — at least the boy and the sailor hadn't seen him.'

'Unlikely Kit would be there *after* midnight.'

'True, but you can see why Inspector Bold is interested.'

'The book — Kit could have lent it. Louis Valentine was his friend. It's probably as simple as that. In any case, there must be dozens of possibilities. Anyone could have got on board.'

'Water-thieves — I know. Scuffle-hunters, rat catchers — the usual river scum after anything they can get — often after a ship has been unloaded. They sneak on board, usually after money and anything valuable, watches, rings, silver. They do it in the dead of night when the skeleton crew — most often the captain and a couple of others — are asleep and slip away again on their own boat. But, Charles, Inspector Bold and John know this, and the thing is that water-thieves don't often murder a victim.'

'The captain might have put up a fight.'

'There doesn't seem to be evidence of that — and nothing stolen, as far as John knows. No, it's someone who had a motive other than robbery. Apparently, the captain's man — name of Pilgrim — is missing.'

'Louis Valentine spoke of him — great friends, they were. I met him after our dinner at Blackwall. Pilgrim came from St. Lucia — had been with him for years. He could hardly be a suspect.'

'Everyone's a suspect, Charles, even you were, once.'

'I know, I remember it only too well.' In a previous case, it had been Charles Dickens who had been suspected of murder. He remembered Inspector Hardacre of Manchester who had entertained some grave doubts about Dickens's relationship with the dead man, and who had looked at him with eyes that glinted like quartz and pierced right through him.

'That's murder for you. It taints everyone — even the innocent. Murder is the stone cast onto the waters, the ripples rolling outwards to the very edge of the lake, and even those at that edge feel the cold touch of the water.'

'Very poetic, Sam, and true, for you, for me, and now for Kit — and Pilgrim.'

'And the fact that he is missing from the ship means that Inspector Bold will wonder why.'

'I know — and I should know. We've been in enough cases.'

'So, let's get your Kit eliminated first, then we can leave it to Inspector Bold and John. You can tell him what you know about Pilgrim.'

They fell silent then, watching the rolling river. They had left Waterloo Bridge behind, had passed the Temple Stairs, and were approaching the frowning Blackfriars Bridge. Sometimes in the dusk there was a flash of light — a duty boat in which an Inspector of the River Police would be on watch. Then came Southwark Bridge and the swirling tide of London Bridge. A collection of sharp-bowed steamers and clippers lay at Fresh Wharf to pick up cargo and passengers. The boats known as Billy-Boys at a trading wharf. Fishing smacks and Dutch eel-boats at Billingsgate.

The great bulk of the Customs House, then the Tower of London and Traitor's Gate — what treacherous creature had stolen into Captain Valentine's cabin in the quiet of the night, armed with a knife? The man who had taken that on board had intended murder, surely. Someone who knew the captain, someone who hated him. But who might have hated that pleasant, if somewhat sad young man?

They passed St Katharine's steam packet wharf from where the continental steamers sailed to Hamburg and Antwerp on the morning tide and into the Pool of London, the river banks bristling with shipping, great tiers of tarred hulls which seemed to Dickens to rise out of the water like black streets. Timber droghers from the Baltic, wine ships from Portugal, Baltimore clippers, West Indiamen, East Indiamen, Gravesend packets, and Geordie brigs unloading coal. Behind loomed the great warehouses packed with goods brought from the great world beyond.

And then they were at Wapping Stairs and the station house where John Gaunt was to leave a message for Inspector Bold, telling him that he, Superintendent Jones, and Mr Dickens were going to Gun Lane in search of Mr Kit Penney, whose book had been found in the cabin where Captain Louis Valentine had been murdered.

5: LIMEHOUSE

The cab took them through a maze of streets choked with wagons and carts and crammed with lodging houses, ancient taverns, small manufactories, sail-makers, sack-makers, and hundreds of odd little shops with little windows with circles in them like dirty eyes winking tearfully at them when lights flickered within, and all packed with goods hanging from poles and doorposts. *Well might they weep*, thought Dickens. Surely there could not be sufficient customers for all those sea-boots, sea chests, oilskins, curiously fashioned sailors' hats and caps, enormous canvas trousers that must have been made from sails or were sails, pilot coats and peacoats, quadrants, sextants, biscuits and baskets — in short enough stores for a man to sail into eternity?

But then, the crowds of sailors made him think again as their cab waited behind a stacked cart. All manner of men congregated here: the swarthy Lascars, the slight Chinese men, men with skin as black as ebony, the pale haired Finns, tattooed arms, ears with rings in them, a hand with two fingers missing, a face with the scar of a cutlass across the cheek, and there, darting into an alley, a man with a dark face whose scared eyes caught his for a moment as he passed under a gas lamp. Everywhere, the noise of a thousand different voices and the smell of tar and rope and tobacco and spices, and always the smell of the river, and the salt sting of the wind which brought the tide surging in from the distant sea.

The cab took them up Old Gravel Lane, over the swing bridge, past the London Docks with their great tea and tobacco warehouses, along High Street to Broad Street then turned towards the river again into Narrow Street where the quaint old houses leant out to the river.

He and Kit had played here on the muddy shore, just below the crazy old tavern. This was where Sir Walter Raleigh had sailed to the New World. They had been him, jumping on and off half-sunk barges, keeping their eyes out for treasure — doubloons was a word to be rolled round the mouth — though quantities of rusty nails were mostly the riches dug up. And the emeralds and diamonds turned out to be bits of broken bottle, but there was the consolation of believing that the bones were those of the pirates once hanged at nearby Executioner's Dock.

They had watched the ships going out, imagining their sails unfolding when they reached the sea, imagining the huge waves rising and falling, the wild winds whistling and howling, and the great ships riding the waves, timbers and masts straining and creaking, towards the lands beyond, to India, to China, and to America — where he had been and Kit had not.

The cab stopped. They were at the junction of Three Colt Street and Gun Lane. A step or two would take them to Kit's shop, and Kit could tell them what he knew of Captain Louis Valentine.

But he could not, for to Dickens's disappointment there was no sign of life or light — the shop appeared to be closed.

Then they saw that the door was partly open. Something of that dread which Dickens had felt on the river returned. He glanced at Jones. John Gaunt stepped forward and pushed cautiously at the door. Dickens and Jones followed him in.

The shop looked exactly the same to Dickens. He had loved the place as a boy, watching Mr Penney's subtle fingers working on the instruments. Mr Penney dealt in maps, too, and globes which he and Kit had spun gently and then traced with their fingers voyages across the world. Kit's hands were like his father's, small and neat with fine fingers made for fine work. Not the hands that had taken a knife to plunge into his friend's neck.

Gaunt's bull's-eye lamp caught the gleaming brass of the various instruments Kit dealt in — spyglasses, chronometers, compasses, levels, gauges, balances, sand glasses and lanterns. Mahogany boxes gleamed and glass winked back at them from the pictures of old ships on the walls, from lenses and bottles, and from a pair of spectacles left on the counter — the spectacles that Kit used for close work on the navigational instruments.

All was quiet. And in that silence, Dickens felt the emptiness of absence. Kit had gone. Not just gone out, but *gone*. Dickens knew it when he saw the spectacles and beside them the dismantled chronometer. It was as if Kit had stopped work, walked out of his door, leaving it unlocked, and vanished into the night.

They looked in the empty parlour behind the shop and climbed up the staircase so narrow and steep it might have been the companion way up to the deck of a ship, but there was no Kit in any of the tiny rooms — and no dog.

'What's out the back?' asked John Gaunt when they went back down to the parlour.

'A yard and alleyway,' Dickens replied.

The second door of the parlour was open, too, and out they went into the small yard the door of which was wide open. Gaunt's lamp showed a tidy yard, boxes and crates stacked neatly. The open door led into the narrow alley, which was empty. Voices came from a yard opposite, the door of which bore the legend: *Sampson Meteyard and Son, butchers*. A dog barked.

'Could he have gone visiting? Just slipped across the alley with the dog?'

'All the doors open, Sam?' Dickens could imagine Kit leaving the back door open, but the shop door? 'It doesn't make sense.'

No, thought Jones, unless you thought that Kit had vanished for a reason — a reason connected to Captain Valentine's death. But he didn't say anything. It was clear from his face that Dickens was thinking the same. He said briskly, 'Let's try the butcher — see if Kit's there or if he knows where Kit is.'

6: DOG-WATCH

John Gaunt knocked sharply on the wooden door. In response the dog barked. It was a deep, hollow sound suggestive of something large and not very welcoming. It certainly wasn't Jam, Kit's dog, Dickens knew. Jam with his lopsided grin and foolish tail, his high-pitched bark that meant nothing but that he was happy.

'The watchdog's honest bark,' murmured Dickens.

As if in reply, the dog barked again and Gaunt knocked again.

'Go round the front, John, see if you can rouse anyone.'

'That's not Kit's dog. I know his bark.'

'But he might be with them. Is Meteyard a friend of Kit's?'

'He is. And so is his son — not a butcher, by the way, despite the sign on the door. The son's a barrister at Lincoln's Inn.'

'Henry Meteyard? I've met him. Sensible sort — always genial.'

'That's Henry. Good-hearted people, all of them. The sign belongs to a time when Sampson thought he might have a butcher son. He once engaged a boy called Slaughter with a view to making him a partner — liked the sound of it. He's a humorous cove.'

'No Slaughter now?'

'Only the usual kind —' Dickens grinned — 'a disappointment, it seems, young Slaughter, a thin rail of a lad, inclined to tears. Sampson had to let him go. Became a vegetarian, I heard.'

Jones laughed. 'Get out with you.'

'It might be true.'

'Aye — if you were writing it.'

'Bean's his assistant now, but, alas for him, there'll not be a partnership. Meteyard told me — he couldn't have stood it, he said, Meteyard and Bean. What's in a name, eh, Mr Jones?'

They heard the sound of bolts being drawn back. A voice hushed the dog, which had barked again. 'Keep him quiet, lad.'

The door opened to reveal Sampson Meteyard, a huge man — in Biblical terms, he had the belly of an ox. He held up a lantern the better to see them. They saw John Gaunt behind him and in the shadows, the outline of a very large dog held by an indistinct figure, but another large one.

Meteyard's face split into a large smile. 'Charley Dickens, good evening to you. The constable, here, says you're lookin' for Kit.'

Charley, thought Jones. Another version of Charles Dickens — the lad who had haunted the alleys and wharves of Limehouse with his friend, Kit. He saw how fondly the huge man looked down at Dickens.

'It is good to see you Sampson. Yes, we are looking for Kit — this is Superintendent Jones of Bow Street — we've been in the shop, but Kit's not there. We wondered if you'd seen him.'

'Evenin', Mr Jones — Henry's mentioned you. Come in, both.'

Dickens and Jones went into the yard. The dog growled, a low rumbling sound that seemed to come from deep within him.

'He's new,' observed Dickens.

'From a man who couldn't pay his bill. Fair exchange. I'm fond of him, and we've plenty of meat. Be quiet, you foolish beast. Don't mind him, gentlemen, soft with friends, he is, but

51

he knows he's big an' he thinks he has to keep remindin' us. He earns his keep — the bark puts off any thieves.'

'I should think it does. You haven't seen Jam, have you?'

'No, I haven't, Charley, but come in, come in.'

They went through the yard into the back kitchen of the house and sat down at a huge, scrubbed pine table. Dickens had been in here before. He had thought as a boy that the table could seat a party of giants at a banquet. The Meteyards had seemed enormous then — still were. Mrs Meteyard was a large woman, as was the barrister. Formidable in court he was. Dickens had seen him.

'What's this about?' asked Meteyard.

John Gaunt told him about the captain's murder and about the book with Kit's name in it, and how they wanted to know more about the captain from his friend.

'And Kit's not in? And no dog?'

'That's it — and I'm worried, Sampson. The shop door was open and the yard door, and Kit's work bench — it looks as if he just walked out.'

'He said he was goin' to see Captain Valentine before he left for Erith, but I don't know if he was goin' last night or today.'

'But, you didn't see him go out earlier today or come back?'

'No, I didn't think about it — I'll ask Joe Bean if he saw him at all. He went out with the dog earlier.'

The butcher shouted for Bean who came in — a brawny young man whose face had the colour of that dish. A young man, Dickens knew, of indefatigable good cheer, who went about the hacking of the bloody cadavers with all the enthusiasm of an ogre hacking his way through the woods. Not a vegetarian — a word which brought tears to Sampson Meteyard's eyes.

'Mr Dickens and these policemen want to know if you've seen anything of Mr Penney this evening — when you took the dog out.'

'What time was that?' asked Gaunt.

'It'd be five-ish, but I dint see Mr Penney. I came back down the alley. It was all quiet.'

'Was the yard door open?'

'No. I think I'd 'ave noticed — old Mug'd 'ave gone noseyin'. Can't pass an open door, 'e can't.'

'The dog,' Meteyard put in, observing Gaunt's confusion. 'Ugly mug.'

'Oh, I see. So you saw no one. No one in the alley?'

'Not a soul.'

'About Captain Valentine, Charley —' Sampson Meteyard looked troubled — 'these gentlemen don't think — I mean — I know Kit said he was going to see him, but he wouldn't have harmed the captain. They were good friends — you know that, Charley.'

'I do, Sampson, and I've told the Superintendent all about Kit and that it's impossible to think that he could harm the captain, or anybody else for that matter.'

'If he does come back, you'll tell him to come to Wapping police station? Tell him to ask for Constable Gaunt, or Inspector Bold,' John Gaunt said.

'I will. We'll keep our eyes open. I've a key to the shop. Shall I lock up?'

'Yes, that would be wise. And if you hear or see any strangers about, you'll let me know?'

'Yes, we'll do that.'

Meteyard let them out through the back door. Dickens lingered for a few moments. Sampson Meteyard's anxious face looked at him. 'This ain't right, Charley, lad, it don't make any sense. Kit wouldn't just leave everything. Do you think...?'

'I don't know what to think, Sampson, but I don't like it. I'm worried. Let me know as well as Gaunt, if you hear anything.'

'What about his ma and sister — what if they come? What am I to say?'

'Oh, lor, Sampson, I hadn't thought of that. I'll have to go and see them — I can't just leave them to find out that he's missing. I'll wait overnight and then if there's no message from you in the morning, I'll have to — he might be there — for some reason. An emergency?'

'Could be, but —'

'I know, I know — look, I'll have to go. Send someone at nine tomorrow. Goodnight Sampson.'

Dickens went into the alley where Gaunt and Sam Jones waited.

'Mr Meteyard mentioned Kit's mother and sister. They live at Greenwich. If he's missing, I ought —'

'Would he have gone there?' Jones asked.

'He might — I mean, if there were some sort of emergency—'

Jones looked grave. 'If he were in danger —'

'From the murderer. Kit might have seen something, or someone had seen him near the ship — someone who followed him or who came to the shop — oh, God, Sam, Kit might —' *Might be dead*, he thought.

Gaunt interrupted. 'I ought to get back to the station to report to Inspector Bold. He'll be waiting, and I need to tell him about all this. We need to search for Mr Penney.'

'And I should get back to Bow Street. Bold won't want me on his case. Goodnight to you, John. Let's hope for the best, Charles. Kit might well be at his sister's.' *Cold comfort*, he thought, looking at Dickens's stricken face, *but I can't push into Bold's case.*

'Will you come back with me, Mr Dickens? I need you to tell the inspector all about Mr Penney, convince him that —'

'Kit might be a victim, not the murderer.'

'You should do that, Charles.'

'I will, Johnno. Goodnight, Sam.'

Dickens watched Jones's solid form dissolve into the darkness. How he wanted him to stay, but he knew it wasn't possible. It wasn't Jones's case. He'd have to be in this one without him. With John Gaunt. Not the same.

7: THE SHIP AGROUND

Long Jodd, Ned Carver, a sailor called Tooth — he had just the one — and another whose name might have been Singer or Slinger, had been rounded up by Inspector Bold's constables. A message from Bold left at the police station had directed John Gaunt to The Ship Aground. Dickens went with him. He might not be welcome, but he wanted to make sure the Inspector knew about Kit.

At The Ship Aground, they found Inspector Bold in possession of a private parlour guarded by two of the constables. 'Old Nick' Barley greeted them, offering brandy and warm as he did so. Dickens and Gaunt accepted. While they waited, Dickens looked round. The place was full of sailors in high good humour, spending their money, singing, stamping their feet, some dancing with wild, whirling girls with bold eyes and raucous voices. A Black man played a piano accordion, his face gleaming in the heat given off by sweating bodies, smoking lamps and tallow candles. He thought about the Black face he had seen in the street — the frightened eyes, and he thought about Pilgrim again as they went into the parlour.

No fool, the inspector. The four sailors had a glass of something apiece — no doubt to loosen their tongues. Of course, their possessions had been searched. Long Jodd had a sea chest and the two others staying at the inn had ditty bags. The fourth who lodged with his sister-in-law had taken his sea chest there. None of the sailors had much beyond a few spare clothes and bits of equipment: his sailor's knife, his marlinspike, his fid — the spike used in splicing rope, his palm

— the hard shield to protect the hand in sailmaking, his bullock's horn of grease and his serving board. Inspector Bold had examined the knives and the marlin spikes and fids. Both the latter could be used as weapons, but none had any tell-tale blood. Of course, they wouldn't. The tidy murderer would have cleaned it off. Nevertheless, he had confiscated them — for the time being, he told them. Carver had been angry. Tooth had just looked bewildered. Long Jodd had stared back at Bold with hard black eyes. 'Fair enough,' he had said. Nothing to suggest he had anything to hide, but Inspector Bold had noted that hard stare. *A challenge*, he thought.

Long Jodd seemed to be explaining himself as Dickens and Gaunt went to take their seats. Gaunt was about to introduce Dickens, but the inspector stopped him with a gesture and gave the sailors' names. Bold knew who the stranger was. He knew it was Charles Dickens. He had read some of the books, but hadn't said so to Gaunt — he hadn't read the book in which the character Kit appeared. He'd liked the books he'd read — not *Pickwick*, though. Sam Weller's perpetual cheerfulness grated on him. His favourite was *Dombey and Son*. Bold had a daughter he called Floy after Florence Dombey. He had hoped his Florence would be as good as gold like her namesake. And she was. Still, no need to talk about it.

'Mr Jodd,' he resumed, 'you were about to tell me about the death of that boy, Potter. How you felt about the captain — you were angry, so we've been told.' The inspector's voice was mild. Fish for the facts was his method, and see what kind of dish can be made of them. No rush.

Dickens turned his attention to Long Jodd. There was nothing remarkable about him at first sight. He was very swarthy with black hair greased back into a pigtail, a silver hoop in each ear, black eyes and very black eyebrows which gave him a foreign look. Asian? It was hard to say, but his voice placed him in London. However, his teeth were noticeable — long, hard, yellow like a horse's — as if he had come into the world to bite it. Dickens looked at the eyes which were looking at Inspector Bold. Black eyes which were unfathomable — hard and shiny as polished jet, but nothing to show what he was thinking or feeling. The eyes were all surface.

Jodd took a swig of his drink. 'Well,' he said, 'I admits I woz annoyed. I'd looked after that lad — looked out fer 'im. We woz turned off at Bombay — bin with the trading boats along the coast. Yer don't get no security with them, but Ben an' me, we wanted ter see a bit o' the country. When we woz turned off we thinks it's time fer 'omeward bound, an' the cap'n took us on — both — I wouldn't leave Ben. Why, I knowed that lad from a babby — 'is ma's my sister. Anyways, I saved old Gammon on the quay. Coulda bin killed, but I pushed 'im outer the way. Dint 'ave no trouble with the cap'n till the lad woz gone.'

'Why should the captain think you had anything to do with it?' Bold asked, still mild.

'The Black — Pilgrim. I sees 'im with Ben Potter, whisperin' to 'im — tol' Ben ter keep away, an' it's my belief that the Black spoke bad about me ter the cap'n —'

'Why would he?' The Inspector's voice was sharp. 'Did the boy tell him something you didn't want the captain to know?'

'Not a thing. Told yer — I looked out fer that lad. Me own sister's boy. Anyone'd tell yer. Yer should be lookin' fer 'im — yer said 'e's gone missin' — well, 'e would, wouldn't 'e?' The horse teeth showed, horribly. Dickens expected him to neigh.

'Why so?' Bold looked at the others.

Dickens watched Jodd and saw how his eyes flicked towards the sailor called Singer, or Slinger, who kept his head down. He seemed to be looking at Jodd's hands. Dickens looked too. Strong, big hands with tufts of black hair on the knuckles — the impression of animal strength. He saw, too, on the right hand the pointed head of a snake tattoo — the body of the snake disappeared up the sleeve — it was horribly real. The forked tongue which darted as Jodd moved his hand made him feel slightly sick. There was something threatening about Jodd — he had a presence.

Tooth gnawed his lip with his one yellow fang. Every inch the sailor, Dickens noted, his hair the colour and texture of oakum, tied in a pigtail, and the silver hoops in his ears and a faraway, sea-gazing look in his eyes. He looked towards the Inspector — back on land and uncertain. 'Dunno 'xactly — just 'e woz — dint trust 'im. Chop an' me thought —' he looked at Ned Carver for help.

'Carver?'

Ned Carver had earned his nickname. His face was almost bisected by a deep, ugly scar, a red-purple groove. It looked like a badly sewn seam, knitting his crooked nose to his cheek.

'Tha's right. Black, see, loner, 'cept fer the cap'n. Knew all about the cap'n —'

Bold was sharp. 'What did he know about the captain?'

'Knew about 'is lady an' well, 'e'd tell 'im all sorts. Yer couldn't trust 'im.'

'The captain did.'

'Sly, see,' said Jodd, ''an 'e drank. Cap'n dint know. There was somethin' abaht the madeira we took on board. Someone 'ad been at it. We all knew 'oo it woz, but, see Pilgrim 'ad cap'n in 'is pocket.'

'So someone else got the blame.'

'Questions woz asked, but it want us an' cap'n couldn't say it woz.'

'And the lad, Potter — how do you think he went overboard?'

Jodd frowned. 'Burn me if I knows.' *You might very well*, thought Dickens — a rogue fit for burning. Inspector Bold waited. Jodd went on, all sincerity. 'Dunno 'ow 'e coulda fell, sir. It was a quiet night — sea as calm as a pond.'

'Do it himself, did he?'

'Why should 'e? We woz on our way 'ome. Mother waitin' fer 'im.'

'Where?'

The Inspector's sudden question seemed to ruffle Jodd for the first time. *Liar*, Dickens thought, *he's no more idea of that boy's mother than the emperor of China. They're all lying except the quiet one. He knows something and he doesn't like it.*

'Gravesend,' answered Jodd.

'You'll let me have the address?'

'Can't rightly recall — we bin away so long — three years near. Ain't been in touch.' Jodd's eyes were steady. 'But, I can find it — down by the docks.'

Bold was bland. 'I'll have a constable go with you — tomorrow. Potter's mother, your — sister — will want to know.' The Inspector paused over the word 'sister', but Jodd didn't flinch. *Hard case*, thought Dickens.

'Aye, right.'

'So, if the boy didn't kill himself and there wasn't an accident…'

'Done in, I reckon.' This was Carver. 'Yer oughter find the Black man — I mean if 'e killed Ben Potter an' the cap'n knew it then — well — stands ter reason —'

'What does?'

Jodd answered for him. 'Funny thing 'appened with an 'angman's knot. Pilgrim taught Midshipman Wilkes 'ow ter do it — the lad woz very proud o' one 'e did an' it went missin' night my lad woz lost. Someone did fer 'im with that rope an' threw 'im overboard — an' now the Black's missin'.'

'Why should Pilgrim kill the boy?'

'Ah, well — whisperin', see. Voodoo, I reckons. Mumbo-jumbo stuff. An' Pilgrim killed the cap'n — that's why 'e's run.'

Bold's expression remained neutral — what he thought about voodoo magic, he kept to himself. 'That's what you all think?'

'Stands ter reason,' repeated Carver.

'Mr Slinger?'

'I suppose it does, but they was always friends, cap'n an' Pilgrim — I don't know.'

Slinger was the name then. Mr Slinger. Dickens noticed how his eyes darted at Jodd. Frightened of him, but not as ready as the others to shift the blame on the missing Pilgrim.

'And you three were here all night?'

''Tis true. Nick Barley'll speak fer us,' Carver answered.

Nick Barley already had. But Bold knew that there was no way of disproving that the three sailors had stuck together. Barley had said that he'd given them a room to share, but any one of them, or all of them, could have gone out and have been on that ship between midnight and six in the morning. They were lying about something, and Jodd was the key to all that.

'Mr Slinger — you were at your sister-in-law's all night. She can vouch for you?'

'I told the constable an' my sister-in-law backed me up.'

'Keepin' 'er bed warm, woz yer, Slinger?' Jodd sniggered.

It was unnecessary. Just done to provoke. *That's the kind of man he is*, thought Dickens. *A bully. He'll have frightened that lad, driven him, pushed him over. And he could have killed the captain if Louis Valentine had known something that Pilgrim had told him about Jodd and Potter. But, Kit — how did Kit come into this?*

'Right, you four, I want you within reach. Jodd, Carver — you'll be here when I want you. Tooth?'

''Ere, too.'

'Slinger?'

'At my sister-in-law's house.'

'And I want to know if you hear anything about Pilgrim.'

Jodd and Carver nodded and stared back at Bold, their eyes unblinking. Tooth looked as if he didn't understand. Perhaps he knew that Pilgrim was already dead. Slinger looked worried. Perhaps he knew, too.

John Gaunt had waited patiently, but he was determined to ask them about Mr Penney and the chandler's shop before the Inspector left.

'Do any of you know the marine chandler's shop in Gun Lane, owned by a Mr Christopher Penney, friend of the captain's?'

Jodd, Carver and Tooth said not. Why should they know? They would know the general dealers, the shops selling oil skins, sailors' clothes, tobacco, rum, but they wouldn't necessarily visit a shop like Kit's which was more likely to be frequented by officers, men who wanted nautical instruments. Slinger seemed to hesitate, thinking about the name.

'No, I don't think so.' Dickens met his eyes very briefly and saw recognition there. Slinger knew who he was, or perhaps he knew Kit, but he looked down quickly and said nothing more.

They left The Ship Aground and walked back a little way up the causeway. Dickens told the Inspector about Kit.

'Not likely the murderer then.'

'No, Inspector, not at all — you'd only have to see him.'

'If he were not missing.'

'I'm worried, Inspector — Kit wouldn't have left all the doors open and his spectacles just left on the counter.'

'But, it's possible that he went to the ship.'

'Not at midnight.'

'Neither George Gammon nor that young midshipman saw him earlier, though Gammon was on board alone at some time in the evening.'

'Perhaps he didn't go at all.'

'No way of knowing till we find him. Any relatives?'

'A mother and a sister at Greenwich. I should go and tell them tomorrow.'

'He wouldn't have gone there?'

'Why would he leave the doors open?'

'Hm. I'll get the night constables to keep an eye out, and for the Black man. What did you think of all that back there, Gaunt?'

'Jodd's a rogue. I didn't believe a word he said about that boy — not after what Gammon and Mark Wilkes told us. And they were very keen to pin the boy's death and the captain's on Pilgrim. And as for voodoo, it makes no sense. Pilgrim been with the captain for years. And the madeira, Jodd had that, I'll be bound.'

'Mr Dickens?'

'Jodd brought about that boy's death — somehow. I met Pilgrim with the captain — they were close, I saw that. There was trust there.'

'Jodd and the captain?'

'Could be — he'd be capable, especially if Captain Valentine knew something that Pilgrim had told him about the Potter boy. But, I don't see how Kit Penney fits into all this.'

'Nor do I — it may, of course, be something quite different. I want Jodd watched. I'll keep a constable in the pub. I want evidence to bring him in. We've only hearsay so far.'

'The quiet one, Slinger, he knew something and Jodd kept his eye on him when he thought you were concentrating on Carver and Tooth. And Slinger wasn't too sure about the accusations against Pilgrim,' Gaunt added.

'I noticed that, and I saw that he came out just behind us,' said Dickens.

'Did he now? We'll need to question him further. We'll get his address from Nick Barley, and then Gaunt, you can make your way to that sister-in-law's. In fact, bring Slinger back to the station.'

'What about Gravesend?' asked Gaunt.

'I don't believe it for a minute, but let's get a couple of constables to take Jodd there. The sister will have moved or died, of course — if she ever existed. It'll be a waste of time, but it'll keep Jodd under our eye. I'm obliged, Mr Dickens, for you coming to tell me about Mr Penney. You can be sure I'll be looking for him, and let me know if you find him at his sister's. Goodnight to you.'

It was a dismissal, but what could he expect? Bold went back to The Ship Aground to talk to his constables. John Gaunt looked at Dickens with sympathy.

'I'd better get after him. He'll not want you involved — he's not like Sam.'

'I see that, but that doesn't stop me from going to places where Kit might have taken refuge if —' He thought again. Not dead. No. He wouldn't believe it. 'The Inspector knows I'm going to Kit's sister. She'll be worried — and his mother. No doubt they'll point me in the direction of other friends.'

Gaunt grinned. 'We might come across each other in our search.'

'We might indeed. I'll keep my eye out for you. Goodnight, Johnno — you'd better get after him for that address.'

8: TEMPEST

Dickens went on his way. He felt despondent. He missed Sam already. And, alone, what could he really do? Try to find Kit — who might be dead. He thought about Scrap who lived with Sam's Sergeant Rogers and his wife, Mollie. Scrap had been useful to them all in their previous investigations. He was smart and could make himself invisible on the streets — just another urchin. Perhaps, he could borrow Scrap from Mollie? Perhaps not. For the first time he felt uncertain. It was all very well investigating with Sam, and with the knowledge that Rogers, Stemp and Feak, the other constables who had been involved in the previous cases, were to be called upon, but just Scrap and himself? Dangerous. He thought of Kit's abandoned shop and a figure in the dark with knife held in a large hand — tufted with black hair, perhaps.

He made to hurry, but he realised that he had no more idea than a blind mole where he was. He thought he knew these streets. But he hadn't been thinking where he was going. Now in this narrow alley, he was aware of darkness. Somewhere voices shouted, and there was the sound of singing. He'd passed a pub before and had registered the noises. Go back then. He turned round and there, further along the alley where a gas lamp spilled its sickly light, someone stood looking at him. A sailor.

He couldn't make out who the man was. Long Jodd? But he stayed where he was and grasped his stick tightly and raised it. The sailor came forward and lifted his hands as if to reassure.

'Mr Dickens, sir, please, I gotter talk ter yer. I knew yer back there — seen yer picture. I thought I could tell yer...'

'Mr Slinger, is it?' Dickens recognised him now. The quiet one. Nothing to fear. The man sounded anxious, not threatening.

'Yes, sir, Tempest Slinger.'

'Tempest?'

The man came nearer, and Dickens could see him smile at Dickens's astonishment at his name. ''Tis, true, sir, I know it sounds daft. 'Twas my pa's notion. 'E was a sailor — 'ad a fancy for somethin' different. I was to be a sailor, o' course.'

'What did your mother think?' Dickens was beguiled by the name despite the circumstances. Tempest Slinger — wait till he told Sam. He felt a pang. Sam.

'Dead, sir, never knowed 'er.'

'I am sorry for that.' Dickens smiled at him. 'She might have liked it. But what is it you want to tell me?'

Tempest looked behind him. 'Not 'ere, sir. Will you come 'ome with me? It ain't far. Just a step or two.'

They walked in silence through another alley which turned a right angle and led them into a wider road — Bedford Street. Dickens knew where he was now. They were crossing High Street from where Slinger took him into Wade Street.

Tempest Slinger stopped at the neat little terraced house where his widowed sister-in-law lived.

'Jennie's my brother's widow. 'E wasn't a sailor — kept a shop, off Castor Street, not far from Mr Penney's.'

'You knew him then? I wondered, when you hesitated.'

'Didn't want ter say, Mr Dickens. It's complicated, see. It's ter do with Long Jodd. Come in, sir, an' I'll do my best ter explain.'

Tempest Slinger opened the door into a little hall, and a woman emerged from a room at the end, a small, very neat woman, shiny somehow like a silver button. She looked at Tempest anxiously.

'What did the police want? I've been that worried — what did they say about the captain? It wasn't anythin' to do with you. They can't think that —' she broke off, seeing Dickens for the first time.

'Jennie, Jennie, let us get in and then I'll tell you. I've brought Mr Dickens, Jennie — I need ter tell 'im somethin'.'

Jennie Slinger came forward. Her anxious expression turned to one of astonishment. 'Mr Dickens — good gracious me — oh, my — I never thought — good gracious —'

Dickens took pity on the flustered woman. 'Mrs Slinger, I am most happy to meet you and your brother-in-law, who I think may have some information for me about my friend, Mr Kit Penney.'

'Mr Penney — we know him. My husband, Mel —'

Tempest interrupted. 'Melvile after the ship, *Lady Melvile*, an East Indiaman — my father sailed in her, way back in 1814. He was lost with *The Kent* in 1825. The ship was destroyed by fire in the bay o' Biscay. It's why Mel wouldn't go to sea. Mel was older than me. I went — in pa's memory, I suppose. Still — sorry, Jennie, you was tellin' Mr Dickens about Mr Penney.'

'In the parlour. We can sit in there.'

The parlour was a little room with a fire and a Dutch clock on the mantelpiece, a painting of an East Indiaman above. It was lit by oil lamps, and there was a deal table in the centre with four chairs. There was a bookcase, too, with some books in the familiar green covers.

'Is there something the matter, Mr Dickens, about Mr Penney?'

'I'm not sure, Mrs Slinger, but, first let Tempest tell you about the police.'

'I don't know what they think, Jennie. They spoke ter me an' Jodd, Ned Carver an' Al Tooth. They wanted ter know about the boy that went overboard an' the captain an' Pilgrim.'

'They can't think that Pilgrim —'

'Jodd an' the others was suggestin' that Pilgrim might 'ave murdered the captain.'

'Stuff — you've told me a dozen times that Pilgrim was devoted to the captain. You spoke up for him, I hope.' Tempest looked sheepish. 'You don't mean to tell me that you let them think — savin' you own skin, was you?'

'It wasn't quite like that, Mrs Slinger. I didn't believe a word Jodd said, and I don't think the police did either. In fact, Tempest, they noticed that you were not keen to implicate Pilgrim. Constable Gaunt is coming to ask you some questions, so I would like you to tell me about Mr Penney first.'

'What's Mr Penney to do with it all?' asked Mrs Slinger.

'I don't know, but he is missing. He is not at the shop, and when I went there with the police, the doors were open and no sign of Mr Penney. Has either of you seen or heard anything of him?'

'No. I sometimes call in when I'm shopping, but not since last week.'

'He didn't come to the ship at all, Tempest?'

'No, not as I know, but the captain would 'ave been sure to see 'im afore 'e went ter Erith.'

Dickens handed Mrs Slinger his card. 'You will, please, let me know if you hear or see anything of him. I am going to see his sister tomorrow. I hope he may have gone there. Now, Tempest, what did you want to tell me about Long Jodd and the others?'

'It was all lies, what Jodd an' them was sayin'. Jodd did torment that boy — Ben Potter — 'e 'ad some 'old on 'im. An' Jodd always said 'is sister was dead.'

'And the others — why should they wish to protect Jodd?'

Tempest looked down. 'Money, sir. We all owed 'im —'

'Tempest Slinger — you ain't sayin' that you owed money — cards, was it — again?' Jennie Slinger's voice was sharp. 'You said the captain didn't hold with gamblin'.'

'No more 'e did, but Jodd, 'e 'ad a kind of power — I don't know — we — just the few of us got drawn in. Jodd was a persuadin' sort o' body —'

'Stuff, again, Tempest Slinger — you should have known better — betrayin' the captain, you all was. Drink, was it?'

The madeira, thought Dickens. Tempest looked ashamed. 'I know, Jennie, but it'd not been an easy voyage — terrible storm. St Elmo's fire — yer know what that means, Mr Dickens?'

'I think so — souls of the dead?'

'Exactly — and then one of the passengers died in the night — sick man, a parson, 'e was. Unlucky, some say. Jodd said. An' the lad, o' course. Captain's last voyage, see — some'ow it seemed all wrong.'

'And Jodd?'

'Unlucky voyage, 'e said, unlucky fer the captain since it was 'is last voyage — Pilgrim, it was, 'e said — seen it afore. A Black — unlucky.'

'But you'd sailed with them before.'

'I know — but me an' Tooth 'ad been mates, so I got drawn in. Tooth ain't very —'

'Simple, Mr Dickens, that's Albert Tooth,' Jennie put in, 'no harm in him, but he'd be persuaded. Didn't know you were simple, Tempest Slinger.'

'You 'ad ter be there, Jennie, yer don't know Long Jodd.'

'An' if I did, he wouldn't frighten me — lot of cowards —'

Dickens came to Tempest's rescue. 'I have met him, Mrs Slinger, and I think I know what Tempest means. So, you were all drawn in and came to owe him money.'

'That's right, an' so we didn't speak out when we saw 'ow 'e was with the boy — should've done, I know, but what proof? An' any one of us could 'ave gone overboard —'

'About the boy? How was Jodd with him?'

'Tormented 'im — made 'im — a slave yer might call it — treated 'im like a dog. Course 'e wasn't Jodd's nephew. An' then 'e saw the lad talkin' ter Pilgrim, an' it was after that the lad went overboard.'

'You think the boy told Pilgrim what was going on.'

'I do — an' Jodd's mebbe after Pilgrim.'

'And you think that Jodd killed the captain.'

'He could 'ave — 'e 'ated the captain an' Pilgrim.'

'You'll have to tell all this to Constable Gaunt when he comes. It might put you in danger.'

'Too bad, sir. Should 'ave — we all should 'ave spoken. If 'e 'as killed the captain, we're all in it. We should 'ave spoken.'

Tempest looked so shamefaced, so wretched, that Dickens felt sorry for him. A good-natured man and a simple one. Not in the way of Tooth, more just uncomplicated, and credulous, he thought. Sailors could be a superstitious lot. Out there on the empty ocean, seeing fire darting in the rigging, two deaths on board, the captain's last voyage, a sense of unease and fear created by Jodd. He could understand why they had kept quiet, but, at least, Tempest would tell Johnno and Jodd could be arrested.

But Kit — he still couldn't see how Kit was involved in all this — unless he had been on the ship at some time. But

Gammon had not seen him. 'I must go now, Mrs Slinger. If you hear of Kit, let me know as soon as you can. Goodnight to both of you.'

Tempest Slinger showed him out. 'Didn't wanter say in front of Jennie, but Jodd — 'e 'ad a lot of stories. Told us 'e'd killed a man wot 'ad crossed im. We didn't know if it was true, but 'e was frightenin' some'ow. 'Ad a kind o' power — way 'e'd stare at yer. Like a snake. Bad 'earted cove. I can believe 'e'd do murder an' think naught of it. Yer'd 'ave ter be there, Mr Dickens.'

'I believe you from what I've seen of him. You must tell Constable Gaunt — everything.'

'I will, an' I'll ask about — see if I can find out anything about Mr Penney. Least I can do.'

'I'll be obliged. Now, go and make your peace with Mrs Slinger.'

Tempest grinned. 'Aye, I'd better. She's a good woman — keeps me in order.'

Dickens went on his way. He would take the train, the Blackwall line, from the station just behind the great West India Dock. It would take him to Fenchurch Street, and he could get a cab to Devonshire Terrace. Bone-weary he felt, and a tight feeling of anxiety seemed like a band about his heart. Kit, Kit, Kit, Kit, his footsteps said as he walked on. And Pilgrim. He thought about that. Two missing.

9: A FRIGHTENED MAN

Peter Best was a frightened man. The Captain murdered. He'd heard that at the wharf when he'd gone to *The Redemption* at Blackwall Reach — just to leave a message for the captain to tell him that he'd left a package for him at the marine chandler's shop — those had been Adam Valentine's instructions. His instinct had been to hide — he didn't want to be involved in murder. He saw the policemen at the ship. And then the fight. His face felt swollen and his left arm was stiff, but he was safe and back at his lodgings.

He had no idea what had happened — he had gone to the shop in the afternoon where the man called Kit Penney had received the oilskin package. A pleasant man with an open, honest face who'd invited him to take a glass of something, but he'd declined because he had somewhere else to be. Tomorrow, he had decided, he would deliver the letter to Mrs Tallis, the captain's sister, but he'd do it late on when it was dark. Just slip it through the letterbox.

Then, he would be free to do as he pleased and to think about his future — he did not want to go back to St. Lucia. Adam Valentine was dying and that meant that his son would inherit, and that meant that his own job would not be secure. Marcus Valentine would want a clean sweep — his own men, especially the foreman's post. Oh, he'd seen Marcus with that man, Jeremie Corneille, down at the old house — the house that had been shut up all those years. Gossip had it that old Adams's wife — the mad one, the first one, Marcus's mother, had died there, and the house had been closed. Haunted, the

73

Black folks said. Not that he'd believed it, but still, the closed shutters and the silence were sinister.

Peter Best knew Corneille. He'd been up at the house to dine, even though his dead father, Ralph Corneille, had been in debt to Adam Valentine. Corneille was arrogant. He'd paid no attention to Best. Something dark about him, as if he cast a long shadow. But Peter Best had seen him shake hands with Marcus by the old house, and he knew, in his heart, what that meant. There was some deal afoot — some agreement. Perhaps it meant that Corneille would be a partner, would get his own estate back. Peter Best didn't know why, but he knew they wouldn't want him — not Adam Valentine's man. They'd want their own man — the foreman at the Corneille plantation, perhaps. He didn't want to go back, but it was a risk to stay. He had money — money he'd sent to his brother, William, and he'd gone to William's as soon as *The Endeavour* had got in.

That's what frightened him. He had a sense that he was being followed. It was when he had come back from William's — out on the Isle of Dogs. It was the same feeling he had sometimes walking past that old house at night, as if the air was too thick and the silence could be felt as a breathing presence. Sometimes, he'd see a light in the trees. It would flicker, go out, flicker again and then be gone, but he never saw anyone. As he had made his way back along that dark road, he'd felt that same breathing quiet, and he was sure, when he turned, that he had seen a light.

And, in the dark when he had come away from the marine chandler's shop, he had felt again that sense as though the air stirred somewhere across the road at the opening to an alleyway that led into shadows. He'd thought to go into a pub where there was warmth and light and company, but as he approached the door, it was flung open and a crowd of drunken, brawling sailors had spilled out, taking him with it into a melee of flying fists and kicks. It had been like being sucked into a whirlpool.

He'd sprawled in the street and felt a few blows from boots; a foot, fortunately bare, had landed on his nose, but, just as he was aware of the proximity of a large boot descending, a strong arm had grabbed him and hauled him to his feet. A hulking sailor grinned at him and dragged him inside — a good-humoured laughing man who had treated him to rum and apologised for his mates. The fight still went on in the street, so the sailor showed him out the back way and directed him to his lodgings at Mrs Cly's off Salmon's Lane.

And that was another odd thing — when the Black sailor had helped him up, he'd glanced back across the road and he thought he had seen a figure there, a man who looked like a sailor, very like the sailor he'd seen at Mrs Cly's, a tall, swarthy man with greased black hair and a ring in his ear, a sailor whom he had seen on the stairs. And, he thought that someone had been in his room at the lodgings — something was wrong. His bag moved on the bed. It was on the pillow — not where he'd left it. Not that there was anything in it. He thought it might have been Mrs Cly. The nosy sort, he'd thought, but now? Now he was sure he was being followed.

And what worried him about being followed was that he had something to hide. Peter Best was not his real name. His brother, William, lived way out in the marshes on the Isle of Dogs. Years ago, they'd lived in Love Lane at Wapping where their father had been a labourer at the London Docks. William had moved away — far enough to live amongst folk who knew nothing and asked no questions.

He had killed a man, and not just any man. His own father. The drunken father who, in Love Lane, had beaten his wife senseless and had beaten his sons, too, until he, home from the sea, had brained him with an iron bar. He had become Peter Best, the name stolen from a neighbour's son who had gone to sea and had never come back. If anyone wanted to know about his old self then they'd learn that he, too, was lost at sea. He had got a berth to St Lucia, where he had worked his way up to become foreman to Adam Valentine. Once he had possessed ambitions as a sailor and had thought he might rise in the merchant service, but he had found himself bound to another tyrant. When the opportunity to come to England came, he had thought then he might not go back to St. Lucia. After all this time, who would remember what had been found on the muddy shore by Execution Dock?

But now, he was being followed. Someone had followed him to William's, he was sure. Someone who might have seen him near the ship — the ship where the captain had been murdered. He shuddered at the thought. Someone from the old days? Someone who recognised him? Someone who had something to gain? Get out. Suddenly, he had a longing for the wide ocean. He would take the letter to Captain Valentine's sister tomorrow night. Duty done, he would get a message to William and then he would go north, to Liverpool, and onward, outward — anywhere.

10: AURORA

Dickens passed a restless night. He had slept fitfully, waking at times to remember Kit and Pilgrim. In the early hours he had lain awake trying to connect them. Perhaps Jodd had threatened Pilgrim, who had run away. Perhaps he had taken refuge with Kit and they had both fled from Jodd. And were lying low — at Kit's sister's house in Greenwich. It made sense. He had felt better then and had slept. He woke, resolved to go to Greenwich as soon as possible. After breakfast. He would go to the office of *Household Words* in Wellington Street, see Harry Wills, the sub-editor, and then take the Blackwall line to Brunswick Wharf from where a steamer would take him to Greenwich. They'd be there — surely.

As he approached the iron gate which led out of his garden, he saw a boy standing outside — a boy about twelve. The lad looked uncertain, wondering how to get in. A message, thought Dickens, but not from Meteyard. The lad was far too small to be Joe Bean. From Mrs Slinger then. News of Kit.

Dickens went out into the street, where the boy handed him a note. It was from Mrs Slinger. Mrs Penney, Kit's mother, was at the shop and she had asked for him. The boy was Mrs Slinger's — Percy. A solid, cheerful lad with brown hair and bright eyes. Dickens would come, he told the lad. They would take a cab to Fenchurch Street and then the railway to Limehouse.

It had always seemed to Dickens that there was something ship-shapish and deck-swabbish about Mrs Penney — Aurora by gift of her sea-faring father — a mixed blessing, she said.

Her aprons cracked like sails and her hands were made for hauling a very weighty anchor. Her husband had called her 'The Admiral'. Whilst her son and husband bent their eyes to the minutiae of cogs and wheels, hers had scanned the horizons, wondering if those dark smudges, no bigger than a man's hand, betokened ships coming in or were omens of storms. 'On watch' had been her motto, but she hadn't seen this coming.

She stood with Jennie Slinger in her son's shop. She was looking at Kit's spectacles and the pieces of the chronometer on the counter, and at the glass lens on the floor. Kit never dropped things, and that, above all, had frightened her. What had so startled her son that he had dropped something? And had not picked it up.

She had arrived at eight in the morning, as she always did when she was to look after the shop. Today, Kit had planned to go to Erith with the captain. When she had found the shop empty, she had gone to speak to Sampson Meteyard, who had told her of the death of Captain Valentine and that Kit was missing, and that two policemen and Mr Dickens had come in search of Kit. Sampson had directed her to the police station to ask for Inspector Bold or Constable Gaunt. No, she had thought. The man she wanted was Charles Dickens. She didn't want any police — if Kit was in danger, then Dickens could go and find him, take him somewhere safe, somewhere naught to do with the captain. Erith, she thought, where the Captain lived and his betrothed. Kit would have gone there. Police were all very well. Sampson might believe that Kit wasn't a suspect, but if he'd run away for some reason then they'd think it — bound to — and she wasn't having that. Get him safe first. That is, unless... She wouldn't think that, but her eyes went to the piece of glass on the floor and she thought of the signs that someone had been up there. Just a few things disturbed, and that smell — the smell of a stranger — no, Kit had fled from danger, and it was something to do with the captain. Mr Dickens must go to Erith, and she would stay here in case Kit came back. Jennie Slinger had offered her boy, Percy, as messenger.

Mrs Penney was a resourceful woman. She had run the shop after her husband had died until Kit was old enough to run it himself. At fourteen Kit had concentrated on refining the skills his father had taught him. Mrs Penney and her strong-minded daughter, Susannah, had done everything else. Kit had been frail as a child — at ten he had been small for his age and hampered by his deformed foot. Charles Dickens had been small, too, no taller than Kit, but he had held himself high and there had been a look of determination in his eyes that she had admired. He stood his ground — even when rougher boys threatened. Once, they'd found a half sovereign when they were searching for treasure and an older boy had tried to take it, pushing Kit over to sprawl in the mud. Young Charley had sprung upon the lad and had punched him in the face. The boy had retreated. Kit and Charley had returned to the shop triumphant, though Charley had a swollen eye.

Charles Dickens was tough in a way that Kit was not, protected by a strong-willed elder sister. Charley's sister, Fanny, had been musical. She remembered that — the two of them performing songs at Christopher Huffam's house. Fanny had a sweet voice, but she seemed delicate, quite unlike strapping Susannah. Charley had gone in for comic songs — *The Cat's Meat Man* was a favourite. She remembered Charley's father placing the boy on a table to sing it. He was clever, too — quick on the uptake. A bright lad and a tough one. He'd had to be. She knew what it meant to him when he had been sent to work at Warren's Blacking. John Dickens was a feckless fellow, she had always thought — always in debt, living like a gentleman, but he'd been good company on those nights at Christopher Huffam's. Now his son was the most famous man in the land, but he still came to see Kit and sent him all his books. He'd be the man to deal with the police and to see that Kit was protected.

The shop bell jangled, and Percy Slinger came in, accompanied by a young girl who was holding Kit Penney's dog, Jam, by a piece of rope tied to his collar. After them came Charles Dickens.

'Rosanna Chibb, what you doin' with Mr Kit's dog?' exclaimed Jennie Slinger.

'In the yard.' Rosanna Chibb was not given to volubility. Terseness was her forte. Actions not words. She looked impassive, thought Dickens, and her dark eyes in the dusky face looked too old.

'Whose?'

'Mine.' Mrs Penney's sharpness made no dint in Rosanna's armour.

'When?'

'Don't know — this mornin'. Knew Mr Kit'd want me to bring him home.'

'How?' Dickens found himself adopting the same staccato method of inquiry — it was efficient at any rate.

'Didn't bark — Mr Kit would have told him not to. Somethin' not right.'

'You didn't see Kit at all?' Mrs Penney asked.

'Nah — just Jam. T'ain't right.'

'True, Rosanna, Mr Kit is missing — we don't know where he's gone.'

'Want me to look?' Rosanna asked.

'Yes. Keep your eyes open — by the river, anywhere you think —'

'Take Perce,' offered Jennie Slinger.

Rosanna looked at Perce, a measuring kind of look. 'Suppose,' she said.

Mrs Penney looked at the dog. 'And Jam — where is he, Jam? See if you can find him.' Jam answered not. He looked most downcast and the foolish tail drooped.

'Don't ask about — unless it's someone you know,' put in Dickens quickly. He thought about Long Jodd and Ned Carver and that subtle knife in the dark. 'Don't ask any strangers.'

'Right.' Rosanna's old eyes looked back at the stranger. She knew what he meant.

'Here,' said Mrs Penney, 'take some money, and come back when you hear the clocks strike one o'clock. Punctual, mind.'

The three went out.

'They'll be all right?' Dickens asked.

'Perce isn't a fool, and Rosanna Chibb has a lot of sense. She doesn't ever say much, but she's tough, I'll give her that. Hard life. Mother keeps a lodging house —' Jennie Slinger looked as if she might have said more, but Mrs Penney interrupted.

'I'm worried, Charley. Someone's been up there.' She pointed to the rooms upstairs.

'How can you tell? Nothing seemed to be disturbed. We looked last night.'

'Well, you wouldn't — I do all the cleaning for Kit. I know every inch o' that room. Things have been moved — the books on the table were on the floor. There was a drawer in the round table. It had been left partly open and when I looked in, papers had been disturbed, and the counterpane — it wasn't on the bed. It was on the chair — tidy enough, but not Kit's way. I know it's small things, Charley, but Kit is so methodical, so neat in his ways. Someone had been up there, I know it — and there was a glass piece from one of the instruments on the floor by the counter. Kit never dropped things. Something frightened him — here — in his own shop.'

'I believe you, Mrs Penney. You know him better than anyone.'

'And I know these rooms — and, upstairs, I could smell him — I could smell a stranger. Old clothes and grease. Bear's grease. Someone was there.'

It all sounded so slight, and as for the smell, Dickens wondered, but, still, looking at Aurora Penney's fierce blue eyes, he was convinced. And Jodd had greased-back hair. Whether Bold would be convinced, he couldn't say.

'I'll tell Inspector Bold.'

'Not yet. First, will you go to Erith, Charley? I thought Kit might have gone there. I thought you could bring him back. I don't want the police getting hold of him. If they want him then they can question him here where I —'

'Can look after him. I know, Mrs Penney, and I will go by steamer directly.'

He turned to go just as the bell jangled again and John Gaunt stepped in. He recognised Jennie Slinger from the night before so the other woman must be Mrs Penney, Kit Penney's mother. She didn't look very pleased to see him.

'I just came by to ask if you'd heard anything about your son, Mrs Penney. I'm afraid I have no news.'

'No, nothing.'

'You have no idea where he might have gone?'

'I don't,' she said, terse as Rosanna Chibb.

'What of Long Jodd?' asked Dickens, filling the gap.

'Inspector Bold and I went straight back to The Ship Aground after I had spoken to your brother —' he glanced at

Jennie Slinger — 'Jodd and Carver had gone. Naturally, Tooth knew nothing — too drunk anyway. I'm on my way to your house, Mrs Slinger, to see if your brother has any ideas about who Jodd and Carver might have gone to — any other of the crew.'

'Has Inspector Bold sent to Erith — the captain's fiancée?'

'Yes, Mr Dickens, he sent Sergeant Cox last night, and he went himself to tell the captain's sister and to take the young midshipman. He asked her about the Black man, Pilgrim, but she knew nothing.'

So, Kit hadn't been at Erith, but he might have arrived after the sergeant had gone. It was still worth trying. He ought to tell Johnno, but he didn't want him with him because if Kit were there, Inspector Bold would want him taken to the station.

'Would you come with me, Mr Dickens? Mr Slinger will talk to you.'

Dickens glanced at Mrs Penney before he spoke. 'I can spare half an hour, then I've another errand. Time and tide and all that.' Mrs Penney understood.

Dickens and Gaunt made their way to Wade Street, accompanied by another constable who had waited outside the shop. Gaunt explained that Inspector Bold was not in a good mood, 'Cursing himself for not taking Jodd in last night and cursing Tempest Slinger for not speaking up sooner. Furious that Slinger followed you and didn't come after us straightaway. That's why I offered to come to see Slinger again — I thought he might clam up if Inspector Bold hectored him.'

'He would — I can't blame him entirely. Long Jodd's not a man I should like to cross. What is the choleric Inspector up to now?'

'Searching every tavern from The Ship Aground all the way to Brunswick Wharf, but Jodd could be anywhere, and we don't know anything about him — family or anything.'

'Tempest Slinger told you that Jodd had always said his sister was dead?'

'He did — just as Inspector Bold thought.'

'The people at Erith didn't tell the sergeant anything?' Dickens trod carefully.

'No, they were too shocked, I think. There's a captain's wife, Mrs Pink. She did all the talking. Said they didn't know anything about the voyage, and they certainly couldn't think of anyone who might want to harm the captain. Sergeant Cox left them — Bold'll go back, I suppose.'

Dickens thought it time to be honest with Johnno. Bold couldn't stop him going to Erith, nor should he mind. He'd be too busy looking for Jodd. 'I'm going to see them — about Kit. They might know something of him.'

'You think he might be there — Sergeant Cox asked, but they said not.'

'I don't know, Johnno, I really don't, but Mrs Penney asked me to go. She wants Kit back before the police get to him — she's afraid Kit might be a suspect.'

'I can see that, but I think Inspector Bold knows it's Jodd. He's not much concerned about Mr Penney just now.'

'But I am. Kit might be in danger. Mrs Penney believes that someone was at the shop and in the room above — things disturbed — not much, but not the way Kit put things, and a smell.'

'A smell?'

'She could smell a stranger, she said — old clothes and bear's grease —' Gaunt raised his eyebrows — 'I know it sounds flimsy, but she is convinced, and I believe her. She's a practical woman — not given to fancy.'

'And the things disturbed? Not much, you say?'

'No, why?'

'Just that in the captain's cabin things had been disturbed — whoever was there had unpacked his clothes and put the things neatly on the bunk.'

'A tidy thief.'

'Just what the inspector said.'

'Somehow, I don't see Long Jodd as a tidy sort of fellow, but his hair was greased. I noticed. But what could he want with Kit? Was he looking for something?'

'That's what we thought on the ship. It's a puzzle. Let's go and see Mr Slinger — see what he can tell us about Long Jodd.'

11: SLY CLY AND CAPTAIN PYE

Silas Cly was no help at all. *A phenomenon of moroseness never before encountered*, Dickens thought — a bilious-faced, ragged-browed, watery-eyed sometime sailor with a wooden leg. Now lodging housekeeper — the house, a tall, peculiarly thin house with a lean doorway and a narrow window beside it.

They had been directed to the house by Tempest Slinger who had, with Dickens's gentle persuasion, recalled Silas Cly whose nickname was, unsurprisingly, Sly. 'Nat'rally,' Tempest had said, 'An', o' course 'e was. Sailed with us — years back before the Captain was a captain, but 'e was always thick with Carver. An' then 'e lost 'is leg an' married a widder 'oo'd lost 'er 'usband in the water — an' she did, Mr Dickens — story there —'

Dickens had seen before how Tempest, like Sam Weller, had a propensity for branching off into byways of history, and he was guilty of a propensity for wanting to hear. Johnno's lips tightened. He wanted to know about Cly, not the "widder", but Dickens, it seemed, was not going to stop Tempest as he nodded encouragingly to the sailor.

'They was walkin' one day Lime'ouse dock way — she stops to talk ter somebody or other. Looks round. Slog's gone.'

'Slog?'

'Jim Sloggett — came up days later at Lime'ouse 'Ole. Stones in his pocket. Takes all sorts.'

'It does indeed, Mr Slinger, but for the sake of Constable Gaunt, I beg you tell us about Mr Cly.' Dickens had sensed Johnno's impatience — he was breathing somewhat heavily.

'Sorry, sir. She 'as the lodgin's in Salmon's Place, off Salmon's Lane 'bout a furlong up on the left as you're walkin' from Commercial Road. Anyway, could be that Ned Carver sent him there — crooked beggar is Sly, an' fond o' money — that's all I can think of. I mean there's others, nat'rlly from *The Redemption*, but, I dunno, Sly's the sort...'

Mr and Mrs Cly were, as Dickens and the constables came into Salmon Place, on their doorstep, gawping up towards an open window of the narrow house. A crowd had gathered, the faces of which were similarly engaged. At the window was propped a black contraption like a slide and coming through the window was a roughly made coffin. The black ladder. Dickens had seen this before — it was a somewhat grotesque manner of removing a corpse from an upstairs room if the staircase of the house were not wide enough, and judging by the size of the house, this was the case here. He and Gaunt watched with the crowd as two men began to lower the coffin by ropes threaded through the handle — and a precarious business it looked, too. The crowd held its collective breath as the coffin made its funereal progress down the slide. It faltered for a second or two. The slide shook a bit. The undertaker's white face looked up. Hands pulled the ropes taut and the coffin moved again and slid gently to the end of the slide. The undertaker, as long and narrow as the coffin, patted it and raised his black-gloved hand to the man above. An urchin in the crowd shouted, 'Stunner!' At which impropriety the crowd roared its approval and dispersed.

Constable Gaunt went over to the undertaker and spoke a few words. The undertaker pointed to the two people standing in the doorway of the house. Silas Cly stood by one doorpost and the woman, whom Dickens took to be the "widder" acquired by Cly, stood by the other. Dickens revised his estimate of Sly's moroseness — Tempest's soubriquet seemed very apt, however — but Mrs Cly, now that he saw her more clearly, was an even more miserable creation, as thin as her husband, with improbably black hair, darting black eyes, and a face that would curdle milk. Mrs Sly, then. As far as he could tell she stood on two legs. They looked like two wooden figure heads carved to fit a particularly narrow ship — a funeral barge, he thought. Mrs Cly did not look pleased to see a policeman approaching her — in fact, she looked positively murderous.

'Who is he?' Gaunt asked, indicating the coffin.

'No need fer no perlice. There's nothin' ter see. Jest a poor old cove. Not niver done no 'arm ter no 'un. An' 'is property's mine — not that 'e 'ad nothin' much, but 'e knew I woz good ter 'im.'

'I want to see that body.'

'Not your business, nor yours neither.' This last to Dickens, upon whom she directed a malevolent black glare. Perhaps she had seen his sceptical look when she used the word "good". He could see why Slog had put stones in his pockets.

John Gaunt was not to be put off. He went back to the coffin. 'Open it.'

The undertaker complied. Dickens went over to see for himself. It was not Long Jodd, just a poor, ancient man who looked like a waxwork figure already. Whoever he had been, he was gone now, absolutely gone. *Death*, he thought; lay death and sleep, side by side, and say who shall find the two akin. Someone had written that sleep and death were brothers — if it were so, then brother death was a gaunt spectre. There was no beauty of repose here in the sharp rigidity of his unsightly countenance.

Gaunt walked back to the pair at the door. 'I'm looking for a sailor named Long Jodd. Know him?'

Silas Cly spoke. 'Not niver 'eard of 'un.'

'Niver knowed no short Jodd neither,' Mrs Cly snorted. It was, perhaps, meant to be a laugh, but it failed somehow and dwindled to a sneer.

'Not niver 'eard of 'un, neither.' Mr Cly had even less sense of humour than his wife — and hers wasn't much.

Another thicket of negatives which, Dickens thought, revealed much about their attitude to life in general, which seemed to be composed of equal parts of disgust and resentment. However, Johnno, undaunted, took a cleaver to this dark forest and cut through it with Carver.

'Friend of Ned Carver. You know him.'

'Not niver seen 'un, neither, not for months.'

Dickens looked at the closed coffin in which the dead man was sealed now forever from life. He thought about Kit. He looked at Mrs Sly's sour face. Leave them to it. Let Johnno, or Bold find Long Jodd, or not. His task was to find Kit, and he should go to Erith.

Johnno, it seemed, was determined to get into the narrow house, so Dickens bade farewell to the other constable and went away back down Salmon's Lane. Crossing St Ann's Place, he stopped to gaze down into the waters of Limehouse Cut. The dead man's yellow face seemed to rise up like the face of a drowned man. There were bubbles on the sluggish, brown water. He thought of a drowning man down there, caught in weeds or ropes or chains, cut off from the light of the living world. Never to come up again from the dark. Full fathom five.

'Shouldn't care to go down there,' a voice said. He turned to see a man standing next to him, a man of the Captain Cuttle persuasion, one of those timber-looking men, stout of heart as well as limb. He had very light blue eyes, faded from wind, wave and weather, and a face criss-crossed with deep lines — the map of his life. It would be possible to trace continents there and read lines of longitude and latitude.

'I was thinking that myself — dreadfully dark down there.'

'Not the sea — always thought it wouldn't harm to go down in the sea's clear water and be washed clean.'

'A sailor?'

'Was, Captain Dick Pye at your service — not Cuttle.' He smiled, offering his hand.

Mind-reader, thought Dickens. *I wonder if he tells fortunes, too.* 'Charles —' he began.

'I know who you are. Remember you as a boy. You sang, as I recall, at your godfather's, Mr Huffam — down there.' He pointed down to Church Lane. 'Your father put you on a table and you sang the song of the cat's meat man. Your father, always a genial man — good company. Ah, the old days, the old days.'

'He was — is, I mean. Did you know Mr Penney and his son?'

'Of course, young Kit. Call in sometimes — at the shop.'

'I'm trying to find him — he is missing, and his friend Captain Valentine has been murdered on his ship.'

'I know, I heard. Know who did it?'

'The police suspect a sailor from his ship — Long Jodd.'

'Not a name I know, but I'll keep my ears open. But young Kit? Is it connected?'

'I don't know, but I thought to go to Erith where the Captain lived. Kit's mother thinks he might have gone there. You cannot think of anywhere else he might go if he were in danger? He left suddenly — the shop door open and his dog, Jam, found by a girl, Rosanna Chibb.'

Captain Pye thought, his eyes gazing along the canal where a sailing barge with its red-brown sails was making its serene way along the canal, bound for Limehouse Hole.

'Mrs Judith Black — the ship owner. Lives at Pekin Place, off Bow Lane. Kit will know her through the captain. He'd know people at the shipyard.'

'I'll try her if I have no luck at Erith. I am much obliged to you, Captain Pye. Here is my card. You'll let me know if you hear anything about Kit or Long Jodd — or anything.'

'I will. When found, make a note of.'

Dickens laughed at Captain Cuttle's words. Then he went on into Church Lane, pausing by Church Row where at number five his godfather had lived in the large handsome house outside the gates of Hawksmoor's St Anne's Church. *Ah, the old times*, he thought, echoing Captain Pye's words, *the old times*. Now the railway bisected the terrace, and the trains came shrieking, roaring and rattling past the old house and the great white church.

It was Christopher Huffam whose contacts with the East India trade were to have been the salvation of the Dickens family in 1824 when debts had piled up, and the young Dickens had become all too familiar with the pawnbrokers. People in the East India trade had daughters to be educated. The idea was that his mother should set up a school by which miracle the family fortunes would be restored. A house was found at Gower Street, and a brass plate bore the legend: *Mrs Dickens's Establishment*. Dickens remembered delivering a great many circulars to advertise the merits of this genteel school. No one came. And that was the end of it — and Christopher Huffam could offer no more help, and, even he, handsome and prosperous, had fallen on hard times and left nothing. Like that poor old man in his pauper's coffin.

He looked at the church — it had been on fire last year, but the great steeple with its clock still rose high into the air like a stone beacon, recording how the river flowed on and on to the sea, and showing the mariners that they were home. Fire, air, water and earth. His eye rested on the graveyard where the poor little ship-boys who had fallen overboard were buried — so many burials for the forgotten, the unknown, the found drowned. All the futures they never had.

With that melancholy thought, he walked on, thinking, in a muddled sort of way, about Captain Pye; longitude and latitude; a Huffam cousin, a ship's surgeon who had died at Madras; and again of his godfather Christopher Huffam, who had moved to Warkworth Terrace on the Commercial Road not long before his death in 1839. His wandering thoughts stopped abruptly at Warkworth Terrace — a name familiar for another more important reason, for there lived the chronometer and clockmaker, Charles Wieland, whom Kit had known. That might be somewhere to investigate — it was minutes away from where he was and not very far from Kit's shop. If Kit were running away, then somewhere near, surely. Ought he to turn back? No, Mrs Penney had said Erith. He should go there first. But, he had two names now: Judith Black and Charles Weiland. There was a chance.

He walked on, quickly now, down Church Lane, into Limehouse Causeway, and from there to the train which would take him to the steamer pier at Blackwall.

12: SHIPWRECKED HEARTS

The door of the tall, bow-windowed house at Erith was opened by a little, white-haired, pale-eyed girl in a dark grey dress and white apron to whom Dickens handed his card. She looked, her pale eyes widened, and she motioned him into the hall, a long, narrow apartment the walls of which were decorated with pictures of sailing ships: in storms, their great sails swollen; listing on foam-capped seas; in calms, the sails at rest; sailing in copper sunsets and pearly dawns; at anchor by wharves in exotic lands. There was one above a table, the ship foremost on a calm sea of peacock blue: *The Redemption*.

The little girl came out, motioned him to the open door of a room on the right, and vanished like a ghost into the grey shadows of a corridor.

He went in. There were three in the room, a young woman in black seated, a tall handsome woman who was standing, and, astonishingly, the pale child whom he had just seen vanishing down the hallway. How had she made division of herself?

The tall woman in black with a lace cap on her grey hair came forward.

'Mr Dickens, you are most welcome. I am Mrs Pink, and this is Mrs Grace Fox.'

Dickens bowed to the young woman in black who inclined her head. She looked stricken. Her face was very pale, and she was absolutely still as though frozen with grief.

'And this is Hope. You will have met her sister, Faith, at the door.' *Ah, twins.* 'The Darlings.' Dickens supposed that they were. 'Orphans — their father, Josh Darling, served under my husband, Captain Pink, and we took them in. Good girls.'

93

'I am sure they are.'

'You can go now, Faith, if you will.'

As Faith went out, a large, one-eyed black cat came in, a big bruiser with a sailor's gait and a bushy, black, waving tail.

'And this is Tar — as in Jack. A sailor once, but retired. His eye. We might have called him Nelson, but —'

'Piratical. The black flag?' Dickens looked at the tail.

Mrs Pink smiled. 'He's soft, really.'

The cat went over to Grace and sat by her feet, leaning against her skirts.

'A very gentle beast. I am so sorry to intrude, Mrs Pink. I hope you will both accept my sincere condolences. This is a dreadful thing.'

'It is. We are shocked into disbelief, Mr Dickens. We could hardly understand what the policeman told us.' Mrs Pink looked at Grace, who had bent down to stroke the cat — for warmth, perhaps. She looked at Dickens and shook her head. He saw her pity for Grace. 'But, you are here about Kit — we know you are his good friend. The policeman asked about him.'

'I am. He is not here?'

'I'm afraid not. We haven't seen him.'

'Can you think of anyone he might have gone to?'

'Shakespeare might know. What do you say, Grace?'

Grace nodded. *I suppose he might*, thought Dickens, *but as he's not here…* What a bewildering household this was, where folk spoke in riddles.

Mrs Pink saw his confusion. 'I beg your pardon, Mr Dickens, I see you are bemused — and well you might be. I should have explained. Shakespeare is Mr Tabor, who lodges upstairs.'

'Shakespeare Tabor?'

'Yes, indeed. His mother was on the stage and she — well, she would, I suppose — she named him for the playwright. It seemed to go with Tabor...'

Dickens murmured, 'I see.' Not that he did.

'Shakespeare and Kit are very good friends. Shakespeare paints ships and Kit bought some for his shop — to sell. So, I think you might talk to him. He is a man of ideas — and he might have an idea about Kit — where he might be.'

'Yes, I should like to speak to him.'

'Mouse will show you up. He'll like that, won't he, Grace? He likes to be useful.'

Dickens wondered about "Mouse" and how it got on with Jack Tar, whose ear seemed to twitch at the word.

'You'll get him, Grace, will you?'

Grace departed to fetch Mouse. Dickens could not help wondering whether the word should have the definite article: was it *the* mouse, or, perhaps *a* mouse, or something else entirely? Another tiny servant? A mouse couldn't...

Mrs Pink regarded him sympathetically. 'Mouse is Grace's son by her first husband, Decimus Fox.'

A menagerie, thought Dickens, *cat, mouse, fox*, but he nodded as if he understood it all.

Mrs Pink continued. 'Mr Fox, the Reverend Decimus Fox, died before his son was born. A very good man, Mr Dickens, full of good works round the docks, but a fever took him — it must be seven years ago, and poor as church mice, they were. Which is why Captain Pink brought Grace here and the baby. Reverend Fox was Captain Pink's sister's child. A very good woman. Dead long since. The baby was called Posthumous, but it is such a mouthful, and he, such a quiet little baby and so small, we called him Mouse.'

'Ah,' said Dickens, 'and Mr Tabor?'

'Decimus's cousin who needed company — a lonely fellow, so we invited him when Grace came. Such a happy family we were, until — Grace will not get over this, Mr Dickens, and as for Mouse —'

She broke off as Grace came back with the boy, who was still rather small with fair hair, a grave little face and wondering grey eyes behind the lenses of his spectacles. Dickens was reminded of his own boy, Sydney, who had the same faraway look sometimes. The Ocean-spectre, Dickens called him.

'This is Mr Dickens, Mouse — you know his books.'

Mouse stared at Dickens, his eyes widening. '*A Christmas Carol*? Scrooge?'

'Yes, indeed.'

'And Mr Pickwick, and Sam Weller, and David Copperfield?'

'Yes, all those.'

'I think you must be very clever,' the boy said approvingly.

'Well thank you.' Dickens bowed.

'Walter Gay's best. He went to sea. I shall go one day with the captain — he'll be home soon. We saw his ship go by. I saw it first.'

Dickens glanced at Mrs Pink. She shook her head very slightly. Then Mouse did not know yet. What a pity, it was. How would they tell him? All these lives spoilt — all their innocent happiness and hope crushed because one man sought to save himself. He thought of Long Jodd, and hoped that he would be found and pay for this cruelty.

Mouse took him up several flights of stairs until they came to a landing, from which another, very narrow flight, rose to what was presumably an attic room. He pointed upwards. 'He's up there. I'll wait for you.'

Dickens climbed up and found himself in a large loft-like chamber which was filled with light and packed with an extraordinary variety of objects: a globe on a table littered with maps, and books everywhere — his own, he noted — and various plays of Shakespeare, most with bits of string or ribbon slipped inside, others open on other tables, sheets of paper held down by a glass paperweight with a ship inside it, a ship in a bottle, several quills and bottles of ink. Some of the papers were covered in writing — blue ink, the colour he used. Perhaps Mr Tabor was writing a book — a play, perhaps. There were paintings of ships on the walls, and an unfinished one on an easel, above which a stuffed seagull perched.

There was a myna bird in a cage — its black feathers iridescent in the dazzling light that came from the skylight and the open doors which gave on to a makeshift balcony made of planks. He could see a balustraded section which made it look like the deck of a ship. On the deck stood a man looking through a spy glass.

The myna bird spoke first. 'To be or not to be.'

'That is the question,' Dickens responded automatically.

'Ship-shape, ship-shape,' the bird squawked.

The man on the balcony came in. 'To be or not to be,' the bird repeated.

'Hamlet — his name,' the man said, indicating the myna bird.

''Tis not alone my inky coat, good mother,' Dickens found he couldn't stop himself.

'Mother, mother,' the bird answered.

'A snapper-up of unconsidered trifles,' Dickens smiled at the man.

'Indeed, he is.' Shakespeare Tabor came further into the room, laughing. 'He picks up anything a visitor says. But, I know you — you're Mr Dickens.'

'What the dickens! What the dickens!' Hamlet asked.

'I wonder myself.' Dickens bowed to the bird.

'I'll put him out —'

Dickens looked at the bird's beady eye. 'Out damned spot.'

'Don't encourage him or he'll monopolise the conversation.' Shakespeare Tabor took the bird and its cage onto the balcony from where Dickens heard him still screeching, 'What the dickens, dickens,' which ended in what sounded like a jeering cackle. It was quite unnerving. Shakespeare closed the doors. 'His manners are not always the best — offensive creature. Tar gives him a wide berth.' He smiled.

'No offence in the world, Mr Tabor,' Dickens offered his hand to the tall, thin man who had a high, very pale, domed head towards the back of which grew a bush of thick, black hair. His eyes were warm and brown and wise behind his spectacles. *Wisdom and constancy*, thought Dickens — this quoting of Shakespeare was catching.

'I am very glad to meet you — very glad, indeed. Your books —' Shakespeare Tabor pointed to the familiar volumes.

'And Shakespeare, of course,' said Dickens, smiling, 'and you write as well as paint?' He pointed to the papers on the table.

'I'm writing a little pamphlet — it's about Shakespeare and the sea. Hope to get it published. Know anyone?' His eyes sparkled.

'Oh, I might — you could send it to me at *Household Words*.'

'It will be a while. I'm just sorting out the quotations — copying them, you know, trying to order my thoughts. Work in progress.'

Dickens wondered whether it might be like Dr Strong's dictionary or Mr Dick's history of Charles the First — doomed to be always in progress. He smiled encouragingly and wondered when he might broach the subject of Kit and the Captain. *Give him time*, he thought. He'll come to it. He knows what I'm here for. Dickens could tell that Shakespeare Tabor knew by the nervous flutterings of his hands. He picked up a quill pen and put it down again, picked up some papers, glanced at them and back to Dickens.

'You know, Mr Dickens, I believe he went to sea. How else could he have known? Storms you see. *The Tempest*, *Twelfth Night*, *Comedy of Errors*, *Pericles* and, of course, Wapping — the stairs from where Raleigh and Drake set off…'

Shakespeare Tabor paused at Wapping Stairs and sat down suddenly. He removed his spectacles and wiped his eyes on a paint-smeared rag which he picked up absently from the table. Dickens waited.

'I beg your pardon, Mr Dickens. I know what you've come for, and I thank you for your patience while I babbled of the sea.'

'Not at all, Mr Tabor — I understand. The captain's death — what a blow it is for all of you.'

'That poor girl downstairs — and the child. We have not told him. I do not know how we are to do it. Such innocence. How could anyone do such a thing?' Shakespeare Tabor looked at Dickens as if he might know the answer. *And I do*, thought Dickens. Greed, revenge, selfishness, fell cruelty — all come to stalk this innocent house.

'Wapping,' continued Shakespeare Tabor, 'where I met Kit and the captain. Now, I think, I should not have brought the captain here.'

'You could not have known. I met Louis Valentine with Kit — a good young man who needed to find happiness, I thought, and he did. That is something, perhaps.'

'Not enough, though — they should have had years, and shall she love again? I think not, Mr Dickens. She waited so long…'

He loves her. I see that. Dickens looked at the weeping man. *But it is an unselfish love, the kind of love that is content to serve.* Grace Fox had something left: her child, Mrs Pink, Captain Pink who would come home to them, and Shakespeare Tabor. Perhaps, one day — he hoped it might be so. But, he said nothing. He waited for the man to recover himself.

'I beg your pardon, Mr Dickens,' Tabor said, wiping his eyes again, 'weakness, I know.'

'We should never be ashamed of our tears, Mr Tabor.'

'Thank you — you have come to ask about Kit.'

'Yes, you know he is missing.'

'I do — but the police can't think that Kit had anything to do with the Captain's death. Not a bad word for anyone — but you know that, Mr Dickens.'

'Of course, and the police suspect one of the sailors. They are searching for him. However, Mrs Penney believes that someone was at the shop and that Kit has fled from danger. She asked me to come. I wonder if you can think of anywhere he might go.'

'There's Charles Wieland — his shop is on Commercial Road — you know him?'

'I know that he is Kit's friend. I shall go there when I return to Blackwall. I should go now for the ferry.'

'And I will send to you if I hear of Kit, and you will tell us if you hear anything more about the Captain.' Shakespeare Tabor's eyes filled again.

'I shall, you may be sure. Good day, Mr Tabor.'

Dickens went down the narrow stairs to find the boy, Mouse, who was sitting silently and patiently on the top step of the next flight of stairs. The child stood.

'I'll take you down.' Mouse took Dickens's hand in a gesture so confiding and innocent that Dickens felt like weeping.

'When Walter went to sea and was lost, I thought he might not come back, but you brought him home, Mr Dickens, to marry Florence Dombey. A happy ending. I liked that.'

And I cannot bring Louis Valentine home — would that I could. Dickens could not answer.

They reached the hall where Grace was waiting with Faith, or was it Hope? They would need both. Grace asked the girl to take Mouse into the kitchen for his tea and asked Dickens if he would take tea in the parlour with Mrs Pink.

'Thank you, but I must not. I have promised Mrs Penney, and Mr Tabor has suggested a place where I might ask about Kit.'

'Do you think they are connected — Kit and...'

The tears gathered at her eyes and ran down her cheeks. She wept soundlessly. Dickens took her hand, and when she raised her swimming eyes, she saw his blue ones gazing at her so tenderly. She felt the warmth of his hand covering hers — so had Louis held her. Never again. She felt a tidal wave of grief where before she had felt made of ice.

'I was asleep — I fell asleep, thinking of him, and he was dying. I should have been awake, I should...'

'It wants time,' he murmured.

'A long time.' She leant against him and he felt her heart beat faintly. Still alive — just. She smelt of violets. Fragile and shy in dim woods.

'It will be so.'

He pitied her profoundly. She seemed to be drowning before him and there was no help he could give, except to stand with her hand in his and wait. At length, the parlour door opened to reveal Mrs Pink, who came out to bid him farewell. Grace murmured, 'Thank you,' and faded away down the shadowy corridor.

'You have done her good, Mr Dickens,' Mrs Pink said. 'I thought she would not weep. It is better that she does.'

'I think so, too. And now I must go to see Mrs Penney. Goodbye, Mrs Pink. I will send to you if I hear more of Kit or the Captain.'

Mrs Pink opened the door for him and watched him walk quickly away towards the pier. Whatever had passed between him and Grace, it had unlocked something. And that was for the good — if there were anything good to come out of this disaster. How she longed for Captain Pink to come home. She looked at the setting sun. Fair weather. Soon. She shut the door and went back into the house into which such darkness had come.

13: THE COMFORT OF FRIENDS

Charles Wieland was an old-fashioned, gentlemanly person who received Mr Dickens most cordially in his shop at Warkworth Terrace. He was about fifty and had been at Warkworth Terrace for above twenty years. The shop was a place of wonder. In the glass cases were all kinds of shining instruments, and, on the counter a fine mahogany and brass eight-day marine chronometer. Dickens thought of the instrument on Kit's counter and the piece of glass on the floor. He asked his question, but Wieland could tell Dickens nothing of Kit. Mr Weiland promised, as all the others had, to send to him if he heard anything.

Dickens trudged back, weary now, to see Mrs Penney, but there was no news there, either. Rosanna Chibb came in with Jam, both looking as forlorn as he felt. He thought he would not mention Mrs Judith Black. No use in getting her hopes up again. He made all his promises and went out to take the train in the opposite direction to Fenchurch Street. Time to go home. Rosanna Chibb and Jam came with him.

'Going home, now, Rosanna? You look tired.'

'I'll find him, Mr Dickens, I will. Me and Jam'll search till, till — next Christmas —' Jam didn't look convinced. His tail drooped and he looked at Dickens with, he thought, the perfect incarnation of a hang-dog expression — 'He's got to be somewhere. Jam needs him, Mrs Penney needs him, an' I…'

'He's your friend.'

'He teaches me — I want —' She fell silent. Her eyes, the colour of treacle, burned with tears, but they didn't fall. 'My pa's dead. I miss him, but Mr Kit helped. He let me come to the shop to learn. I want to know.'

'What does he teach you?'

'All about the instruments an' how to make them. He said I was good — I could be his apprentice. Mrs Penney wasn't sure, but Mr Kit persuaded her. Why shouldn't a girl make the clocks an' chronometers? Why not?' There was a challenge in her eyes now. She'd defy the world, this one.

Why not? Dickens thought about Katey, his daughter, about the same age as Rosanna. He thought she might be a painter. Judith Black, the shipyard owner; Mrs Gaskell's novels; Lady Ada Lovelace, Byron's daughter. The Enchantress of Numbers, Charles Babbage called her. He thought of the child, Ada, sucking her feathered quill, working out her equations. But a child from a common lodging house? He looked at the dark eyes glinting her face. She might — with Kit's help.

'You can, and Mr Kit will come back, I'm sure of it.'

But she knew he wasn't. She saw too much. Her old eyes looked at him with something he thought was pity. She didn't believe in him. Well, he didn't believe in himself just at that moment.

'Which way do you go?'

'Back of Three Colt Street.'

They walked together in silence until Rosanna said, 'Captain Valentine was Mr Kit's friend. Someone killed him, and now Mr Kit ain't here. No one's said anythin' — no one tells kids anythin'. They think we don't see. I saw it in your eyes, Mr Dickens, but I've been thinkin', an' you said to be careful before. You think he's dead, don't you?'

He looked her straight in the eye, meeting her challenge. The truth then, for this brave girl. 'I don't know, Rosanna, and that's the truth, but I hope and so must you — hope to the end.'

They walked on until they came to a turning into a little court.

'Home's down there where ma is — she runs a lodgin' house. The Black sailors come cos of pa. I help — washin', shoppin', cookin' — but there's got to be more, Mr Dickens, there's got to be — or there's no hope. My grandpa was a slave — why must I be?'

Dickens had a thought. 'Did you know Pilgrim, the captain's friend?'

'Yes, he came to stay sometimes. Knew pa, but I haven't seen him this time. Thought he'd gone to Erith.'

'No, Rosanna, I've been there.'

'He's missin', too? Could he be with Mr Kit? They can't both be dead.'

'No, I don't think so — perhaps they are together. Keep looking, but be careful Rosanna — I beg you.'

'I will. I've got Jam.'

'And Percy Slinger?'

'Sometimes, but I know more places, an' no one notices a girl an' a dog.'

He looked at her proud face — she'd be a beauty. Was — almost. He saw the fine bones of her face, the slender neck, the dark curly hair worn loose and short. Her dress was of some drab material, but she had tied round her neck an old red silk handkerchief which gave her the rakish look of a boy. She'd be noticed. He felt a tremor of fear, suddenly seeing Long Jodd's tufted hands, and remembering a boy, perhaps pushed over the side, his body plunging down, gasping for breath, his lungs bursting, until he lay, forgotten, fathoms deep in the cradle of the sea.

'I mean it, Rosanna — no going about in the dark.'

She saw that he did. His intent eyes held hers. He could be fierce, this Mr Dickens. But then she should have known that. Mr Kit talked about him and he had lent her some books. The girls weren't up to much, she thought, but he knew about folk, how they lived, what they felt — just ordinary folk. The kids in *Oliver Twist* — she knew plenty like them, and Limehouse, he'd described it just as she saw it, and he was angry about it, even though you laughed sometimes. You could trust him. Not many you could. She promised. She wouldn't take risks. But she wouldn't take Percy Slinger, either.

Dickens went on his way. From Fenchurch station, he decided, he would take a cab to Bow Street. He wanted to see Sam, just to talk to him. He needed something, comfort, apart from a glass of something warm, and food, he thought, remembering that he had eaten nothing since Percy Slinger had fetched him from Devonshire Terrace. It seemed an age ago, and nothing to show for his peregrinations. Nothing but a sense of defeat and pity. Until he had listened to the child and watched Grace Fox dissolve before his eyes, he had not thought much about poor Louis Valentine. Kit had occupied his mind, but seeing them all at Vernon House had brought home the terrible price of murder.

He thought of rooms left empty where the dead were absent now; he thought of the empty bed where the pillow bore the imprint of the beloved head; the unused brush in which the hair was still wound; and the silver-backed mirror marked by the faint stain of a breath, but which now reflected only the empty sky.

He quickened his pace. Long Jodd must be found, but what could he do? Inspector Bold seemed a determined fellow, and Johnno too. Perhaps they would find Jodd. But Sam, he thought, Sam was the man he needed, yet he couldn't help — except that Dickens could talk to him.

At Bow Street, Jones took one look at him and took him straightaway in a cab to his own house in Norfolk Street where Elizabeth, his wife, took another look and brought hot tea, soup and bread, and Dickens was ordered not to speak of anything until he had drunk the tea and eaten the bread and soup. He felt better then, not just for the food, but for the warmth of their care and concern. Sometimes, he thought, a person just needed looking after. No questions asked. He supposed that he gave the impression of such purpose and unlimited strength that he needed no such things — but, oh, that want of something, something he had not had, how it possessed him in his lonely moments. That something that Sam and Elizabeth had, and which showed so vividly in their unspoken glances. Elizabeth had known without Sam's telling just what their guest had needed.

Jones regarded him gravely as he ate his soup. He remembered the other night when Dickens had spoken of his ills — something eating away at him. His face looked older tonight, haggard with weariness and misery, and his eyes glinting with unshed tears. There were lines he had not noticed before. Jones felt sad. Dickens was getting older. Jones had always thought of him as a young man. Fatherless Dick, he had once called himself. And all day he had been tearing about, looking for his friend. He would wear himself into shreds.

Jones gave him a brandy. 'And now you may tell me all.'

'Superintendent, Sir,' Dickens smiled and was more like himself.

Dickens told of all he had done that day, first of Mrs Penney, Johnno, Silas Cly and his Missus. 'A mouldy swab as ever broke biscuit, he, and, she with a face like a slab of cold veal.'

Jones chuckled. 'I'd know them as soon as I saw them.'

'I tell you she reminded me of that Maggie Brine we met when we were looking for that young man, Theo Outfin, when Scrap went missing.'

'Yes, I remember — I'll not forget her vitriolic gin in a hurry.'

'Heroic, you were.'

'She thought you were temperance. Drink up. Medicinal, of course.'

Dickens laughed. The shared memories warmed him, too. He told of Captain Pye, Mrs Pink, and Shakespeare Tabor at whose name Jones interrupted with an astonished, 'Who?'

'I know, I know, extraordinary, ain't it — his mother was on the stage. A most cordial fellow most grieved about the captain and his affianced lady, Mrs Fox.'

Dickens went on to speak of Grace and Mouse. 'That poor, poor girl — if you had seen her. I thought she would drown of her grief. I thought then of poor Louis Valentine as well as Kit. It's all so hopeless, and I feel so helpless.'

'I don't know what more you can do, but if you would like, I will give you a hand tomorrow. Keep you company.'

'It is just what I would like, if you can.'

'Well, if, as you say, Bold is convinced that Jodd is the murderer, he won't take it amiss if I help you look for your friend. Have you any other leads?'

'Shakespeare Tabor mentioned the ship owner — a lady, it seems, who runs a yard at Blackwall and lives at Pekin Place, off Bow lane, not far from the East India Docks. I hadn't the strength to go today, but I thought tomorrow.'

'I can come with you. Shall I collect you from Wellington Street at 10.30?'

'Yes, I'll go to the office early. I ought to see Harry Wills. I didn't even leave a message this morning.'

'I'll walk with you — part of the way.'

'You do me good, Samivel, as always.'

'Perpetivally at your service, Mr Pickwick.'

They went out into the street just as a cab drew up on the opposite side. A policeman jumped out.

'Sir, Sir,' he shouted.

Jones recognised the voice of Constable Feak. 'What's up?'

'Body, Sir. Sergeant Rogers said to come. An' Constable Dacres is injured.'

'Tell the cab to wait.'

Feak did so and came across the road.

'Dacres — is it serious?'

'Don't think so.'

'Where?'

'Portugal Street, Sir, just by the gates of the burial ground. See, Sir, Mr Meteyard found 'im —'

'The butcher?' exclaimed Dickens.

'No, sir, the barrister, an' Mr Rogers thought you should come, Mr Jones, as you know Mr Meteyard.'

14: BURIAL GROUND

Henry Meteyard, son of the butcher, Sampson Meteyard, and barrister at law, had just rounded the bend on Portugal Street which led to Portugal Row, on his way to his apartments in Lincoln's Inn Fields, when he heard the shout. Recognising the voice, he ran back towards the burial ground.

Portugal Street burying ground was known familiarly as 'the green ground' — not that there was anything green about it nowadays except the noxious gases that rose like mist from a swamp. The gates were in Portugal Street and it was, conveniently, if you had a mordant sense of humour, next door to King's College hospital whose windows looked out over the dead, affording the patients a grim reminder of their fate, as if the cholera, typhus fever, bronchial disease, or gangrenous leg, or the deaths of their children, had not already done so.

In a region which Dickens had called a wilderness of dirt and misery, the burial ground at night had a sinister aspect. There were plenty of folk about though the hour was late — comings and goings from the hospital; idlers lounging at shop windows; a woman with several children huddling in a doorway; a knot of men grouped by a cart, the wheel of which had come off so that it slumped in the street, its load of pots and pans and miscellaneous iron bits scattered on the ground; an unseen woman screaming and another screaming in answer. And someone laughed madly, somewhere down an alley, as if from some dark future about which only he knew the joke.

Yet, it was quiet, as always by the burial ground — the smell, perhaps, put off even these denizens of the pernicious stews and alleys, whose poisoned lives were spent in squalor and desperation. Or, more likely, the sight by day, and the thought by night, of the mist rising, and the dead rising from their graves. These dead tended to rise by day, too. Sometimes open coffins were left stranded in a sea of putrescence while the gravediggers made room in the hole — some second guest to entertain. Bones, severed hands, legs, arms, had all been seen scattered on the saturated ground, waiting for the day when they might be reassembled to meet their maker.

Henry Meteyard had said goodnight to Doctor Allan Woodhall, member of the Royal College of Surgeons, which was in Lincoln's Inn Fields. Doctor Woodhall practised at the King's College Hospital on Portugal Street just below Lincoln's Inn Fields.

Neither the burial ground nor nearby Butcher's Row held terrors for Henry Meteyard; he was familiar with the stench of blood and the sight of dead meat from the slaughterhouse behind Gun Street. It was the living with whom he was concerned — as was the doctor, or often, the nearly dying — dying from typhus fever caught from, he firmly believed, the open cesspits in the alleys and courts and the poisonous gases which rose from the burial ground and seeped into the hospital wards. The doctor wanted, above all, to see the removal of the burying ground, preferably before he went to his own grave. And, the slums, of course, but that would take longer, until eternity, he supposed in his pessimistic hours — as if the Burial Grounds Commission were not taking long enough. However, he had given his evidence to it, as had Henry.

It was of these matters that they had been talking as they walked up St Clement's Lane. They had talked of Henry Austin's report on the burial grounds, and of Mr Dickens's powerful article: *A December Vision*, a terrible portrait of a diseased and infected city, published just last December in *Household Words*.

Allan Woodhall had turned the corner into a pool of blackness which was the space before the steps that led up to the gates of the burial place. There had been a lamp once — but it had long gone out. He heard a noise — a kind of grunt, as of someone in pain.

'Do you need help?' he cried out, peering into the darkness and making out, he thought, the figure of a man, seemingly bending over something black on the steps. And then something erupted from the darkness and crashed into him with such force that they both staggered. Woodhall shouted out and attempted to hold on to the struggling man.

Henry Meteyard arrived just in time to see Woodhall fall. The assailant's left fist had shot out and struck him a powerful blow to the chest which knocked Woodhall down. The stranger saw Meteyard, thrust past him, and ran off down Portugal Street. Seeing Doctor Woodhall begin to get up, Henry gave chase, but the fallen cart impeded him, and some public-spirited citizen stuck out his leg and Meteyard fell, too. The assailant ran on. A police constable appeared, but he, too, was felled, and landed amongst another knot of idlers who cheered. Henry Meteyard stood and looked about him, but whoever had tripped him had vanished, too. Pity, he'd liked to have punched his head in — growing up in Limehouse had meant he was handy with his fists.

The policeman lay in the mud. Henry went to help him. The crowd, seeing the tall, powerful man with his fists at the ready, deemed it politic to retire. Henry helped himself to the policeman's rattle and swung it, bringing two more constables from the end of the street.

'Take charge here,' Henry ordered, 'and one of you, come with me — my friend was knocked down by the same man.'

'Stemp, sir, Bow Street,' said the taller of the two constables. 'Superintendent Jones?'

'Yes, sir.'

They went back down the street to find the doctor kneeling by the body of a man lying on the steps of the burial ground.

'Murder,' he said.

The cab dropped Dickens, Jones and Feak at the end of Portugal Street. Jones could see Stemp standing guard with his lamp and the burly figure of Henry Meteyard. Sergeant Rogers came out and greeted the Superintendent who asked, 'Dacres?'

'All right, Sir, bump on the head. The doctor had a look at him. Feak brought him back to the station. I came straight here, saw Mr Meteyard, and sent for you.'

Jones turned to Henry. 'As well you were here. What does the doctor say?' He gestured to the step.

The dead man was sprawled on the steps, his face down on the cold stone, one hand reaching out to the gate as if he were pleading to get in; the other arm was invisible under the body.

The doctor looked up at Jones. 'Allan Woodhall. I've not moved him. Your Sergeant told me to wait for you. A stabbing, I think, in the throat, but I need more light.'

Dickens stepped forward. 'Poor fellow.'

Henry Meteyard looked at Dickens. 'Mr Dickens — you here?'

'Yes, I was with Superintendent Jones, telling him about my attempts to find Kit Penney.'

'My father told me about it and Captain Valentine's death.'

'Doctor Woodhall, would you turn him over?' Jones said.

Rogers gave his lamp to Henry Meteyard and helped the doctor turned over the dead man. The head lolled backwards, and the doctor steadied it. His throat had been cut. They could see the wound. Blood had poured from it. The victim's coat was sodden, and there was blood on the steps.

'If one of you could hold the head?'

Rogers went to kneel by the dead man's head, which he cradled in his hands.

'Just tilt it backwards a little. That's it.'

They waited and watched the figures in the lamplight. They looked at the dead man's face, so still and pale with the dreadful gash at his throat. *So sudden*, thought Dickens. His life extinguished like a candle flame. Out, out, brief candle. Death had come and gone, a fleet assassin in the night.

The doctor was quite still, too, as he looked at the wound. It might have been a painting, the light falling on the two faces, Rogers, a shadowy figure, only his strong hands illuminated. Then they could see the doctor's fine white hands gently pulling away the shirt and cravat, both blood-stained. They saw the hands delicately exploring the wound and the back of the neck. He looked up at them, his pale face long and haggard in the yellow light.

'A deep incision, so deep that it has divided the windpipe, the gullet and severed the carotid artery and the jugular vein. He would have died very quickly. Certainly, he was dead by the time I had struggled with the murderer, picked myself up and came to see. And look how the hands are clenched, which tells us that the attack was sudden and there was no resistance from the dead man.'

They looked at the hands. 'What's that paper?' In the hand that had been concealed under the body, there was a torn piece of paper. Doctor Woodhall gently prised open the fingers and handed the paper to Jones.

'It often happens that the victim is found with something still held firmly — I once examined a woman who held on to a snuff box — it was clearly murder as this is.'

In the lamplight they could see that it was part of an envelope on which was some writing. Jones looked closely.

'Hard to tell. An address, perhaps. It looks like a capital *M* and then *a* and *d*; then there's a tear and what looks like a capital *T*. Underneath —' Jones raised the paper to see more closely — 'a capital *R* then *e* — the next letter's partly torn off. Could be a *d*. Take a look Rogers, you've good eyes.'

'I think it's an address — the capital *R* is sloped, not under the *M*, and there's a small *s* and a space before the *M*, and what might be part of a capital *L* after the *d*.'

'Red Lion Square, perhaps?' Henry Meteyard offered.

'Or Red Lion Inn,' the doctor said.

'Could be,' said Rogers, 'they're just over the road, across Holborn — he might have been goin' there.'

'He might. Not that it helps at the moment since we've no idea who he is. Anything in the pockets, Doctor Woodhall?'

The doctor felt in the pockets of the jacket, trousers and waistcoat. 'Nothing — no money, no papers, not a thing to tell us who he was.'

'Can you tell us anything of the murderer?'

'Not much — it's so dark just here and it was so quick. I heard a groan or a grunt and shouted did he or they need help. Someone burst out from the gateway, here, shoved into me. I tried to hold on, but he struck out and I went down, then Henry came running. Thick, dark coat, taller than me, strong as the devil.'

Jones turned to Henry Meteyard. 'What did you see of him?'

'I ran after him and when he turned to look back, I saw his face just fleetingly as the moon came out. Dark face —'

'Not Black?' Dickens asked.

'Hard to say. He wore a cap of some kind. I did get an impression of something shiny — it just caught the light. An earring, maybe, and added to that, I just thought — like a sailor. A pea jacket and wide trousers. I could be wrong, but —'

'You've seen plenty of sailors in Limehouse,' Dickens finished for him.

'Exactly.'

Doctor Woodhall looked up from the paper. 'Henry, can you shine your light here — I wonder if the *s* here just before the capital *M* could form *Miss* or *Mrs*, then *M* — *a* — *d* — *e* —, and I think the next letter could be *l*. The second name begins with a *T* and then —' he peered more closely — 'an *a* — I wonder if it might be —'

Henry interrupted, 'Mrs Madeleine Tallis who lives in Red Lion Square.'

'Lord, Sam, she's Captain Valentine's sister. Johnno told me. The sailor might have been Jodd.' He turned to the doctor. 'You didn't see his hands?' Dickens was thinking of the tattoo.

'I'm afraid not.' He turned his eyes to the paper which he had been contemplating.

That was a leap, thought Jones, more cautious, from a possible sailor to Long Jodd. Once Dickens got an idea, it was hard to shift him. Still, he might be right. He often was, and he was observant. He would notice the mote in a man's eye where another might just see the beam.

'What do you know of Mrs Tallis, Mr Meteyard?'

'I know them. Mr Justice Tallis is her husband.'

'Then we will go to see them. She might know who this is.'

'I can get the body taken to the hospital mortuary and let you know if I find out anything more when I've examined him and from the post-mortem.'

'I am obliged to you, Doctor. I'll come in the morning. Mr Meteyard, would you be willing to come with us to the Tallis house — it might help as you know them and have met Captain Valentine.'

'I will — gladly.'

'Rogers, I want you to wait while the doctor goes to get assistance with the body. Stemp can stay too. Then have a look about — see if anyone'll tell you what they saw. Not much chance, I know, but —'

'If he is a sailor, someone might have noticed — worth a try.'

Just as they made to go, Stemp called out. 'Found an 'at, Sir.'

He came forward, holding out a low crowned hat.

'Not the sailor's cap,' observed Henry Meteyard.

'The dead man's, maybe,' said Jones. 'Take it, would you, Doctor Woodhall, and keep it with the rest of his clothes. Now, we'll bid you goodnight, my thanks for your help.'

Doctor Woodhall went off to the hospital; the three others made their way to Red Lion Square, leaving Rogers, and Stemp, solid and imperturbable as ever, standing guard over the murdered man whose sightless eyes gazed up at the now hazy moon, staring back like an all-seeing eye. The eye saw the black river moving inexorably to the sea; it saw the great ships which on the dawn tide would unfurl their wings, ready to sail across the wide oceans to different worlds. Come morning, the eye would close, and open again on a house on an island far way where a man lay dying, his swollen heart ready to burst, and where another waited for news.

15: CROSS EXAMINED

Their way took them across Holborn into Dean Street, across Eagle Street, the birthplace, Dickens recalled, of the eccentric dentist, Van Butchell. He, who had sported a thirty-year-old beard and had exhibited the mummified corpse of his wife in his shop window — the corpse was now housed — if that was the word — at The Royal College of Surgeons. And, oddly, the dentist Samuel Cartwright had been born in Eagle Street, too. Something in the air? Teeth, he thought. Had the attacker been Long Jodd? He understood Sam's caution, and he still could not understand where Kit fitted into all this. Well, His Honour Mr Justice Tallis might have some answers.

He couldn't help glancing at the end of the large building on his right at the end of Dean Street: Day and Martin's Blacking Factory — the blacking polish used by Sam Weller at the White Hart Inn where Mr Pickwick had met him. Not Warren's — Dickens had enjoyed his revenge on the place of his servitude at Hungerford Stairs. He hurried to catch up. Leigh Street led them into Red Lion Square — teeth again and Leigh Hunt's tale of a lady of quality who lived in the square and had, according to Hunt, an alarming propensity for letting her false teeth slip out, then cramming them in again. All the better to eat you with, Dickens supposed. Henry Meteyard smiled at him as he went up the steps to the house. Good, strong, white teeth — a man you could trust. He wondered about the judge's teeth.

Not that he saw much of them. Much too high, the judge. Tall as Henry Meteyard, but much narrower. He could have been no other than he was. He had a head made expressly for a wig, a gleaming hawk's eye, a high-bridged nose, and the firm handshake of a man confident of his powers and repute. The hall seemed full of alarmingly tall men. Dickens felt insubstantial, and feeling that hawk's eye upon him, he rather wished he had not created Mr Justice Stareleigh. There were Pell, Dodson and Fogg and Serjeant Snubbin. And Sampson Brass, Quilp's slippery attorney — Dickens's lawyers tended to the ridiculous or the sinister. Henry Meteyard found it all very funny, but Judge Tallis had a disapproving air — the long nose, he supposed. Guilty as charged. And he was going to do it again — he thought of a half-finished article to be entitled *Red Tape*, which would take a very sharp knife to the law's entanglements.

The judge showed them into his library. The hour being late, he had answered the door himself. *Very late*, Jones had thought guiltily, seeing the judge frown at their presence on his steps after ten o'clock. He had, however, smiled, albeit thinly, at Henry Meteyard, and let them in.

Henry asked about Mrs Tallis, but the judge regretted that she was asleep. 'She is most distressed about her brother, as you may understand.' His eye regarded the Superintendent rather coldly. 'You may state your business to me, Superintendent.'

Jones explained the events of the night, and showed the paper. 'This was in the dead man's hand. Mr Meteyard and Doctor Woodhall wondered if the name might be your wife's, and the letters may well be part of your address.'

The Judge reached for his spectacles. Dickens half expected him to put on his wig — there was something so much of on the bench about him. He examined the paper and delivered his verdict. 'It may well be, but I cannot think who might be the bearer of such a letter — you assume that the attacker took the letter.'

'We do,' Jones answered, 'and the reason we are particularly concerned is that the victim was murdered in the same way as Captain Valentine. Mr Meteyard thought he saw a sailor running away — the man who knocked down Doctor Woodhall and my constable.'

Judge Tallis regarded Henry, who prepared to give his witness statement. Dickens wondered if the "thought he saw" accounted for the steely gleam in the judge's eye. Even Henry looked a little doubtful, but he spoke up.

'It was an impression, sir, of dark skin, an earring catching the light, a peacoat —'

'An impression?' Very much the judge.

'Yes, I am afraid that is all I can say.'

'Hm. Superintendent, perhaps you would be good enough to explain the connection with the murder of my poor brother-in-law.'

'Inspector Bold of the River Police is looking for a sailor called Long Jodd who, it appears, harboured a grudge against the captain, and who has vanished. Mr Dickens was there when the Inspector interviewed members of the crew of *The Redemption*.'

'And your part in this, Mr Dickens?'

'I am seeking Captain Valentine's friend, Kit Penney, who is my very old friend who disappeared on the night the Captain was killed. I am very concerned about him.'

'You discern a connection between the disappearance of Mr Penney and the death of Louis?'

The wording of the question seemed to Dickens to have in it a suggestion that Kit might be nefariously involved. Jones saw a dangerous glint in Dickens's eyes, the same glitter that he had seen when he had mentioned Inspector Bold's interest in Kit. He waited rather apprehensively, wondering if Dickens might metaphorically unsheathe his sword. The judge might tower over Dickens, but Dickens roused could be very formidable.

Dickens retained his composure. 'I do not know, but there were signs of a disturbance at Mr Penney's shop and house which suggested precipitate flight of a fearful, not a guilty kind.'

Touché, thought Jones. He understood the natural inclination of the judge to cross examine his witnesses, but he felt a growing impatience. They weren't in court. Nevertheless, he looked quickly at Dickens. *Softly, now*, his glance warned.

The judge looked at Dickens. 'You knew Louis?'

'I met him — a good young man, and I met Mrs Grace Fox and all that kindly household. Mrs Fox is grief-stricken — I do not know how she will go on. She has not told her son yet — the little boy expects the captain hourly.'

Bravo, Jones cheered inwardly. Mr Justice Tallis had stood over them, every inch a judge. He sat down suddenly — a human being. Dickens felt as surprised as if he had seen the judge in his night-cap.

Tallis addressed himself to Dickens. 'I beg your pardon, Mr Dickens, I forget myself sometimes. It is second nature. Henry can tell you —' He smiled then, and Dickens saw that his teeth were white and even — 'But, I will speak frankly to you now. I love my wife, and I was very fond of Louis. We met Mrs Fox and her little boy — an engaging child. We have no children. You have made me realise the deep significance of it all. Forgive my brusqueness. You, too, Henry, and Superintendent Jones. How may I help?'

'I should like you to think of anyone connected to the captain who might come here.'

'I can think of someone connected to my wife and the captain. She was expecting a letter from her stepfather, who lives on the island of St Lucia — Madeleine and her brother were brought up there. Their story is quite a complicated one, but I need not dwell on that. Some weeks ago, my wife received news that her stepfather's agent, Mr Peter Best, would be coming to England on *The Endeavour*, which was due in the West India Dock some days ago. Naturally, she expected to hear from him, but the news of Louis' death put it out of our minds. I cannot help you as to identification of your victim. Neither my wife nor I have ever met him, but the sea-faring connection is there.'

'And it is one that I shall investigate, sir. I can send to the shipping offices for news of *The Endeavour* and her passengers. Thank you for your time, Mr Tallis. I must be on my way back to Bow Street.'

The judge escorted them to the door. As Jones and Henry went out, he touched Dickens's arm. 'I hope you will come back, Mr Dickens, to tell me news of your friend, Mr Penney. I hope you will find him. And my wife would like to meet you, I am sure. You might talk to her of Louis and Grace and the boy — she will want to see them, in time.'

'Most certainly, I will, Mr Tallis. Goodnight.'

They paused at the corner of Holborn Row where they would part, Henry going to his rooms at Lincoln's Inn Fields, Dickens and Jones to Bow Street.

'I always had a feeling that Tallis might be human, Charles, and you found it out in minutes. I take my hat off to you. It's taken me years.'

'Nobody would suppose it, Henry, nobody ever supposes it, bar the Superintendent, here, who is a man of superhuman perspicacity, but I am naturally a bashful man, and your words bring a blush to my cheeks which only the darkness conceals.'

Jones laughed. 'Shyer than my maiden aunt.'

'Not quite,' said Dickens, 'a lady so retiring that no one has ever seen her.'

'I certainly should never have supposed it,' laughed Henry. 'Let me know what I might do, Charles. My father is most upset about Kit. Whatever help I can give, Superintendent.'

'If you go down to Limehouse, keep your ears open, Henry — you might hear something.'

'I will. Goodnight to both of you.'

Dickens and Jones went on along great Queen Street. 'Check to the judge,' observed Jones.

'I saw your warning glance, otherwise I might have said more than I ought.'

'What you said pierced his legal breastplate — you brought home to him the meaning of Captain Valentine's death.'

'I suppose I remembered how it was brought home to me. He thought only of his wife, and I thought only of Kit until I went to Erith.'

'And we have a name, perhaps.'

'Peter Best — but who killed him?'

'And why?'

16: WHO IS HE?

'Nobody knows nothink, I suppose,' Dickens remarked. It was morning and he had come to Bow Street after flitting into the office to see Henry Wills, the sub-editor. He was conscious of the many different businesses for *Household Words* that he had left with Henry Wills. *Sir Giles Overreach, I am*, but he had turned his back on his overflowing desk.

'That's about it.' Jones was recounting the adventures of Rogers and Stemp who had searched in vain for the vanished assailant. 'Nobody saw anything, nobody heard anything, and, as you say, nobody knows anything about anything at all.'

'Blind, deaf and dumb.'

'Quite. It comes on them very suddenly. Just one thing. Some old law writer on his way to Took's Court was knocked off his feet by a running man — thought nothing of it — happens all the time — and Rogers got the impression that he was never steady on his feet anyway — smell of brandy. Sailor, the old man thought. They went up the way he pointed. Called in at The Ship Tavern on the reasonable grounds that the name suggested the ocean. Nothing doing. But it was very crowded — quite a party going on. I don't suppose the drinkers would have noticed any stranger, and you know how knotted the lanes are round there. Same story at The Seven Stars. Nothing.'

'Nothink will come of nothink, as the Stratford man might have said,' observed Dickens somewhat gloomily. Jones laughed. 'Well, he might have picked up a bit of the cockney when he was down at Cheapside.'

'The equation's just the same, however he said it.'

'There was a clerk called Lear at the solicitor's where I worked as a young sprig — nothink came of that, either. I used to drop cherry stones on passers-by to pass the time. Ah, noiseless time, the greatest spinner of them all...'

'And we're wasting it. I am due at the mortuary. Moreover, in the hope of adding something to our meagre store of knowledge, I've sent Rogers to the West India Dock office to find out if a Mr Best was actually a passenger on *The Endeavour*.'

'I am bound for Mrs Judith Black in Pekin Place — I suppose she'll speak only Chinese.'

'Very droll. I shall have to go that way myself. I must parley with Inspector Bold and Johnno; if these two cases are connected — and they may well be if last night's victim is Peter Best — then co-operation is required.'

'I'll come with you to the mortuary then. Could we go to Mrs Black after you've seen Bold?'

'We could.'

Swift strides took them across Drury Lane and on to Blackmore Street. Somewhereabouts was Clare Court, where Dickens remembered buying a half-penny plate of beef at Johnson's a-la-mode Beef-house. He had been twelve then, and he could still taste it. They went through clamorous Clare Market where butcher's beef from the Portugal Street slaughterhouses lay in ghastly piles of fly-covered, bloodied flesh, the iron smell mingling with the smell of dung and mud, the charcoal smoke from braziers, rotten vegetables and unwashed humanity. Bleary-eyed oysters gazed at them; very old chickens with scaly legs were piled high — 'Fresh poultry,' the vendor cried, with scant regard to any truth — skinned rabbits, pigs' trotters; pots and pans and paupers; saveloys, scissors and sneaks and scavengers; housewives, fishwives, dabs and dolly-mops; beggars and butchers; bartering, bargaining, brawling and bawling — all the teeming, stinking life of the city, and a stone's throw from the high houses of Lincoln's Inn Fields and its garden with its trees and quiet walks. And a stride from their neighbours — the dead.

A nifty turn or two through the crowds brought them to Portugal Street. They passed the burial ground, which looked no better by day. Dickens noticed a figure with a large basket bending down to pick up something, putting what he found in the basket, and bending again — very like a gleaner, a gleaner of bones or of souls, perhaps. Earls and costermongers, lawyers and crossing-sweepers — all here, jumbled together until the Day of Judgement. What if a lawyer were reassembled with the wrong head? Would he answer on the Day: 'I don't know nothink'?

Then they were past and up the steps of the hospital. Jones was in a hurry.

The mortuary was cold as a tomb, and the dead were there under their winding sheets laid upon marble slabs like carved effigies on sarcophagi in country churches. But the smell was not of dust and age, more of carbolic and that underlying sweet-sick scent of corruption.

Doctor Woodhall greeted them courteously, saying then, 'Your man is here.' He lifted the sheet to expose the face of the dead man. He was not Black, though his face had once been burned by the sun. Death had made it paler, like wood that had been bleached by the sea. There were scars on the side of his face — they looked like old burn marks.

'He has lived abroad, I fancy, but his hands are not those of a sailor —' he lifted the arm — 'a strong man — well developed arm muscles, but he has not always been a labouring man. A penman. See here, the carbuncle on the middle finger where the pen or pencil has pressed habitually.'

Dickens imagined the strong arm raising a whip to the slaves on that faraway island — but Peter Best had perhaps been upon the island after slavery had been abolished. He thought of Pilgrim — perhaps the Captain had plucked him from slavery in the place where he had been brought up.

'Well-nourished and good clothes. Well paid, I should say.'

Jones was talking. 'The agent of Mrs Tallis's stepfather, perhaps. The Judge told us last night that she was expecting a visit from him. He arrived recently from St Lucia. His name is Peter Best.'

'Ah, now that is odd. You remember the hat that your constable found. I examined it closely because I felt something hard. Sewn into the inside of the crown were a couple of sovereigns wrapped tightly in a letter.'

'Not to Mrs Tallis?'

'No, it was addressed to William Lambert of Chapel Farm Cottage, Dolphin Lane, Isle of Dogs.'

'Signed?'

'Yes, but by someone called Francis, William Lambert's brother. I could not say that it is in the same hand as the fragment we found, but it is —'

'Worth investigating. May I see the letter?'

Doctor Woodhall passed the letter to Jones, who looked at it closely, Dickens peering over his shoulder. It was brief:

Dear William,

I cannot come back. I have felt certain that I am being followed — I felt it on the night we went to The England's Arms and at other times, too. I am very afraid that someone might have recognised me from the old days — someone who might think to gain something, who might know what was done. I must leave very soon. I enclose the two sovereigns which will help you for the time being. I shall write when I have got well away from here and send more.

 Your brother,
 Francis.

'So, this dead man may be one Francis Lambert who is connected in some way to Mrs Tallis. He may have been delivering a letter from Peter Best — on his behalf, perhaps.'

'Someone who had reason to be afraid,' Dickens said.

'So it would seem, whichever he is.'

'They could be one and the same — it is not uncommon for a man to take another identity. We can never always know even who our living patients are — never mind the dead,' observed Doctor Woodhall.

'He refers to "the old days" — something done which he wished to keep hidden — something which had sent him abroad.'

'Something so dreadful, Sam, that he was ready to flee again.'

'I cannot help you with that,' said Doctor Woodhall, 'I can only tell you what you knew last night. He was murdered. The attack was swift and violent. Death follows quickly — in seconds — with a wound of a large artery like the carotid. It was done, I imagine with a razor, or a knife.'

'And as you pointed out, Charles, Captain Valentine was murdered by knife, and this man, whether he is Peter Best or Francis Lambert, was found with the address of the captain's sister. There must, surely, be some connection which we must find out by going to Dolphin Lane on the Isle of Dogs. I'll take the letter and the two sovereigns. I could do with knowing who he is before the inquest tomorrow. It should be straightforward, Doctor Woodhall, with your evidence.'

'Yes. It'll take place here, upstairs. The coroner and jury will come down here to view the body. Henry will give evidence, too.'

'Good. It will be adjourned while the police are pursuing enquiries — murder by person or persons unknown, and if we don't find anything at Dolphin Lane, then the identity of the victim will have to be unknown, too. Thank you, Doctor Woodhall, I shall see you tomorrow.'

They made to go. Before they reached the door, Doctor Woodhall spoke to Dickens. 'I had not time to speak last night, but I wanted you to know that I read your *December Vision* and was much moved.'

'I hope it may do some good, but we need deeds as well as words, I think.'

'Very true — Henry and I have given our evidence to the Burial Commission and so have others. Those burial grounds must be removed — I am firmly convinced that lives can be saved.'

'I, too, and I shall lend all the support in my power. I hope to join the Sanitary Commission Deputation to Lord John Russell at the end of the month — some good may come of our efforts.'

With that they left the doctor to examine his other corpses, known or unknown, remembered or forgotten, but irretrievably lost to the life they once had.

17: GROG COURT

Jack Straw, sergeant of the River Police at Wapping Stairs, was not a man of that material. Nor was there anything of the rebel about him. He was stocky, barrel-chested, red-faced and genial, beaming at Dickens as if they were old friends. He looked like a sailor and had the gait of a man on a rolling ship.

He answered the Superintendent's question. 'Inspector Bold's gone with Constable Gaunt — man dead. A sailor, so it seems. I don't know 'is name as yet. You'll find the Inspector at Grog Court, Sir, if you wants to go that way.'

'I do. I need to see him — another matter of a dead man.'

'Grog Court, eh?' said Dickens.

'Aye, Mr Dickens — it's not far. There's a pub there — The Anchor — all the sailors knows it.'

'Sailor once yourself?'

'Waterman — like my father. My brother Fred's a lighterman, but the steamboats — things are changin' an', well, I wanted a change, despite the captain — that's what we call the old pa. He admires your writin's, sir. Got us all down to a T, he says.'

Watermen, judges, charwomen, tailors, threadbare clerks, countesses and costermongers — even the Queen herself — they all read Dickens. *It's a wonder we aren't mobbed in the streets*, Jones often thought. But Dickens went unnoticed most of the time in company with the tall policeman, in clothes darker than usual and a low crowned hat. Sometimes he wore an old pair of spectacles given to him by Zeb Scruggs, an old clothes dealer. Occasionally he had sported ones with green lenses — he was fond of those, but Jones had vetoed them on the grounds that Dickens was always walking into walls, lamp posts, even people. An indignant old woman had made to strike him with her umbrella — naturally, Jones had caught the blow. Sometimes Dickens masqueraded as a lawyer; on one occasion as a poor old man; on another as an undertaker — it all appealed to his sense of drama — and it was useful. And Jones knew that Dickens would dearly like to get into a uniform — he loved dressing up. *A step too far, but he'll get his way, I'll bet someday.*

But, 'Grog Court?' he reminded, aware of time flying.

'Sorry, Sir — at the north end of Nightingale Lane, by the New Cut, north of Fore Street.'

'I know Nightingale Lane,' said Dickens. It was not far from Church Lane.

Through a low-browed arch they entered the aptly named Grog Court, which was a dank, miserable dungeon of a place behind The Anchor. Here they found sitting on an upturned barrel a wretched boy with his head wrapped in pickled brown paper — one eye was staring at a constable with the face of one ordered for immediate execution. The other eye was half-closed in his sickly yellow face. Another man who looked rather sick, too, lounged against a wall.

'Inspector Bold?' asked Jones. 'I'm Superintendent Jones from Bow Street. I need to see him.'

'Through there, sir.' He pointed to another little archway.

They went through and found themselves in a narrow alley where Inspector Bold and John Gaunt were looking down on the body of a man. Inspector Bold turned as they came through and addressed himself to Dickens.

'It's Ned Carver.'

'Is it, by God? Any idea who did it?'

'Superintendent Jones, Inspector,' Jones put in, 'I have some business with you after you've dealt with this.' He nodded to John Gaunt.

'Right. And, to answer your question, Mr Dickens, we've a strong suspicion. Some sort of fight o' course. A lot of broken heads, a couple of broken legs, a quantity of black eyes, bruises, split lips, but nothing to write home about. The landlord's a cooperative sort and got the police when they found the body. Most are nursing sore heads, but, let me ask you both, what do you see?'

Jones and Dickens stepped forward to have a look at Ned Carver, for it was he. Dickens could see the terrible scar standing out livid in the bloodless face.

'Not a bruise, not a black eye,' Jones said, 'anything broken?'

'No — the doctor had a look.'

'So, how did he die?' asked Dickens.

'Stabbed in the back.'

Dickens thought about the stabbing of Captain Valentine. Had the same knife cut Peter Best's throat and also been plunged into Ned Carver's back? Three murders by the same black tufted hand?

'Somebody took advantage of the fight to kill him,' Jones put in.

'That's exactly what I think, Superintendent. Here's the story: group of sailors — known to the landlord — boozing, singing, dancing — generally enjoying themselves.'

'Carver was there?' Dickens asked.

'He was — and having a grand time by all accounts. Plenty of money, it seems. Some sailor came and sat with him. The landlord, Dick Lobb, seemed to think it was the stranger who started the fight — over a girl. The stranger tried to muscle in — and here's an interesting bit — the girl's man was Black, and the stranger made a few insulting comments — you remember, Mr Dickens, what Long Jodd said about the Black man, Pilgrim. All hell broke loose and spilled out into the court.

'Young Mealy out there was carried along in the swell, and got a broken head in the process. He's the pot boy. Get him, will you, Gaunt. You can see how, in all that chaos and shouting and everyone throwing punches, no one's likely to know who did what. Mealy, however, did see something.'

Mealy came in. He looked at the Inspector nervously. 'Meantersay, I want doin' no 'arm — bleedin' madman nearly knocked me 'ead off — it 'urts chronic.'

'Long Jodd, we think,' offered Gaunt. 'The landlord described the stranger — well, if you don't count half a dozen others with earrings and dark faces, but who else? It sounds like he set it all up.'

'Mealy?' Inspector Bold looked hard at the poor boy.

'Same as wot biffed me wiv 'is bleedin' great fist — right 'ook like Ben Caunt's. Niver seen 'im afore but meantersay if I sees 'im agin, 'e'd better watch it — tha's all.'

Ben Caunt was a renowned pugilist — Dickens had joked at the resemblance between himself and that grim-looking individual in the portrait that William Boxall had started. Dickens had called it off. He suppressed a desire to laugh at the idea of little Mealy taking on the likes of Long Jodd. Mealy's skinny legs in a pair of dirty nankeen shorts looked like two spindles. Not a muscle on him.

'Did you notice a snake tattoo at all?' asked Bold.

'Dint see nothin' 'cept stars.'

Dickens kept a straight face. Mealy wasn't laughing.

'When was Carver found?' Jones was thinking about Peter Best murdered last night.

'Not until this morning. No one missed Carver — why would they? Nor the stranger — people come and go all the time, and the party went on — all friends together after the fight. Some went off, some stayed. The landlord didn't go out into the alley until an hour ago.'

'But why kill Carver? They were thick as thieves the last time we saw them,' said Dickens.

'Thieves fall out,' said Bold, 'and Carver knew too much about him, and Captain Valentine, perhaps. There's no money left on the body, either.'

'It was about the Captain I wanted to speak to you. Mr Dickens and I are away to the Isle of Dogs in search of one William Lambert, brother to a murdered man with a connection to the captain's sister. It happened last night at ten o'clock so it's unlikely that Jodd could have done both, though I don't suppose anyone knows what time the stranger came.'

'Trouble is it was an all-night affair, though Carver's been dead a few hours, I'd say. Post-mortem will tell me more.'

'Can we meet later, after Mr Dickens and I have been to the Isle of Dogs? I can give you all the details of last night's murder then.'

'Very well. Let's meet at The Grapes on Narrow Street at five o'clock. Gaunt can get the landlord to give us the upstairs room. He knows us, and we'll be quiet there.'

'Until five o'clock then.'

John Gaunt came over as they left. 'Is there any news of Mr Penney?'

'No, Johnno, I am sorry to say, and nothing of Pilgrim, either. We will tell you all we know later.'

Dickens looked back. Little Mealy with his mask of brown paper was staring after them. What did death mean to him? Not much. But it had meant much to him. As a very small child, he had been terrified of a masked face — even then, perhaps, it had seemed to him some remote suggestion and dread of that death which would make every face still.

18: ISLE OF DOGS

An obliging police boat took them along the river towards Chalkstone Steps. It was, John Gaunt had assured them, quicker than the land route. A cab would have to thread its way through crowded streets, cross bridges, and circumvent various water-filled basins in order to reach their destination.

'I'm thinking,' said Jones as they settled themselves.

'Spill your beans.'

'Carver was stabbed, so was Captain Valentine and a blade was used to kill Peter Best. Long Jodd?'

'Could be, but I sense a doubt…'

'There's the timing. If Long Jodd has killed Carver then he was, by all accounts, probably deep in drink last night when Mr Best was killed. And, I do wonder if the murder of Mr Best — or Mr Lambert — is a different matter altogether from the murder of Ned Carver. Captain Valentine and Best are connected to St Lucia. As far as we know, Jodd is not.'

'And, if the letter were from her stepfather in St Lucia to Mrs Tallis, then it's hardly likely that Long Jodd would steal it. Perhaps it has nothing to do with anything between the captain and Long Jodd.'

'Moreover, what has Francis Lambert's secret to do with anything?'

'Deep waters, Sam,' Dickens said, as a particularly sloppy piece of river leapt into the boat and over his boots. 'Very prompt, Father Thames. No, what I mean is that the trouble with Jodd and the dead boy, Potter, on *The Redemption* can surely have no connection with a letter from St Lucia — or none that I can think of in my present damp state.'

'It may even be that the murder of Mr Best or Lambert has nothing at all to do with *The Redemption* — the letter shows him frightened that he was being followed and that he had reason to fear his pursuer — it would suit me if the death of Best/Lambert is separate from Carver's. Then I don't need to entangle myself with Inspector Bold — not that I mind him, but it would be less complicated. Perhaps Lambert is not Best.'

'William Lambert may yet enlighten us, but I need to entangle myself with the captain's murder — Kit is still missing.'

'So he is, and we will go to see Mrs Black after we have seen Mr Lambert.'

The police boat brought them round the great bend in the river, past Limehouse Hole and the great West India Docks, into Limehouse Reach, past Cuckold's Point on the opposite bank, and then to Chalkstone Stairs. They climbed the stairs to find themselves opposite The England's Arms and nothing much else along this windy stretch of the Deptford Road, the haunt of smugglers and those on the run from the police, or from themselves.

Along the road to the north there were an oil manufactory, iron foundries and docks, and a couple of streets of mean little tenements for the workers. To the south of the inn were the wrecks of some of the windmills which had given Mill Wall its name. But across lay terra incognita — the low, flat marshes where standing water gleamed dully in the fading light, and a wind keened ghostly through the grasses.

There were some cottages here and there and a few half-finished buildings which had an orphaned, melancholy look as if they had been forgotten. As if someone had left them undone and gone off to make his profit elsewhere. *He'd be back*, Dickens mused; the great wheel of progress would turn and these buildings would multiply, and the iron manufactories and rope works would double and treble, and the isle would, perhaps, lose that rather sinister aspect that he had felt as a child when he and Kit ventured this way sometimes to take a fascinated, half-terrified look at the old chapel. They always turned back from there. There was another iron foundry there now, but you could still see the sails of the old windmill they had explored when he was Don Quixote and Kit his Sancho Panza — or a single footprint in the mud would set them off as Crusoe and Man Friday.

According to the constable who had ferried them, Dolphin Lane was reached by taking a turn right by the oil manufactory. Chapel Farm was down the lane. There was a cottage, he thought, somewhere beyond the farm, in the fields.

The farmer pointed them towards what looked more like a shack than a cottage. There was a little twist of smoke coming from a little chimney. A straggling footpath led to the house and this they took, losing sight of it where the footpath turned, seeing it, losing it again, and aware all the time of the darkness coming, the cold wind and the sense of melancholy loneliness.

The farmer had been one of those taciturn, incurious men who, Dickens reflected as they picked their way along, lived so isolated lives that the doings of even their nearest neighbours held no interest. He was like a stunted tree bowed by the wind and bent on survival. There was a black, red-eyed dog tethered by a rope to a post. It had barked furiously at their approach. The farmer had only grunted when Jones asked about William Lambert and indicated the footpath with a jerk of his thumb.

William Lambert looked anxious at seeing a tall stranger at his door, and even more so when Superintendent Jones of Bow Street introduced himself. He gave a puzzled look at the second man, but he had no choice but to let them in.

The house was little more than a shack — it appeared to have two rooms downstairs. A ladder rose up to what must be a bedroom. There was a meagre fire on a stone hearth and a smell of damp and earth. There were a deal table, a stool, an upright chair, and a ragged armchair by the fire. Surprisingly, on the table were books, and in the light of a smoky oil lamp, Dickens could see some of his own.

Dickens tried to think if this slight, worried looking man in his thirties, perhaps, bore any resemblance to the man in the mortuary. But he could not tell. This was an unremarkable face, bony and angular. He looked undernourished as if worry had worn away his youth and hope. The dead man's face had been similarly bony, but that was all. Any two men might look like this — except that there was something hunched about this man, as if he were always expecting a blow.

Jones was showing him the letter. 'Do you know this hand?'

'It is my brother's. Francis wrote this. Where did you get it?' He looked at his visitors' faces. 'Something's happened to him.'

'Mr Lambert, we need to sit.'

Dickens fetched the stool and a chair for Jones. William Lambert sat in his armchair.

'Tell me first, did your brother ever use another name?'

William Lambert's face turned white and his brown eyes filled. 'You know it all. Someone has peached — we are done.'

'I know nothing of your past or your brother's secret, but I need to tell you —'

'He's dead —' William Lambert wept. His thin hands covered his face and his shoulders heaved. Grief poured out of him — it was as if all the weeping he had never done had been saved for this moment. Jones handed him a handkerchief and Dickens went into a little scullery to fill a tin cup with water from a barrel.

The sobs gradually ceased, and William Lambert drank his water. Then he said, 'I am ready. I have waited fifteen years for this.'

'Tell me about your brother.'

'He called himself Peter Best, and fifteen years ago he went to St. Lucia where eventually he became foreman to a sugar plantation owner, Adam Valentine. He came back on Mr Valentine's business. Now someone has killed him. I know it. Who? Tell me who.'

'We don't know yet — he says in the letter that he was being followed. You seem to understand this.'

'It lies in the past — the secret that has come back to destroy us.'

'What secret, Mr Lambert?' asked Dickens.

'The stars had it in their twinkling, the water in its flowing, the leaves in their rustling. It lurked in strangers' faces, and their voices. Everything had lips on which it always trembled — your words, Mr Dickens.'

Dickens looked at him in astonishment. 'Barnaby Rudge.'

'I know who you are, sir. And I know all you know of secrets — those words I said just now spelt the truth to me. I brought it with me, my secret, to this lonely place where, at least, the leaves and the stars and the water, if they told it, could only tell it to the air, for I have no friends or neighbours to whom I might have told it. Only my brother, and you tell me he is dead.'

'I am profoundly sorry, Mr Lambert.'

'I know you are, Mr Dickens. You have been my friend these lonely years, and my sole companion and teacher, and when I tell you both the secret, you will understand it.'

'And you will tell it?'

'I need to know, Mr Lambert,' said Jones, 'I need to know if the death of your brother is linked to the death of a Captain Louis Valentine —'

'Valentine? He is connected to Mr Valentine of St. Lucia?'

'He is the stepson of the man your brother was agent for and whose business brought him to London.'

'How did he die?'

'He was murdered — by a sailor, we think, but I must know about your brother and whether his death leads me to the death of the captain.'

William Lambert looked bemused. *Well, he might*, thought Dickens. *We are all bemused.*

'The act was not mine.' William Lambert looked at Dickens — his words, again, or rather the words of Barnaby Rudge. 'And unlike Barnaby Rudge, I did not do it. It truly was not mine. My brother left London because he killed my father — for my mother and me, for our sakes. My father was a drunken brute and a bully. When I was a child, Francis was at sea, but he came back when he was nineteen and I was twelve. He saw what was done. Our mother was already an old woman, with no teeth, abused and beaten, and I, so brutalised that I was no more than an animal. I could hardly speak; I couldn't read or write. I ate like a beast with my fingers. Our father threw food on the floor for me and laughed to see me gobble it. When Francis came in, he saw me eating from the floor like a dog. He protested, but our father knocked him down — to show him that nothing had changed. Francis might be grown, but he must submit. Francis said nothing and our father knocked him down again, and then he turned him over and kicked the coals on his head.'

William Lambert drank more water and began again. Only the few sea coals on the fire stirred in the silence. 'Our father went out then. Our mother bathed the burns. Francis took me into the yard and washed me. He went out and bought food and fed me with a fork as if I were a baby. He put me to bed and made my mother lie down with me. He sat in the chair by the fire with the poker in his hand.

'Our father came in. Drunk. He stood swaying at the door. Francis stood with the poker behind his back. And when our father came at him, roaring, Francis struck him with the poker. He fell, and Francis struck him again and again until he knew he was dead.

'In the dark, in the early hours, we, he and me, dragged him to a cart and took him to the river down by Execution Dock. We tipped him in the water. The tide was high. I remember the bubbles rising as he went down. I believed he would never come up.

'Francis went away — he left money. No one knew that he had been — at least, that is what my mother and I believed.'

'Perhaps someone did,' said Dickens.

'Our father's body was washed up. We could not help the police who came. People knew what he was — it was thought that he had been in a fight. We couldn't say.'

'You went away.'

'I did. My mother died when I was sixteen. Francis always sent money. I went to school and after her death, I came here and waited for my life to begin. But it did not. I couldn't make friends, love or marry, or have children — the secret, Mr Dickens, and Francis, too, kept it. I waited for Francis — or for this.'

He seemed to shrink before their eyes, a withered leaf of a man. They could only look and pity, for there was nothing to hope for now. *Only*, Jones thought, I do not believe that the secret is the reason for Francis Lambert's death. Not after fifteen years. Not that it would matter to this man. Still, to tell him might be something.

'I do not think it is the secret, Mr Lambert. I think that your brother's death is to do with Captain Valentine, whose stepfather was your brother's employer. I think your secret is kept.'

'I do not care who knows it now, and you, Superintendent, you may take me where you will — as an accessory to murder.'

'No, Mr Lambert, I will not — it is too long ago, and you have suffered enough. You were a child. It is your brother's death that I must investigate now. The inquest is tomorrow.'

'Must I be there?'

Jones made a decision. 'No, Mr Lambert, your brother is Francis Lambert. The murder victim is Peter Best and is to do with St. Lucia. His past, here in London, is not relevant. It would be better you were not there. Do you know anything of his employer's business here?'

'I don't — only that Francis was to take messages to the captain and his sister. Francis thought he might not go back to St. Lucia. That gave me hope. All is lost now. An inquest will make no difference to me or to him, but I see that you must investigate his death. I shall go back to my books, Mr Dickens, and find my comfort there.'

'I hope you will.'

'One last thing Mr Lambert, where did your brother lodge?'

'In Limehouse — Salmon's Place. A Mrs Cly, he spoke of.'

Well, well, thought Dickens, but he made no comment, only glanced at Jones.

They went away then, leaving the broken-hearted William Lambert seated by the fire in his lonely house, the door shut against hope. They concentrated on finding the footpath, using Jones's bull's-eye lamp to keep them on it. They had no idea what marsh lay on either side.

'Watch your feet,' warned Jones, leading the way, 'it's treacherous in parts.'

'I can't even see them, though I suspect their presence by a chilliness about the ankles. It's bleak, ain't it?'

They passed the dark huddle of the farmer's house. They stood still, getting their bearings. No sign of life. All was silent under the fitful moon. Dickens looked back. It seemed to him that there was a flickering light somewhere near the house. Then it was gone. The wind made its low, mourning whistle. The light reappeared then vanished — a willow the wisp sort of thing. Jones walked on.

They heard the farmer's dog bark behind them. Then it howled, and the cry was taken up by another, and another, so that the howling took on a ghostly, echoing quality as if phantom dogs were calling from ruins far away on the empty marshes.

'Isle of Dogs, eh?' Dickens said, not that he felt very cheerful. That black dog and its unseen companions gave him the shivers — the dog was always black in legends. They were said to haunt gibbets. He remembered seeing a gibbet years ago, outlined against a bleak sky in Hogarth's picture of the idle apprentice being sent to sea. There were the remains of gibbets on the shores of the Isle of Dogs where pirates had hung. And he had seen one himself with Kit — somewhere on the shore over yonder. He hoped Jones knew where yonder was.

'Art thou there, truepenny?'

'A piece of me — we're back on Dolphin Lane now, I think. Ah, there's a light.'

It was the constable who had thought to come to meet them and light their way back to Chalkstone Stairs.

19: BIRDS OF A FEATHER

'Salmon's Place, eh, where your Mrs Cly takes tender care of her lodgers.'

'She's murdered the lot of them, I shouldn't wonder. A face made for hanging.'

'I can't wait to meet her — and we'll have to go there. See what she has to say about Peter Best. If anyone came to see him or he mentioned any names — I doubt it, but we'll have to ask.'

'And his murder is not to do with the secret?'

'Not now, I'm sure — it's too long ago.'

'What about Long Jodd? We don't know for sure if Long Jodd was at Salmon's Place, but, if he was —'

'I know. Damn it. He will keep butting in.'

'Like King Charles's head. Coincidence?'

Jones thought. 'Hm — I never like coincidence where murder is concerned, but I still find it hard to believe that Jodd is connected to the murder of Best.'

'It is interesting that Peter Best came here to London with a message for the captain. What a pity he didn't tell his brother.'

'Judge Tallis said that the background of his wife and her brother was complicated. I wonder what that meant.'

'I suppose I could ask him. He invited me back.'

'Ah, yes — useful, that. And we must ask John if he found any trace of Long Jodd at Mrs Cly's.'

'What are you going to do about the inquest? I mean about Doctor Woodhall and the letter.'

'I think he will understand when I tell him about what we have found out. I shall ask him to omit any mention of the letter. What good would it do?'

'You don't want me there?'

'I do not — I want it quick. No sensation provided by the celebrated author, thank you.'

'And here was I vowing never to desert Mr Micawber. No, I see that it will be better to keep it simple.'

They watched the river as the constables rowed them back the way they had come. Dickens thought about William Lambert. *Nothing now to hope for. Not even in my books.* He thought of how the books he had read as a child had kept alive his hope for something beyond the blacking factory. But William Lambert was not a child. It was all over with him.

'Don't leave off hoping, Sam, or it's of no use doing anything. Hope, hope, to the last.'

Jones raised his eyes, surprised at the passion in Dickens's voice. His eyes were hot. 'William Lambert?' There was more, perhaps, but it was enough to concentrate on the matter at hand.

'Yes, and that poor girl, Grace Fox, and Kit — we must not give up hope of finding him.'

'We shall not — I never shall desert Mr Dickens.'

Dickens grinned at him. 'I believe you, Sam. You do me good — as always. Shall you have time to come with me to see Mrs Black?'

'We'll do it — after we have spoken to Inspector Bold. See how the land lies.'

'It lies close enough now.'

It did. The constable steered the boat towards the old, wooden Kidney Stairs which led directly up to The Grapes public house wherein, they hoped, Inspector Bold and Johnno would be waiting.

Another phenomenon of moroseness, thought Dickens, as he and Jones entered the upstairs room of The Grapes. Inspector Bold was looking gloomily into his pot of ale as if he might find an answer there. Long Jodd had not been found then.

It was so, the Inspector told them as Johnno poured them some of the ale from an earthenware jug. 'No sign, but we do have Tooth in custody. Not that he's much help, but it felt like something to do and it'll keep the poor simpleton from Jodd's clutches.'

'We've questioned him about Jodd and possible acquaintances — he knows Silas Cly, but I found no trace of Jodd there,' Johnno said.

'Naturally, we couldn't find any sister in Gravesend — dead end, that's what it is.'

'Salmon's Place came up when we went to the Isle of Dogs,' Jones said. He went on to explain the circumstances of Peter Best's death, the double identity, the relationship between Best, Captain Valentine, his sister and the plantation owner, Adam Valentine, in St. Lucia, and the messages to be delivered to the captain and his sister. He didn't mention the secret.

Inspector Bold listened intently, his eyes sharpening at the reference to Best and the captain. 'You think that Best's murder and the captain's murder are to do with St Lucia and not Long Jodd.'

'I'm beginning to. Not that I rule out Jodd entirely. Blades were used in all three murders. A sailor's knife might have been used in the murders of the captain and Peter Best.'

'Open mind, eh, Superintendent. And you want us to cooperate on this?'

'Yes, I'd like your thoughts.'

The pot boy — another Mealy sort of boy in a greasy apron — brought a dish of rather good-smelling stew and some plates and cutlery.

'Let's eat while I think.'

Not bad at all, thought Dickens as they fell upon the food. Jones ate with relish — always patient, ready to wait for the Inspector's thoughts. Fools rush in. Sam Jones never did.

'Well, Mr Jones, I've thought. The murder of Mr Best took place on your ground, and you'll want to have charge of that, and since Captain Valentine's murder was done, as I begin to think, by the same hand, then you'll want to investigate that. Meanwhile, I have the murder of Ned Carver to look into, and the missing Black man — I'll come to Mr Penney in a moment, Mr Dickens — and we know that Long Jodd bore a grudge against Pilgrim so it's not beyond reason to think that Pilgrim is in danger from Jodd. What I think is that I must concentrate on Long Jodd before he does anything else while you, Superintendent, follow the lead you have in Salmon's Place.'

It was what Jones had hoped for. Always let the other man, if he were your subordinate in another division, take the lead. It was Bold's right. He said, 'I agree, but where our cases converge, and well they might, I shall pass on the information.'

'I shall do the same.'

'And Mr Penney?' asked Dickens.

'The same — if I find out anything I'll let you know, and if you do then you'll tell me. I'm sorry that I can't do more.'

It was as much as he could hope for. Dickens was rather inclined to think that he and Sam might find out more because it seemed even more certain that Kit's connection to the captain must be the reason for Kit's flight. He thought about the letter Peter Best was to deliver to Mrs Tallis and about

Peter Best's message for the captain. Now he wondered if Peter Best had delivered something for the Captain at Kit's shop. Not that he knew whether Kit received letters for Louis Valentine, but it would be worth asking Mrs Penney.

Inspector Bold had stood up and was preparing to go. 'Gaunt, you should go with the Superintendent to Salmon's Place. See if you can help shake any apples from that tree. Now I'll bid you goodnight, Superintendent and Mr Dickens.'

'Salmon's Place, Johnno. I am sure Mrs Cly will be delighted to see you again.'

Mrs Cly was not delighted. In fact, she looked more murderous than before. Sly was nowhere to be seen — *stones in his pocket*, thought Dickens. She lost herself in her usual impenetrable thicket of negatives, the gist of which was that: dint she already tell 'em that they'd niver 'eard of no Jodd, long or short, not niver, not no'ow, an' woz 'e deaf? This last to Gaunt.

The Superintendent, at whom she looked with more caution, explained that they wished to see the room which had been occupied by Mr Peter Best. 'Don't tell me you haven't heard of him. I have it on good authority that he lodged here.'

'Dint niver say 'e dint, did I?' she asked rhetorically.

'Indeed, you did not,' said Jones. 'Much obliged.' He shouldered his way past her with Gaunt at his heels. However, she seemed to have taken an unreasoning dislike to Dickens. She gave him a look of contempt which would have withered an anchor and attempted to bar his way. 'An' 'oo the dickens is 'e when 'e's at 'ome? Three's a crowd.'

'He's with me,' said Jones curtly before Dickens had chance to ponder who, indeed, he was — when he was at home. Such philosophical questions, however, seemed redundant at this moment, though he couldn't help thinking of the myna bird's similar enquiry. *Standing on shaky ground, I am. 'Oo, indeed?*

Mrs Cly stood back to let him pass, favouring him with one of her murderous glances.

'Ma'am.' He bowed slightly, adopting the meek servility of a curate, and followed the others up the narrow staircase.

'Two pair back,' she shouted after them, indicating that the room was up two flights of stairs. 'But 'un's gorn, that Best. Niver comin' back. Niver no more.'

Truer than you know, Dickens reflected. Never more, quoth the raven.

The narrow room was empty, and the bed made up. For all her sourness, Mrs Cly was a decent lodging house-keeper — this wasn't a doss house. The room was basic, but clean. They made a search of the drawers in the chest, of the cupboard with a hanging rail, and of the fireplace, but there was no sign that the dead man had been here. *So*, thought Jones, *the murderer took his bag as well as his money and papers. Peter Best had been intending to leave town.*

They went down again. Mrs Cly was waiting. 'Nothin' there. Coulda told yer. When they goes, they niver leaves nothin' be'ind.' She seemed to regret this — no pickings. Vulture rather than raven. 'Still 'e paid up — not like t'other 'un.'

'What other?' Jones asked sharply.

'Sailor.'

'You didn't mention him when I came earlier. I asked if you had any sailors staying here.' Gaunt was indignant.

'Gorn, I jest told yer.'

The equivocation of the fiend, thought Dickens — *she ought to have been a Jesuit.*

'What was his name?'

'Jack Dawe.'

151

The words ran together. Jackdaws, mynas, ravens, vulture — an ornithological cornucopia. Dickens wouldn't have been surprised to see Sly come in with a parrot on his shoulder. He thought of the fall of a sparrow. Damn Jodd and the other, if there be another.

'Jackdaw?' Jones asked.

'Jackdaw — 's'wot I said.' Seeing Jones's face, she said, with weary resignation, as to one whose idiocy confounded her, 'Jack — Dawe — sailor.'

'When did he go?'

'Dunno — not nothin' left when I looked yesterday mornin'. 'E owes me fer a night.'

'And he came when?'

'Three days ago — two nights 'e thought. Paid me fer one.'

'What did he look like?'

'Sailor — they all looks the same. Dark — not Black. Pigtail, earring. Dint say much, but —'

Heavens, thought Dickens, *she is thinking*. He watched as she blinked — once, twice, three times, then four, as if the rusty cogs of her mind were turning — painfully slowly.

'Mrs Cly?' Jones sounded anxious. Perhaps he thought she was about to have a seizure. Heavy breathing accompanied the eye blinks.

'Thinkin', I am.' She blinked twice more. 'Somethin' queer about 'un, Jackdaw — niver seen 'un. Bed not slept in — but that woz 'is look-out. Whorin' I thought — I'll not 'ave that 'ere.'

'Did he have anything to do with Mr Best?'

'Couldn't say. Mighta met on the stairs — 'is room was the front o' the two pair.'

Jones nodded to John Gaunt, who went back upstairs to look at the room.

'Yer'll not find anything.'

'Mr Best, if you please, Mrs Cly.'

'Mr Best was a gent — from foreign parts. Decent sort o' cove. Quiet. Why d'yer want to know about 'un, anyways?'

Jones saw no reason not to tell her. 'He is dead, Mrs Cly. He was murdered last night — so if you know anything more about him or about your other lodger, I'd be obliged if you'd tell me.'

Even Mrs Cly demonstrated something other than resentment or disgust. 'Gawd, what a thing — poor divil. You don't think it woz that Jackdaw?'

'I don't know, Mrs Cly — what else can you tell me?'

'I dunno, sir, wot I said — jest a sailor an' I niver seen nothin' of 'un.'

'Did Mr Best have any visitors or anyone asking about him?'

'No, sir, not as I knows.'

'Well, if anyone asks about him, you must send to Constable Gaunt, here, at Wapping Station. You understand.'

'Yes, sir.' She was a bit cowed now, but whether she would bother to report anything, Jones and Gaunt doubted, but it was worth asking.

'The man who wasn't there,' Dickens observed, as he, Jones and Johnno stood at the entrance to Church Lane.

'Long Jodd wasn't there either,' said Jones, 'at least, I don't think so. She was willing to admit to Jack Dawe. I can't see any reason why she would have denied Long Jodd — he wasn't an old friend like Carver.'

'I'm beginning to agree,' Gaunt said. 'From what you said earlier about Best and the messages, it looks more likely that the murder of the captain is to do with St Lucia. Still, we'll be looking for Jodd as the killer of Ned Carver, and I'll ask about for Jack Dawe unless Jodd gave a false name.'

'Whoever he was, he'd left by yesterday morning. Best was killed last night,' Jones said thoughtfully.

'Anything in that?' Gaunt asked.

'Might be — he could just be a sailor passing through or he could be Jodd. Ask about, anyway.'

'I will. I'd best get back to the station.'

'And we are bound for China to Pekin Place where the ship-owner, Mrs Judith Black, lives. I thought she might know something about Kit.'

'And,' Jones added, 'she might be able to tell us more about the captain's background.'

Gaunt went on his way. Dickens and Jones would have to walk about a mile along the East India Dock Road to Bow Lane.

20: A COLD WIND IN THE EAST

'Silks and shawls and sandalwood, and spices, dyes and drugs — the east comes upon the wind, Sam.'

'Snow, more like, if you ask me.'

It was, in truth, a bitter east wind that blew them past Canton Place, after which Kedgeree Street, Oriental Street, Canton Street and eventually Bow Lane which led them to the row of three handsome terraced houses which comprised Pekin Place, comfortably situated, despite the associations of its name, next to All Saints Church. What the saints thought of their eastern neighbour, they did not say. Not that there was anything of the mystic east about the houses which belonged to the reign of William IV. The central house which bore the legend *Pekin Place* was a three-storey house set back behind a railed area over a basement. Two arched windows on either side looked at them with an air of perpetual surprise. A smartly painted front door stood at the top of a flight of six steps. *Money*, thought Dickens.

The ringing of the bell brought a neat maid to whom Jones addressed his business, asking to see Mrs Black about Captain Valentine. The maid, whose face took on a solemn look at the reference to the captain, bade them come in and took the card away.

They were invited into a well-furnished drawing room, where Mrs Black rose to meet them. He caught the scent of her hair as she nodded to dismiss the maid — a heady scent of rose and musk — Fleurs de Bulgarie. Expensive. He thought of the tender, innocent scent of violets. How different she was from Grace Fox. A handsome woman, in her thirties, perhaps. She wore an elegant black gown which set off her shining blonde hair and pale, perfect complexion. She was beautiful in an austere way, and commanding. But then she ran a shipyard — not unheard of, but rare enough to lend her a quality of authority.

Jones introduced himself and Charles Dickens. She inclined her graceful head, but looked at him curiously. The scent reached him again. *Too much*, he thought.

'Superintendent, you told my maid that you wished to speak of poor Captain Valentine. I hardly expected to see you, Mr Dickens.' Her teeth were white and small, but, he fancied, they looked sharp enough to make a neat and painful bite.

'I came to find out if you know anything of the captain's friend, Mr Christopher Penney, who is my dear friend, too. He is missing — he vanished from his shop on the night of the captain's death.'

She invited them to sit. 'I am afraid I cannot help, Mr Dickens. I know Mr Penney, but he has not come here.'

'Not to your yard?'

'Not as far as I know — if he had, I am certain I would have known about it.'

Dickens was disappointed. Mr Wieland and Mrs Black were the only leads he had — both were hopeless now. It was difficult to imagine Kit skulking at the shipyard without anyone knowing — still, it might be worth a look.

Mrs Black was looking at the Superintendent. 'I have spoken to the police already — I do not know what else I can tell you.'

'There has been a development. Peter Best, an agent of Captain Valentine's stepfather in St Lucia, has also been murdered — in the same way as the captain. I believe the two are connected, and I wonder if you can tell us anything about the captain's background in St Lucia. I have spoken to Judge

Tallis. He tells me that the history of the captain and his sister is complicated.'

'I wonder that you do not ask him for more information — he will know better than I.'

She was very cool. Very self-contained, a characteristic which tended to arouse suspicion in Sam Jones — why should she be reluctant to speak of a man whose history she must know, a man who had met a violent end? She spoke of 'poor Captain Valentine' as of a distant acquaintance whose death was politely regretted, but a death which had not disturbed the even tenor of her ways. Jones could be cool, too.

'I certainly shall ask Mr and Mrs Tallis, but, as I am here —' *and not going anywhere just yet* — 'I should like to know more about Captain Valentine.'

She inclined her head. 'I do not see what bearing my knowledge of Captain Valentine has on his death —' she observed Jones's face and added graciously — 'but I will tell you what I can. The captain was married to my sister-in-law, Alice. She died in childbirth three years ago. And my husband, James Black, died five years ago. He was never well, and I ran the business for him after his father retired. My husband's will left the majority share of the shipyard to me. Alice's smaller share went to her widower, Captain Valentine. I had hoped that we would become partners —' there was a slight flush at her neck — 'business partners. Louis, however, wanted to marry again and make his home in Erith with Mrs Fox's family. I intended to buy out his share of the business.'

Ho, ho, thought Dickens — the green-eyed monster. Business partners, forsooth — why should she wish to buy him out when she learned he was to marry? Interesting that she should use his Christian name in the context of marriage.

'Did Captain Valentine wish to sell his share of the business?'

'I do not know — it was something I was going to discuss when he came back from this last voyage.'

'And now?'

She raised her perfectly arched brows. 'Now?'

'What happens to the captain's share of the business?'

'It reverts to me.'

'And of his history in St Lucia?'

'His father died sometime in the early 1820s, and his mother remarried. His father had an adopted brother, Adam Valentine. He was not related to them. Etienne Valentine's father had brought him from London where he had found him — an abandoned child, living on the streets. He didn't even know his own name. Etienne's father gave him the family name. When Captain Valentine's father died, Adam Valentine inherited the estates and married Louise. I do not know why the adopted brother should inherit, but, it seems that Louis and his sister, Madeleine were happy enough. However, after their mother died, they both came to England. After school, Louis entered the merchant service with Money and Wigram — the Blackwall Line — and Madeleine lived with her cousins until she married.'

'And did Captain Valentine correspond with his stepfather in St. Lucia?'

'I believe so.'

'Would he inherit the estates when his stepfather dies?'

'No, Adam Valentine has a son by his first wife — I know nothing about her — but Louis assumed that the son would inherit. I do not think he minded — St Lucia seemed to hold painful memories of his parents' deaths. He said he had no desire to go back.'

'Does the name Peter Best mean anything to you?'

'I am afraid not. I really do not think I can tell you anything more, Superintendent.'

'Just one more thing — have you heard of anyone by the name of Jack Dawe?'

'No, it means nothing to me.'

'Thank you, Mrs Black. We'll bid you goodnight.'

They stood up to go, but Dickens had one more request. 'You will let me know if you hear anything of Mr Penney. I am most anxious about him. Here is my card.'

She said that she would, and the parlour maid came to show them to the door.

'The wind's in the east there,' said Dickens as they turned down Bow Lane, but before Jones could reply a veiled woman in black glided out from the church gates opposite.

'Sir, if I might speak with you.' She stayed where she was, so they crossed the road.

'I am Mrs Skillett, Mrs Black's housekeeper. The maid told me you wanted to speak about Captain Valentine. I was coming to the church, so I thought I might wait for you.'

'Have you something to tell us about the captain? If so, we can go back to the house.'

'No, that won't be necessary. I can talk here.' She led them into the shelter of the lych gate. *Doesn't want to be seen from the house*, Dickens thought, but they followed her.

'If you would lift your veil, madam, I'd be much obliged. I like to see who I'm talking to.'

She complied. She smelt of eau de cologne. It was hard to make out her features in the darkness, but she was no beauty like her mistress. No expensive perfume for her.

'What is it you wish to tell me?'

'She had words with the captain before he left — wanted him to be her partner and more than just business. In a fury, she was, afterwards — she's hard, that one. Wants all her own way.'

'And this is significant because?'

'Thought you ought to know — with the captain being dead. You'd want to know all about them.'

'You are suggesting that your employer, Mrs Black, may have had something to do with his death.'

'Well, it wouldn't be the first time. Young Mr Black died — suicide they said. Took poison. Grief, she said, after his sister's death, and because of his own illness.'

'What ailed him?'

'Wasting disease. Weak as water. He couldn't do much for himself. She had it all her own way. They had a nurse, but she wasn't there when he took the poison.'

'And this was all given in evidence at the inquest?'

'Er — yes.'

'Medical evidence?'

'Doctor Stephens. He —'

'Testified to Mr Black's illness?'

'Of course, but, we all knew — close she was to the doctor — like she was with the captain.'

Jones was remorseless. 'And you didn't voice your suspicions then — you are, I take it, accusing Mrs Black of poisoning her husband in collusion with the doctor. A very serious allegation, Mrs Skillet.'

She looked frightened then. 'You're twisting my words — I'm just saying that you ought to know what kind of woman you are dealing with — that's all.'

'I hope that is all.'

'Just trying to do my duty,' she said sulkily.

'Thank you for your information. I won't detain you.' Jones pushed open the gate. She passed through and went towards Pekin Place.

From an upstairs room, Judith Black watched the black-veiled woman come towards the house. She had seen her meet the visitors. She had seen them go into the shelter of the lych-gate. *Skillett*, she thought, *how I hate her — a sneaking, sly toady of a woman with that long red nose poking into everything.* A woman who saw too much. Judith had no love for any of her servants. She hated their creeping servility which they thought disguised their resentment. She had known what they had said about James.

She felt the heat rise in her face. She would never forget the old housekeeper insisting that the sheets were always washed after a wedding night. Gossip in the laundry, the scullery, the kitchen, on the stairs. They all knew that James Black was impotent. She'd got rid of all the old servants over time. But Skillett was just as bad.

She heard the door close. So, she was back. Judith could imagine only too well what Skillett had been talking to the policeman about. She'd have been repeating the gossip about James's death, and her relationship with Doctor Stephens — and, no doubt, telling of the failure of her plans for Louis. Skillett knew because she listened at doors. Another humiliation. She could not forgive that. How she had wanted to get rid of the long-nosed creature. Now, however, it was time she got her sailing orders. What else might she know? She wanted to fly downstairs to accuse Skillett, to slap that simpering face. *Wait*, she thought, *wait. Patience. Keep the enemy close. Keep her sweet. A little present, perhaps.* She went to her dressing room.

'What do you make of all that?' asked Dickens.

'No love lost there — I should think Mrs Black would be an exacting employer. I don't think it helps very much.'

'Nor do I — the pot, or in this case, the skillet, calling the kettle black. A nasty little woman with a grudge, I'd say.'

'And I hardly think Mrs Black would be sneaking about one of her ships after midnight with a handy dagger.'

'No, but I can imagine her with the poison bottle. Cool, wasn't she, until she referred to Louis.'

'Yes, I noted the tell-tale flush. I suspect that Mrs Skillet just wanted to stir things up a bit, but she went too far for her own comfort. Nevertheless, Mrs Black did lie about her business dealings with Louis Valentine. She said she was going to discuss the matter of the shares in the business when the captain came back, but Mrs Skillett said they had high words before he sailed — if we are to believe Mrs Skillett.'

'Pride, perhaps. I get the impression that Judith Black was used to getting her own way. In any case, there's Peter Best to consider.'

'Right — no reason to think that Mrs Black would have anything to do with him way over in Portugal Street. However, I think I might send Stemp to the shipyard just in case Kit is there. It's worth a look.'

'It is. I ought to turn my face towards Gun Lane before I go home. Not that there's anything to tell, but Mrs Penney will want to know what I've been about.'

'Yes, and I've an idea. I sent Rogers to the West India Dock to ask about Peter Best and *The Endeavour*. Now, I want to know who else was on that ship from St Lucia — anyone he might have talked to about his purpose here.'

'I had a thought, too — about letters. You wondered if Mr Best might have had some communication for the captain. I wonder if Kit took any letters for him — as a regular thing, I mean. I can ask Mrs Penney to look if there's anything.'

'A good notion. In the meantime, I'm going to see a man I know — Michael Simpson of the West India Docks Police. He lives in one of the police cottages in Garford Street. I shall ask him to get me the names of other passengers from St Lucia who disembarked in London.'

'You'll come to the shop afterwards so that we can go back together.'

'I will.'

Dickens went on his way to Gun Lane. But the shop was closed, and there were no lights in any of the windows. The door was locked this time. He went down the side alley so that he could see if there were a light at the back. All was in darkness. Mrs Penney had left her post. Why? He wondered at that. What could have taken her away?

He could go in and ask Sampson. The butcher's yard door was open. He heard nothing of the barkable dog. Perhaps brawny Bean was walking him somewhere. In he went to see Mug lying in the capacious doorway of his kennel. Mug eyed Dickens as he might have measured a mutton chop and found it wanting. The Newfoundland raised his massive head as if in preparation for a bark, but changed his mind, yawned, and made himself more comfortable with his head on his paws.

Brawny Bean appeared from an outhouse. 'Thought I 'eard someone come in — Mug musta known yer or 'e'd 'ave barked.'

'I'm just stepping in to see Mr Meteyard.'

Dickens pushed open the back door to see Henry Meteyard, barrister-at-law, sitting in his shirt sleeves at his mother's kitchen table. Mrs Meteyard was delivering a pair of hot buttered crumpets to a plate.

'Crumpets is 'olesome,' he observed as he stepped in.

'Charley Dickens! Come in and let me give you a kiss.' Dickens did as he was bidden. Mrs Amelia Meteyard was a handsome woman in a meaty way — it ran in the family — with arms the colour of ham and a face red from the kitchen range. He felt the warmth of her kiss. 'What a sight to see you — a bit on the thin side, I'd say, but there was never much of you. All in the head, I suppose.'

'Fit to burst sometimes.'

'Same as Henry — you think too much, you young men. You need looking after.' *I do, I do.* 'But crumpets you shall have. Henry, my lad, pass one of yours to Charley and you shall have two more each, and, Henry, pour some tea.'

Henry Meteyard did as he was told. His dignity in court he never forgot, but he left it in his wig case. He never brought it to Limehouse. *Perhaps I should leave Charles Dickens somewhere when I go home — in a locked trunk at a railway station. I could collect him when I need him.*

When they had tasted a crumpet each, and Mrs Meteyard had seen that they had every comfort, she left them. Dickens asked Henry if he knew where Mrs Penney had gone.

'Greenwich — she knows that Kit wouldn't come here, but he might go to his sister's. My father's out — just having a look and keeping an eye on the shop.'

'I just came to enquire. I have no news. Sam Jones and I have been to the Isle of Dogs in search of Peter Best's brother.'

'So Allan Woodhall said.'

'Poor fellow — he has waited for years for his brother to come home, and now, this.'

'Do you think it's anything to do with Kit?'

'I do. Sam and I begin to think that the sailor, Long Jodd, is not the killer of Captain Valentine. Inspector Bold of the River Police believes he has killed another sailor from *The Redemption*, but we think the connection between Best and the captain lies in St Lucia.'

'Peter Best had a letter for Mrs Tallis — could he have brought something for the captain?'

'I had the same thought. I was going to ask Mrs Penney if Kit ever received letters for him, but it will have to wait. What do you know about Mrs Tallis?'

'Delicate, it seems. There are no children, as the judge told us. Gossip — there's always gossip at the Inns, especially about judges — gossip has it that the lack of children has hit her hard. He, too. Men like a son, they say.'

Dickens laughed. 'Not six. Not that I regret them — well, not often. Sometimes they seem twice that number, racing up and down stairs in double-soled boots, but they're good lads — all different. And you, Henry Meteyard, no sons for you?'

'Shush — not a thing I speak of. Ma, there, she wants me married, but a man has to make his way these days. And he, if he comes, won't be a butcher, I daresay.'

'Sore point?'

'Not really, they're proud of me, and there's hope on the Meteyard and Son horizon —'

'Not Mrs M —' Mrs Meteyard was fifty if she was a day.

Henry roared and wiped his eyes. 'Don't say so. She'd be mortified. No, a cousin of my father has a son who has a most chopping boy — aged about ten now and has inherited the

Meteyard brawn. Bloodthirsty little beggar — takes a great interest in the carcases and certainly a potential son.'

'But not for you.'

'No, Charles, not for me, though I wouldn't care now that the Meteyard succession is secure, so to speak, whether it be son or daughter.'

'I have three daughters — the last just a baby. I like daughters.'

'But would you want one of them to marry a butcher's son?'

'Ah, that's it, is it? Too refined are they, the daughters of the law?'

'That's about it. I want a good-hearted, strong-minded, independent girl who'll like Sampson and Amelia, butchers or not.'

'Well said. I shall look about me.'

'Mrs Amelia will be much obliged.'

'But Mrs Tallis, do you know anything about her origins in St Lucia?'

'I'm afraid not — I don't know them that well. She and the judge are reserved, I would say. However, I do know that her solicitor was Ernest Lovelock. Lovelock and Imm at Symond's Inn. I shouldn't think so now, but, perhaps Louis Valentine used them still. They might be worth a try if you are looking for background.'

'Indeed, I shall suggest them to Sam — who may well be here, judging by Mug's bark. He did not bark for me.'

'He has criminal tendencies — Mug, not the Superintendent. He's been known to help himself at butchers' shops — not ours, of course. I think he might sense the advent of the police.'

The door opened to reveal Sam Jones, who came in with Sampson.

Sampson promised to keep looking and to let them know, and to keep an eye on Mrs Penney in the shop. It was time to go.

Hearing the dog bark, Dickens remembered. 'Where is Jam?'

Sampson knew. 'With Rosanna Chibb — that girl's convinced that Jam will lead her to Kit.'

21: CLOUDS ON THE HORIZON

A man with a long beard, dressed as a sailor, leaning over him, brandishing a wrench with which, he supposed, the madman would use to take out his teeth. The madman's mouth was the mouth of a horse with great teeth which turned into tombstones which became one tombstone bearing the inscription: *Fathom Five*. He awoke from drowning, surprised to find tears on his face. Dickens shook his head to banish the dream.

Somewhere a child was crying — little Dora. The crying stopped. Catherine must have gone to her. Poor little mite — she seemed so delicate. And Catherine never well, either, faint and giddy and suffering from those headaches. What to do about that? He felt seriously concerned — she was sometimes so confused and nervous, and he felt guilty. He knew he had been irritated with her, and he knew that there was something in him that failed her. He could only be practical. He couldn't talk about what was wrong with her — or him, for that matter. He couldn't imagine Sam unable to talk to Elizabeth.

Well, no use dwelling on all that. He needed to consult the family doctor. And he must go to see his parents at Keppel Street. His father was under the care of Mr Davey, the surgeon in whose house his parents lived. But his father was failing, he knew it. And, yet, he couldn't talk to his mother, either. And Kit was probably dead. The familiar sense of loss swept over him as he lay there, beached, he felt, on a lonely shore where a cold wind blew, chilling him to the bone. Intimations of mortality — not quite what Wordsworth had said, but it was what he felt just now.

But the life of the house stirred: doors opening and shutting — *slamming, rather*, he thought. Walter probably — his own chopping boy. Sounds of feet on the stairs. Laughter somewhere. Get up, hide your heart and do your duty. In fact, do more. He rose, took his daily shower, dressed and went upstairs to the nursery, kissed his wife and played with the little girl whose tiny smile made him feel better. *I should have called her Lucy*, he thought, his mind running on Wordsworth. The child is father to the man.

Things at Keppel Street were dreary. He spoke of Dora and how she had smiled at him. His father put on a cheerful countenance; he always did, but it was clear that he wasn't well. His natural buoyancy was subdued — he had always been an optimist, avowing that he was like a cork — push him under in one place and he would bob up elsewhere, none the worse for the dip. Well, he was sinking now. His longevity was, indeed, exceedingly problematical. He remembered his father's words about an old friend who was sick. So characteristic of John Dickens — six words, more usually, where one might do. Mr Micawber. He hadn't had to invent much. The blossom is blighted. The sun goes down. Floored. John Dickens was floored.

His mother asked about Fred and he knew he had displeased her by criticising his brother's improvident and foolish marriage. His mother was fond of easy-going Fred — she would be, he thought gloomily, giving her a five pound note. She hadn't asked, but he knew, and he gave it because he didn't love her. She gave him a perfunctory kiss as he left for Wellington Street. She'd got her money. He couldn't help thinking of Amelia Meteyard's warm, floury embrace. Too thin, she had said. His mother never noticed. *My fault, I suppose. I should be more... Damn it.* He walked away, fast — running from the past that dogged him like his murderer.

He sat at his desk in Wellington Street, his mind filled again with images of the sea. Foaming breakers, howling winds and lashing waves in an article for *Household Words* on lighthouses, and next a piece on coral growing fathoms deep, even an article on slavery which brought to mind the missing Pilgrim. *How all occasions do inform against me.*

He was conscious of things pressing and knew that there was nothing more he could do about Kit. Sampson Meteyard, Rosanna Chibb and Perce were looking. And where would he look anyway? He could spend hours trailing around the wharves, alleys, and lanes of Limehouse — what a nook-shotten place it was. No man need go to Australia to hide his head. He could do it just as well in any part of London.

What with the Sanitary Commission, his involvement in the debate about the paper tax, his *Child's History of England* and all the general botheration of *Household Words*, he had enough work on to last until eternity and beyond. He had the first shadows of a new story hovering about him. Befogged, bewildered, blue-devilled, that's what he was. He sat with his pen poised.

'Attend to me!' insisted *Household Words*. *I will, I will.* He bent to his work, editing, altering, deleting, inserting, scoring out, inking in with his iron pen until the proofs resembled an inky fishing net — which watery idea brought him to a full stop.

He had not told Sam about the lawyers mentioned by Henry Meteyard. Now that was something he could do. He and Sam could go and find out, perhaps, something about Louis Valentine's history in St. Lucia which might give a clue about Peter Best and whether he had brought some message for the captain, and that reminded him of his idea about Kit's possibly receiving letters for the captain. He would have to go back to see Mrs Penney. But finish all this first.

'Just what we wanted.' Sergeant Rogers was a satisfied man and so was Superintendent Jones. Doctor Woodhall had agreed not to mention the letter and had given his evidence most succinctly, as had Henry Meteyard. Superintendent Jones had said he had the case in hand; he was gathering evidence about the dead man's identity and would need more time to complete his investigation. After a brief consultation between the coroner and jury, it was decided that the inquiry should be adjourned.

'And Inspector Grove says that Charles Darden was denied bail,' continued Rogers. The case was a recent one. Charles Darden had stabbed a policeman. 'It was quite clear from the evidence of Inspector Grove and Feak that Darden knew what he was doing, drunk as he was, and that sailor, George Bird, saw it all.'

'Good. And what of Caleb Davis?'

'On the mend — it was a nasty wound. Darden twisted the knife in Caleb's thigh. That went against him.'

'Good. Now, of sailors, I've had word from Michael Simpson about the passengers on *The Endeavour*. I saw him last night and asked him to send me names of men travelling on their own, and who came off in the West India Docks — I thought Best might have had or made some acquaintance on the long voyage.'

'We're lookin' for a connection between Mr Best an' someone who has come to London.'

'We are — Mr Best's entry says that he resided at the *Belle Regarde* Plantation, which confirms what we knew — he was the agent of Mrs Tallis's stepfather, Adam Valentine, and was on his master's business in London. I looked for anyone who resided in St Lucia first and then any likely person who was coming home from St Lucia.'

'Did you find anyone?'

'There's one man who lived in St Lucia — French man by the sound of it — Gaspard L'Estrange. His address is *Douce Bouche* estate — a sugar plantation I should think. The name means sweet mouth. Don't be too impressed, Alf,' he said, looking at Rogers's admiring gaze, 'it's about all the French I know.'

'Any forwarding address?'

'Mivart's Hotel, and there's a couple of others who live in London: Sir Napier Moss of Montague Square —'

'They'd be first class passengers, though, wouldn't they? I mean, I don't suppose Mr Best would have —'

'I should have thought of first class — well spotted. Still, Mr L'Estrange might be useful if he owns a plantation. He might know the Captain's family — he might know of Mr Best.'

'That's true. Anyone else?'

'Father Gerard Mole — St. Patrick's, Soho Square. And, going back to Sir Napier Moss, I'm wondering if he knows Mrs Tallis or the Judge. Montague Square is not that far from Red Lion Square. I'll have to go and see him.'

'Shall I go to the church — might be worth a try.'

'Yes, he might have come across Mr Best. I think I may need Mr Dickens for Mivart's Hotel. It's a bit grand for the likes of me.'

'Any news of Mr Dickens's friend?'

'Not a thing. I wish there were some news. Mr Dickens is eaten up with anxiety.'

'Comin' today?'

'No — he's at his office in Wellington Street. There's nothing he can do but wait.'

'Not a thing he likes — always on the move. Don't know where he gets all that energy from — an' writin' the books and the magazine. Like a steam engine, he is.'

'And even they run out of fuel at times. However, I'll see him later. You get off to the church and I'll try Montague Square.'

Jones tidied his papers, thinking about the sailor, George Bird, the handy witness in the Darden case. That's what they needed, a handy witness or two, or more, preferably, but no one had come forward to say they had seen Long Jodd, or, indeed anyone else at The Ship or The Seven Stars. It was all so tenuous. Henry Meteyard had seen a man who might have been a sailor, or might not. Long Jodd might have murdered Ned Carver. A man called Jack Dawe might have also been a sailor and might have had contact with Peter Best at Salmon's Place. Passengers on *The Endeavour* might have talked to Best. Too many mights. He stood, lost in thought.

'Penny for 'em?' Dickens came in.

'I was thinking about a sailor.'

'Anyone in particular? We seem to have a surfeit of sailors.'

'And not one of 'em any use in this case. There was a sailor called George Bird who witnessed the stabbing of a policeman, and I was thinking we could do with a handy witness. You've not one lurking outside have you?'

'Alas, no, I came to say that Henry Meteyard mentioned lawyers whom he thought Louis Valentine might have used. I wondered if we should go and see what we might find out about St. Lucia and the complicated history.'

'Who are they?'

'Imm —'

''Oo?' Jones grinned.

'Very funny. Imm and Lovelock of Symond's Inn.'

'I know them. And I've been looking at the passenger list of *The Endeavour* on which Peter Best came in to see if I could find anyone who lived in St Lucia and might have known of Best.'

'Find anyone?'

'A French man staying at Mivart's — I was going to ask if you would come with me to see him later, and I was going to Montague Square in search of a Sir Napier Moss who came in on *The Endeavour*, but we'll go to Symond's Inn first.'

On their way out, Jones told Constable Feak where they were going. Feak was to make sure that he took any message from Sergeant Rogers. In the meantime, he and Mr Dickens were going to Lovelock and Imm —

Feak's mouth shaped itself into a circle.

'Not "oo" — Imm with a capital "I",' Jones explained.

Feak's mouth stayed as it was, but no sound emerged. Dickens laughed. 'It's a name, Constable Feak — I-M-M.'

'Oh, sorry Sir,' said Feak, not quite certain where he had gone wrong. 'I'll tell Mr Rogers where you've gone, shall I? An' take any message.'

'Thank you, Feak, I shall be back in an hour, I should think.'

As they walked briskly towards Chancery Lane, Dickens thought about Mr Ernest Lovelock — a ladies' man? A swell with a smooth, handsome face, a neat moustache, a curl on his brow, the languid brown eyes of a lover — he had him. A butterfly on a pin.

'Have you met Mr Lovelock?'

'I have.'

'And?'

'Wait and see.' Jones's eyes were amused. 'Wait and see if you're right.'

'I am on the tip-toe of expectation.'

22: DRY AS DUST

'More wiglomeration.'

Jones laughed. 'Not a word I'm familiar with.'

'No, I just made it up, but you see my drift. I always feel a chill upon me like the inside of tomb when I venture into these musty precincts. I laboured here once amid the pens, the pounce and parchment, and the dust — an inky little clerk, property of one Charles Molloy whose chambers I inhabited. I was the eagerest boy to run an errand — any errand so long as it took me into the streets. Off to the Errors Office I sped, to the Essoigns Office, the Outlaw Office — where I had hopes of meeting Robin Hood — to the Papers', the Peace, the Pipe, and the Pells' — whoever they were. The mysteries of the law, Samivel — the heart of which is never to be plucked out.'

'I hope it will. Come on, let's get in and see the lawyers.'

Time had stood still here in this dusty spot where old Symond, obviously a sparing man in his way, had constructed his inn of old building materials which took kindly to the dry rot and to dirt and all things decaying and dismal, and perpetuated Symond's memory with congenial shabbiness. It was a little, pale, wall-eyed, woebegone inn like a large dustbin of two compartments and a sifter. Quartered in this dingy hatchment commemorative of Symond were the legal bearings of Imm and Lovelock.

The outer door of the chambers of Lovelock and Imm opened into a hall which even at this middle part of the day held no light. The fanlight above the door was obscured by dust and only a faltering gaslight breathed out a dull blue flame. There were mysterious doors leading from the hall, but none bore any legend. A pale finger at the end of a ghostly hand severed from its body pointed up the stairs.

'It marshals us the way that we are going.' *Like Macbeth's dagger*, Dickens thought.

They peered up into the dark recesses of the staircase. All was silent.

'Are you sure this is right?' Dickens found himself whispering.

'No, I only met Mr Lovelock in court.'

Their breath stirred the thick air. Dust settled again. Dickens could not imagine Captain Valentine or anyone at all in this untouched place. Were they the first for years and years?

Upstairs someone sneezed so loudly that dust spilled down the stairs.

'Bless you,' offered Dickens.

'I have most need of blessing,' a voice said cheerfully, and feet clattered down the stairs. A merry young face came at them through the gloom. 'Much obliged, sir. Amen.'

'Lovelock and Imm up there?' asked Jones.

'Not Imm —' the cheerful young man laughed — 'always wanted to say that.'

''Oo then?' supplied Dickens.

'Oh, very — oh, I say, Mr Dickens.' A pair of the brightest blue eyes widened in astonishment. 'Great heavens, fancy you here. What a thing — my word, *David Copperfield* — what a wonder! Is it possible to shake you by the hand?'

'It is,' said Dickens, smiling and offering his hand, 'and I am much obliged, Mr?'

'Tom Lomax — not Traddles — law's not for me. Uncle Lovelock will tell you. Best not ask, though. I'm a disappointment to the law and to my uncle. He thought I might — well I didn't, so I'm off to Antwerp soon. In the cloth trade now.'

'Exciting?'

'Not yet, but I shall enjoy the travel. I shall go further one day — across the wide, wide sea.'

'Fresh air rather than dust?'

'Exactly. Does Uncle Lovelock know who's coming to visit?'

'No, not yet.'

'You'll be more welcome than I am. He's up there in his den, poor fellow. I am a trial to him. The dust always makes me sneeze. Pains him. He likes the dust — keeps everything quiet.' He sneezed again. 'Well, I ought to be away. So good to have met you, Mr Dickens. Wait until I tell the fellows. Charles Dickens!'

He was gone in a whirl of dust. Dickens and Jones went up the stairs quietly and knocked at an oak door with a frowning ecclesiastical air. Had a bishop appeared they would not have been surprised, but it was only an elderly man in rusty black who motioned them in, nodded when Jones gave his name, and vanished into an inner chamber.

They heard whisperings as of old leaves stirring. The speechless old man came back, leaving the door open for them to pass through into Mr Lovelock's room. Dust, parchment, dust, red tape, dust, law lists, dust, tomes, and more dust. From amid the dusty piles, as if rising from a sarcophagus, Mr Lovelock slowly appeared. There was a faded, dried tea leaf sort of look about Mr Lovelock. He had one of those faces which seem to be squeezed into an expression of anguish as if the very world pained him, but he must, perforce, be in it. Not a ladies' man, disappointingly. A secret sorrow? That'd be it. Lovelorn. Dickens did not look at Jones, who was explaining their business as Mr Lovelock unfolded himself into an upright position. It took some time.

He gave the small dry cough with which all elderly lawyers began their grave considerations. 'Ah, Superintendent Jones, yes, yes, I remember you. Cribb and Cratchit — most distressing. And Cribb killed himself — a reverend gentleman, too. Debts. Money's a dangerous thing. And now murder, you say. Ah, Mr Jones, the world, the world... This Mr Best you mention, murdered, too, like the poor captain. You think the two cases are connected?'

'I do, and I wish to know anything you can tell me of Captain Valentine's history and affairs.' Seeing Mr Lovelock glance at Dickens, he added, 'Mr Charles Dickens is looking for a Mr Christopher Penney, the captain's friend and his. Mr Penney is missing.'

Mr Lovelock gave Dickens a pained glance and coughed again before saying, 'Oh, Mr Dickens, I see you now. You know life do you not? And the law — dear me, your lawyers. Troubling —' Dickens felt guilty again, as if he had contributed to Mr Lovelock's suffering — 'A most distressing set of circumstances. Poor Captain Valentine had been my client for many years. Very distressing indeed. Very much so...'

Jones waited. Clearly a man who would take his own time — eternity, probably. Dickens waited. Ernest Lovelock straightened a perfectly tidy cravat; smoothed an imaginary stray lock from his forehead; adjusted the precisely arranged pens on his desk; saw that they were disarranged, and put them back again, all the while the expression of anguish deepening the lines about his mouth so that he appeared to be sucking on a lemon.

'Mr Lovelock, I haven't a great deal of time. If you would oblige me —'

'Ah, yes, yes, dear me…'

Mr Lovelock told them much of what Judith Black had already revealed about the inheritance of the estate by Captain Valentine's stepfather, but added, with a shake of his dusty grey head, that the captain's father, Etienne Valentine, had committed suicide. His widow had married the foreman of the estate, the man who had been taken as a boy from the streets of London. The boy had been adopted and it was he to whom Etienne Valentine had left the plantations.

'No blood tie. Most unusual, Superintendent Jones. Most irregular, but, then the family was French. French…' His anguish returned. 'The French were once in possession of the island so I suppose twenty-five years ago or so, Etienne Valentine might have thought it safer to leave his property in the hands of an Englishman — his children were young — I don't know — but the captain did not discuss the matter with me.'

'Did the captain leave a will?' asked Jones.

'He did. He made a new one before he sailed. He was to be married, but, careful of the perils of the sea, he wished to provide for his affianced lady. His money goes to Mrs Grace Fox, with express provision for her child. His share of the shipyard reverts to Mrs Judith Black. It was very straightforward.'

'Who was the beneficiary before Mrs Fox?'

'His sister, Mrs Tallis, though the shares in the ships and yard would still return to Mrs Black — he thought it only fair. He had inherited them through his first wife, Mrs Alice Black.'

'You have not received any letters for the captain from St Lucia or by the agency of Mr Best?'

'No, I believe the captain's correspondence, should there be any, would be addressed to him care of Mr Penney — your friend, Mr Dickens. It was more convenient for the captain.'

They stood outside the outer door, contemplating a scrawny cat with its eye fixed on a meagre sparrow pecking at the dust. Dickens moved his feet and the sparrow flew up into the dreary sky. The cat glared at the man who had robbed him of his dinner and walked away, a picture of offended dignity.

'Well, what do you think?' asked Jones.

'What I may think before dinner is one thing, Mr Jones, and what I may think after dinner is another, and upon that philosophical point, I suggest we confer after a small beefsteak pudding and a pint of small ale at The Old Ship Tavern where your constables failed to find the murderer, but where we might ask a question or two of Daniel Stagg, a particular friend of mine.'

'I know him. A *small* beefsteak pudding, you say?'

'With two kidneys, a dozen oysters, and a couple of mushrooms thrown in — a pudding to put a man in a good humour with everything except the two bottom buttons of his waistcoat.'

'Lead on.'

Daniel Stagg, the landlord, greeted Dickens as an old friend and the Superintendent with rather more caution.

'Two of your beefsteak puddings, Mr Stagg, and two glasses of pale ale, if you will oblige us.'

They took a table in a corner of the parlour where they might not be overheard. It smelt of sawdust, tobacco smoke, tallow, sea coal from the fire, and of spirits and beer. The round table was a bit sticky with the rings of pots and tankards. In the centre of one, a finger had traced the word 'ded'. Dickens gazed at the word. Dead? A warning? An epitaph? The three letters seemed peculiarly menacing, somehow more final than the usual four.

However, Daniel Stagg came and swirled a clean tablecloth over the marks in the manner of a magician. Dickens half expected the table to vanish, but knives and forks followed and two glasses of pale ale.

The puddings came and proved as tasty as Dickens's description. The pale ale washed away the dust of Symond's Inn. It was time to ask a question or two. Dickens called over the landlord, congratulated him upon the pudding, received his thanks, and Jones asked about the night on which the constables had come asking after a sailor.

'I remember, Mr Jones, but it was busy, an' we do get sailors — all sorts o' strangers. I didn't notice any sailor in partikler. I told the constables an' they could see fer themselves 'ow crowded it was. There was an inquest earlier in the day, so folks was in talkin' about it all. We knew 'im, see — well, we knew 'im by sight. Rum cove — loner. Overdose of opium.'

Ah, "ded", thought Dickens. Epitaph, then.

Daniel continued, anxious to justify himself, 'I would 'ave 'elped if I could, an' then there was the 'Armonic Meetin' — always a good crowd fer that — Little Swills — 'e's a comedian — took off the coroner. A treat it was — so yer see Mr Jones, what with one thing an' another...'

'I understand, Mr Stagg. Who else was serving?'

'The lad, yer might as well ask 'im. He's a noticin' sort o' boy is Pips.'

The boy, whose head was not unlike the small kidney pudding, appeared at the landlord's cry of 'Pips!' He looked a bit more substantial than poor little Mealy down at Limehouse, and his eyes were bright in his round face.

'These gen'lemen want ter know if you remember a sailor who mighta come in late last night. Tall — in a peacoat — on his own.'

Pips scratched his head. 'Dunno — 'twoz that busy. Quite a few sailors — can't tell one from another. Oh, wait a bit, I remembers now — I went out into the skittle-ground — jest next door. Dog woz barkin'. Knew it wan't skittles — folk don't play at night — too dark, see.' They nodded to show that they understood this piece of wisdom. 'There was someone there. Said 'e woz feelin' queer. Could I get 'im a brandy.'

'Can you remember anything about him?'

'Dunno — dark skin. Foreign, mebbe. Coulda bin a sailor — yers, I remembers now. 'Ad an earring.'

Dickens saw Long Jodd in his mind's eye for a moment, and he recalled Mealy and his reference to Ben Caunt's right hook. 'Just the one earring?'

Pips screwed up his eyes, thinking. 'I think so. Gold.'

'Did you bring him the brandy?'

'Yers, and 'e give me two bob —'

'Left or right-handed?'

The boy screwed up his eyes again. 'Left — remembers now. An' 'e drank off the brandy in one go, stood up, pushed past me an' went. Dint stay fer 'is change.'

'You didn't notice a snake tattoo on his hand?'

'No, sir.'

Dickens handed the boy a shilling. 'Thank you, Pips, I'm obliged to you. Most helpful.'

The boy went off with Daniel Stagg. Dickens turned back to Jones, who said, 'Well?'

'Long Jodd wears two silver earrings, and he's right-handed. Mealy — you remember — said that the man at The Anchor had a right hook like Ben Caunt's —'

'And Doctor Woodhall said that his attacker hit him with his left fist.'

'And Jodd had a particularly horrible snake tattoo on his right hand — surely Pips would have seen it. Bold asked Mealy about it.'

'So he did, though Pips might not have noticed. Still, I'm inclined to think that it wasn't Long Jodd who was here.'

'The invisible Jack Dawe had an earring.'

'As does every sailor from here to the Nore Light — we'll have to wait for Gaunt on him. Now, this stranger that Pips met — the old law writer pointed Rogers and Stemp this way after his brush with a sailor.'

'And Pips said the sailor might be foreign and that he'd said he felt queer — well he might if he had just murdered Best and knocked down Woodhall and Dacres. And he went off in a hurry.'

'All true, but what worries me is that if the murderer is another sailor, Jack Dawe or anybody else, it won't be easy to find him. I'll have to go back to *The Endeavour* — assuming that our murderer came from St. Lucia — trace the crew.'

'But you might be able to narrow down the likely suspects. Someone connected with the Valentine estate — somehow. Oh lor, Sam, I can't think how.'

'Neither can I. In any case, the sailor seen by Pips could be any old sailor. It's no use dwelling on him for the moment. Let's think about motive. What's at stake here?'

'It must be to do with St Lucia.'

'This estate business — could that be it? Lovelock said, and Judith Black, that the estate passed into the hands of the adoptive brother of Captain Valentine's father —'

'But both said that the captain was not concerned about it. Louis Valentine's father killed himself — perhaps he didn't.

Murder, Sam.' Dickens's eyes gleamed. 'Could Louis have known that his father was murdered, and someone wanted to stop him talking?'

'But it was a long time ago — Louis Valentine has had plenty of time to expose a murder. And why was Best killed?'

'True. And, I forgot, Mrs Penney said someone had been in Kit's room upstairs — someone who was looking for something —'

'The murderer was looking for something that he believed the captain to have, or that he believed Peter Best had.'

'Something so important that he killed them to get it — something that he believed Kit had. Does that mean that Kit is dead too, that the murderer then went after Best, having searched Kit's place? Oh, God, Sam — it must mean that.'

'No, wait, wait. If he was going to kill Kit, surely he would have done it in the shop. Let's suppose that Kit tried to resist him, denied having anything belonging to the captain; then he would have killed him as he killed the captain and Peter Best. That's how ruthless he is. Kit can't have been there when whoever he was searched the place.'

'So, where is he? He must know something. He could be in danger still —'

'Unless the murderer took something from Peter Best as well as the letter intended for Mrs Tallis. He might well be on his way back to St Lucia — and even if we found out that a ship has sailed or is due to sail, we can't find him because we don't know who he is.'

23: MISSING

Sergeant Rogers was waiting for them at Bow Street. John Gaunt was with him. Rogers had found the priest at St Patrick's in Soho Square, but Father Mole could tell him nothing about Peter Best.

'No confession of dark deeds?'

Rogers looked at Dickens, his face blank for a moment, then he grinned, 'Oh, I get you. No — nobody's confessin' to anythin', worse luck.'

Jones turned to John Gaunt. 'What's the news, John?'

'It's about Carver. The body was taken to the bone house by St Anne's church, where a surgeon examined the wound. The victim had been stabbed as we know, and here's the important bit. The surgeon found a sliver of wood about half an inch long adhering to the lip of the wound — he believes it is broken off a sailor's fid, which we now believe to be the weapon.'

'Long Jodd's?'

'Could be. We confiscated their knives, marlin spikes and fids, but they're easy enough to get. We know that Best's throat was cut. You said it was a deep wound made with a blade. You couldn't cut a man's throat with a fid. Our surgeon in Limehouse is familiar with sailors' fids — it's not unusual as a weapon, but it's not a blade.'

'What about Captain Valentine? Could it have been a fid?'

'We assumed it was a knife or dagger — it went into the soft part of the neck between the clavicle and shoulder blade. The surgeon still says so. He called the wound an incised puncture, and it was a clean cut on both edges — a double-edged blade.'

'That's clear enough, John. It was good of you to come.'

'I wanted to come myself because —'

Dickens looked at Gaunt's face. He seemed troubled now. 'Something else, Johnno — there's other news. Not Kit!'

'No, Mr Dickens, not Mr Penney, it's the girl, Rosanna Chibb. This morning, Jam came back without her. Mr Meteyard went out to look, but there's no sign of her. I thought you two ought to know.'

'She wouldn't abandon Jam — she was insistent that the two of them would find Kit. She's been good about reporting back to Mrs Penney, too. She wouldn't just go off and leave them. Shall I come back with you?'

'I think Mrs Penney would like it. Inspector Bold has the constables looking.'

'I ought to go, Sam — what will you do about Mivart's and the French man?'

'We'll go tomorrow. I'll go to see Sir Napier Moss — he lives not far from Judge Tallis, and he returned from St Lucia on *The Endeavour*. I thought I might find out more about Captain Valentine's family over there, and whether Sir Napier knows anything about Peter Best's reason for coming here. He might not know anything, but it's worth a try.'

'Right,' said Dickens, 'I'll come to Norfolk Street later, shall I, if I can?'

'Yes. Let us hope that Rosanna turns up — hope to —'

'I know — never give up hoping.'

Aurora Penney was at the door of the shop. Jam looked thoroughly miserable. They both were looking up and down the street.

'Charley — it's good of you to come. I can't think where she's got to. She always comes back — at lunch time, teatime, and I told her not to go about in the dark.'

'She promised me she would be careful — we should have stopped her after the murder of Carver. I should have thought —'

'I should have thought, Charley, not that Rosanna would have given up. But it's no use sayin' what we should have done — it's what we should be doin' that's more important.'

'The constables are looking, Mrs Penney,' Gaunt said.

'I know, I know, lad — you're doin' your best, but you haven't found Kit, or Pilgrim for that matter.'

Gaunt was saved from further comment with the arrival of Sampson Meteyard and Henry, but their faces showed that they had not found her.

'We've been all over the place — all sorts of nooks and crannies, down by the wharves, along the shore where the old windmill is and all those old wrecks of boats. There's a family lives there. Rosanna knows the daughter, Lizzie Hexam — but she hadn't seen her, not since a day or so when Rosanna was askin' about Kit. The father's a waterman. Said he'd keep an eye out —' Sampson stopped then. They all knew what a waterman might find.

Dickens knew the places — the old windmill with its warty excrescence which showed where the sails had been, and he had seen the watermen who fished for dead bodies which were taken to the bone house. She could be drowned; she could be murdered. What if, as she was making her enquiries about Kit, the murderer, who wanted whatever he had wanted from the captain, from Peter Best, from Kit, had heard and thought she might lead him to Kit, had led him to Kit?

But he only asked, 'What about her mother?'

'I've seen her,' said Mrs Penney. 'I don't think she really understands. I didn't enlighten her about what's gone on. Rosanna's always been a law unto herself. Mrs Chibb thinks she'll be back — of course, she needs Rosanna to help in the lodgings. She was annoyed that Rosanna had been disappearing all the time. She didn't like it when Rosanna came here to see Kit. Didn't see the point — she had Rosanna's future all mapped out.'

'Slave to her and the lodgers,' Dickens said.

'That's about it — mind, I'll admit I wondered if Kit was giving her false hope, but he didn't see any reason she shouldn't learn about the instruments. I don't know — it's hard for a girl, but he said she had something…'

Sampson said, 'She did — does. Tough is Rosanna; I wonder if she's found out something about Kit.'

'But she wouldn't abandon Jam, and she'd have come to tell me.'

'She might have told Jam to come home — he'd do as he's told. Maybe that's the message — she's tellin' you that she's found out somethin'. Well, maybe…' Sampson scratched his head. 'She's got sense, Rosanna, sense enough to keep out of danger.'

'She has,' said Henry. 'Father, you should tell Ma what's happening. Mrs Penney, go in and sit for a bit while I talk to Mr Dickens. See what we can think of next.'

Mrs Penney looked at Henry suspiciously. Not much got past Aurora, but she went in and Sampson went down the alley to talk to his wife.

'I wanted to have a word.'

'So I gathered — what are you thinking?'

'I'm thinking that there have been three murders.'

'Long Jodd murdered Ned Carver. We're sure of it,' John Gaunt said.

'So you think Captain Valentine and Peter Best were murdered by the same hand — the person who searched Kit's rooms for something?'

'Sam Jones thinks so and I do,' Dickens said, 'but Sam wondered if the murderer has found what he wanted — we assume he took Best's money and papers, but, now…'

'Rosanna is missing and that's what worries me. Apart from Rosanna, what about Mrs Penney? Might he come back?'

'You mean if he thinks that whatever he is searching for might still be here, or Mrs Penney might know something?'

'Exactly, Constable Gaunt, and that's why I wanted to talk to you both. I know the police can't be here all the time, and neither can you, Mr Dickens, but I can. I've no pressing business. Mrs Penney could go to her daughter's. I could be in the shop. He'll not get past me, and Sampson's not far away. I could borrow Mug. What do you say?'

'I say aye, Henry, if you can persuade Mrs Penney — she's used to being in charge. I always thought she could storm a town single-handed with her hearth broom.'

Henry grinned, 'An arm-lock might do it. What say you, constable?'

'It's a good idea and would ease my mind, and the inspector's.'

'And I've another idea, Henry. I could get you a boy with very sharp eyes and ears, and very sharp wits.'

'Young Scrap?'

'The very same — he'll be glad to do it. I have a feeling that life has been a bit too quiet for him lately. He could be useful — he's used to shop work, and he'll find his way about in no time. He has a nose for places.'

'I ought to go,' Gaunt said. 'I'll tell Inspector Bold, and we'll keep the beat constables on the watch for Rosanna.'

'I'll get Mrs Penney to go in to my mother. Father and I can have another look round, but it's getting dark. I doubt we'll find her tonight. Let's hope that my father was right, and she'll come back.'

John Gaunt went away. Henry Meteyard and Dickens stood silent, brooding on the missing girl. Dickens thought of the murderer with his knife; the knife that had cut through the soft flesh of Louis Valentine's neck. Death where is thy sting? In the cold kiss of the steel's point on the warm skin. He could feel it and shuddered. It seemed more terrible than the brutal slashing of Peter Best's throat — more subtle, more sinister. That the same hand could do both. And, perhaps another killing had already taken place. Rosanna Chibb somewhere in the dark — that spark put out, sightless eyes staring into the black, implacable sky.

'I have a horrible feeling about this, Henry.'

'I do, too. I should go in to Mrs Penney — tell her what we've decided. Will you come in with me?'

'Back you up?'

'Yes, she'll listen to you — she values how fond you are of Kit.'

'I don't know — I still feel like little Charley Dickens who sang the song of the cat's meat man when I'm with her — and your mother.'

'Bless 'em — we'll always be boys to them, but we must persuade her.'

'All right — bring your hearth broom.'

Half an hour later, Dickens was on his way. He had asked about letters for the captain, but Mrs Penney didn't know of anything recent. She would look. Dickens approached the matter of Henry's being in the shop. Mrs Penney had agreed — not without persuasion. 'Protection! Me!' She had glared at them both, but Dickens had impressed her as Henry knew he would. He had told her that she must be safe for Kit. He told her that Superintendent Jones, a man he would trust with his very life, believed that Kit was in hiding. How would it be if he came back to find his mother dead? Even 'The Admiral' had flinched at that.

Dusk was descending, bringing shadows with it. The streets were quieting now. The wind got up — that east wind again. They said it carried fever. Perhaps it did. Something rushed in his blood. Fear.

24: AT BEDFORD SQUARE

Sir Napier Moss was a most obliging man with a good-natured face, browned from the St. Lucia sun, a man who lived well and had the means to do it. Superintendent Jones had noted the elegance of the white-pillared house, the spacious hall and the luxurious furnishings of the library into which Sir Napier had ushered him, offering brandy and cigars, explaining all the while that Lady Napier was at a reception with their daughter, that he was alone, that he would help in any way he could, that he knew Judge Tallis and his charming wife, had known her in St Lucia where he had property. Jones, breathless, accepted the brandy and sat down.

Sir Napier rattled on. 'Sugar — it's all sugar there, Superintendent. Fortunes made, including mine. Not but what I was glad to see the end of slavery. Always felt guilty somehow — my father didn't. Called me a fool when I voted for Wilberforce's bill. Didn't expect I'd give up my fortune to ease my conscience. He was right, of course. Dead now. I'm wanting to sell. I thought old Adam Valentine —' He took a sip of his brandy.

Jones took advantage of the pause. It would be brief, he saw, as Sir Napier kept his glass at his lips. 'You know him?'

'I do. You want to know about him in connection with Louis Valentine's murder?'

'Yes. And the murder of his agent, Peter Best.'

'Yes, bad business all round. Tallis told me. But Adam Valentine — a formidable man, Superintendent. Hard as nails, respected, feared at times, but never much liked. Something of the gutter about him. He had a look —' Sir Napier closed his eyes as if to conjure the man — 'the look of a man who knew what you were — that you were soft and he could buy and sell you if he chose. Successful. Runs his plantation with an iron hand. Not a whip, you understand. His workers are well fed, decently housed and looked after, and, unlike some, he's no slaver. Shrewd enough to adapt to the times. He made enemies of some of the older families when he took over the Valentine plantation. Plenty in debt to him.

'But he's dying, rumour has it — heart, they say. And his son will get the estate. That's another thing. Valentine has no time for his son, Marcus. The mother, Adam Valentine's first wife, was mad, they say. By all accounts, Louis was his favourite, but when the second wife died, Louis and his sister came to England for good. There was talk — St. Lucia's a small place — that there must have been some double-dealing, that Louis and his sister were cheated. But it could just be that with their mother gone, there was nothing to keep them there. Painful memories, perhaps.'

'The father killed himself?' Jones wanted to know how.

'Yes. Shot himself. He left all the business matters to Adam Valentine and lived like a gentleman. Drink, cards and mistresses. There were a number of children said to be his. Broke his wife's heart. I saw him before he died — a wreck of a man. Syphilis ate him up — almost blind at the end, and insane. General paralysis of the insane, they call it. No one was surprised, knowing Adam Valentine, that the estate passed to him, nor that he married Louise. Surprised at her, though. Beautiful woman — good family.'

'And the agent, Peter Best, what do you know of him?'

'I met him — a quiet, hard-working, decent sort. I spoke to him on the ship. He just said that he was taking letters to Louis and his sister. I wondered if Adam Valentine was leaving something to them.'

'Part of the estate?'

'I shouldn't think so. They don't need it. Louis owns shares in the ships and the yard, and these captains don't do badly from the cargoes. In any case, he was not a man to want wealth. Mrs Tallis is well provided for — Tallis isn't a poor man. I shouldn't think they'd want any part of it. It's a burden, I can tell you. I don't want to keep going back and forth. I'd be glad to be shot of it at any price. My sons don't care for it.'

'Another passenger on *The Endeavour* was a Frenchman called L'Estrange — staying at Mivard's. Do you know him?'

'Yes, I do. Owns a plantation. I dined with him on the ship. He could tell you more, probably, about the Valentine family.'

'He is not one of the families in debt to Adam Valentine?'

'Good Lord, no. A shrewd man is L'Estrange, and a wealthy one.'

Jones stood up. 'I am much obliged, Sir Napier, for your assistance. It was good of you to tell me all that.'

'Don't see that it helps you much, I daresay, but you'll judge for yourself. Tallis said you'd taken Mr Dickens to see him about a missing friend.'

'Yes, we haven't found him, either.'

'Tallis took a liking to him — Mr Dickens. I must say, I'd like to have met him. Give him my compliments, if you will. I so enjoy his work — all that about the lawyers makes me laugh. Tallis wasn't amused when I chaffed him about it, but he's the serious type. He liked Dickens, though.'

'Most people do, sir — he has the gift of friendship.'

'Well, I hope you can find his friend — and solve your case. You'll let me know.'

'I will. And now I must bid you goodnight.'

Sir Napier took him into the hall where a footman waited to open the door. Jones went out into the night. He would walk back to Bow Street. The night inspector was Ben Jolley, a constantly worried man whom Dickens had described as one who knew the world was coming to the end and, out of pity for his fellow men, kept it to himself. It was very apt. Jolley would appreciate his visit. Then home.

He walked down Charlotte Street towards Broad Street. Much to think about. The stepfather was dying and had, presumably, wanted to communicate something to his stepchildren. Someone had not wanted those letters to reach Louis Valentine and Madeleine Tallis. And to get them he had murdered the captain and Best, and had threatened Kit Penney.

The answer lay in St Lucia and what was in those letters. Could be money — murder and money were familiar bedfellows. Dickens had wondered about murder in Saint Lucia. Now, he couldn't help wondering how a nearly blind, insane man had shot himself. Unless someone had handed him the gun. Perhaps that was the family secret. What Louis Valentine knew. But where did the letters come in? Adam Valentine's son was to inherit, but suppose that the inheritance had been got by foul means? When did that wreck of a man write his will? Suppose that Adam Valentine's letters contained a confession. Louis Valentine had not known any secret, but he was going to be told one. And that secret might mean that Marcus Valentine's inheritance would be in jeopardy. Not that his speculation was much use unless they found the letters, and, as he had thought before, they might well be sailing away to St Lucia. But, the girl, Rosanna Chibb, was missing — she who had searched for Kit. The dog had come back without her. So, it might be that he, whoever he was, still had not found them. Did Kit Penney have them? But, like the girl, he was missing. Who was he? Someone sent by Marcus Valentine to intercept the letters. Someone. Someone.

At Bow Street, Inspector Jolley gave him what passed for a smile. He reported with his air of melancholy resignation on the various arrivals during the evening: the girl who had stolen a gold watch; the man who had tried to shoot his wife — he'd missed; the man who had been apprehended with a stolen barrel of oysters which he had attempted to roll down the street; the couple who had accused a respectable lawyer of insulting the wife then attacked him; the five lads who had been taken from a den of thieves under an archway.

'Dacres and Johnson were looking for stolen goods and traced them to the place. Set proper, it was — fireplace, cooking stove; straw beds; the whole place secured by boards and canvas covering the entrance. Home from home. And a line and coat hanging from it. Some kidsman teachin' them to pick the pockets. The constables had to crawl in backwards, and they couldn't stand up.'

'Fagin's kitchen.'

'Just so, Sir, and plenty of watches, bits o' silver and trinkets — all stolen. But, a quiet night, really — so far.' He sighed. 'No parents o' course — you can see why they do it. Still, they'll have to go before the beak. Couple o' months and out to do it all again — makes you wonder.'

'It does, indeed.'

With a faint grimace at that inadequate response, Inspector Jolley resumed making the entries in his ledger — the neatest of hands he had.

Jones went home to Norfolk Street where the young servant girl, Posy, let him in. As she took his hat and coat, his wife Elizabeth came from the kitchen down the hall. As the door opened, he heard the sound of voices.

'Visitor?'

'Scrap's in there with Eleanor — they are reading together and seem to have some secret which they, or Scrap in particular, wish to divulge to Charles. He was rather hoping that he would be coming with you.'

'He might come later.'

'And Scrap is convinced that you are investigating a murder. Mollie Spoon told him about it at the shop. He is wondering why his services have not been called upon. Most indignant he is.'

'Ah, well, the trouble is that I think the answer lies in Limehouse, which is where Charles has gone. I'll tell you all when I've eaten.'

'There's a stew on the range. Posy made it — all by herself.'

'My, from soup to stews — it'll be lobster and caviar next.'

Elizabeth laughed. 'She is so determined to do it all herself. I offered a recipe, but she preferred the one from her book. "Needs doin' proper for the Superintendent," she said. The rest of us clearly are of no account.'

'She has made such progress — thanks to you.'

Posy had come to them by Charles Dickens. She had been selling artificial flowers in the street and was half starved — a pitiful, undersized, illiterate orphan who had been apprenticed to a milliner after the orphanage, but the milliner, not a very skilled one, had gone out of business and Posy went out into the streets to sell the few flowers the woman had given in lieu of money. Good food, clean clothes, and, above all, kindness, had done much.

They went into the kitchen where Eleanor and Tom, Elizabeth's and Sam's adopted children, sat at the table with Scrap, who placed his book very carefully to one side. Jones loved coming home to a full house. It had once been so empty — after their only daughter, Edith, had died at the age of twenty-one, and her new-born child with her. He thought of her often, but without the terrible emptiness which had possessed them both for years afterwards. Eleanor and Tom Brim had been orphaned at the death of their father, who had entrusted them to Sam and Elizabeth. A year had passed. Tom Brim, now six, seemed to have forgotten most of what had happened, though Elizabeth made sure to talk of papa and how happy he would be to know what a good boy Tom was at his lessons. With Eleanor, it was different. She was eleven and had seen her father at the last. She had known all, and she remembered her mama who had died when Tom was born. Papa had relied on her. She would not forget easily.

Jones greeted Scrap, who looked at him with narrowed eyes which seemed to say that he knew something was going on, but he only said, as if it were a casual enquiry, 'Mr Dickens comin'?'

'I think he might later.'

'Only I wanted ter discuss somethin' with 'im — I've a bit of a surprise fer 'im.' He looked across at Eleanor, who clearly knew the matter to be discussed. 'Awright if I waits fer 'im?'

'I don't know when.'

'Mollie knows where I am. Told 'er I 'ad somethin' important fer Mr Dickens.' Mollie Spoon, wife to Sergeant Rogers, managed Mr Brim's stationery shop and Scrap did the errands — when he was not assisting the police — a role he relished and, he thought, looking at the Superintendent's face, there was somethin' doin'. Where woz Mr Dickens? 'E woz in it somewhere, an' Mr Jones is worried about somethin'. *I'm stayin' till I finds out.*

Later, long after the children had been in bed, Elizabeth came down with a blanket.

'I take it he's not going back to the shop.' She smiled at Scrap, who was fast asleep on the sofa. She laid it gently on him, giving him the fleetest of kisses. It didn't do to be too demonstrative with Scrap. He was grown up now — he thought. At thirteen, he was still small, but he had filled out. Like Posy, good food, a job to do, responsibility, and, above all, being needed, had given him happiness he had never known on the streets.

'I'll bet he told Mollie that he'd be staying the night.'

'Interrogated, were you?'

'Yes — you know how tenacious he is. But I explained that the case was really to do with Limehouse, and it was a bit far for him to be nosing around, but I would send if I needed him. I promised, but I can't really see that I will want him.'

'Did he mention Charles?'

'No, and I didn't ask, but I am wondering where he is.'

Jones told Elizabeth about the missing Rosanna Chibb. 'I don't know the girl, but Charles was convinced she wouldn't have left the dog — Kit Penney's dog.'

'You're worried.'

'I am. She was looking for Kit, who we think may have received a letter for Captain Valentine; Kit is missing; the captain's servant, Pilgrim is missing, and now the girl. They have to be connected to the murders of the captain and his stepfather's agent from St Lucia.'

'And you've no idea who might be looking for those letters?'

'Not a clue, except that I think there must have been someone on the ship in which Best arrived. I've followed up two, Sir Napier and a parson. There's a Frenchman staying at Mivart's hotel who I intend to interview tomorrow. See if he knows anything about Best, the agent who was murdered, or anything about the estate.'

'Might the Frenchman be a suspect?'

'No, I don't think so — Sir Napier spoke well of him. A wealthy man, by all accounts.'

'Does anyone else benefit from the captain's death?'

'His betrothed, Mrs Fox, and the lady who runs the shipyard and has the majority shares in *The Redemption*, the captain's ship — Mrs Judith Black. She inherits the captain's shares in the ship and the yard.'

'A lady in the case?'

Jones grinned at the reference to Mrs Crupp, David Copperfield's landlady. 'I hope not. There was something about her, though, some feeling for the captain. We saw it — just a faint flush at the neck when she said his name. She referred to him as the captain as if he were a distant acquaintance, but the name "Louis" brought that flush to her neck.'

'Love? Jealousy — a woman scorned?'

'I don't know. Not the loving sort, I thought — an icy sort of woman. There is some talk of suspicion connected with her husband's death — her housekeeper, a malicious little body, told us that. Charles said he could imagine her slipping a drop of poison into a drink, but she couldn't have killed Peter Best. Henry Meteyard and Doctor Woodhall saw a sailor at the scene who ran off. It's to do with those letters from St Lucia, I'm sure.'

'Are you sitting up for Charles?'

'A little longer, I think. I'll build up the fire.'

Elizabeth kissed him goodnight and left him to stare into the revived flames. He thought about Gaspard L'Estrange, who would not be staying at Mivard's and committing murder in his spare time. Surely there could be no motive there. Still, anything was possible. *I ought to see him as soon as I can.* The boy, Pips, had said the stranger in the skittle-yard was foreign.

25: IN FIVE-BELLS PLACE

Dickens walked quickly up Three Colt Street towards the turning which led to Five Bells Place where Rosanna's mother kept her lodging house. A gust of wind nearly blew off his hat. He stopped to right it. Bits of paper and rag swirled about his feet and as he kicked them away, he caught sight of something red. He bent to look. It was a piece of old silk, torn now, but there was a knot in it. It was a kerchief — he had last seen it round Rosanna Chibb's slender neck.

What best to do? Go back and get Sampson and Henry? Have a look down the court? She might just have lost it — then he would have created alarm for nothing. He looked at it again. But, it was torn. He knew that this meant something dreadful had happened. Just a quick look then.

He went down the alley past the Five Bells and Blade Bone public house from where he could hear the sound of a fiddle and the noise of feet stamping. Then it was terribly dark and quiet suddenly. He started at the sound of a window banged shut. There was a gas light at the end above an archway. He made for that, stopping there, listening, hearing his heart knocking at his ribs. Then there were voices coming in his direction from the pub, perhaps. Two men. Sailors by the look of them. They came up to him. What was a gent doing here in the alley? He saw suspicion in their faces and stepped forward.

'I'm searching for Rosanna Chibb.' He regretted the words as soon as he spoke them — he realised what they would think.

The taller of the two loomed over him menacingly. 'Want a girl do yer?'

A gust of meaty breath, the sickening stench of decay, sweat, grease, stale tobacco and liquor. Dickens attempted to move away, but the second man twisted his arm round his back. 'Filthy toff — gerrout out of 'ere or yer'll get more than yer bargained fer.'

'Ere, wot's this?' Dickens had dropped the red kerchief. The first man picked it up. 'That's Rosanna's — wot yer done wiv 'er?'

'Nothing. She's missing — I found it and thought —'

The flash of a blade. That icy kiss he had felt before. The knife touched his throat. To die here in a stinking alley before he was done. He tried to twist away, but the second man yanked his arm again and he felt the blade scratch. He saw the hand holding the knife, the blackened fingernails and the tattoo on the thick fingers, spelling out 'HOLD FAST.' The man's other hand suddenly grasped his cravat, pulling his face to him. Hard eyes looked into his. He felt that he shrivelled in the glare of contempt.

'After the quim, cock robin. Thought yer'd dirty yer gent's 'ands — not wiv our Rosanna, yer don't.' The face touched his. Meaty breath again. But words failed him. His blood turned to water. The knife caressed his cheek.

'Could take yer filthy eye out — ow'd yer like that, cock robin?' The sailor smiled, revealing black teeth. 'Little muck swiper.'

A dog barked. A good, barkable dog. He glanced to the left. Someone was coming into the alley. Someone very large. He cried out. Just the one word. 'Sampson!'

The dog bounded forward. He came like a vision of the hound of hell, black and barking, red eyes blazing. The man with the knife fled, dropping the red kerchief. Mug, for it was he, leapt on the other man, bringing him down. The man screamed as Mug worried at his arm. Dickens heard the ripping of cloth. Mug's jaws glistened with saliva and he growled low in his throat.

'Leave,' shouted Sampson. Mug stopped, but remained with his huge paw pinning the whimpering man down. There was the sudden acrid stench of urine. Dickens looked down at his attacker — a pitiful, small weazen of a man, now sobbing in terror, all his cocky bluster gone, his filthy trousers wet.

Sampson came, huge and menacing in the gloom. He nudged Mug aside and hauled the man up by the scruff of his neck. He dangled there, a puppet with broken strings.

'Sling yer 'ook.'

The man picked himself up and went off in a shambling run, still whimpering. Mug followed, stopped dead at the archway, barking his throaty farewell.

'What the hell?' Sampson looked at Dickens, his rumpled coat and collar and the blood at his neck.

'A slight misunderstanding,' Dickens said, straightening his coat. His legs were trembling, and his voice sounded hoarse.

'Good God, Charley, it looked more like murder. What happened?'

'I found this.' He picked up the piece of red silk. 'I think it's Rosanna's. I came down here to have a look. Those — er — gentlemen thought I was looking — er — with a different purpose in mind. I imagine they are Mrs Chibb's lodgers. Protecting Rosanna, I suppose, but I didn't have chance to explain and I was somewhat hampered by a knife at my throat.'

'He's cut your neck. There's blood.'

Dickens was surprised it wasn't water. 'I felt it — a scratch I think.'

Sampson looked closer. 'It doesn't look deep. You'd best come back with me and get it cleaned up.'

'Thank God you came.'

'Just havin' a look about — hopin' — you know.'

'I do — you may have saved my life — and Mug. I thought it was the hound of hell come.'

Mug looked at him reproachfully. 'Sorry, Mug, I didn't mean to offend you.' He tousled the dog's great ears and heard a little rumble in his throat. Friends again, he hoped.

Dickens stood upright from the wall against which he had been pinned. His legs felt weak, but he mastered himself, picked up his fallen hat, and went with Sampson and their bodyguard back to Gun Street.

'What the devil?' exclaimed Henry as they came into the shop. 'I thought you'd gone home half an hour ago.'

'Charley was attacked when he went lookin' after Rosanna.'

'I found this at the entrance to Five Bells Place. The wind blew it to my feet.'

Henry looked at it sombrely. 'Rosanna's.'

'Yes. I went to have a look. Two sailors came down the passage, and like a fool I said I was looking for her.'

'Oh, I see, they thought … but what about you? There's blood —'

'An uncomfortable encounter with a knife, but it's just a scratch. I was lucky that Sampson and the heroic Mug arrived in time.'

He felt faint suddenly. Sampson brought a chair. 'Get some brandy, Henry.'

Henry turned to go, but there were footsteps on the stair. Mrs Penney appeared.

'Dear God, Charley — been in a fight? You'd best come upstairs, and I'll clean you up.'

The blood was washed away, the wound dabbed with iodine, the coat dusted off and the hat brushed so that Dickens looked more like himself. Mrs Penney gave him brandy, listened to the story and looked at the red kerchief.

'Someone's taken her.'

'I think so. That's why Henry and Mug must stay here.'

'I know, I know.' She looked defeated now. 'What else can we do, Charley? I've never felt so hopeless, not even when George died. I knew it was going to happen. I was prepared, but this — it's like the end of everythin'. I've always found answers, reasons, some kind o' strength, I suppose. Now I feel the life's sucked out of me.'

Dickens took her hand, felt its work hardness, big hands for a woman — no better sign of a brave heart than a hard hand, but her face seemed changed, the determined outlines somehow made vague by her grief. 'Kit escaped, Mrs Penney, we know that — he had time to leave Jam. He's somewhere, he must be.' He looked her in the eye. 'Bear up, Old Salt, fly the colours.'

She looked back into those blue eyes. So bright, though there were lines now. Somewhere, sometime, he had grown up and he was looking at her, giving her strength. She hadn't thought she needed it until he had said again that Henry Meteyard must stay. But she couldn't help smiling. 'Charley Dickens, you were always a sharp little devil — but you're right. And don't you go gettin' into any more fights.'

'I won't.'

They sat for a few moments longer, her hand still in his, and he watched her face reappear as if she had come back to herself.

Henry came up. 'I'll find a cab to take you home — all the way.'

'You will take the kerchief to Inspector Bold.'

'I will, and I'll send a message if there's any news tomorrow. Don't come unless... We'll take care of things here.'

'Thank you, Henry.'

They went down. Sampson was waiting. Henry went out. Dickens said, 'Sampson, would you find those men? They might be at Mrs Chibb's. I don't want Inspector Bold looking for the wrong man. Explain if you will, and tell them, no hard feelings — well, only hurt ones.'

The cab rolled away. Norfolk Street, he had told the driver. Bone-tired and shaken as he was, he had to see Sam. The rest was a dream, a horrible nightmare in which Death had touched him with an icy finger and had whispered his name. But Sam was real, solid, and he needed him.

26: CONFERENCE

A familiar double tap on the window woke Jones from his dozing by the fire. He went and opened the front door. Dickens was there. There was blood on his shirt collar. His face looked shrunken in the blue gas flame.

'Bloodied but unbowed — just about,' Dickens said, observing Jones's quick glance.

'Come into the parlour.'

Scrap was awake too.

Revived by brandy, Dickens told his tale. Scrap listened intently, never taking his eyes from Dickens's face — the red kerchief, the man with the knife, the tattooed fingers, the hound of hell, Sampson, the gigantic — an' 'e'd missed it all.

He gave Jones a look and turned to Dickens. 'If I'd bin there, Mr Dickens, I coulda — well — I coulda done something — chased 'em off. Remember that time in them alleys when that Itie threw the knife. It woz me pulled yer out.'

'I know, Scrap, and I shall never cease to be in your debt. And, of course, I would have been glad of your company.'

Don't encourage him, thought Jones. But he didn't comment.

'An' that girl, Rosanna, yer wants me to find 'er?'

'Well, I do have a proposal —' he saw Jones's face — 'for both of you, but only if Mr Jones agrees.'

Big bad wolf. Thank you, Mr Dickens, hero of the hour. 'I'm listening.'

Dickens grinned at the dryness in Jones's voice. 'I mean it, Scrap.' The words he'd spoken to Rosanna Chibb. No good had come of that exhortation. Try harder. 'The Superintendent knows best. Orders is orders.'

'Get yer. 'S'awright, Mr Jones. I knows yer knows best.'

'Mr Henry Meteyard, Scrap, is the son of Sampson, who came to my rescue with his dog. Henry Meteyard is looking after my friend Kit's shop. So I thought you could be useful to him — a sharp pair of eyes — and ears. You know the sort of thing — anyone hanging about the shop who seems wrong. Someone watching.'

'Erran's an' that. I might 'ear things. Wot d'yer think, Mr Jones?'

Jones thought. 'I don't need to tell you to be careful, to think about Mrs Jones and Eleanor and Tom. I know you will be sensible and not go looking for trouble. So, yes.'

'I'll not let yer down.'

'I'll come for you at the shop tomorrow morning after I've been to the office. I'll explain to Mollie that I need you for a few days.'

'Mollie won't mind, Mr Dickens, not if yer tell 'er I'm needed on a case.'

'You're not going to be doing any more searching alone down dark alleys, Charles, I hope.'

'No, Sam. I'll come back after I've seen Scrap settled in.'

'And that applies to you, Scrap. Daylight hours only. Settle back on your sofa, or I'll have to answer to Mrs Jones. I'll see Mr Dickens home.'

As they began to walk, Jones said, 'I mean it. This case is difficult enough without you haring off on your own. I know you think you have the keys of the street, but this man's dangerous, as are those Limehouse alleys. You're not indestructible. Inimitable — not immortal.'

'I know. I was a fool. I am sorry, Sam. You are not angry about Scrap, are you?'

210

Dickens looked so anxious, his face like a penitent boy's, and his eyes so guilty that Jones had to say, 'No. I can't stop him now. We have used him before, and it's not fair on him to say that we don't need him anymore. It's always a risk — for you, for him —'

'And for you.'

'I get paid for it. And, in all justice to you both, I have not turned you down before. Perhaps, I ought —' He wondered, not for the first time, if it were right to use either Scrap or Dickens. Then he smiled, thinking, *try to stop them*.

Dickens watched the doubts chase across Jones's face, and then he saw the smile. 'I know how responsible you feel, old 'un, but it means a lot to me — all this — us — together. I know what we risk. Living's a risk. Risk your head under every open window. Risk your heart. We are all hurt in action, but we must fight on.'

'But not necessarily with a couple of ruffians with a knife.' Jones smiled at him. 'Just so long as you keep remembering that there is real danger.'

They walked on. Jones told Dickens about Louis Valentine's father. 'And I asked myself about the suicide of a half-blind madman and about that same man's will, leaving his estate to Adam Valentine.'

'You think Adam Valentine might have helped him on his way and that he has stolen the estate.'

'I do, and I wonder if in those papers there is some confession by the dying man to Louis Valentine.'

'And someone wanted to stop Louis Valentine from reading those papers and claiming what was really his own. Someone who might want to keep what he expects to inherit — Adam Valentine's son?'

'I wonder if he has sent someone to do his work and if that someone was on the ship, so I'd like to go to see Mr L'Estrange at Mivart's tomorrow — early evening. I want to know if there was anyone else on that ship — someone I missed from Michael Simpson's list, someone who knows the Valentine family. Can you manage that?'

'I can. You think it's someone other than the sailor at The Ship Tavern?'

'Well, think about it — if we are right and Adam Valentine's son sent an agent to do his work, then surely he would choose a man he knew and trusted. Not a common sailor, surely?'

'No, that makes sense. But what if…'

'What?'

'Suppose you're right and there was someone on *The Endeavour* and that someone disguised himself as a sailor — think about that — around Limehouse, around *The Redemption*, who would notice a sailor, a sailor who went on board *The Redemption* in the night?'

'Just a crew member — late back. Easy. But who the devil else was on *The Endeavour*? I went through the list —' Jones stopped — 'Charles Dickens, I'm a blockhead — a blind fool —'

'Sam, for heaven's sake, what?'

'What if there was another ship from St Lucia?'

'Oh, Lor, Sam, we never thought of that. Our man came on another ship — risky though. It must have come before *The Endeavour* if Marcus Valentine was to be sure that he had his man in place — waiting for Peter Best.'

'Then first thing tomorrow morning I must go back to the West India Docks and see Michael Simpson. He'll know about ships and what routes they take from St. Lucia. For God's sake, I hope I find a name.'

They walked on up Cleveland Street to the corner of Carburton Street, from where Dickens had only a short way to walk to Devonshire Terrace.

'He is still here, isn't he? And he has taken Rosanna Chibb because he thought she would lead him to Kit, which means that Kit is not dead and that he might still have those papers.'

PART III: WRITTEN ON THE AIR

27: THE SINGLE GENTLEMAN

Harry Wills stared at his chief. A thin, serious, rather dull man, so thin that Dickens joked that he slept in a flute case.

The morning after the night before. Wills was concerned. Dickens looked so pale.

'Are you sure that you are quite well?'

Dickens reassured him that he was, but that he would be going out shortly — to see the Superintendent at Bow Street.

'About the piece?'

'The piece?' Dickens wished Wills would go. He meant well and his concern was touching, but he would hover. And he so wanted to look at the newspaper that was sitting on his desk.

'*A Night at the Station House* — you know you wanted us to put in a piece about the workings at night.'

'So I did, so I did. Certainly, I will mention it.'

Wills hovered anxiously for a few moments more, then mercifully departed, leaving Dickens to snatch up the paper in which were written the four words which had so startled him: *Hide and Seek Boy.*

The words were the first in an item in the personal column. There it was, amid the advertisements for ladies' maids, valets, grooms, cows, *The Memoirs of Marie Antoinette*, a novel by the Earl of Belfast, artificial teeth. He would not have paid any attention, not being in need of a lady's maid or artificial teeth, or a cow, for that matter, but he had noticed the words for two reasons. Firstly, they had been magnified by the lens of the disguise spectacles that were lying on top. Secondly, the phrase referred to the boy who talked to Little Nell in the graveyard in *The Old Curiosity Shop*.

He looked at the whole message: *Hide and Seek Boy. Information from single gentleman. Brass Court, Bevis Marks. Mr D. S. Sign of the Crescent.*

His heart seemed to knock at his ribs, and for a moment he could not breathe. The *Hide and Seek Boy* — Kit? *The single gentleman* — Nell's grandfather's brother. *Brass* — Sampson Brass, Quilp's lawyer who lived at Bevis Marks. *Mr D. S....* *Mr D. S....* By the Lord, Dick Swiveller, who was at Brass Court too. The writer meant him, surely, and therefore Charles Dickens. What the sign of the Crescent was he had no idea. But it must be that the notice was about Kit and was meant for him. Information to be found at Bevis Marks.

But from whom? From Kit — he knew the novel. The book that had started it all for him. That innocent book found at the scene of the crime. Kit's book and now the reference to the *Hide and Seek Boy* — that was what Kit called the boy who loved Nell. No one else would know that. From someone with whom Kit had taken refuge? Or from someone who had taken Kit. Mmm… Whoever had written it knew that he would come.

The single gentleman — that good man who had sought and found Nell and her grandfather. He gazed at the notice. Not threatening, he was certain. Dick Swiveller was a good sort too. It was witty, clever, and intimate. He would go.

He remembered Sam the night before, Sam seeing the blood on his collar, Sam doubting, and Sam saying: "Just as long as you remember." Risk. Go to Limehouse with Scrap. Come back, see Sam. Then answer the message. Go now to Sam, but Sam was at the West India Dock pursuing his enquiries. He would not be back for ages.

His heart was beating fast — he wanted to go now. Delay was drawn daggers, and this was what it was about. Taking a risk — you had to. He had to, or rust and die.

Get Scrap. Scrap could watch and wait outside the sign of the crescent. If he didn't come out — after, say half an hour — then Scrap could fly to Bow Street. Calculated risk, then. Sam would understand. He looked at the spectacles on the desk. Yes, take precautions. He swept them up, took a long dark coat and a low-crowned hat from the coat stand — just in case. You never knew who might be watching.

At the door of the stationer's shop in Crown Street, Scrap was waiting — very much the urchin again. Not too ragged for an errand boy at a marine chandler's shop — a worn jacket, a cap, patched trousers, but neat and fairly clean.

Scrap also had the keys of the street and sometimes he needed to use them, to unlock those streets — to be out and about, sniffing the air like a dog on the scent. And not just on errands — on business — crime business. Not that he wanted to go back to life on the streets, thieving a nose-wipe, filching a bit of bread, an apple from Covent Garden — well, more, if he were honest, listenin' to his pa an' that woman in their sweatin' sheets, feelin' the sting of a palm and worse. Let 'em rot. Some folk yer could do nothin' fer. 'Opeless, they woz. *I ain't niver goin' back ter that.*

But the rush of the streets claimed him sometimes, the noise, the crowds, the markets, the match girls, the sweeps with blackened faces, the crossing-boys, the running-patterers, the muffin-men, the pie-men with their portable stoves, the coffee-sellers — pies, buns, fish, eels, whelks, oysters, hot spuds — yer could buy wot yer wanted an' eat it right there on the street. No knives an' forks. The river an' the boats an' the mudlarks.

'E'd done that. Found a silver cup once. Pa 'ad sold it. Good as drunk it. But mostly it woz old bones, bits of iron, wood, bottles — not worth much.

As poetical a Mayhew as Dickens himself, Scrap knew it all: the netherskens, lodging houses, slop-sellers, pawnshops, twisting alleys, broad streets, spacious squares, narrow courts, and he could read their lives in their faces: gaunt faces; faces fat with riches; girls' faces, haunted; pocked faces; blue faces of the cholera; faces cocky with greed fulfilled; thieves' faces. A mother's face, a long time ago like a dream of another possible life that never came true. And a murderer's face once, close to his and haggard with loss — lost it, Scrap had thought then, lost the life he should have had. He knew what they all were, and he'd know a wrong 'un when he saw him.

Dickens smiled to see him waiting. He waved his hat. The boy waved back. Scrap, his other self — Scrap who knew him, he sometimes thought, better than he knew himself. Scrap to whom he had told that he had gone to work at a blacking factory when he was twelve. The great secret. Told it, Scrap had observed that he supposed it was the way of things, sometimes, and had gone on eating his pie. Scrap who answered the call of the streets when the desire for freedom surged in his veins — just as he did himself. That's why he was taking this risk — to be free.

'A change of plan,' he told the boy whose blue excited eyes mirrored his own.

'Secret, is it?' Scrap indicated the long coat. 'Yer got yer disguise. Where we goin' then?'

'I am not quite sure — to Bevis Marks to find a house under the sign of the crescent.'

Scrap's eyes opened wide. 'Cor — wot's it mean?'

'A crescent is like the new moon when it is just a half hoop in the sky. It's a symbol — of hope —' by God, so it was. Then there was nothing to fear. 'It's used by Turks and Arabs on flags and buildings — out there in the East.'

'Like the Arabian Nights wot Mrs Jones read to us — me and Nell?'

'Just so. Anyway, I think that whoever lives under the sign of the crescent knows something about my friend, Kit, who is missing.'

'An' them murders?'

'Might be.'

'Could 'e be dangerous, this crescent cove?'

'That's why I need you — to watch for me. If we find the place, and I don't come out, say, after half an hour, you should fetch Mr Jones or Sergeant Rogers. When we get nearer, follow me, but we're not together.'

'Got yer. Yer mightn't see me, but I'll be there. Don't yer fret none.'

'I won't, but be careful.'

''Ow many times we done this?'

My foot, my tutor. He could have laughed at Scrap's patient wisdom. 'I know, but I don't want Mr Jones to think I've put you in danger — or, Mrs Jones, for that matter.'

'Promise yer, I'm just an erran' boy about 'is business.'

'Got yer.' Dickens resisted the temptation to spit on his hand. 'Let's be off to the sign of the crescent.'

They found a cab which would take them all the way along Holborn, past the frowning jail at Newgate, into Cheapside, past the great bank, into Threadneedle Street where they got out. Dickens wanted to approach Bevis Marks on foot with Scrap keeping his distance. They parted at Bishopsgate just as the clock of St. Helen's Church struck the hour. Dickens looked back at Scrap and pointed to the clock. Scrap should listen for the chime on the half hour. He then walked on while Scrap paused to refasten a bootlace.

A right turn into Camomile Street led to Bevis Marks where Sampson Brass, and sister Sally in her brown gauze scarf like a vampire's wing, had their premises and where the mysterious single gentleman lodged, and where Quilp popped up at the window like a particularly grotesque jack-in-the box. Quilp — where had he come from? Dickens sometimes shuddered at his own imagination. Best not to dwell on Quilp just now.

He walked along, looking down alleys in search of Brass Court, occasionally darting a glance across the road or behind him. Scrap was nowhere to be seen. Wearing his invisible cloak.

There was a boy, however, seated on some steps, staring with fixed concentration at a very large stone. The philosopher's, perhaps. He looked like one who was puzzling over a great secret. Dickens hoped so, and that he would not throw it.

Dickens halted before this philosophical phenomenon and enquired for the sign of the crescent. The boy transferred his gaze to Dickens, who he seemed to think had dropped from the moon — crescent or not.

'Where's this come from?' he asked. 'Tha's wot I'd like ter know. Want 'ere afore.' He looked up for an answer to the gloomy air above. 'Never bin 'ere afore.'

'I'm afraid I don't know much about stones.'

'Thought I did. Throws 'em, gen'rally. At folk passin', an' sometimes I drops 'em on 'eads an 'ats — from up there.' He pointed to an open window. 'Should see 'em dance — rich folks, not poor. 'T'wouldn't be fair. Poor folks 'as enough trouble.' He sighed and gazed upon the mystery once more.

'Not as big as this. Kill 'em, I suppose.' He relished the thought. 'Dead. Dead as wotsits.'

'Door nails.'

'Tha's right. Door nails.' The philosopher thought. 'Yer could drop them if they wozn't fixed in doors.'

At least I only dropped cherry stones. 'I wonder —'

'Where's it from — so docs I.'

Dickens felt like one in a labyrinth — one of those mazes which took you round in circles. 'The sign of the crescent — do you know of anywhere that —'

'Down Golden Court — third 'ouse along — left.' He pointed to where Dickens could see a turning. Brass Court — of course.

Dickens gave him a sixpence at which he looked in a considering manner. He looked at the stone again. 'Done,' he said and vanished up the steps.

Well, I'm blowed. Bought a stone, have I? He laughed out loud. Not that he knew what to do with it. He could hardly put it back. The boy might be watching — from that open window. He walked on quickly just in case. As he reached the turning, he glanced across the road. A messenger boy was looking up at the houses. An errand to do. Dickens turned the corner into Golden Court, dropping the philosopher's stone as he did so.

28: A CABINET OF CURIOSITIES

The door knocker was a crescent moon — worked in brass. This was it then. Dickens knocked and waited. The door opened to reveal a Black boy in an embroidered red jacket. He wore a white turban embellished with a golden crescent badge. He said nothing, only looked with wary eyes at the stranger.

'Mr D. S. to see the single gentleman.'

The boy gave him a wide, beautiful smile. The door opened wider, and he entered a space like a little box. Another door was opened; he stepped into a museum of curiosities, a curious triangular shaped room with black wooden panelling. The door closed behind him. The boy had vanished. He was standing at the base of the triangle. Opposite was another door. He looked about him. Light came from a silver lamp, which descended from a ceiling of stars and more crescents. There were ledgers and boxes in shelves on one wall and on the other side more shelves with an extraordinary collection of objects: a snake with jewelled eyes winked at him; something which might have been — probably was, now he looked at it — a shrunken head withered to the size of a little leather ball; an alligator with its jaws open; a stuffed monkey with an old man's face — something Quilpish about that; an ivory tusk; ivory and silver boxes; a painted ostrich egg; silver cups, curiously chased with obscure symbols. And a little, soft kid-bound book of secrets.

He had a sensation of being watched. He looked up to see that a shadow had come into the room, though from where he could not tell. It was simply there. It seemed to inflate itself, moved into the silver light and became a man whose suit shone as if it were made of wax.

'Mr D. S.?' A soft voice like a hiss.

Dickens felt a tingling at his neck. 'The single gentleman?'

A strange, lifeless eye, the colour of mud, which stared at him as if reading all that was there. Unnerving. The other was a blank socket. 'Not I. Mr Kaprillian. We did not expect you so soon. But he is above in his cabinet, musing over his treasures. You will be interested, sir, I daresay, to see them, silver and gold gee-gaws, from foreign parts.'

'Well, yes, but I should like to meet your master, Mr —'

'Riddle, sir, Riddle, Mr Simic Kaprillian's confidential clerk. You know all about it, I daresay.'

'I —' Dickens stopped himself from saying 'daresay' — 'I know nothing of your master.'

'From Persia, though Armenian by birth — a rich history, and a strange one. A most knowledgeable man, you will find.'

'Might I go up to see him?'

'I daresay you might. Indeed, you might. I will go and see. Mr D. S., you say.'

'I do.'

The shadow vanished through the mysterious door. The monkey gazed at him, its ancient eyes glinting as if it were alive. He didn't know whether to be afraid. Always suspect everybody, Sampson Brass had said. But somehow, he didn't.

Riddle, the shadow, came back and ushered him through the door and pointed up the black staircase. 'He is waiting.'

He was. A man of about Dickens's own height — not tall but not a Quilp either. He was conventionally dressed in a dark frock coat and a shirt of startling whiteness. His face was ageless, smooth and satiny, and of a tawny, copper colour. Dark, penetrating eyes. An aquiline nose like a blade. Like the wind from the east on the night of Kit's disappearance, bringing its sand and dust, the Armenian brought not only the treasures of the east, but the sense of a remote past, mysterious and secret. The room suited him, as did the one downstairs. There was a black desk — ebony perhaps, on which a skull with pearls for eyes grinned at him.

Simic Kaprillian came forward with a smile. 'Mr D. S.— Mr Dickens — I should say — welcome. I knew you would come. We tread the steps appointed for us, and the man whose steps are appointed must tread them.'

'I did — your message appointed so. And I hope it tells of something more than a mystery — I am hoping that the hide and seek boy is found.'

'He is, Mr Dickens, I have him safe. You shall know all.'

'I have a boy waiting outside — I must tell him that all is well.'

'Will he like to see the treasures?'

'Most certainly.'

'Then my little Black boy shall bring him in and show him all.'

Mr Kaprillian went to the door. Dickens heard him call, running steps on the stairs, and a conversation in a strange tongue.

'All is arranged. You must sit now, Mr Dickens. You will take refreshment — I have coffee here, strong and sweet, and the airiest of cakes. When you are refreshed, you shall hear the tale.'

They sat by a black marble fireplace in which a fire glowed. The coffee came in tiny silver cups and the cakes on a lacquered tray. Dickens tasted the coffee — it was strong and thick. He ate two of the cakes — like eating sweet air which dissolved on the tongue and vanished, leaving an impression of having tasted nectar. He composed himself to hear. *Like the*

Arabian nights, he thought, *and I am the King Shariah to his Scheherazade*. He knew that he must be patient.

Mr Kaprillian pointed to the skull. 'He whose death is decreed to take place in one land will not die in any land but that.'

'Memento mori,' Dickens said.

'Not just for me. I like my customers — the ones who want jewels and silver and gold — to see that for all their riches, they will come to this.'

'And worms will eat them.'

Mr Kaprillian laughed. 'That, too, Mr Dickens, but the poet says that there is no writer that shall not perish, but what his hand has written shall endure. Therefore, he says, "Write nothing but what will please thee when thou seest it on the day of resurrection."'

'If I did that, I should never finish anything, and as you do, I have my customers to please as well as terrify.'

'Well, it is true that we must live in this world until we are numbered among the people of that other world.'

'And a dirty world, this is, at times, but I am glad to know that my friend, Kit, is still in it. I began to fear —'

'He said you would, and that it would be safe to send you a message. He knew that his mother would contact you and that you would search for your hide and seek boy. I am to be Scheherazade and tell his tale as he told it to me. He came here, of course. How necessary it was that he should flee and hide we understood when we knew of the captain's murder.'

'How did you know of it?'

'I went down to Blackwall to take a message from Kit to the captain about the papers and to warn him that he might be in danger. Alas, it was too late.'

'And did you hear of the murder of the agent of the captain's stepfather, who was taking a letter to the captain's sister?'

'We did, and so we knew that the packet delivered by that same man to Kit was somehow the reason for those deaths — the decree I spoke of earlier may be given in any land, and I think that the captain's death was decreed in a far land, and that it was to happen here.'

'You have the packet. There are letters?'

'We do, and it is here, safe and unopened, but, Mr Dickens, let me tell you the tale so that you will understand more. You must take some sweet wine of Cyprus for it will soothe you.'

Kaprillian took a silver jug and poured the wine into two crystal goblets. He put more wood on the fire — something aromatic so that the flames leapt up and a genie seemed to appear. Kaprillian looked at the flame, nodded and said, 'I will begin.

'In the early evening of the day on which the captain was to die, a man came with an oilskin package for the captain — to be given only into his hands by Kit. The package, he said, was from the captain's stepfather in St Lucia. That man, I think, must have been Mr Best. Yet, Kit thought, he seemed nervous, glancing about him as if he were afraid of a watcher or a follower. He went away and Kit, intending to take the packet to the ship in a little while, put it in his pocket.

'A little while later, the shop bell jangled again and another man, a common sailor with a dark face, black hair, and a gold ring in his ear, came in. This sailor asked if Kit had seen a friend of his from St Lucia, a Mr Best whom he wished to meet.

'Something about this man of the dark face seemed untrue to Kit, and that impression was made more vivid by the reaction of Jam, that most foolish and amiable beast, who growled low in his throat. The man looked at Jam with an expression of such venom that Jam whimpered. Yet the expression on his face was most cordial when he looked again at Kit. But Kit had seen, and he remembered Mr Best's fear, so he denied that he had seen Mr Best. His visitor went away.

'Kit was much disturbed; he could not settle to his work. His fingers seem to have lost their accustomed agility — so much so that he dropped a lens. He resolved to go to the ship immediately with the package. Bending to pick up the lens, he heard the faintest jangle of the bell and then a stealthy turning of the door handle. Someone was coming into the shop. Someone who made no sound. He crept away upon his knees, motioning the good dog to go with him and to make no noise. He went out to the back yard, through the yard door, leaving the house to tell, as the poet says, "its fate to those who come to seek but do not find."'

'The house told its story — the open doors, the unfinished work, the empty rooms told me that he had fled. And his mother read the tell-tale details of a dropped lens, the smell of hair grease and a counterpane in the wrong place.'

'A most observant lady.'

'She is, and she is waiting most anxiously for news of her son.'

'Which she shall have, for it is time now for me to take you to see your Kit and to decide what must be done.'

'I must tell you that the two murders are being investigated by Superintendent Jones of Bow Street, a man I trust and revere — he is my close friend and I must tell him everything. He ought to see that package. It must give us a clue as to the reason for these murders.'

'It will be greed, the desire to have at all costs what the murderer believes is his, by right. Every man ought to set bounds to his desires, Mr Dickens.' Kaprillian sipped his wine.

True, thought Dickens, *but I am not sure I can set bounds to my desires — or to anything. A satisfied man, this. I see it in those dark eyes. What might it feel like?*

Seeing that Dickens was not going to answer, Kaprillian continued, 'Mine are, I bless heaven, amply indulged; to have more than enough is needless, is a burden; "too much rain does not nourish, but causes the earth to rot and decay. There is a wind which filleth the sails of the mill, and there is a wind which destroyeth by overmuch power."'

'There has been destruction enough in this case — two dead and the brother of Mr Best left without hope. I have seen the brother who was waiting for Mr Best. Even if we find the reason, we must still find the man.'

'For which the resources of your policeman must be employed. Do you wish him to come with us to see Kit?'

'I do.' Dickens thought that he must send Scrap. He could not go further without telling Sam. 'I will send the boy who came with me. He will bring the Superintendent to — where?'

'My warehouse is in Bury Street, just round the corner. Tell your boy that it is the third building. There is a gas lamp under which they will see the sign of the crescent. Mr Riddle will wait outside for them. Let me get the package.'

He opened a safe hidden behind a picture, while Dickens thought about how to broach the matter of Riddle's trustworthiness or otherwise. He dredged in his mind for the poet of the Arabian Nights. 'Did not the poet say, "Keep not company with the one-eyed man for a single day?"'

'Ah, poor Riddle. You wonder why I employ the shabby man with his dirty eye. In many ways so much a thoroughgoing

Englishman — shrewd, suspicious, loyal, pig-headed, practical, bigoted, but that eye sees much. Mr Riddle in his lamplight measures my visitors. He watches them watching my treasures. Does that man's eye narrow into a hard, greedy stare? Or that other man? Do his eyes open in wonder? The first man we do business with, but we do not trust him; the second we may do business with, but we will trust him and never cheat. Mr Riddle saw your wonder.'

'I am glad I passed his test — for Kit's sake.'

'I knew you would, but Riddle is of a naturally suspicious nature. He is not a warm man, but he senses warmth in others. But you, Mr Dickens, would have given him warmth if you had created him. You would have given him a pretty little daughter — a good fairy. Alas, I could only give him a job, and he will wait in the cold for your Superintendent while we attend to Mr Kit.'

29: A NAME

Jeremie Corneille. Jones had discovered that *The Pursuit* had come in from St Lucia three days before *The Endeavour*. Of the names on the passenger list, that was the one he had picked out. Jeremie Corneille of the *St. Catherine* Sugar Plantation. Jeremie Corneille who had given his forwarding address: Mivart's Hotel. Surely, he knew Gaspard L'Estrange who knew Adam Valentine. He had wondered if the conversational Sir Napier Moss could tell him something. That was where he went first. To be sure, there were other names, but this one, he had thought, was important. He had asked for the other names to be copied and sent to him at Bow Street — just in case, though he dreaded the thought that he might have to follow them all up, including the no doubt dispersed crew.

Sir Napier Moss had been most forthcoming. The Corneilles were one of the families in debt to Adam Valentine — and they had resented it. Yes, they still lived in their fine old house, but they had watched, as had plenty of others, when the furniture, silver, paintings and heirlooms had been sold. They had watched as Adam Valentine had put in his own foreman. Old Raoul Corneille had seethed to see his son, Jeremie, employed under the foreman as a clerk. It had killed him, they said.

What a hot-bed of gossip, thought Jones. A small community feeding on its own. He felt the heat of the place. Enervating — unless you were Adam Valentine — and poisonous. He thought of heavy-leaved trees, secret dark places under their canopies, silent natives, even more silent snakes. He would have hated it. He never minded the cold, and loved frosty days when even London could sparkle. It was dirty, but it was familiar. It was home.

Heart, Sir Napier had said, ironic that it was heart trouble that was killing Adam Valentine. The young Corneille inherited the old house and nothing else. Everyone was waiting to see what would happen to him when Marcus inherited the plantation. Those two were friends of a kind — as unlike as chalk from cheese. Marcus, an unattractive fellow, not liked, not even by his father. Corneille, tall, handsome, confident, charming despite his poverty. Popular with the ladies.

Jones had gone back to Bow Street. It was time to go to Mivart's. He wouldn't wait for Charles. He had no idea when he would come back from Limehouse. Time to act. He would take Rogers with him.

At that moment, Rogers came in. Scrap was with him, looking as though he might burst with excitement.

'You're supposed to be in Limehouse.'

'I knows but Mr Dickens, 'e 'ad a message ter go ter a place — sign o' the crescent. Mr Jones, it woz astonishin' — yer ain't niver seen sich things — stuffed snakes wiv jewels fer eyes, an' 'ead — shrunken it woz. 'Orrible thing, but a monkey — dead, but lookin' all alive. An' secret spells an' magic an' a locked chest of treasure an' a lamp with a genie or some such. An' a man wiv one eye an' a Black boy in a turban wot showed me —'

'Scrap, slow down — what message? Who from?'

'Sorry, Mr Jones. A message about Mr Kit — the 'ide an' seek boy, 'e called 'im.'

'Who?'

'The man wot sent the message — 'e's got Mr Kit at a ware'ouse in Bury Street — sign o' the crescent. Mr Dickens 'as gone wiv 'im an' Mr Dickens said you should come.'

'Does he have a name?'

'Mr Kapril or somethin' like. Furrin, anyways. 'E's Kit's friend an' 'as bin lookin' after 'im. An' Mr Dickens said to tell yer that there's papers, secret papers wot will solve the murders. Secret.' Scrap's eyes shone at the magic word 'secret'. Jones doubted if Dickens had actually used the word, but Scrap appeared to be fired by this tale of magic and heaped treasure. Still, he got the gist, put on his coat, and followed Scrap, who was already at the door.

'Alf?'

Rogers was staring after Scrap with an expression of such astonishment that he did not answer. Trust Mr Dickens, he was thinking — you never knew what was comin' next — stuffed monkeys, shrunken heads, genies in lamps. Like the Arabian Nights, it was. *Wait till I tell Mollie.*

'Alf — are you coming?'

'Sir.'

Bury Street was but a step from Bevis Marks, a street with many warehouses connected to the India Trade, for the magnificent East India House was only down Lime Street. They were unremarkable buildings, dark and closed in the unremarkable street, yet they contained the riches of a continent. Dickens felt a thrill as of one about to be shown a mystery.

He walked with Mr Kaprillian, Riddle following them.

'Just one more thing, Mr Kaprillian, before we meet Kit; there is a girl of whom he was fond — Rosanna Chibb. He was teaching her. She went looking for him with the dog, Jam, and now she is missing. Jam came back without her. Am I to tell him? Or should I wait until he sees his mother?'

Mr Kaprillian stopped. 'Kit told me that he had taken the dog to her. He spoke of her as a girl with much spirit, much desire to learn. There was a quickness to her, he said, something uncommon. This is grave news, indeed. The murderer, perhaps, believes she can tell him where Kit is.'

'That is what I think, but must I tell Kit? He will think it his fault.'

'You must tell him,' Kaprillian smiled, 'for as our poet says, "truth only may walk through the world unharmed." Consider what harm may be done if you do not tell him.'

'A wise man, your poet. I will tell Kit.'

They were at the warehouse. Mr Kaprillian took out his key to open a door which was set in the larger double doors through which the wagons from the docks would go. Riddle waited outside.

Kaprillian lit a lamp. It was very ordinary. Packing cases and bales were stacked high and there was an aisle through which he led Dickens. The anonymous crates and cases and bales might have contained anything, but the East was present in the perfumes and spices that scented the air. At the end of the aisle they turned a corner and then another, through more, narrower passages. Here the cases were smaller. Dickens caught glimpses of packages with strange writing like messages from far-off lands. Occasionally, there was a flash of colour: blues, crimsons, golds and silver shone briefly from silks which peeped from their wrappings. The spicy scents were heavier here, and the shadows suggested caves and hollows, treasures hidden from human view. He thought of the warehouses of Abudah, the merchant of *The Tales of the Genii*; the fortunes of nine viziers; pearls, the size of eagles' eggs; rubies, blood red; and diamonds glittering in the darkness.

Kaprillian turned to see if he was keeping up. The lamplight threw shadows on his face — the face of a magician, an alchemist, a sage. He whispered as if he had read the mind of his follower, 'The talisman of Oromanes —' he grinned at Dickens, a good-humoured man again — 'you think of *The Tales of the Genii.*'

Dickens laughed, 'I can't help it — it's the scents in the air.'

'We are here now.' Kaprillian pushed open a door between two tiers of high shelves. Kit had been very well hidden.

And there he was, getting to his feet from an easy chair beside a warm stove in a little, comfortable room which Kaprillian had, no doubt, magicked from a storeroom.

'Charles — you answered the message. I told Mr Kaprillian you would. What news of Ma?'

'She is anxious, but stalwart as ever, searching the horizon for her missing lad. Henry Meteyard is at the shop — just to be sure. Mr Kaprillian told me all the events of that night.'

Kit's face fell. 'I thought only of Louis, that it must be important for him to receive the package. Mr Best was obviously frightened of something, and when the stranger came back — so stealthily — I thought there must be some danger. I took Jam to Rosanna Chibb's and came here, but when I learned of Louis' death, I wished I had given it up.'

'But Louis was already dead. I think the murderer must have followed the agent to your shop. He did not find the papers with Louis, so he followed Mr Best.'

'And killed him to no purpose — what a waste of two lives.'

'My friend, Superintendent Jones from Bow Street is investigating now — I have asked him to come here so that we can open the package to see what it's all about.'

'What does he think so far?'

Dickens told him what they knew about the estate in St. Lucia and that they wondered if Captain Valentine's stepfather had bequeathed the estate to the captain rather than his own son. 'We wondered if Adam Valentine had got the estate by some nefarious means. Do you know anything about Louis's father?'

'Louis told me that his father had committed suicide — that he had gone mad after a long, slow decline. His mother married Adam Valentine, but after her death, Louis and his sister came to England. But he didn't talk much about his childhood — I had the impression that the death of his mother whom he loved intensely shattered the fragile structure of the family. He said that he felt that the ties that linked him to Adam Valentine and his son, Marcus, were broken.'

'He never thought that Adam Valentine had acted dishonestly?'

'He did not say so — St. Lucia was just a dream place. Gone forever. He said he would never go back. That was why he chose Money and Wigram when he started out as a midshipman. India, he wanted. The past was the past — over and done with.'

It never was. Under the glittering surface it lay, dark and threatening, like some sea creature waiting to come up. You saw it when the still water was disturbed, a shadow underneath. Poor Louis Valentine. The shadow had risen from the depths. And a shadow loomed over his reunion with Kit — Rosanna Chibb.

Kit saw him frown. 'What is it? Something else?'

'Rosanna Chibb was looking for you with Jam. Jam came back without her. We don't know where she is.'

'She'd never abandon Jam. Could he — whoever he is — have taken her? He saw Jam at the shop. He'd think, perhaps, that she knew where I was — Oh, God, Charles, this is my fault. I should not have left Jam with her. I should have known—'

Dickens didn't dare tell him about the red kerchief. It was too much to bear. He only said, 'You could not have known, Kit — and no one could have stopped her. She was determined to find you. I told her to take care.'

'I need to go back — I ought to look for her —'

At that moment Jones came in with Scrap. Kit turned to him to ask if he had heard anything about Rosanna. Jones told him that he had heard nothing. Kit asserted that he must go home, help to find her. 'This is all my fault — I should have stayed to face the stranger. Just given him the damn papers.'

'He would have killed you anyway. He had already killed Louis,' Dickens offered.

'Better me than Rosanna Chibb or poor Mr Best — a coward, I am.'

Jones stepped in. 'Murder does this to us, Mr Penney. It leaves us all with a sense of having been wanting — in sense, or wisdom, or courage, or having failed in some act that might have prevented it all. But you must not lose sight of the murderer — it is what he does in secret that confounds us. We feel we should have thought, but we can't imagine what such a man might do when we have no knowledge of his character, his motive. The murderer belongs to the dark, and you live in the light. How could you, or any of us, know what a stranger might do? I am not offering an easy way out of your feelings, Mr Penney; I know what it is to feel that I could have done other than I had done, but it is, at the last, the murderer who bears the responsibility — not you.'

Oh Sam, Dickens thought in the silence which followed, *my wise old friend, how well you reason; and Kit must listen for he, it is true, lives in the light. He is too good a man to know the mind of the murderer. Would that I could say the same for myself. If anyone should have known, it is I. Even Sam cannot fathom the depths of my guilty mind. All the things undone which ought to have been done.* He could not think of a single thing to say.

Simic Kaprillian spoke. 'Listen to the wise Superintendent, Kit — all that he says is true. The poet tells us that the good in the world is the gift of Allah, but the evil is the choice of his creatures. That man chose his wicked path.'

Kit looked at Dickens, who found the words he wanted. 'It is true, Kit. You were doing what you felt was your duty to Louis, your old friend. Superintendent Jones is right — murder taints us all, and we cannot help that except to act. Henry and Sampson will look for her. They'll do everything they can, and Mr Jones is doing all he can to find the man who did this. The important thing for you now is for us to let your mother know that you are safe.'

'Am I to go to her? What is best, Superintendent?'

'I don't think you should go home, Mr Penney. If, and I say if, the murderer has taken Rosanna, then it means that he thinks that you have those papers. You must stay away from the shop.'

'You can stay at my house in Highgate, Kit. My wife is there — she will be pleased to have your company. It is far enough away.'

'A good idea, Mr Kaprillian. There must be no sign at the shop that you have been found — we will send word to your mother.'

Scrap piped up. 'I can go. I'm serposed to be goin' ter 'elp.'

'Then Sergeant Rogers will go with you — in plain clothes. Henry Meteyard has met him. What do you say, Mr Penney?'

237

'I don't suppose I have much choice. Thank you, Mr Kaprillian. I am most grateful.'

'Now, Mr Kaprillian, I take it that you have the packet of papers which began all this.'

'I do, Superintendent.' Kaprillian took the packet from his pocket and handed it to Jones.

Kit sat down again. Dickens saw that his face was haggard and miserable. He thought only of Rosanna Chibb. Dickens saw again that little piece of red cloth — so eloquent of Rosanna's character, her unique spark that set her apart. All her budding beauty blasted. She was dead, he felt sure. That torn-off scrap told him so. Violence had been done. And Dickens felt anger — these papers would tell of a man's attempt to atone. Redemption. Was that what Adam Valentine had wanted? To make up for a past sin. The sin of greed. But there could be no atonement, for the dying man's greed had tainted his own son who had sent his own agent to thwart his father's desire, and greed for his reward had, no doubt, urged that agent to kill.

Jones had undone the package. He scanned the contents — there was a letter to the captain in which Adam Valentine confessed to having forged Etienne Valentine's will. He did not confess to a murder. He handed the letter to Dickens and looked at the true will and the deeds which made Louis Valentine owner of the *Belle Regarde* plantation.

'It is as we thought, Charles. The papers prove the ownership of Captain Valentine.'

'He never wanted it,' said Kit. 'He had enough. He had everything, he told me, Grace whom he loved and the little boy, and his shares in *The Redemption* and the shipyard. What a waste. Poor Louis, poor Grace. Is it Marcus Valentine who has done this?'

'I think he has sent someone to intercept the papers, though whether he intended murder, I cannot say, but I am looking for the man he sent.'

'Have you any clue, Superintendent?' asked Kaprillian.

'I have some enquiries to make about a passenger who came on *The Endeavour* who might be able to give me information about a French man who worked for Adam Valentine. This man is also in London. He came on a ship called *The Pursuit*.'

'You will let me know through Mr Kaprillian if you find the man who did this and if you have news of Rosanna. Pray God you may find her.'

'Yes, I will. Charles will send to you. Now we must go, and you must go to Highgate.'

'I will take you to Highgate straightaway. Mr Riddle will find us a cab.'

Simic Kaprillian went out to arrange the cab and Rogers came in. Jones gave him instructions. He was to go to the stationery shop to change from his uniform. Then he and Scrap would take a boat to Limehouse, though they must keep apart on the boat. Scrap was to follow Rogers to the shop.

'You must not be seen together, but, Scrap, you must go into the shop just after Sergeant Rogers. Time to look about tomorrow — in daylight.'

Jones took them out, leaving Dickens with Kit. 'Superintendent Jones will find him, Kit. Depend on it.'

'I will, but Rosanna, he will have killed her, I know it. You know it.'

Dickens saw the desolation in Kit's eyes. He was reminded of Shakespeare Tabor then. Kit was changed irrevocably. Something of innocence had gone from him, as it had gone from Mr Tabor and Grace Fox. Mrs Pink, too. That's what murder did. It was the thief of innocence. It tainted all those involved, their goodness marked with a stain — a bloodstain which would fade, but leave a mark, however faint, on the silken fabric of their lives. Despite all he had said to Sam about hoping to the last, he knew the uselessness of false hope, hopefulness more painful than a sorrow faced.

'I think so, Kit. We must face that and our own failures —' Kit looked at him in surprise — 'I told Rosanna to be careful. It wasn't enough. But you must take care now, and I must take care of your mother — rather, Henry and Sampson will do that. And Mug, of course.'

Kit smiled at last. 'And poor Jam. He and Mug are quite friends.'

'Perhaps Mr Kaprillian will have him at Highgate.'

They embraced then and stood silent, waiting for Mr Kaprillian to return.

A cab was found to take Dickens and Jones to Brook Street. On the way, Jones told Dickens about *The Pursuit*, the ship that had arrived three days before *The Endeavour* and had brought from the plantation named *St. Catherine's* to London a man whose forwarding address was Mivart's Hotel, a man whose family was in debt to Adam Valentine, a man who was a friend of Adam Valentine's son, a man whose name was Jeremie Corneille.

'As Mr Kaprillian's poet would say, "it is written upon the pages of the air".'

'I had rather it were written in the register of Mivart's hotel.'

'Bring me a table of geomancy and a pen of brass —'

Jones laughed. 'You're as bad as Scrap — head full of magic and sorcery.'

'And as if by conjuration, here we are at Brook Street. All will be revealed — I hope.'

30: NIGHT LIFE

Mivart's Hotel in Brook Street occupied a row of grand houses, once the homes of earls and their countesses, viscounts and barons and their various ladies of high birth — or low, sometimes, though they rose to the rank of their husbands and glided about their marbled halls to the manner born. Now it was the haunt of royal highnesses, courtly diplomats, and wealthy merchants from across the world. The hotel was renowned for its French cuisine and its discretion. The Prince Regent had kept a suite there, valuing the same discretion and privacy — not that either virtue seemed particularly efficient since everyone knew of the Prince's amorous dalliances behind the stuccoed whiteness of number fifty-five. Dickens had lent his Mrs Skewton a temporary splendour by allowing her to borrow a house in Brook Street from a stately relative — in order to further her ambitions to marry her daughter Edith to gloomy Mr Dombey. An ill-starred alliance, that one.

And Mrs Skewton, like the Prince Regent, was all surface, powder and patch, false hair and teeth, and behind the painted front a slovenly bundle in a greasy flannel gown, though she had been a beauty, legend had it, in the Prince's day. Just so, hidden behind the stucco and brick of the glittering hotel, were the mews properties in hideous little streets containing stables, coach houses and dung hills. Mayfair tended to make Dickens think of dung hills.

Jones, who never thought of dung hills unless he trod in one in the pursuit of some miscreant, went up the steps and through the door to find someone in authority who would direct them to Monsieur L'Estrange. Dickens went after him. Mr Dombey's marital strife was of no relevance here, though he did catch sight of the spectacularly unhappily yoked Lord and Lady Smythe. It was his task to make the enquiry. Several glittering personages hailed him as he went by. A woman with feathers in her hair smiled at him with someone else's teeth — he bowed and hurried on. At the reception desk he offered his card. The gentleman in power was all politeness. If Mr Dickens and his companion would care to wait in the little salon, he would send a message to Monsieur L'Estrange, who was dining at that moment.

Gaspard L'Estrange appeared quite soon. 'I came quickly, Mr Dickens. I am astonished that you should wish to see me.'

'I am afraid, sir, that I have practised a little deception — it is my companion, Superintendent Jones of Bow Street, who wishes to speak to you. We thought it more tactful to give my name.'

Monsieur L'Estrange was not a whit disturbed. An elegant man in perfectly cut evening clothes, he smiled a charming smile, flicked his coat tails elegantly and sat on a gilded chair. *The pineapple of perfection*, thought Dickens, resisting the temptation to take out his comb and order his unruly hair — a habit he thought he had grown out of. He felt dusty after his day in the East.

'I am, of course, charmed to meet the great Mr Dickens, but —' he turned his shrewd brown eyes to Jones — 'I take it that your visit is to do with the death of Captain Valentine.'

'It is, and I wanted to ask you if you know of a man called Jeremie Corneille — I know something of his history with the Valentine family, and I know he has come to London. I wish to find him to ask him what he knows about the Valentine family — whether he knows anyone else who has come here in search of the captain, or whether he saw the captain before his death, or Peter Best, the agent, for that matter.' Jones was carefully vague — Mr L'Estrange might be a friend of Corneille's. He didn't want Corneille warned about police interest in him. And Jones was interested, given Corneille's indebtedness to Adam Valentine.

L'Estrange gave him a penetrating look. 'I see. I will say to you only that I know him, but I would not say that I am a friend of his.' Jones nodded. They understood each other. L'Estrange continued, 'However, I have seen him, though I do not think he saw me. He was here, I am certain; then he was gone. Of course, I asked about him. I was curious. He was well-dressed, and I did wonder if he had come into money. This is an expensive establishment. One is always curious about one's neighbours, but they told me that he had gone away on business.'

'You don't know where?'

'No, but I saw him once more — at Kellner's in Leicester Square. You know it?'

Dickens knew it — a café chansante where there were concerts: Spanish guitars, German horn players, Italian tenors. It was popular with the French and Germans because of the music and the pretty French barmaids. He nodded.

'I went there — a night off — from all this. Sometimes one wants a little gaiety —' he smiled. *Gaiety*, Jones thought, *that's what you call it. Gaiety*, thought Dickens, *I wish* — L'Estrange continued, 'I saw him with one of the French girls — not a barmaid. Something else, I should think. Very well dressed — most attractive. They left together. I asked about her of an obliging waiter. Her name is Marie Louise.'

'When did you see him?'

'It was the night after I saw him here.'

'Could you describe him to me?'

'Tall, clean-shaven, dark, glossy hair, a thin face, an air of one who believes the world will be his for the taking — even when he was chained to Adam Valentine's foreman at the Corneille Plantation, he retained that confidence.'

So, Jones thought, *nothing like the sailor seen by Henry Meteyard and Doctor Woodhall, but he might have employed someone to do his dirty work.* Perhaps he was living somewhere with his French girl. Still, it would be worth trying to find her. 'Would you take us to this Kellner's? You would know the French girl again?'

'Most certainly — a very striking young woman. Of course, I will take you. There is one more thing you should know. Corneille's mother was English, and she had family here. Corneille knows his way about. He came to school in England.'

'Where?' asked Dickens.

'Eton — he knows London.'

Well, well, Eton where Dickens's eldest son, Charley, was being educated — to be a gentleman and scholar. Doing well, too, though Dickens had his doubts about a future there. What he didn't want was a boy who thought the world owed him a living — the world his for the taking. Hard work and self-sufficiency made a man.

'You might say that he can be an English man in London and a French man in St Lucia — or Paris, perhaps.'

And a common sailor, maybe, when he chose — all murderers were actors. They had to be. How else does a man live on after such a deed? Think of Claudius, taking his brother's wife to bed, having murdered the man, politicking in Denmark's court, giving his reasonable fatherly advice to his cousin Hamlet whom he dared call his son. Such daring. He could believe it. Corneille acting his part — relishing it. He knew about that — nothing better than assuming a role, throwing off the chains, becoming somebody else. *I know him,* he thought, *just as I knew Bell in that case in Manchester.* Bell was a good actor — and a murderer.

He heard Jones asking where the English family lived and paid attention to L'Estrange's response. 'Richmond — but I don't remember the name, I'm afraid. I'll let you know if I do recall it.'

Their way took them down Regent Street into Coventry Street, which led directly to Leicester Square. Here there was glitter too, but cheaper, more feverish and louder than the aristocratic dignity of Grosvenor Square and Brook Street. Leicester Square was crowded with lovers of the night — the clerks, the medical students, the shop boys, the common street-walkers, and the part timers, who were seamstresses or milliners or servant girls by day, plying for hire by night; the fashionably dressed courtesans with their gentlemen; the lonely widows meeting a lover on the sly; the ladies of intrigue looking for customers to take home to their houses of assignation — all the hierarchy of women: the French, Germans, Italians, Poles. All drawn like moths to the bright lights. The music hall advertised music for the million; there were cafés, cheaper hotels, gambling dens. All the eyes were hot with desire for food, for drink, for winning, for love — for a night in which you could cast off the penury, the drudgery, the hopelessness, the blankness of the future. Tomorrow might never come, and if it did you might have money to burn again, even though the sharks outside the gambling den looked at you with cold eyes and wolves' teeth in mouths that closed like traps.

Gaspard L'Estrange led the way into Kellner's. The café was packed. Jones followed, threading his way through the tables. When he looked back, Dickens was just coming in. Jones looked at him in amusement. He might have been watching a perfect stranger. Dickens had put on the spectacles and was now wearing the long coat he had carried all the way from Bevis Marks. He had combed back his hair, adopted a stoop of the shoulders, walked with a slight hesitancy of step, and glanced about him with an expression of fearful timidity. He could have been a country parson, a banking clerk, a lawyer's clerk. Whoever he was, he was not Charles Dickens.

Herr Kellner, recognising L'Estrange, bustled up, offering cigars, brandy or coffee. L'Estrange gestured vaguely to his friends — there was no need for introductions. He looked with some surprise at Dickens, and then they were led to a table in a quieter corner.

'I hardly knew you, Mr Dickens,' L'Estrange grinned at him.

'All to the good, better that I'm not known.'

After the coffee and brandy came, they looked about. The café glittered with gilded mirrors in which they could see, as if looking at a dream wreathed in blue smoke, all the marble-topped tables, the shining silver and glassware; the waiters gliding from table to table with heaped trays; and all the men, young and old, with their girls, some very young, half afraid, their red lips opening and closing like so many innocent fish. Others older, more experienced, laughing and allowing kisses and caresses under cover of the crowds. Hard eyes, frightened eyes, languorous eyes in painted faces floated in the mirrors. Satins and silks in crimsons, blues and yellows swirled; and the lights shivered and splintered; and somewhere music sounded, blending with laughter — all part of the dream. At a nearby table, Dickens saw a tragic-eyed woman in red satin, her gaze averted from the hungry mouth of the old man with his hand on her knee. *There must be*, he thought, *more broken hearts in London than in any other place in the world.*

246

L'Estrange spoke. 'There — Marie-Louise — in black, by the bar.'

She stood out in her black close-fitting dress. She seemed to be waiting, looking for someone. Perhaps Corneille was coming. Was that him? A young man approached her, handsome, sure of himself. She bent towards him, touching his chest with her closed fan, whispering. It was a 'no' then. He walked away, and Marie-Louise turned to the bar. Perhaps he was not prosperous enough.

'Go now,' said Jones, 'before she's spoken for.'

In the mirror, they could see Marie-Louise look up with interest at the approach of the handsome French man who bowed. She smiled. He kissed her black-gloved hand. He leant to whisper.

'The master of seduction, eh, old 'un?'

'Remove your eyes, my boy.'

They were coming over now, followed by a waiter with a tray on which there were glasses — and champagne.

She smiled at them all. Dickens was aware of her perfume. Fleurs de Bulgarie — that was it. Same as Judith Black — what would she think of that? Mind, the Queen used it, so they said. What might Judith think of Marie-Louise? Marie-Louise had thick hair, rich brown in colour with wonderful golden lights in it. She wore it piled up in a great cloud to accentuate the length of her neck and her small head, and glossy ringlets fell upon her shoulders. Her eyes seemed to be of green-gold colour, narrowing like a cat's as she studied them. Her skin was thick and rather yellowish. She was not pretty, exactly, certainly not beautiful, but he couldn't help imagining for a moment that magnificent hair tumbling about her shoulders — the richness of it, the scent. She was certainly alluring — more so than the icy Judith Black, of whom he thought suddenly with a shiver.

Marie-Louise glanced at him — a knowing look, as if she read his thoughts. He almost blushed, but her eyes moved on and her lips curled a little. He looked a poor creature. Dickens felt her disdain — not a feeling with which he was familiar. Still, all in the cause of justice. He adjusted his spectacles and arranged his face in an expression of fastidious disapproval.

Dull little man. Wouldn't he like to... Marie-Louise looked at Jones. What she saw pleased her. Older, certainement, but kind eyes. She liked grey eyes. Not exactly handsome, but strong looking. Money? Perhaps. Would he like to...? She thought not. He seemed very English. She turned back to Gaspard, who was pouring champagne. Dickens saw Jones's lips twitch.

The champagne was drunk. Marie-Louise drank hers with healthy relish; the clerk — whoever he was — sniffed at his suspiciously. His nostrils dilated slightly as if the glass contained something unpleasant. He took a cautious sip, and Jones saw how his eyes were lowered modestly. Even his eyebrows, usually so eloquent, arched humorously or quizzically, seemed to take on a kind of frowning timidity. But, Jones knew, he would take it all in and he would describe Marie-Louise as exactly as if he had painted her in oils.

'Now Mademoiselle Marie, my friend here —' L'Estrange motioned to Jones — 'who is a very important man would like to know something about a countryman of mine — Monsieur Jeremie —'

She interrupted with a smile, 'Ah, Monsieur Crow, of course I know him — charmant, so gentil, I like him very much —'

Jones saw that L'Estrange was going to interrupt but he was quicker, hearing simultaneously that Dickens drew a quick breath. 'Where is he now, Miss Marie?'

She narrowed her eyes at Jones. 'Why do you wish to know this?'

'I am a policeman, Miss Marie, and I want to ask him some questions about a possible acquaintance of his from St. Lucia — who is missing.' He did not want to mention murder. Always better to keep it vague.

Gaspard refilled her glass and his own. She drank before she said, 'I do not know, monsieur. I dined with him a few nights ago, then he said he must go from London on business. He would come back, he said, in a few days and we would take supper again. I look forward to it.' Her pink tongue, cat-like, caressed her lips.

'Well, if he comes back, perhaps you would contact Monsieur L'Estrange at Mivart's Hotel —' Jones looked at L'Estrange, who nodded — 'I should not like to alarm Monsieur Crow with talk of the police and a missing man.'

'Certainement, monsieur, I will be delighted to tell Monsieur L'Estrange.' She smiled at Gaspard. No doubt she would be very pleased to see him again.

Gaspard L'Estrange escorted them to the door of the cafe, promising that he would return to Marie-Louise. 'I shall take her to supper — perhaps I might find out something more about Corneille. Odd that he used another name.'

'I think so, too, which is one more reason that I should like to find him. You will tell me, Mr L'Estrange, if he returns to Mivart's, or if Mademoiselle brings news to you.'

'I will. Goodnight, Superintendent. Mr Dickens — it was a pleasure to meet you.'

Dickens was looking back at dark-haired Marie-Louise. He asked one more question of L'Estrange. 'Do you know Mrs Black, the ship-owner?'

'Madame Judith — why, yes. The captain introduced me. A most charming woman —' he looked back at Marie-Louise, who was smiling up at a silver-haired gentleman — 'intriguing.

She came to dine with me here a few nights ago. I am meeting her again, I hope.'

'Did she speak of Louis Valentine?' asked Jones.

'No. We talked of other things. She is interesting to me. There is something about her. Fire and ice — a riddle to be solved, perhaps.'

I expect you'll solve it, thought Dickens, remembering the flush at her neck when she said the name "Louis". They bade L'Estrange farewell and went out into the night to make their way towards Regent Street.

'Well?' said Jones, regarding Dickens's face, which bore the expression of one who had discovered a great secret and was dying to tell. 'Well, tell me what you found out there.'

Dickens's eyes gleamed. 'Well, indeed — Jeremie Corneille, Jem Crow and Jack Dawe.'

'Jack Dawe? Where does he come in?'

'I have a poet's words for you.'

'Spare me another word from the wretched poet.'

'Ah, Samivel, not that poet. Quite another. When has the Inimitable let you down? Perpend to these words which shall be written upon the air.'

'Magic spell is it? Get on with it.'

'Listen, then, to the magic words:

"The Conclave determin'd to make him a saint,

And on newly-made saints and Popes, as you know,

It's the custom, at Rome, new names to bestow,

So they canoniz'd him by the name of Jem Crow."'

Jones frowned. 'Who? Wait, wait — I know this. A bell rings faintly — the children — a poem — yes. By Heaven, Charles, well spotted. The Jackdaw of Rheims. I remember it. Well, I'm blowed. Jack Dawe. Lord, Charles, what would I do without you?'

'I am too 'umble to say, Mr Jones.'

'So Corneille is Crow to Mademoiselle Marie and is Mrs Cly's Jack Dawe. Why should he choose those?'

'I am in a scarlet fever of modesty, but I confess, with not a little pride, that I can tell you that, too.'

'Why am I not surprised? Amaze me.'

'I shall. Corneille is the French word for crow.'

'Good God, I am amazed, but that means —'

'But me no buts — allow me my undiluted triumph. Corneille's our man, surely.'

'So it would seem.'

'He has motive — the loquacious Sir Napier Moss told you that the Corneilles were in debt to Adam Valentine and resented it. Adam Valentine is dying, wants to make good to Louis, own son gets wind of this, sends Corneille. Promises Corneille reward — his own estates back. Corneille —'

'You needn't go on. It makes sense, of course, but —' Dickens opened his mouth — 'don't interrupt. I shouldn't have — I hope to God that Marie-Louise doesn't tell him about the police asking —'

'She'll be more interested in L'Estrange now. In any case, I doubt if he'll come back to Kellner's. He'll still be after the papers.'

'That's a point. In the meantime, we need to go back to Mrs Cly — she's the one who knew Jack Dawe.'

'True, Sammy, true as turnips. Though, as you may recall, Mr Cly, Tempest Slinger's old friend Sly, was not present last time. I wonder if he might remember more about the man who wasn't there.'

'Salmon's Lane it is then, though I don't hold out much hope of the Clys telling us anything unless there's money in it. They're a greedy pair — and cunning. Greed, Charles, that desire to have what you think is your right, come what may. That's what drives Corneille.'

'Aye, that catalogue of human passions — greed, cruelty, the abuse of power which bring to mind our catalogue of murderers. Name one that hasn't been possessed by a passion so strong that its flood has not created havoc in its way.'

'That's why they're dangerous — why he's dangerous. Come on, Charles, let's get moving. No use loitering in this cold.'

'Still, Sam, it's my belief that there never were greed and cunning in the world yet, that did not do too much, and overreach themselves.'

'But in that overreaching, what's yet to come?'

Dickens had quoted the words of David Copperfield to Uriah Heep, but the last words he could not say aloud. They were there in his head. "It is as certain as death."

31: FEVER IN THE BLOOD

Jeremie Corneille, or Jack Dawe, sailor, to another new landlady, lay on his grimy cot under a threadbare blanket, shivering, watching the shadows slide into the room where they flickered in the light of the oil lamp and played on the cracked ceiling. Odd shapes emerged: a dog, a horse, a hunchback like a ragged figure in a magic lantern; a man in a top hat seemed to lean down at him, as if to touch him with some weapon. He closed his eyes to shut it out.

He felt ill, delirious almost. He sat up, reached for the brandy bottle and took another swig. He needed warmth. Perhaps the slatternly girl would bring him soup or something. Ada — that was her name. She'd looked frightened of him. He mustn't draw attention to himself. The landlady would remember a sick man. The girl might remember that he'd frightened her. He should have been more careful. He ought to move on, but he was too weary tonight.

He could have wept. It had all seemed so easy. He was sure Best had gone to *The Redemption* — but no papers there. That shopkeeper denied seeing Best — but he was there, he must have been. But the shopkeeper had vanished. Then Best on his way to the sister's house. It was easy to take him near that burial ground. He might not have killed him if he hadn't heard that voice — but Best hadn't had the papers — only that damned useless letter. And nothing in his bag, either. Corneille had thrown that in the river.

He had known then that the shopkeeper had them. And when he saw the girl with the man's dog, he'd followed her down the alley. She had turned, unsuspicious, and had asked if he wanted lodgings. He would have said yes, he would have waited, got friendly with her, but the damn dog had growled and barked. She was suspicious then and backed off. When he approached, she turned to run. The dog ran ahead, still barking, but he had grabbed her and dragged her by the kerchief, pulling it tight; but she fought back, and the kerchief tore. She nearly got away, and when he put his hand over her mouth she bit him so hard that his hand bled. It was damned painful now. He wouldn't have killed her if she hadn't struggled so fiercely. He pulled her head back with such force that he heard her neck snap. It was over in seconds.

He felt sick, thinking about it — stupid little bitch. He'd heard voices at the entrance to the alley. Terrified, he had scooped her up and taken her down another narrower alley to dump her. He'd gone through a broken-down door into the yard of an abandoned house where there was hole in the ground, underneath which there was a kind of cellar or vault. He had put her down there, but when he looked down and saw her exposed body, he knew that he would have to go down and cover her. It had not been easy, but he had squeezed himself through the hole and hidden her under a pile of old sails. There he had waited — for an interminable time, it had seemed, his hand throbbing, and the knowledge of that girl with his blood on her mouth. He had almost wanted to uncover her and wipe it off, but to see her again was insupportable. He hadn't thought about Best at all after he'd done it. The captain's body had not touched him — only with anger. But the girl, she would be his undoing.

He had almost felt like lying down there beside her, giving it all up, but the thought of the rope forced him to his feet. He had listened, straining his ears. Somewhere, a dog had barked. A different bark this time. Deep — the sound of something large and frightening. There were voices again. When it was quiet, he slipped out of his hiding place, covering up the hole with old lumber and planks. Then he piled on bits of old metal so that it looked like a heap of scrap. She wouldn't be found — not until he was long gone. He hoped. Then he made his way through a nest of verminous alleys until he came to the river, from where he found his way to this squalid room in a mean little tenement off Hill Place by the Commercial Road.

So, what now? He looked at his swollen hand where a bruise was appearing under the broken skin. A human bite — it might be infected. He'd got dirt in it, he knew, from that filthy cellar, and rust, and God know what else. He'd cleaned it, but it looked worse now. Iodine, that's what he needed. Perhaps, the slattern? He thought again about giving her money — but that was no guarantee. If anyone came looking, she'd spill it all and still have his money in her pocket. Could he bear to fuck her? She'd probably be willing. Promise her he'd come back. She was unkempt, greasy and smelt of fish, but not ill-looking. He'd noticed that and the voluptuousness under the dirty gown. But he'd catch something — sure to. He thought of Etienne Valentine and his madness. He'd seen him on the veranda, stick thin and raving, his nose eaten away. He and Marcus had fled, horrified.

Marcus. He couldn't go back to St Lucia — well, he could. The captain was dead — he could report that to Marcus, but suppose the papers came into the sister's hands. She'd inherit, he supposed. But suppose they were lost. Marcus would get it all, and he wouldn't need to give Jeremie Corneille anything and he wouldn't have the bargaining power. Convince Marcus the papers were out there somewhere and that the sister might turn up to stake her claim? But Marcus still wouldn't have to give him anything, and Marcus hadn't killed anyone. He had. That gave Marcus the power.

Damn, damn. He had to get those papers, or all was lost. The shopkeeper must still have them. He had watched the shop. That old woman must be the shopkeeper's mother. But to get at her? He'd seen the tall man — the one who had chased him after Best's death. He seemed to be on guard there. He'd seen the police constable come and go and another, smaller man, well-dressed. Somehow important. The old lady seemed glad to see him. Relative, maybe. Lawyer? Perhaps the smaller man knew where the shopkeeper was. The shopkeeper might have given him the papers and he'd gone to tell the old mother. Worth a try — wait, and if he came back then follow him.

And to do that he needed help. So, Ada it was then. The rope or the pox. He laughed then. The pox it would have to be. Move on, take her with you. Clean her up, buy her some clothes. Charm her. Use her. Promise her anything. By God, that would do. Spin her a tale and she could watch as well. She could go into shops nearby and listen. She didn't look too stupid.

He got up, took another mouthful of the brandy and went to the door. He felt better.

32: WITNESS FOR THE PERSECUTION

Silas Cly at second sight was no more appealing than he had been at first. His face was still the colour of tallow, and in his surprise at the suddenness of Jones's shouldering entry into his inner sanctum, his mouth opened and closed like a codfish. Words of protest formed, but it was too late to utter them. The tall man was in the parlour, the smaller one following. Cly recognised him and directed his indignation to the innocent party.

'Prosecution, that's wot it is.' He followed his uninvited guests into the parlour.

'It might well be,' said Jones drily, understanding Mr Cly to mean persecution, but refraining from correcting him. Prosecution of anybody was just what he would like at the moment.

Witness for the persecution. Dickens was reminded of Mrs Gamp. He looked round for the equally unlovely Mrs Cly, but that lady was absent, it seemed, unless she were laid out in the curiously long chest under the window of the narrow room in which the smell of fish was almost overpowering. Its narrow airlessness gave the impression of a coffin, albeit furnished. Not exactly luxurious — Mrs Cly's taste was for the utilitarian. Apart from the chest, there were a table on which lay a plate bearing the remains of a fish supper and a bottle of beer, three chairs, and a dresser on which stood a Dutch clock which had struck the hour as they entered the room.

'Wot bleedin' time d'yer call this?' Cly asked truculently.

'I think your clock struck ten,' observed Jones mildly.

'I can bleedin' count — meantersay, it's late ain't it?'

'Never too late for police business. Superintendent Jones of Bow Street. Your wife will have told you about my previous visit. You had a lodger — name of Jack Dawe. I want to know all about him.'

'Dint niver know nothin'. Dint niver seen much of 'un. Came an' went. Owed us rent.'

'You shall be paid if you tell me all you can remember. He was here at the same time as Mr Best, who was murdered.'

'Think 'e did it. Gawd, the bleeder.'

'Now you see why I need to know — and, Mr Cly, what you tell me will be confidential and what I have told you is the same. No loose talk — you don't want Mr Dawe back, but if you see him, I want to know.'

'What abaht me an' Lavender? She won't like it — nervous, she is. Meantersay, wot abaht us — dangerous, it might be if 'e comes back. Meantersay, we wants payin' — meantersay, yer pays fer information, don't yer?'

Jones kept his patience amid the meantersays. 'It depends, Mr Cly, on what you can tell me. First, when did Mr Best come?'

'More'n a week ago. Friday it woz. Said 'e'd come from St Lucia — on business. Dint say wot.'

'When did Jack Dawe come?'

'Dunno 'xactly — mebbe couple o' days arter Best came. Come when it woz dark.'

'Did he say which ship he had come on?'

'No, jest that 'e'd come from the dock — West India, I thought.'

'Did he say how he knew to come here?'

'Jest like any of 'em. Ask abaht, unless they knows about us from other sailors. Word gets round. Good lodgin's us is — not like some.'

'I'm sure they are. Now, did Jack Dawe have anything to do with Mr Best?'

'Couldn't say. Queer cove. We niver 'ardly saw 'un. Lavender —' Dickens fought the urge to laugh. *Lavender, forsooth. Dried long since.* Cly continued. 'Lavender, she thought 'e was 'idin' somethin'. I thought — I dunno —'

'Thought what, Mr Cly?'

'I dunno. Somethin' not right. I was a sailor — dunno — 'e want genuine — tha's it. No more a sailor than my wife. Somethin' o' the gent abaht 'im...' Cly's ragged eyebrows drew together like a thatch over his eyes, which disappeared under the jutting forehead. They waited as he thought. Like his wife's, his cogitations were almost audible. His eyes opened. 'I knows wot it woz — I remembers. It woz 'is 'ands — not sailor's 'ands. Them 'ands niver caulked a boat nor niver knotted a rope.'

'Was he left-handed?' asked Dickens.

'Dunno — niver noticed, but 'e want no sailor —' Cly turned to the Superintendent — 'Do it 'elp, sir?' Hoping for his payment, no doubt.

'It may well do, thank you, Mr Cly. And you have no idea where he went?'

'Nah, jest dint come back. An' I 'opes it stays that way. I pays my taxes — t'ain't right. Murderers in the 'ouse. And rent not paid — disgrace, tha's wot.'

Whether Mr Cly was demanding a reduction in his taxes for housing a murderer, Jones could not quite make out, but he gathered that the rent money might assuage the respectable citizen's ire. 'How much did he owe?'

Cly thought. Dickens could see him working out how much he might get away with — by how much the nerves of the fragrant Lavender might be soothed. 'Two guineas.'

Guineas, indeed. Jones put half a sovereign on the table. 'I can give you this, Mr Cly, in gratitude for your assistance. Consider yourself fortunate that the murderer is hardly likely to return to pay his debt. My compliments to Mrs Cly.'

With that they left Silas Cly contemplating his half sovereign. *Not bad*, he thought, exchanging it for a florin in his pocket. Lavender would never know.

'Farewell, thou art too dear for my possessing,' Dickens murmured as they went down the steps and away down Salmon's Lane.

'It was the first coin I touched — I was hoping it would be a florin, and that's more than the room was worth. Lying rogue — two guineas, my eye. And, what's more galling, is that we are not much further on.'

'Only that we can be sure — Cly realised that Dawe was not what he purported to be.'

'True — but look around you.'

They had crossed the Commercial Road at the point where Dickens had met Captain Pye and were making their way towards Gun Lane. Dickens looked about him at the crowds in the street, going in and coming out of the public house, coming away from the late-night market and the shops that were still open.

'See what I mean? We know his names, but he is disguised as a common sailor. Which of them do you think is he?'

Jones was right. There were plenty of sailors in gangs or with girls. He could have been any one of them. So many pigtails, so many earrings, peacoats, caps, oilskin hats, wide trousers, dark faces, lighter ones, ugly ones, scarred ones, bearded ones — too many, too many. Yet, an idea came to him — nothing momentous, just a thought.

'I understand, but there is one thing that might help, especially if we have Gaunt and some of Bold's other men, and Henry, Sampson and Scrap. Jack Dawe will be by himself. These are all in groups. They might notice one on his own lurking about the shop — he must be watching, hoping for some clue as to Kit's whereabouts. He must believe that Kit has the papers.'

'He must if we are right about his taking Rosanna. I'll go along to Wapping Station and leave a message for Bold with the night inspector. Are you going to the shop? I'll come back for you.'

'Yes, I will. I've had another thought. I met a Captain Pye when I was coming from Salmon's Lane the first time, and I asked him to keep his ears open for the name of Long Jodd. I could ask him to do the same for Jack Dawe —'

'Or Jem Crow — unless he's taken another name.'

'Pope, Cardinal, Saint, Rheims, even — that's French, too.'

'Don't — it makes me despair to think of it. I'll get on my way and see you at the shop in about half an hour.'

'Keep your eyes peeled for a lorn, lone sailor.'

Dickens saw that there was light in the shop and knocked. Henry let him in. Scrap, it seemed, was with Mrs Amelia and his new-found friend, Mug. He'd rather taken to Bean, whose younger brother he was to be. Not that anyone would be much interested — people came and went all the time — sisters, brothers, cousins, uncles, spinster aunts, lunatics, orphans, temporary lunatics, temporary orphans, temporary uncles or aunts. Most families had a floating population on the sea or off it. Bean and Scrap had taken Mug out earlier so that Scrap could get his bearings.

'Bright lad,' observed Henry, 'doesn't miss anything — even in the dark. Mrs Amelia's quite charmed.'

'Yes, you get fond of him. He's got that something, but don't let him stray too far. Sam Jones — and his wife — would not forgive me if anything happened to him. It was my idea, after all, that he should come. And after Rosanna... No news, I suppose.'

'No, your friend, Constable Gaunt, has been to keep us informed and we've all taken turns to look. Tempest Slinger and his nephew have been round and about too, and Mrs Penney.'

'She's all right?'

'Now, yes, apart from Rosanna. She's with Amelia. We've made her stay there. She was relieved when Sergeant Rogers came with Scrap and told us about Kit. What a tale. Scrap told us all about Mr Kaprillian who, by the way, is going to come here for her to take her to see Kit.'

'I bet he did. Mind, I felt as if I were in the Arabian Nights. I'm glad that she will be going to see him. Rogers told you all about the papers?'

'Yes — it sounded crazy, really. To come all that way for them. And then murder, but it's been done for less. A day in court tells you that. Rogers said that you and Mr Jones had gone to Mivart's in search of information.'

Dickens told him all that they had found out about Jeremie Corneille. 'Not that we know where to look. I just wonder if he might be noticed — a sailor on his own, though he could be someone else by now. It's all a bit hopeless. Do you know a Captain Pye, by the way?'

'No, but my father might, or Tempest Slinger. Why?'

'I met him a day or two ago and asked him to keep his ears open for mention of Long Jodd, the sailor we thought might have been the captain's killer. I thought he might do the same for Jack Dawe.'

'I'll mention it. Let me get you a drink. Brandy?'

'It would be most welcome. Sam shouldn't be long.'

Henry went upstairs to fetch the bottle and glasses. Dickens felt the silence of the room settle around him — when he thought consciously it seemed like a weight on his shoulders, but it was the weight of dread — dread of what had happened to Rosanna and the weight of hopelessness. They might never find her — or him, for that matter. Sam seemed downhearted, too. Failure, then, and Grace Fox, Mouse, Shakespeare Tabor and Mrs Tallis all bereft, left not knowing. They should take the papers to Mrs Tallis, he supposed. The Judge would have to deal with the inheritance.

Just as Henry came down the stairs, Jones came in to tell them that he had delivered his message. He accepted the brandy. Henry thought that Mrs Amelia could make them something to eat, but they wanted to get on their way — somehow they were not hungry.

In the cab, Dickens asked, 'What now?'

'We wait, though for what, I haven't a clue.'

'Doomsday?'

'It happens sometimes. You know that. Remember the Eliza Grimwood case. The Inspector found those gloves under her pillow and smelt the cleaner on them. He went to every glove cleaner in London. They found a man who'd been seen getting in a cab with her, but he wasn't convicted. The murderer was never found. He's out there somewhere.'

'Hidden from all human knowledge.'

'We may have to accept that. I'll take the papers to Judge Tallis and he will have to deal with the inheritance. He's the lawyer.'

'Something might turn up.'

'It might, indeed, Mr Micawber.'

'But, you are not in hourly expectation.'

'No, I'm afraid not.'

The cab rolled on. Jones got out in Norfolk Street. Home and hearth, he thought gratefully. Dickens went on to Devonshire Terrace. It was raining now, but there was a light in an upstairs window, just a faint one. Then it went out. He stood in the wet darkness. He should feel glad to be home, but there was that feeling he often had of belonging nowhere. Home is where the heart is — but where did his reside?

33: MR DICKENS TAKES THE TRAIN

Rain again, sheeting down, pouring off roofs, the pavements ankle deep in mud, the streets running with thick, gluey water, horses splashed up to their blinkers, a stray dog stopped dead, gazing at his muddy-booted legs, and fractious pedestrians shoving their way forward. Every man or woman for himself or herself. The leaden grey sky pressed down like a lid. Dickens was making his way to Wellington Street. He supposed it might never stop and they would all be drowned in a sea of mud, and crocodiles or alligators would wallow in the slime.

The street was blocked by the collision between a cab and a Black Maria — from Bow Street, no doubt. The cab driver cursed the police driver; pedestrians cursed them both; from inside the Black Maria, prisoners cursed their fate, the Lord Chancellor, and every judge in the land. Only the two horses stood patiently amid the general infection of ill-temper. One shook his heavy head and the other, catching Dickens's eye, sighed gustily. What fools these mortals be.

Dickens laughed, cheered up, and slid through the shouting mob, avoiding the jostling umbrellas, crossed the road, and went in. No news. No message from John Gaunt, or from Jones. Three days now. Scrap was still at Kit's shop. Mollie would want him back. Henry Meteyard would have to return to his chambers, too. Face it, he said to himself. Worse for Sam who would, by now, have reported their failure to Judge Tallis, and the newspapers would be recording the lack of progress by the police in investigating two murders and a missing child, one victim the brother-in-law of the distinguished Judge — and so on, and so on. He could have written it himself.

To work, then. Leave the newspaper. Make an effort, as Mr Dombey's sister would say — even to the dying Mrs Dombey. Well, he wasn't dying, except in the sense, he thought, that we all are. Unlike poor Mrs Bacon, about whose murder at Rochester he had just read. Killed by her servant-girl. Ordnance Road — he knew it and the house. Perhaps he had even seen Mrs Bacon, who had been seventy-eight at her death. He'd left Chatham and Rochester when he was a boy of ten — Mrs Bacon would have been fiftyish then. Mr Bacon, also deceased, had worked at Chatham dockyard. Perhaps John Dickens had known him.

He put away the thought of his father and looked at his letters — ramparts of them. Would he, he read, contribute two guineas to the Governess's Benevolent Institution? He supposed he would. Two guineas. He thought about the two sovereigns that had been found in Peter Best's hat and should be given to William Lambert. He thought of that unhappy hopeless man. He ought to go to see him, at least take the two sovereigns. When he went to collect Scrap, he would go there first. He realised that he seemed to be facing the failure. Tomorrow, then. Give it one more day.

There was a letter from Charley — from Eton. Eton, by God. Now that was an idea. He would read the letter later — now he had a train to catch.

He whirled out of the office, passing the astonished Wills, taking the stairs two at a time and racing until he reached the cab stop. His old friend the cab driver, Hob, was there with Bob, who was about to put his nose into his bag of oats.

'No time for wittles, Bob, my lad. Hob — Great Western railway terminus and quick as you can.'

At Bow Street, a sombre-faced Jones was listening to Constable Feak, who had given evidence in the case of a servant-girl who had strangled her bastard child with a handkerchief. She had sent the corpse in a box to her sister, who lived near Retford. In the box was a blood-stained apron marked with the servant's name. Defence counsel, according to Feak, had argued most eloquently that the prisoner had been mad with fear and desperation. She had been seduced, abandoned, and was terrified of losing her place. In a moment of madness, she had committed the dreadful deed. The jury had agreed and had found the girl not guilty by reason of insanity.

Feak looked troubled. 'What do you think, Sir — was it right? I mean, she killed that baby. Strangle 'er own kiddie, I don't know.'

'Neither do I, Feak, but we'll never be in that situation — we'll never know her desperation. She'll be locked up, that's sure, in a safe place. She might have been hanged. What does your mother say?'

Mrs Feak was a nurse and a nurse who knew much about the plight of young women — Jones called her the Sybil of Star Street for her wisdom.

'Same as you, Sir — not to judge what I couldn't know enough about. I suppose the girl was mad at the time, but yer can't say that about the man what killed Mr Best. 'E knew what 'e was doing.'

'He did, indeed — there is no excuse for him.'

'Do you think 'e took that kiddie?'

'I do — there has been no sighting of her for days now.'

Feak went off about his business. No, Jones thought, Corneille was not mad. He knew exactly what he was doing and what he wanted. He just wished he knew where Corneille was. He couldn't go back to Saint Lucia — well, not as Jeremie Corneille. Stemp had been down to the West India Dock. Corneille was not to be allowed to sail on any ship that was going to the West Indies. But he could go anywhere, in any disguise, under any name — that was the devil of it.

'Drown-dead?' Jones asked.

'Very nearly — I left in such a whirl that I forgot my umbrella,' Dickens replied, taking off his coat and shaking himself like a dog.

'You didn't get that wet just coming from Wellington Street.'

'No, indeed, Samivel, I have been to Windsor.'

'Her Majesty at home, was she?'

'Didn't enquire. No, my business was of a more scholarly nature.'

'Eton!'

'It came to me all at once. I had a letter from Charley. I remembered L'Estrange saying that Corneille had been there, so I bethought myself to take a train and ask about him. I thought the records might show the name and address of his English relations.'

'And they told you?'

'Of course — the Sparkler of Albion sparkled and said that he was in search of an old friend's cousin, but that he had — strikes head in dramatic flourish — lost the address. It was easy.'

'And?'

'The name is Robinson — Mrs Julia Robinson of Bank House, Richmond, and, my boy, I know it. I spent many a time in my long-lost youth rowing along the river before taking a quencher at The Star and Garter. The house is on the river — "silent, slow, serenely flowing" — as the poet —'

'Don't.'

'As you please, Sammy, my lad, no poetry then, but here's geography for you. The house lies between Richmond Bridge and Eel Pie Island.'

'You can find it?'

'I can and I will: "My boat is on the shore,

And my bark is on the sea…"'

'You weren't thinking of rowing us there, I hope.'

'Steamer, Sammy, takes us to Richmond Bridge — from there 'tis but a step.'

Dickens was back in his coat before Jones had time to stand up. He didn't move. He was glad to see Dickens so cheerful again, but it was very easy to be carried away by his impetuous eagerness. *Fools rush in*, he thought.

'Old 'un?'

'Just wait a minute.'

'What?'

'Remember Smith Street last year and who we found there. One of my men shot — that's what came of rushing in. Think about it — Corneille could be there at his aunt's, enjoying a glass of madeira and seed cake as blameless Jeremie, or he could be holding his aunt at knife point.'

'Lor, Sam; so he could.'

'Now, let me think. If he is there with his aunt, possibly other family, that might make it easy. The story is that I want some information about St Lucia. That should get us past a parlour maid or butler.'

'Then?'

'I shall arrest him — and for that I need Rogers and Stemp, though I think he's clever enough to co-operate. He'll not want a fuss in the house. And if he's up to no good, well, Stemp's very handy with his fists.'

'But have we enough evidence?'

Jones smiled. 'No — but we'll have him off the streets. Mrs Cly knows him as Jack Dawe, Marie-Louise as Jem Crow. Rosanna is missing. Let's say he has questions to answer.'

'Just a thought — about Pilgrim. We have almost forgotten about him, but you know, he disappeared on the night of the murder of Louis Valentine. He must have seen something. Rosanna Chibb knew him — I forgot to tell you with all the business of her disappearance and going to Mivart's. Perhaps Johnno could ask at Mrs Chibb's. I didn't mention him to Kit, either. He might know where Pilgrim might have gone or who he knows.'

'Good idea. I'll send Feak to see Inspector Bold, and Dacres can go to Highgate.'

'He's got over his bump on the head?'

'Oh, yes. He's a tough lad. Right, I'll go and sort it all out.'

Dickens waited and thought again about that night in Smith Street where an armed murderer had shot a policeman. That had been close, as had the consequences when his own life had been threatened. Good job Sam knew what he was about. Suppose Corneille were at the house. They might have walked into something very dangerous. Thank goodness he had decided not to go to Richmond on the way back from Windsor. He had been tempted, but he had thought of Sam.

Jones came back with Rogers and Stemp. Stemp was his usual imperturbable self — a taciturn man, always dependable, courageous, too. Sergeant Rogers, to whom Dickens owed a life, was another of the same mettle with a good deal of common sense. *It was Sam*, he thought. He inspired loyalty.

'Now, Charles, tell us about Bank House and its location.'

He had to dig deep into the past, remembering his younger self rowing along the river in its early summer morning placidness, pausing with the oars resting in the rowlocks, gazing round at the tranquil riverbank. It was 1836 — the time when *Pickwick Papers* was coming out. Oh, the joy of it. He remembered sitting there and feeling the sun warm on his back and all the promise of the future towards which he was travelling. The scene was as vivid in his memory as if it were yesterday. 'It is almost on the edge of the river — just the tow path dividing the garden from the water. There is a gate in the trees — I imagine it leads to the garden. You can't see much of the house in summer. There will be a clearer view now.'

'And there shouldn't be many people about on a cold afternoon,' Rogers said.

'True. You've not seen the front of the house?' Jones asked.

'I don't remember that, but it is fairly isolated. The gardens are extensive. I remember chimneys of the other houses, but a distance between Bank House and those.'

'We'll get an idea of the lie of the land when we get there. Now, we'll keep apart on the steamer. Let's not draw attention to ourselves. Mr Dickens and I will go down the tow path from Richmond Bridge. Give us a bit of time before you two follow.'

34: GIRL IN THE MIRROR

Ada Pitt stared at her reflection. Granted, the mirror was cracked from side to side and a bit greenish in hue, but what she could see was, she said aloud, 'Astonishin'.'

Clean fer a start — a bath at the washhouse. Jack had told her that he went there. An' 'e woz clean. She'd felt ashamed when 'e said she could stay. She'd got the iodine for his hand. A dog 'ad bit 'im. Nice 'e woz — different from wot she'd first thought. 'E'd seemed a bit frightenin', as if he woz angry at somethin'. The bite, she supposed. Gave 'er two bob for goin' an' said would she keep quiet about it. Shared the food she'd brought. Only bread an' cheese, but still she'd enjoyed it.

She looked in the mirror again. She had never seen herself wholly before. Her hair was clean — she'd never seen its proper colour. Chestnut, Jack had said, 'is favourite. Beautiful. An' the dress fitted proper. Second-hand, true, mebbe third, but clean. Only a patch or two on the skirt. Not but what she'd have liked the red one. But Jack said not to draw attention — his business was to be kept quiet for the time being. Secret, 'e said, an' then 'e'd looked at 'er. She saw something hard in his eyes, like 'e woz angry again. But then 'e'd kissed 'er. No bed, yet, 'e said. 'E thought too much of 'er for that. An' 'e did. 'E'd give 'er a present — the first she ever remembered. An 'andkerchief, all smellin' of flowers. That proved it.

No other bugger 'ad ever thought anythin', never mind too much, of 'er an' when Jack said ter leave Aunt Lilian's, she'd bin glad ter go. Lilian was a slave-driver. She told Jack all about it over the bread an' cheese. An' the brandy. That woz nice — gave yer a nice, warm feelin'. In the night they'd gone. Flitted an' no rent paid. She owes you, Jack 'ad said, serves her right. Mean old cat. Ada wouldn't miss her.

Left with Ada, Lilian told folk, a leavin' present from 'er sister — twin, too. That's why there wasn't a mirror in the house. Lilian always said that she never wanted to see Lou's face again and she'd meant it. The hated face was banished. The lodgers were sailors who were not particular about grooming. Thank Gawd Ada dint look like 'er, Lil 'ad said, though Gawd knows 'oo she do look like. Ada didn't know either. Once, she'd seen a bundle of greasy rags reflected in a shop window. She had realised it was herself, and that was the only time. Now she saw that she was not at all like Lilian — nor the long-lost Lou.

Lou 'ad just gone. Devil knows where, Lilian 'ad said — often. Ada must have been about eight then. She couldn't remember Lou. She'd imagined a better version of Lilian, but that woz jest dreamin'. 'Ow could she be any better, when she'd left 'er daughter like yer might leave a shawl or somethin' which yer couldn't be bothered ter come back fer? An' yer left 'er with a woman who jest treated 'er as a skivvy an' worse. Lilian had not minded offering Ada in case a lodger needed a bit of company. Plenty did. An' they 'adn't minded the dirt or the smell, Ada remembered. She felt ashamed now, but sometimes they'd given her money for herself, not just Lilian — what else could she do?

Jack was different. Jack minded. 'E told 'er she'd be beautiful if she got cleaned up, an' 'ere she woz an' the mirror told 'er that she wasn't half bad. Jack liked 'er. Said 'e'd look after 'er. An' 'e woz a gent. Told 'er that, too. Only disguised as a sailor. She didn't quite understand the business. Somethin' ter do with wot 'e woz owed by them wot 'ad cheated 'im. There woz papers to prove it. Jack thought a lawyer 'ad them, an' she woz ter watch a shop in Gun lane — tell Jack the comings and goings. 'Not too obvious, mind, Ada. Go into the other shops. Listen for the gossip.' There was a butcher's shop and a greengrocer's. She could shop there.

Jack stayed in the new room fer a day or two ter get 'is hand right, but 'e woz out now, gettin' wine and brandy ter keep 'em warm — in bed. That's wot 'e said.

It was just the one room with a rickety old bed, a fire with a bit of grating where she could cook and boil the kettle. Jack had bought clean sheets. 'Now you're clean, Ada, my darling, you shall sleep cleanly.' Jack wanted 'er. She knew that, but 'e only put 'er hand there. She knew what to do. She'd had plenty of experience. 'Not yet, Ada, not until we move somewhere better and you shall have that red dress.' He had kissed her goodnight. She'd never slept so well.

She went in close. The girl in the mirror smiled back at her. Not Lilian, not Lou. Someone new. She bent forward so that her forehead touched the cool glass. The girl in the mirror did the same. Their lips met.

She sprang back as the door opened. It was Jack.

'Admiring yourself, are you? So you should.' He kissed her, holding her head back. His lips kissed her throat and his hands parted the fabric of the bodice. She felt his mouth on her breasts and smelt the brandy on his breath. Then he stopped.

'No more now. I've a little job for my lovely Ada. I want you to get me some clothes — as decent as you can, though they'll have to be second-hand — for the time being. A black coat, shirt and trousers, dark as you can. And some boots. You'll have to take one of these for the size. This lot,' he said, stripping off his sailor's garb, 'you throw in the river. The clothes are for your brother if the old clothes man asks. And no more talk than is necessary. Oh, and get rid of this.' He took out his earring and gave it to her. 'In the river.'

Ada went. Jeremie Corneille lay down on the bed. When she came back, it would be time to move their lodgings.

But he needed money. He hadn't expected it all to take so long. He had thought he would be back at Mivart's, having cashed Marcus's banker's draft. He'd taken some cash on the first draft — enough for a few days. Not too much — Limehouse was full of thieves and pickpockets.

That was a thought. Ada might be persuaded. But she'd get caught — the simple creature. He should have told her to pick the pocket of that pig of a woman, Lilian. But he had just wanted to get her away. Anyway, it wouldn't do to tell her that there wasn't enough money.

But there was another way. And Ada could be very useful for that.

35: THE HOUSE BY THE RIVER

They took a steamer from Waterloo Bridge. Dickens and Jones stood on the upper deck while Stemp and Rogers remained below. Mercifully, it had stopped raining. Jones felt better for action; he could see that Dickens did too, and the journey down the Thames, even on a gloomy winter afternoon, was soothing because there was nothing you could do yet, but watch the changing landscape as you left the smoking city behind and passed under Chelsea Bridge and Battersea then Putney, Chiswick and Kew, gazing at all the various river craft, the wherries, a luff-barge, even a shallop with its awning sheltering the late afternoon rowers making for the other Star and Garter at Putney Bridge.

They found the house by walking from Richmond Bridge along the tow path towards Eel Pie Island. It was an old brick house surrounded by leafless trees and dark spreading evergreens. The garden reached down to the towpath so that the owners could come through the little gate right onto the riverbank. It would have been lovely in the summer. As it was, there was a dripping air of melancholy about the place.

Rogers and Stemp caught up with them. Rogers was to stay by the gate of Bank House and Stemp was to see if he could find a way to the front of the house. There was a very narrow footpath which they thought might lead to a road at the front. If he could not find a way, he was to come back and stay with Rogers. There was no one else about.

Dickens and Jones went through the gate and into the bare garden, sodden now with the afternoon rain. There was a little conservatory built onto the house at a later date with plain and coloured glass windowpanes. Ominously, there were several broken. The place had an abandoned look, as if its summer residents had flown to warmer climes. A crow cawed in a tree somewhere. It was as if some ancient ghost laughed at their coming. They saw its black shape fly out. It perched on the roof of the old conservatory, cawed again, rose into the air on its ragged wings, and vanished. Bank House. Bleak House, more like.

Instinctively, they remained in the shadow of a tree and stood silent until the sense of cawing echo faded. They looked at each other. Somehow, the soothing effect of the river journey had vanished. It started to rain again. They heard the drops falling on the evergreen leaves. Then they saw Stemp appear at the side of the conservatory. Jones stepped out briefly and Stemp, seeing him, went back round the front.

'I wonder if he is here,' whispered Dickens. 'It would make a good hideout. He wouldn't expect to be found. I can't help hoping not.'

Jones looked out cautiously. Something moved at an upstairs window — a shadow. Impossible to tell what it was in the descending twilight. The movement of a branch, perhaps.

'We'd better find out then.' Jones moved forward. There was no sign of life at the back of the house. Of course, he might be watching from that window, but no use skulking in the bushes. 'Round to the front.'

They took the path round to the front of the house. Here the paintwork was blistered and crumbling, and there was another broken window at the side of the front door. The front garden was overgrown and neglected. Stemp vanished into the bushes. There was a light at one of the upstairs windows. Someone was home. There was a bell, too, which Jones rang, sending a cracked-sounding peal which they imagined splintering silence, travelling through a darkened hall and up uncarpeted stairs to come to a sighing rest in whatever chamber the lonely inhabitant dwelt. Then there was silence. Perhaps whoever was in there was waiting for them to go away. Jones lifted his hand to ring again.

His hand froze in mid-air. Someone screamed — shattering the silence like glass. They heard feet coming downstairs — hurried and stumbling. Someone in fear? They heard bolts being drawn back, a key being turned, and then someone opened the warped door very slowly.

'For God's sake, be quiet, or she'll start again.'

The speaker was a woman, who came out into the porch. She dressed in black with an apron, the starched whiteness of which was stained with red. *Blood?* wondered Dickens. The terrible cry had suggested violence, but this apple-cheeked woman in her lace cap could surely not be the perpetrator.

'I am very sorry, Mrs?'

'Landless. What is it you want?' She looked anxiously at the two strangers.

'I am Superintendent Jones of Bow Street Police Station. I was hoping to see Mrs Robinson.'

'That's not possible, sir, it was Mrs Robinson who screamed. I daren't let you in just now. Would you wait while I go upstairs? The nurse is with her. I need to see that they are settled.'

She left the door ajar, and they moved quietly forward. They heard her footsteps, brisk and certain now, as she went up. A door opened, and they heard someone cry out in anguish, 'He is here, he is here.' There was sobbing — a dreadful sound of grief. The door closed.

A few minutes later they heard the footsteps coming down the stairs. They stepped back, and Mrs Landless opened the door fully.

'There's a little parlour off the hall. We can go in there, but please, be very quiet.'

Mrs Landless led them into the small room in which there were a round table and four chairs. The room, though dark and shabby, smelt of wax polish and oil. At her invitation they sat at the table.

'What is the matter with Mrs Robinson?' asked Jones.

'She is a sick woman, sir, mad — not raving — well, not all the time. Did you come by the tow path?'

'Yes, we came into the garden.'

'She will have seen you. Sometimes she goes into that room to look out. The twilight upsets her, and if she saw you she will have thought that he was coming and when the bell rang, she screamed to go down and let him in.'

'Who? Who did she think was coming?'

'Her son, Arthur. He drowned, you see, out there on the river. Her only child. It drove her mad. She has been in the asylum, but they said she could come out. And she is quiet usually — like a child — no trouble. But just now she was upset. I was trying to give her a cordial, but the bell rang, and it spilled down my apron.'

'I am very sorry, Mrs Landless.'

'Well you weren't to know. We never have visitors late on — hardly at all, really, except for the groceries and meat.'

'There are just you and the nurse?'

'Yes, there are two nurses, one in the day and one at night. The night nurse comes at seven o'clock. I am the housekeeper and supervise them, but they are both good nurses, kind and gentle with her. Mr Robinson pays well.'

'He is not here?'

'He lives in China, sir — a tea merchant. He went away after Arthur died. He comes home occasionally, but she doesn't know him. The solicitor, Mr Crabtree, looks after his affairs. Mr Robinson employed me to look after the house, and I engaged the nurses when Mrs Robinson came from the asylum. But, sir, what did you come for — it can't be to do with Mr Robinson?'

'No, Mrs Landless, I came to enquire after Mrs Robinson's nephew, Mr Jeremie Corneille. It is to do with events in St Lucia.'

'He hasn't been here. Only Mrs James — that's Mr Robinson's sister. She comes every month or so to see how we are getting on, but Mrs Robinson doesn't know who she is.'

'Did you ever meet Mr Corneille?'

'He came once, about four years ago. Mrs Robinson was in the asylum. He just said how sorry he was and went away. I believe he used to be here a lot when he and Arthur were boys, but I suppose it all came to an end when Arthur died. Poor Mr Corneille was with Arthur when he drowned, and another boy, Stephen Winter. He still lives in Richmond.'

'Do you have his address?'

'He lives at number five, Church Terrace. I know his housekeeper, Mrs Pinn.'

'Mrs Landless, I think Mr Corneille may come here and I need to speak to him urgently about events that are connected to St Lucia. I must leave one of my constables here. Is there anywhere he can bed down? Not in the house, of course.'

'There's the old boathouse. I could make a bed for him in there. It's not been used since — well, you know when. But there's nothing in it — just a few old bits of furniture. I can bring him food, but he mustn't come into the house.'

'He won't. Is the boathouse locked?'

'Yes, I can get the key. It's still on its hook.'

They went out to the porch to wait while she fetched the key. She looked worried when she came back. 'What am I to say if he comes?'

'He won't get past my constable.'

'But he will need some rest — what if Mr Corneille comes at night? You've seen what might happen.'

'You must not worry, Mrs Landless, I will arrange for Constable Stemp to be relieved during the day. He will be on watch all night. However, please keep the doors and windows locked.'

Mrs Landless's round face crumpled in fear. 'Locked? What has he done? All these precautions — you must think he has done something, that he is dangerous. You'd best tell me, sir. I need to know how careful I should be.'

Jones was reluctant to tell her too much, but it was only fair to tell her something. Not that it would diminish her anxiety. He looked at her kindly face. She had enough to contend with. Damn Corneille.

'I think he may be in need of money. He is involved in some fraud. He might come here in the hope that he could get something from his aunt or uncle. I want to speak to him before he decides to go back to St Lucia. If he's desperate, he might try to break in.'

'Very well, I'll be careful. Now, I'll go and get some bedding for your constable.'

Stemp emerged from the bushes, and Rogers came round from the back.

'No one came out, Sir. I heard the scream, but I only came into the garden — just in case.'

'I'll explain that later, but it was nothing to do with Corneille. However, he does know the house so Stemp, I'll want you to stay here. You know what to do if he comes. In the meantime, Rogers, you will stay here, too. Keep an eye on that tow path. I'm going to the police station to tell them what we've been up to and I'll arrange for a man to relieve you during the day, Stemp. You'll need some rest — better you on watch at night.'

Mrs Landless came out with blankets and an oil lamp and led them to the boathouse. Jones managed to turn the key in the rusty lock. There was nothing inside but an overturned rowing boat and the smell of damp. Stemp righted the boat. There was a pair of broken oars and the seat had broken in half.

'I can sleep in this,' said Stemp, taking the blankets.

They bade farewell to Mrs Landless, who went back to the house.

'Keep a sharp look out — there are only the three women in the house. The nurses change over at seven. Make sure no one else gets in.'

'I know, Sir. I'll stay awake.'

'I'll come back with the constable from V division.'

'Shall I go to see Stephen Winter while you are at the police station?' Dickens asked as they walked back towards Richmond Bridge.

'Yes, you do that. See what you can find out — whether Corneille's had any contact with him.'

'Interesting about the boy's death. Corneille was with him. I wonder what Stephen Winter has to say about it.'

'Something useful about anything, I hope.'

'Do you think Corneille will come to Richmond?'

'It's not unlikely. Stemp's reliable, and there'll be a constable from the station here to relieve him during the day.' He stood still, thinking about Mrs Landless and that poor mad creature upstairs. Only women in the house. 'I'll send Feak, too — I don't want to take any chances. I want that house guarded front and back.'

They crossed the bridge and came to Paradise Road. Church Terrace was a turning off to the right. Jones was to go up to Princes Street and the police station of V division.

'I'll go back to Bank House with the constable and to fetch Rogers. Meet me at the pier in an hour. I'll wait for you.'

'It might not take long, this Winter's tale, but I'll hang about if I'm there before you.'

36: BAND OF GOLD

Ada talked. Of course she did. It wasn't her fault. It was that Lizzie Snook askin' all them questions. Ada couldn't help it somehow.

The gold earring glinted in the lamplight. Ada looked at it on the third finger of her left hand. Just like a weddin' ring. Married — well, good as. She remembered his lips on her breasts. When they'd done it properly. When Jack got 'is money.

She hurried on. She had sense enough not to go to the shop where she'd bought the dress. Jack would be pleased when she told him. An' Lilian said she was stupid.

There was a shop off Albion Street. Far enough from the lodgings off Globe Alley. She needn't give a name, or she could say 'Mrs Dawe'. She smiled at the thought. She thought of the hardness in Jack's eyes. Best not. At the shop she looked at the clothes hanging on poles outside. Too ragged for Jack. Sailors' jackets, canvas trousers, a soldier's jacket, some old boots and shawls. A red dress, but stained. She'd have coveted it once. For the first time ever, she felt that something wasn't good enough for her.

She went in. The bell jangled, and while she waited she looked at the better coats and trousers.

'Can I 'elp yer?' Ada turned. 'Ada? Ada Pitt. Blimey, it is you. Gawd, yer look like a lady! Come inter money 'ave yer? Lilian copped it?'

'No, Lizzie, I've left 'er.' It was Lizzie Snook. They were old friends. Lizzie lodged with Mrs Betts, Lilian's friend — of sorts. She'd not seen Lizzie for ages. Didn't know she worked in this shop.

'Got somethin' ter sell?' Lizzie saw the sack that Ada carried. The sack that should have already gone in the river.

'I'm buyin'.'

Ada moved to the counter and put down her sack.

'Ada Pitt — married!' Lizzie looked at the ring.

'Not yet — it's just —'

'Over the broom, is it? 'Oo is 'e then? Tell us.'

'Nobody you know.'

'Does 'e 'ave a name, this nobody?' Lizzie mocked.

'Jack Daw — k — kins. I'm buyin' some clothes fer 'im. We're goin' away ter — ter get married. I want somethin' decent, Lizzie.'

'I'm not invited then. Fine way ter treat yer old friend.'

'I jest don't want Lilian ter know. I'll let yer know when I'm settled. Yer can come ter tea or somethin'.'

'Tea, is it? Fancy! Well yer've done well, Ada. Yer do scrub up well, I'll say that. Now, what can we find for yer fancy man?'

Ada chose the black clothes and the hat that Jack had asked for and a pair of newish leather boots.

'Give yer a good price for these,' Lizzie offered as she opened the sack to put in the new clothes.

'Oh, I dunno. Jack —'

'A fancy man like 'im don't want these back. I can sell 'em, and you get yours cheaper.'

What could she say? It would be daft to insist that Jack wanted them. Don't draw attention to us, Jack had said. Easier to agree and get away quick.

'All right. But, Lizzie, don't tell anyone yer've seen me. I don't want Lilian after me. I'll niver get away from 'er, an' Jack

— well she's not fit ter know 'im. It's my chance, Lizzie, the only chance I'll get.'

Lizzie looked at the pleading face and saw the tears pooling. *Poor cow*, she thought. She knew fine well what Lilian was.

'I won't tell, Ada, I promise. 'An' all luck ter yer. 'Ere —' she took a piece of old lace from a basket on the counter — 'weddin' present.'

Ada hurried away. It don't matter, she told herself. Lizzie won't tell. She promised. Nevertheless, she threw the ring into the river as she passed and she felt, with a shiver, that she had thrown away her chance.

Jack was waiting. He approved of the clothes, which fitted well enough, and the boots. 'You've done well, my girl.' He looked hard at her. 'And you threw the others away?'

'Yes, Jack, in the river — with the earring.' She crossed her fingers behind her back.

'Good. Now a drink for my good girl.'

The brandy eased her guilt. They ate scrambled eggs and drank some wine. Jack undressed her, kissed her and she kissed him back, but that was all. 'You've drunk too much, and so have I.'

Ada sat on the bed. She didn't care about being drunk. She just wanted to forget what she'd said to Lizzie Snook and to forget those clothes. Jack took off her dress. 'Now, just one more — to celebrate… We'll soon be away from here.'

Ada took another swig. 'Where we going, Jack?'

'Anywhere we like, Ada, my lovely — abroad, if you want. Paris, Antwerp…'

'Where's Ank…werks, Jack?' Ada asked, barely understanding what these words meant.

'Somewhere, Ada, somewhere. In the meantime, tomorrow we're going on a little trip, up the river.'

'Whatferwegoin'?'

'To look at a house — at Richmond.'

Jack went for the bottle of brandy. He poured a generous slug into Ada's tin mug. Her eyes were closed. She didn't see the drops of laudanum. He held the cup to her lips and looked into her sleepy eyes. 'Drink up, that's my girl.'

She lay back. He waited. He heard her mutter in her half-awake state. He thought she said 'Lily' — Lilian, the pig aunt. *Well, I am afraid, Ada, ma petite, that you shall have to go back to her when I've finished with you.*

She muttered again, 'No, Li… Ankwer… Anke…' He couldn't make out what she was saying. She grunted. The drug was working.

Now she was breathing deeply — snoring, her mouth open. She looked what she was — a simple, gullible, trusting servant girl. *Good*, he thought, for what he planned at Richmond. In the meantime, however, he had somewhere to go. Somewhere those papers might be.

37: DROWNING

Church Terrace was a row of prosperous looking, tall eighteenth-century houses. It was quiet in the evening lamplight, sequestered from the busier thoroughfares. Number five had a smartly painted black door with a knocker in the shape of a cherub. The railings were black and the stairs leading down to the area were clean, as were those leading up to the front door. There was a light in the hall and in the windows on either side of the door, but the house had an air of quiet, of undisturbed, reclusive lives lived timorously, perhaps, but comfortably. Whoever Mr Stephen Winter was, he was clearly well-off. Dickens imagined tea served at half-past four on a shining round table for one, a kettle singing by a cheerful fire, crumpets, sandwiches and little cakes, a thin white hand hovering over a flowered plate and shy eyes behind glinting spectacles. He felt hungry — he wouldn't mind an extra place at that round table.

He knocked, not too loudly. They would hear in the quiet dusk. Be startled. Who would come uninvited at this private hour?

A smart maid opened the door. She looked anxiously at the caller who gave his card and asked to see Mr Winter. She would ask. Moments later, a woman he assumed was Mrs Pinn — neat as — came with the card in her hand.

'Mr Charles Dickens?' She looked flustered. 'Mr Dickens, the...'

'Yes, is it possible for me to see Mr Winter?'

'Oh, you must come in — I will go and see Mr Winter. I am sure he will want to see you. He — we all — admire your work, Mr Dickens. I won't be a moment.'

He waited. He had an impression of quiet disturbed by his presence, as if he emanated waves of electricity, sending alarming messages through the air. He looked at the pale watercolours in their narrow gold frames. There were scenes of tranquil fields, haystacks, faint church spires and empty country lanes curving away into distant woods. Somehow they told of hopes unfulfilled, longings unassuaged, journeys uncompleted. He thought of a boy who had seen his schoolfellow drown. He wondered if the artist were Stephen Winter, but as he moved closer to see the signature, Mrs Pinn came back.

'Please, come this way. Mr Winter will be most happy to see you.'

He followed her into a room furnished as a library where the tea-table set for one was positioned by the fire. The shy eyes behind the spectacles looked at him in a bewildered way.

'Mr Dickens, you are welcome, but I cannot help wondering why you have come here. How you can know anything of me?'

'I am much obliged, Mr Winter, and beg your pardon for intruding, but I have just come from Bank House. The housekeeper, Mrs Landless, told me of you.'

Stephen Winter put his hand to his forehead. His cheeks appeared to shrink, and his shoulders sagged. He looked haggard suddenly, like an old man, though he could only have been in his early thirties. He looked like a man who had heard something deadly in the name "Bank House". He regarded Dickens so fearfully that he wished he had not come, but Winter recovered himself sufficiently to ask Mrs Pinn if she

289

would bring tea for Mr Dickens. He waited for her to depart before he spoke again.

'I have not been to that house for over twenty years. I hoped never to hear of it again. I take it Mrs Landless told you what happened there?'

'She did, but it is not really about that matter that I came, but it is to do with the man called Jeremie Corneille.'

Stephen Winter flinched. 'I had hoped not to hear that name again.'

'I am profoundly sorry to distress you, Mr Winter, but you may understand better if you will allow me to tell you why I need to know about him.'

'Then please sit down, Mr Dickens. Let us wait until Mrs Pinn brings your tea, and I will ask not to be disturbed.'

They sat by the fire, but the sight of Stephen Winter's stricken face dispelled Dickens's fancy of a wholesome tea. Again he wished he had not come to disturb the man's peace, but they had to know if there had been any communication between Corneille and his old school friend.

Mrs Pinn came in to pour the hot water from the kettle. She served their tea and left them. Winter offered sandwiches or cake, but Dickens had lost his appetite. So, it seemed, had Stephen Winter, though he drank as a man parched.

'It is a long and complicated story, Mr Winter, which involves —' he thought of the pictures he had seen, of lost hopes — 'certain matters to do with St Lucia — matters of inheritance. I am afraid that the police wish to find Mr Corneille, who is in London, and, having traced his family to Richmond, they wish to know if he has been in contact with any old friends.'

Stephen Winter's hand shook slightly as he replaced his cup and saucer on the table. Dickens poured him some more and drank his own.

'But, what is it all to do with you, Mr Dickens? I can hardly understand.'

'It began with the disappearance of a very close friend of mine who had received some papers for a Captain Valentine —'

'Captain Valentine who was murdered? I read it in the newspaper.'

'Yes.'

'And Corneille is involved in that?'

'I am afraid so. I cannot tell you more. I only wish to know if he has been here.'

'He would not come here, Mr Dickens. Were he to do so, I would bar the door against him.'

Dickens looked at the other man's anguished eyes. What had he seen as a boy all those years ago, which made him loathe the very name of Jeremie Corneille? Softly, softly. 'Is your feeling to do with the death of Arthur Robinson?'

Stephen Winter looked back into the other man's eyes — dark, dark blue like a distant sea, and mesmerising somehow. He felt something shift about his heart. 'It is. I have never spoken of it to anyone since I was asked by the police what had happened, but I will tell you. And how it changed the course of my life — how it blighted my hopes and my future. It will not be quite what you think, Mr Dickens, but of all men, you will understand. I have read your *David Copperfield*, and it is of a child's feelings I speak. I remember the day of Arthur's death as if it were yesterday. I saw it from the riverbank. Arthur and Jeremie Corneille had been rowing — I was left out. Jeremie Corneille had a way of excluding a third and, though at school Arthur and I were fast friends and Corneille was older, it was in the holidays that he held Arthur in thrall. Corneille, handsome, daring, seemed to hold the world under a spell.

'I saw that they were in the middle of the river. Corneille threw a cushion at Arthur, who caught it, though the boat rocked with his exertion. He threw it back, and Corneille half stood to retrieve it and throw it back. Arthur stood and the boat tipped over. I heard Arthur shout with laughter. I thought they would soon right themselves and come back, soaked and laughing, but only one came up. A man on the tow path went into the water and brought Corneille to the bank. He tended to Corneille and went in again. Meanwhile I ran for help. Mr Robinson and some servants came, but it was too late.'

'You blamed Corneille.'

'Not out loud, Mr Dickens — people thought it was just boys fooling. They thought it was an accident. That was bad enough — I could, I think, have recovered from that. I was only a boy. Time would have erased the shock and sorrow. But it was Mrs Robinson's grief that I shall never forget. She looked at me. She could not believe that I was alive and Arthur dead. I, as a boy, saw that someone wished me dead. I never told anyone. It was too big a thing. It would have meant acknowledging that I was somehow not worth wanting — and that others might have felt the same, even my own mother and father. They were not demonstrative people, old when I was born, always distant. I was not a longed-for child.'

'What secrecy there is in the young under terror,' observed Dickens.

'Exactly so. And I never grew out of that feeling. Mrs Robinson went mad. Mr Robinson went abroad. I felt it was I who had caused such suffering by being alive. I never felt worthy again.'

'And Jeremie Corneille?'

'Even then, I felt he was pretending — he lay upon the bank as though he were half-dead, but when I looked at him, his eyes opened, and in that look I saw triumph. He dared me to speak. He was taken to bed, treated as an invalid, and after the inquest, he went back to St Lucia.'

'What was his story at the inquest?'

'They were just playing — Arthur stood up and he, Jeremie, tried to steady him, but they both fell. Jeremie tried to save his cousin, but he couldn't find him in the dark water. Of course, the impression was that it was Arthur's fault, though no one actually said that. All the pity was for the boy who nearly drowned trying to save his cousin.'

'But that is not what you saw.'

'It is not.'

'Did you say so?'

'No, I only said that I heard the splash and a shout. I was afraid of Mrs Robinson, of all of them. I imagined they thought I should have done something, that I was a coward. I felt that my father thought so. I never measured up to his expectations.'

'Was it an accident?'

'I do not know for sure, Mr Dickens, but I knew that it was Corneille's fault. He threw the cushion first. He stood first —' Winter stopped. He was remembering something more. Dickens saw how he struggled to speak. 'There is another thing — I have never dared think of it, never dared say it, even to myself —'

Dickens waited, seeing the pain in the man's face.

'I thought — I thought I saw them struggle in the water. I thought I saw Corneille push Arthur away. Later, I could not be sure, so I was too afraid to speak. I thought he might come back to school. I was sick with that thought too — a coward, as my father thought.'

'You were a boy, only a boy. How could you swear? It was burden enough to see your best friend drown and to know that Mrs Robinson was mad. Too much, Mr Winter, for any boy to make sense of.'

'I see that now — I can see it for the first time as a man sees it.'

'And Corneille went away unscathed.'

'I doubt if he thought of Arthur again. So, tell me, Mr Dickens, do you believe that he is — has murdered Captain Valentine?'

Stephen Winter took off his spectacles, rubbed his eyes and looked at his famous visitor. Dickens saw trust there. He owed the man at least part of the truth. If Corneille was caught, it would be in the newspapers, and then what would Stephen Winter think of the man to whom he had confided his deepest secrets and that man had lied to him? 'I think so.'

'I hope you find him.'

'Thank you for your confidence, Mr Winter. I hope I have not distressed you too much.'

'I will be the better for telling. I never thought that I should be telling Charles Dickens. I am grateful to you, sir — perhaps you have felt better for the telling of some secret by way of your book. The last one, *David Copperfield*, is partly your own story?'

'It is.' He could say no more.

'Then I shall not forget our meeting, Mr Dickens. For a brief while, you have been the nearest to me than any other human being.'

Dickens went away, shaken to the core. A stranger had told him everything that was in his heart, but he had not the courage to do the same. David Copperfield's childhood was very nearly his own — the blacking factory was Murdstone and Grimby's bottle factory; the secret agony of David's soul was his, and Stephen Winter had divined that, for he had known the same secret agony. *Secrecy is Charles Dickens's habit*, he thought, too deep and abiding, and there was nothing to be done about that, and the scar on his heart seemed to pull as if it were opening.

He walked swiftly back to the bridge, thinking, too, of the contrasting lives of two men whose childhood sufferings had produced such different reactions. Stephen Winter's had been flight, and his own had been fight. The battle of life. And what of Jeremie Corneille? Had the death of Arthur Robinson hardened him into a murderer?

38: MOONLIGHT ON THE MARSHES

Stemp and Feak were ensconced at Bank House — gardener and gardener's lad. Jones had thought to send Feak in plain clothes with a basket of clothes for Stemp. He wanted his own men there. Then the grocer or butcher, or whoever might call would not gossip about policemen at Bank House. Inspector Drake of V Division at Richmond had assured him that his beat constables would be looking out for a sailor, or any stranger in the vicinity of Bank House or the tow path. Jones thought that Corneille would be unlikely to go to Bank House dressed as a sailor. And they would keep an eye on number five Church Terrace. Dickens had told him about Stephen Winter and the death of Arthur Robinson. Corneille would have no reason to go there. He would hardly expect a welcome there, but you never knew.

Jones did not know what more he could do. Part of him hoped that Corneille would go to Richmond and then it might be over. Part of him hoped he might still be in Limehouse. He worried about those women at Bank House. He had issued Stemp with a flintlock pistol. He could be relied on to use it only if he had to. Jones dreaded to think what effect the sound of a gunshot would have on poor Mrs Robinson or Mrs Landless and the nurse, for that matter. But Corneille was dangerous. Better to kill him than have defenceless women attacked or murdered.

There had been no news from Limehouse. Rosanna Chibb had not been found, which meant that she was probably dead. There was no point in his going there. John Gaunt would be in touch if there were anything to know.

It was time to go. He was due in court — a case of forgery. One Ernest Merlin, a gentleman, it seemed — of sorts — accused of forging two bills of exchange with intent to defraud. Some five hundred pounds involved — a lot of money. Greed, of course. Ernest Merlin thought he would get away with it because he was a gentleman. *Merlin*, he thought, no magic for him. A cold damp cell, Jones hoped.

Dickens was on his way to Limehouse. It really was time Scrap went back to Mollie. He didn't think that Rosanna Chibb would be found anytime soon. Then he would take the two guineas to William Lambert. He ought to have that money — perhaps it would be a comfort to know that his brother had thought of him — enough to send a present, even though he was desperate to leave London. He would take him a signed copy of *Barnaby Rudge* too, and some brandy. He thought of that cheerless cottage. There was nothing else he could do for William Lambert except spend an hour over a glass of brandy.

The shop was closed. Of course, Mrs Penney was at Highgate, at Kaprillian's house with Kit — she would have been fetched from Sampson's. Perhaps Scrap was there with Sampson and Mug. He could take him to the Isle of Dogs — he would enjoy that. And Scrap with his cheerful smile and eyes eager for life might well reach to the sadness in William Lambert — Scrap was hope personified, evidence that things could change.

But Scrap was out. Sampson told him, 'We all keep lookin' for Rosanna. Your lad won't give up. Says he can't let you and Mr Jones down. But I've told him to come back before dark. He has Mug with him, o' course.'

'That's very like him.' No chance of taking Scrap back to Mollie. 'Tell him I'll look in on my way back. I'm away on a visit to the Isle of Dogs.'

'Not a place Mug's fond of. Nor me, come to that — gives me the creeps, all them empty marshes. You watch your step, Charley, and get back before it gets too dark. You don't want to get lost out there.'

Dickens went out of the butcher's shop. The sky did look threatening. It would rain, perhaps. Ought he to bother? Still, he'd come all this way. He thought about William Lambert — he really should go. He wouldn't spend an hour. It was about a mile's walk — say twenty minutes at a fast pace. He could be back in just over an hour.

He walked away from Gun Lane, down Emmett Street, across the entrance basin to the West India Dock which route took him into Mill Wall Road, across another bridge and into Ord Street, past the iron works and the windmill. It was busy just here with the noises of the iron foundry and oil manufactory. There was the reassuring sound of human voices, but it was quieter further on towards Chalkstone Stairs. He hurried on to the turning into Dolphin Lane and made his way across the marshes.

The clouds had been driven on by the wind; the sky was ashen grey and away to the east he saw the faint shadow of the moon beginning its rise. All human sound had ceased. There was something unearthly about the place — no wonder Mug and Sampson didn't care for it. The bare sky above and the wilderness below might have been another planet — the moon, he thought, might look like this, if it looked like anything at all. The great dismal swamp someone had called the isle. A man might take a wrong step, be sucked down, trapped until the mud and waters closed over his head.

He trod very carefully, keeping to the path that he and Jones had taken, and eventually he came to the old farmhouse. There was no sign of the taciturn farmer. No dog barked. He could see William Lambert's little house, but there was no twist of smoke coming from the chimney. Odd that.

Feeling exposed suddenly, he moved into the shadow of one of the bent trees where he stood watching the cottage. There was no sign of life. He walked a little further, choosing always to hide as best he could in the lee of the stunted trees. He waited again, aware of his heart bumping too fast and the loneliness of the place. The wind was very cold; it made that eerie mourning sound he had heard before. Something had happened at that lonely cottage.

He remembered then the wandering light he had seen that night. Surely Corneille could not have known anything about William Lambert. He knew Francis Lambert as Peter Best from St Lucia. But Peter Best had not been here, as far as they knew. Wouldn't William have said? But then he had been so bowled over with grief. And they hadn't asked.

Corneille had been at Mrs Cly's. Corneille had been at Kit's shop. Corneille had followed the man he knew as Peter Best to Portugal Street. Followed him. Now Dickens felt as if an icy finger were tapping along his spine. But his senses were sharp. The moan of the wind. The smell of the sea. The suck of mud beneath his feet. The pricking of the bark where his hand gripped the tree. He remained absolutely still, scarcely even breathing. Even his heart seemed to have stopped. He strained his eyes, but nothing moved at the little house. The silence was almost palpable, as though the world had frozen.

And into that silence came, as if the sound filled the whole island, the unmistakeable click of a gun being cocked — behind him.

Turning cautiously, he saw the old farmer with his gun and his dog. He didn't know whether to be more frightened of the silent little house or the farmer whose black eyes regarded him with naked hostility. The dog wasn't too friendly, either. The old man gestured towards the farmhouse and walked behind Dickens towards it. Dickens glanced at the cottage, but there was still no sign of life.

The farmer pushed him through his own door. He felt the sharp prod of the rifle barrel in his back. He supposed he could have whirled round and fetched the old man a blow with his stick. However, the gun might go off and, worse, the shot might bring someone from William Lambert's house. Someone who might be just as dangerous as a man with a gun. The farmer spoke for the first time.

'Turn round.' Dickens turned. The gun was still trained on him — it looked like a blunderbuss — there'd be a damn great hole in him if he wasn't careful.

'Yer done that?' The farmer gestured in the direction of the cottage.

'Done what?'

''Un's dead.'

'How?'

''Anged — saw a cove in the night goin' there. Come mornin', door's open. No smoke. Went an' looked. Found 'un.'

'I wasn't there in the night. I came to bring him something.'

The farmer peered at him. 'Saw yer afore with the other man.'

'He's a policeman. We came to tell Mr Lambert that his brother was dead.'

'Yer a policeman?'

'I work with them, yes. There's no one there now?'

'Only dead 'un.'

'You'd better show me.'

The farmer lowered his gun. Dickens exhaled — he felt he had held his breath for an age. They went out and down the lane to the cottage, the farmer still holding his gun at the ready. The dog came with them.

As they went into the little room, Dickens looked up. He saw first the head cricked to one side like that of a man measuring the room. But the red eyes bulged, the face was purple, and the swollen tongue stuck out of the livid mouth. A stool had been kicked over — the same one he had sat on when William Lambert poured out his grief. His eye took in the knot. Expertly tied. A sailor's knot. Perhaps his brother had taught him. Suicide? Dickens turned away. He did not want to look again at that bloated face and those bulging eyes.

He looked at the clock with its vacant face, its hands lifeless. Dumb witness to this death. But someone else had been here. The chairs had been overturned. The few books had been scattered on the floor. Dickens picked them up: *Barnaby Rudge* and *The Old Curiosity Shop* — Kit's book. The book that Corneille had thrown down in Louis Valentine's cabin. He wondered if Corneille knew that. It was Corneille. He had been here in search of those papers.

Upstairs, the sackcloth palliasse had been cut open, straw everywhere, and the covers torn off the bed, pillows ripped, and the drawers of a chest turned out.

Dickens went down again. 'You saw the man who came here?'

'Dog barked. Moon woz out. Saw 'im. Tall — taller than you, now I think on it. Clothes looked black — long coat, low-crowned 'at like yours.'

'Could he have been a sailor?'

'Couldn't say — like a black shadder 'e was. Didn't walk like a sailor, though.'

Corneille had run from Henry Meteyard, had sat when the boy, Pips, had brought him the brandy, then he'd hurried away. Cly had glimpsed him on the stairs. No one had commented on his walk, but you saw what you wanted to see. You saw the clothes of a sailor, the earring, the pig tail, so the stranger was a sailor. But without those trappings, the old farmer had seen a man. Not that it mattered — they had thought he would alter his appearance, but, still, they would not be seeking a sailor in the crowds of sailors swarming round Limehouse, and the description might be useful to Stemp and the police at Richmond.

'I need to get the police.'

'I'll stay — doubt 'e'll come back. I'll light you a lantern.'

'And I'll give you this to keep you company.' He gave the farmer the brandy bottle.

'Keep me warm, that will. Much obliged to ye.'

Dickens made for the path. The moon had risen — wisps of cloud drifted across it. He walked on, holding the lantern in front of him. Shadows like small creatures seemed to run past him, liquid as cats. And, away over in the impenetrable dark, a dog howled, and an answering bark came from the farmer's dog. He'd be glad to get back to Ord Road. He didn't look back. The weary moon looked down on him with its bandaged face.

39: MUG ON THE SCENT

Scrap was standing at a derelict wharf with Mug, watching the river. He was thinking about the Black boy at that Mr Kaprillian's place. That lad knew a thing or two. All them queer things. Curiosities, the boy 'ad said. They were that — from all over the world, brought in on great big ships. He could see the masts of one going into the West India Dock basin. He had watched with Bean and Mug. Bean had told him of the vast warehouses. Rum from Jamaica, spices, sugar. The captain wot 'ad bin murdered 'ad sailed from India — Mr Jones 'ad told 'im of cotton, tea, silks, pearls, diamonds. Some folk must buy 'em, folks with so much money it couldn't fit in a bank. Wouldn't keep it under the bed, he supposed — there wouldn't be one big enough. Funny, though, 'ow some folk ad 'all them riches an' others 'ad nothin'. Not fair, really, but that woz the way o' things.

The masts were disappearing — they went into a great big dock, Bean said. Could 'e be a sailor? He thought about standing high on the mast of a ship. Crow's nest, they called it. Crow — name o' that murderer. Where woz 'is nest? An' where woz that girl? He'd been everywhere, fetched up 'ere at the bottom of some rotten wooden steps. He could have a last look.

But the tide was coming in. Soon this little creek would be filled with the cold brown water. Imagine goin' down in it. He'd seen the handbills offering rewards for the drowned fluttering above the high-water mark. Mebbe not a sailor. 'Sides, 'e couldn't swim. Not many sailors could, so that one they called Tempest 'ad said. Blimey, that woz daft. *Catch me settin' off on a sea voyage not knowin' 'ow ter swim!*

He saw that it would be dark before long. Time to go back ter the shop. Promised Mr Meteyard he wouldn't stay out in the dark. His eyes swept over the jumbled muddle on the muddy foreshore: wrecked boats, broken oars, old nets, crates, rusty anchors, chains as fat as coiling serpents, torn sails, rusted rings, and something that looked like a pair of sailor's trousers, lying there as if the owner had stepped out of them and gone naked into the water. And his sharp eyes caught something glinting in the mud. A last gleam of sunlight picked it out.

Scrap looked at the water. Just a quick look — might be worth somethin'. 'Stay 'ere, Mug.' He went down the steps and across the mud, avoiding broken glass and jagged bits of wood. Reached out. The gold was a ring — a sailor's earring. There were other clothes besides the trousers — a peacoat, a waistcoat, a shirt, a pair of sailor's pumps, all in a heap there by the wreck of a little boat. Perhaps the man had gone into the water, gone under. Scrap shivered. Not right to take 'em, poor divil. Stealin' from a dead man — not likely.

A noise. Something reared up at him from behind the boat. A naked man who shouted and reached out for him, caught him by his jacket and swung him screaming into the air.

''Old yer noise, yer little bleeder. If yer knows —'

The man shut up. Mug was barking. Two black eyes and the longest, yellowest teeth that Scrap had ever seen, and stinking breath in his face. Scrap brought his booted foot up sharpish right between the man's wide legs. There was a yell of surprised pain and he was dropped into the mud, from where he twisted like an eel and was off across the muddy shore before his assailant had the chance to stand upright. He glanced back. The man was full length. Tripped over the rusty chain. Mug was standing at the bottom of the steps.

'Gotter go, lad. Leave 'im.'

Scrap went up the steps with Mug beside him. Best get back.

On his way back down Five Bells Place, Mug pulled at his leash, wanting to turn down a narrow alley.

'We bin that way, Mug, I'm sure we 'ave. Ain't no use —'

But Mug, it seemed, was determined, and Mug, bent on some desire of his own, was not to be resisted. Sampson could have stopped him, but Mug was too much for Scrap. He gave in and the dog led him down the dark passageway until they came to a broken-down door at which the dog stopped and gave one deep bark.

'In there?'

Scrap followed Mug into the yard. It was full of old lumber, bits of metal, old nets and boats, an old anchor over which he nearly tripped. In the middle was a heap of timber and metal sheets to which Mug made his way. He barked again and sat down. It was quite clear that Mug was going nowhere. Scrap sniffed the air. Something rotten. Something was buried under there. *Gawd*, he thought, somethin' dead, buried under this mound of trash. Could be. What ter do? Get Sampson? But Mug wozn't goin' ter leave an' 'e couldn't leave Mug. Serpose someone came. Serpose someone came now. But Mug'd protect 'im, an' a murderer wouldn't come back. If there woz a murderer. He felt sure. *It's Rosanna Chibb under there.*

There was nothing for it but to dismantle the pile and see what was under it. It was nearly dark now, though the moon gave some light, and Scrap set to. It wasn't difficult. The heap of rubbish had been loosely piled and when he had moved the metal sheets, the wooden bits were easily pushed over to reveal the hole in the ground. He couldn't see much in the dark. He'd have to go down.

The moon shifted and shone down through the hole. He found her then, under the pile of old canvas. A girl with blood on her mouth.

The cab which Dickens had found by the dock on Mill Wall Road took him to Wapping Police Station. He thought that he couldn't have walked another step. He turned from paying the driver to see Sam Jones staring at him in astonishment.

'How did you know I was here?'

'I didn't. I have just come from the Isle of Dogs. William Lambert is dead.'

'How?'

'I think he hanged himself.'

'Think?'

'Someone had been there — the place was turned over. Drawers emptied, the palliasse cut up, pillows torn.'

'Corneille. Looking for the papers. But how the hell —'

'Did he know about William? Peter Best must have been there — I thought about it. We know he followed Best to Kit's shop, we know he followed him to Portugal Street, and he was at Mrs Cly's so —'

'He followed him to his brother's. God, Charles, I should have asked — we should have worked that out before. Corneille could have murdered him.'

'I don't know, Sam. Why would he hang him? Go to all that trouble. He would have stabbed him, surely. I think William may have been dead already — we saw how despairing he was. I didn't look too closely — but the smell — anyway, what did he have to live for?'

'We'd better go inside and tell Bold. But what were you doing there?'

'I took two guineas and some books. The old farmer saw me and told me.' Dickens didn't mention the gun — no use adding to Jones's burden. 'I left him there with the body — and his dog. But he saw him, Sam, in the night. The dog barked and he saw a tall man — not a sailor, he said. Long coat and low-crowned hat.'

'A similar man was seen at Richmond. That's why I came to see Bold. And there's more. A young woman went to Bank House asking for work. Stemp was in the front garden, cutting bushes — playing the gardener. He asked her what she wanted and what had brought her to that particular house. She was very vague — and shifty, Stemp said. Nervous, too. When asked, said her name was Lilian Snook. Somehow he didn't believe her. He told her there was nothing doing, went back to his pruning until she was out of the gates. Then he went to look, but dodged back when he saw a man — as you've described — on the other side of the road. He wasn't with her, but Stemp was sufficiently suspicious about two strangers in that quiet neighbourhood. He went round the back of the house to get Feak. He thought they might go for the steamer. Feak was to follow on the boat, but there was no sign of them at the pier. Vanished into thin air, it seems.'

'They could have gone for the train.'

'So Stemp thought, but by the time Feak came back, after watching at the pier for an hour, it was too late. Stemp didn't want to leave the house.'

'He was right — the stranger could have come back. It could have been Corneille — but a woman?'

'Why not? Different clothes, a woman in tow, another person altogether. However, Stemp got a good look at her.

Quite a pretty little body, dressed in black. She looked like a respectable servant. The clothes were not new — he noticed a patch on the front of the skirt. Black bonnet — a bit rusty looking, and a shawl. As she walked away, he noticed there was a piece missing from the fringe.'

'As many eyes as buttons on his coat.'

'Very true — Stemp's the strong, silent type, but he doesn't miss much. My idea is that he should come back to Bow Street then to Limehouse. He'll know her again. Bold's men will be looking too. I've given them the name of the girl, even though it's probably false.'

'There's often a grain of truth in an alias — I'll bet the two names belong to someone she knows. First names she thought of.'

'True enough. Anyway, I'm sending Dacres to take Stemp's place — I still want two there. Now we should go in and tell Bold about William Lambert.'

'Any news of Rosanna or Pilgrim?'

'Not a thing — Gaunt went to see Mrs Chibb and talked to some sailors there, but no one's seen Pilgrim.'

'Long Jodd?'

'Vanished too.'

When they arrived at the shop, Sampson was just leaving with Bean. Mug was with them.

'Mug came back without Scrap.'

'He's missing?' Dickens asked.

'Don't fret, Charley. Mug's just come back. He knows where Scrap is — he'll take us. Mebbe Scrap's found something.'

And maybe someone's found him. Dickens glanced at Sam, saw his lips tighten. They were thinking of the same thing — of another case when Scrap had been taken. But Jones merely said, 'Let's be quick then. Have you lamps, Mr Meteyard?'

'We have.'

They strode away, following the dog which seemed to know exactly where he was going. To Five Bells Place.

Mug barked. Sampson shouted and they heard Scrap answer. 'Down 'ere. I can't get out. 'S too 'igh.'

Sampson's lamp picked out Scrap's face looking up at them.

'I found 'er, Mr Jones. Mug led me 'ere. She's dead.'

'Right. We'll get you out.'

'I'll get down and lift him up,' said Dickens, 'and you can haul me up after.'

Dickens was slight enough to ease himself down the hole. He landed by Scrap, who pointed to the pile of canvas. He had covered her up again. Dickens lifted the canvas to look, to be sure it was Rosanna. In the light that Sampson dangled from the hole, he saw the dried blood on her mouth. She had been hit, perhaps.

"E musta bin tall to get out, Mr Dickens. I couldn't reach up. Knew Mug'd fetch Sampson. It woz Mug wot brought me. Smelt — yer know.' His child's face looked as it had a few years ago before Mrs Jones had taken care of him — pinched and worn before its time. But you couldn't take away what he knew then and what he knew now. 'What a thing, eh? She looked like someone yer'd like ter know.'

'She was, Scrap.'

'T'ain't right — ter steal a life. She shoulda bin able —'

'I know — to have her life and to make something of it.'

'Mr Jones'll find 'im.'

'He will. Now, let's get you up.'

When Scrap was lifted out, Sampson and Brawny Bean took an arm each and hauled Dickens out.

'It is Rosanna.'

'I'll get off to tell Bold. I'll come back to Mr Meteyard's when all is arranged.'

Mrs Amelia fed them and gave them hot tea. Sampson went to tell Mrs Chibb and when he came back, he sat with Dickens in the parlour.

'Numb, I think. I ain't sure she really knew what I was sayin'.'

'Shock and disbelief come first. She'll feel the truth of it later.'

'Aye, not that she had much in the way of love for the child. Didn't understand her. Rosanna was too independent. Unusual — and not just her looks.'

'Who was her father?'

'Black sailor. They were always together, Rosanna and her pa. Everyone knew them. Fine figure of a man. Handsome — carried himself like a prince. Kept a good house, too. When he died, things went wrong between mother and daughter. Mrs Chibb didn't feel it, see, but Rosanna's heart was broken. Then Kit looked after her. She was a clever girl, Kit said, but, I don't know, Charley, if she could have escaped — it's difficult for girls hereabouts. What can they do? Be servants, marry sailors, have too many kids, lose their husbands at sea. Get old before their time. Glad I had a son. I can't help hopin' that Henry finds a sensible wife, Charley. It's a lonely life for a single man.'

And sometimes for a married one, Dickens thought, but he didn't say so. Henry was old enough to make the right choice — you could be in too much of a hurry. He only smiled and observed that Henry, he was sure, would find the right one. Fortunately, they were interrupted by Jones, who came back to tell them that Rosanna had been taken to the bone house. The surgeon had come and had told them that her neck had been broken.

'I thought I saw blood on her mouth.'

'Yes, there was, but no injury. He surmised that she might have been held round the neck, had struggled so he had forced her head back and the neck had snapped. She was only slight — the sudden force could have done it. There was blood and skin on her teeth. He thinks she may have bitten her attacker.'

Rosanna would have fought; Dickens was sure of that. He hoped that it had hurt and that Corneille, if it were he, was suffering. 'She wasn't stabbed?'

'No, but Bold and I still have Corneille in mind. He had reason to take her.'

'It would have been a stranger,' Sampson said. 'Folks knew her. And those sailors who attacked you, Charley, I spoke to them. There's mostly regulars at Mrs Chibb's. They know each other.'

'Bold and his constables are out and about looking for a tall man whose hand bears signs of a bite. And a woman, possibly named Lilian Snook, with a shawl that has a piece of fringe missing. I'm sending Stemp tomorrow — he'll know the girl if he sees her, and he might know the man.'

'I hope so, Mr Jones. It's a bad business about young Rosanna — Kit will be heart-broken.'

'I know, Sampson. He'll blame himself, but he'll have to know.'

40: LIZZIE COMES FOR TEA

Time to get out. He'd seen that so-called gardener at the shop. What was a gardener from Bank House in Richmond doing in Limehouse? Police. But how the hell had they known? He could imagine that they had traced Best to his lodgings at Mrs Cly's. Mrs Cly might have mentioned the sailor, Jack Dawe, but Jack Dawe was nothing to do with Jeremie Corneille who had family in Richmond.

They couldn't know that Jack Dawe was Jeremie Corneille. It wasn't possible. Not that it mattered now. Ada had told him that a girl's body had been found off Five Bells Place. That was all she knew. It had to be that girl. But who the hell had found her underneath all that rubbish? And Ada — the gardener had spoken to her at Bank House. She had been flustered. He could tell when she came out. Damn, damn — the so-called gardener might remember her. Time to get rid of her, too.

Pity about Richmond and about the Isle of Dogs. The man was dead — hanged himself, he supposed, but he'd found nothing. The lawyer must have those papers. It was too late now. He could only save himself — grim sight that hanged man, and that would be him. All that ugliness. He'd drown himself, rather. Like Arthur Robinson. Arthur who had struggled with him, almost dragged him down into those weeds. Well, he'd shoved him away. Every man for himself. And that white-faced little runt, Stephen Winter. What had he seen? Nothing, Winter had said. But he had. Jeremie had seen him. Winter had known it was Jeremie's fault. Not that he'd meant harm to Arthur — he was just fooling, but he had felt his own power when they were in the water, that surge of desire — to live. And when Winter had looked at him lying on the bank, he had seen that Winter knew. And was too frightened to say. Well, he had survived then, he would survive now.

It was time to go. The question was: where?

The continent — easy enough to get a steamer to Antwerp. He still had Marcus's banker's draft. It would be a risk, but it was time to cash it in. Then, from Antwerp get to Paris. He had been before. He could make a life there. He thought of Marie-Louise. Pity, but not a good idea to go back to Kellner's. Move on. Forget the papers, forget Marcus, forget St Lucia.

And Ada? He'd tell her they were going abroad now. She'd like that. Some brandy. A few drops of laudanum. She'd wake up in the morning and he'd be gone.

Ada Pitt was frightened. Of all the people she didn't want to meet — Lizzie Snook, full of the story of the murdered girl. Neck broken, they said. Talk was that the girl — name of Rosanna Chibb — had bitten her attacker. Blood on her mouth, they said. Lizzie had heard it from her landlady, Mary Betts, who'd heard from Alice Straw whose husband's cousin was a policeman and, said Lizzie, her eyes glittering with the horrid details, Mary Betts said Jack Straw was investigating the murder of that sea-captain, and, they said — whoever they were — that the two murders were connected, and a body had been found at a farm on the Isle of Dogs — a man had hanged himself.

'Makes yer think,' said Lizzie, 'yer don't feel safe in yer bed. An' that man shot by the canal — same feller, prob'ly. Sounds like a madman's on the loose —'

Lizzie rattled on with her talk of escaped lunatics, murdering sailors, defenceless women, slaughtered babes, but Ada wasn't listening. She was thinking about that girl biting the murderer. That was what really worried her. Jack 'ad bin bitten — by a dog, 'e'd said. 'Ow could yer tell? No, 'e wouldn't 'ave. But, she thought about Jack's anger over Richmond. It was as if it was her fault. She came back to Lizzie, who was saying something about Jack.

'Still yer'll be safe, Ada, wiv yer Jack, eh?' Lizzie's face was greedy for more information.

'Serpose,' Ada said. 'I gotter go, Lizzie.' She thought of the gardener to whom she'd given the name Lilian Snook. She wished she hadn't, but he'd been threatening somehow. She'd told Jack, proud of her quick thinking. It had been a mistake. Jack hadn't been pleased at all.

'When yer flittin'?'

'I dunno — soonish.'

'Where yer goin' ter, then?'

'Richmond — abroad somewhere.' The word was out. She was so flustered she'd said the first place she thought of.

'Richmond ain't abroad. I knows that. It's upriver. Toffs up there. I'll be 'avin' tea there then, will I?' Lizzie laughed in a way that told Ada she didn't believe any of it.

Ada walked away. She knew Lizzie was watching. Hoped ter God she wouldn't foller. That'd be like Lizzie — could never keep her nose out. She'd given too much away. Jack wouldn't like it — but then 'e wouldn't know.

She stood in the street, uncertain and afraid. She glanced over to that shop where she saw a policeman talking to a huge man with a huge dog. Another man stood in the shadow of the doorway. The policeman turned round. He was looking at her. Turning down the nearest alley, she hurried away. She'd have to get back to Jack — she had to trust him. That's all there was.

'What's the news?' Jack asked. He looked in a better humour.

'Nothin' Jack, only I saw a policeman outside that shop. About that girl, I serpose.'

'What girl?'

'The one I told yer about — what woz murdered. Rosanna Chibb, she woz called.'

'Oh, that one — I'd forgotten you told me. Poor kid.'

'Shame ain't it —' Ada was reassured. Jack didn't know anything about it — 'they said —'

'Who said?'

'Nobody. Jest folk gossipin' —'

'You haven't been gossiping, little Ada, have you?' He came over and put his arms round her. He felt her tremble. He held her hair with one hand and the other was on her breast. He forced her head up to look at him. 'Ada?'

'No, Jack, honest.' It was the word "honest" that did it — in Jeremie Corneille's experience, it usually meant the opposite. He tightened his hold. 'I jest 'eard folk talkin' about the murder.'

'And what did these folk say?'

'That the girl —' She didn't dare say the word "bite", but her eyes gave her away. She looked at his hand.

'What did they say?'

His eyes were hard now. He was forcing her head further back. She couldn't think what else to say, except, 'Yer 'urtin' me, Jack.'

There was a knock at the door. The landlady, perhaps. 'Get rid of her.'

Ada opened the door to find Lizzie Snook.

'Yer dropped yer glove, dear. I follered yer ter give it back.' She held out a black glove.

'Ain't mine.'

'Oh, sorry, Ada. I'll come in fer that tea, shall I — yer can introduce me ter Jack.'

'No, I'm — er — busy just now.' She spoke louder. Jack might think it was the landlady. 'We don't need nothin'.'

Lizzie's eyes flared with anger. Her voice was too loud. 'Oh, too busy for yer old friend, Lizzie Snook. Jack Dawkins too good fer me, is 'e? Ta very much. Yer can keep yer Richmond an' yer tea party.'

Ada stood at the door, watching as Lizzie flounced down the stairs. She heard the front door slam. There was only silence behind her — the kind of silence that made yer feel sick an' hold yer breath. She wanted to run after Lizzie, run anywhere, away from the silence that seemed to harden round her.

'Come in, Ada, my love, and tell me all about Richmond, and Lizzie Snook, and Lilian Snook — that was the name you used, I recall.'

41: MRS GAMP'S CLUE

'Lilian Snook?' John Gaunt asked. Constable Jack Straw thought.

Stemp had noticed the girl staring at the shop. She had turned away suddenly and vanished down an alley, but not before his keen eye had seen that part of the fringe on her shawl was torn away. He went after her into the impenetrable tangle of lodging houses, shops, grimy little courts, yards and alleys. It might have been St Giles's or Seven Dials, but he knew his way about there. Here, he was baffled, but he was sure it was the girl who had given the name "Lilian Snook". She had stared at the shop and had vanished when Gaunt had turned round.

Gaunt and he had returned to Wapping Police Station where they waited now while Jack Straw thought about the name.

'Snook — Snook — there's Snook's Dock. An' there's Snooks in Low Shadwell —Three Cups Court.'

'Any Lilian?'

'Not that I knows. Oh, 'ang on, there's a Lizzie Snook what lodges with Mrs Betts — Mary Betts, friend of Alice Straw, that's my cousin, Bob Straw's wife. She's the sister of —'

'The address, Jack.' John Gaunt was not interested in the convolutions of Straw's family life.

'O, aye — Albion Terrace, off Hill Street.'

At Mrs Betts's lodging house, she, Lilian Twigg and Lizzie Snook were enjoying tea and gossip. Lizzie's anger at Ada's dismissal had not abated. She'd remembered the present and how she'd felt sorry for Ada. Aw right, the glove 'adn't bin

317

Ada's, but there'd bin no call ter send 'er off like some servant. Gettin' too 'igh was Ada — wot woz wrong with Lizzie Snook that there'd bin no tea an' no meetin' the fancy man? Too good fer Lizzie Snook, woz 'e?

Nursing her wrath to keep it warm, she had made her way to Albion Terrace. Seeing Lilian Twigg and Mary Betts ensconced by the fire, she hadn't been able to resist. She wasn't usually invited to the secret conclaves of the two gossips, but when she said that she had news of Ada, a cup of tea and a crumpet were offered with satisfying suddenness. She told them everything.

'Can't say I'm bothered,' Lilian said. 'Thievin' little cow. Went off with the miserable sod in the night — 'im without payin'. Dint like 'im — looked at yer as if yer woz dirt under 'is feet. Serposed ter be a sailor.'

'So wot's 'e want with Ada?' Mary Betts mused. 'Yer'd 'ardly call 'er a beauty. Wot's 'e after?'

'She dint look 'alf bad when she came ter the shop — said they woz gettin' married, goin' ter live in Richmond — or abroad.'

'Richmond,' snorted Lilian, 'abroad, my eye. Well it can't be 'er money, cos she ain't got none. She'll be back when 'e's finished with 'er.'

'Still,' said Mary, 'yer'd want ter know wot a man like that'd be doin' with a scullery girl.'

'All cats is grey in the dark.' Lilian knew that very well.

The three laughed, but Mary, terrier like, pursued her theme. 'Crook, I'll bet. One o' them swell mob. On the run, usin' Ada as a — as a — decoy.'

'That's ducks innit —'

Whether it was or not, they were never to know, for all three jumped at the sound of a very loud banging at the door.

'Gawd,' said Mary, heaving herself up, 'yer'd think the 'ouse woz on fire.'

She came back with Gaunt and Stemp. 'They're lookin' fer someone called Lilian Snook. I've told 'em I've got two 'alves o' that name 'ere, but we don't know no Lilian Snook.'

'Which of you is Lilian?' asked Gaunt.

'I'm Lilian Twigg an' this is Lizzie Snook. What's this about?'

'We're looking for a servant girl who gave the name Lilian Snook at a house in Richmond.'

'Blimey,' said Lizzie, 'it's Ada.'

'Ada who?'

'Ada Pitt — she's my niece. Went off with 'er fancy man, an' Lizzie saw 'er yesterday. She said they woz goin' to live at Richmond — abroad, she called it.'

Gaunt turned to Lizzie. 'What's the man's name?'

'Jack Dawkins, she said, but she dint seem all that sure. Went ter see 'er yesterday.'

It had to be, Gaunt thought. Quick then. 'Where?'

'Lodgin's — off Globe Alley. Walnut Tree Court.'

'Off Nightingale Lane?'

'Yes.'

'Was the man there?'

'Dint see 'im — Ada was that flustered, she —' Lizzie thought about Ada then — 'she looked scared. Dint want me there anyways, despite I give 'er a weddin' present an' all when she woz buyin' clothes fer 'er fancy man.'

'What clothes?' Gaunt asked.

'Black coat an' trousers, boots, an' a black 'at — decent, she wanted. She left some old sailors' slops. 'Is, I serpose.'

Gaunt looked at Stemp. Confirmation — the sailors' slops exchanged for a black coat — the coat seen by Stemp at Richmond.

'Take us to Globe Alley.'

'She's my niece — I oughter come.' Lilian wasn't going to miss this. *Give 'er a piece o' my mind*, she thought, *serves 'er right if 'e is a crook.*

'All right. Not you, Mrs Betts,' Gaunt said. He'd seen Mrs Betts pick up her shawl. He didn't want all three witches.

It wasn't far, just down Island Row, across the Limehouse Cut Bridge, into Nightingale Lane.

'Down 'ere,' Lizzie told them, turning off suddenly into the darkness of the alley and leading them to the romantically named Walnut Tree Court. It was even darker. No tree grew there, and no child either. It stank. Pools of stagnant water filled the lane, and refuse was piled in the deep black mud. *Useful hiding place*, thought Gaunt. They'd never have found him here. Lizzie pointed to a door upon which Gaunt knocked — very loudly.

A haggard-faced child opened the door and looked at them with uncomprehending eyes.

'Lodgers — where are they?' Gaunt barked.

The child blinked. 'One pair back. Up there.'

Gaunt and Stemp took the stairs two at a time, followed by Lizzie and a wheezing Lilian. Just the one door. Gaunt knocked and the door opened. He stepped in. He heard Stemp take a breath.

Ada lay on the floor by the hearth. Gaunt went over, leaving Stemp to bar the door against the two women, but they had seen.

'Gawd, is she dead?' Lilian asked, peering round Stemp's back.

He looked at Lilian, saw the excitement in her greedy eyes, and didn't answer. He knelt down. He could see that she had hit her head on the brick hearth. There was blood coming from a wound on her temple. But someone had hit her in the face. There was blood on her mouth and nose. Broken, he thought. He leaned over. She was breathing — just.

'Stemp, I'm going for a doctor. Workhouse infirmary's just across the way. You,' he said to Lilian, 'apply some cold water to her head, and you, Miss Snook, talk to her. Keep her alive.'

The two women came in. "'E's done it, I bet,' said Lizzie. 'Told yer she was scared.'

Gaunt hurried out. They heard his heavy boots on the stairs.

Gaunt and Stemp sat by Ada's bedside throughout the long night. She had been taken to the workhouse infirmary. Her wounds had been cleaned up, but she was still unconscious. The doctor thought there was hope that she might wake up. Gaunt had sent Lilian and Lizzie home. He was not moved by Lilian's desire to stay with Ada. All that "me niece wot I brought up — good as a mother, I've bin ter that girl" cut no ice with him. He had seen her hard eyes. A matter for the police, he had told her. A message would be sent to Albion Terrace when there was news. Lilian and Lizzie went off to Mary Betts's — he knew they would. Gin and gossip, he thought.

By morning, they began to think it was hopeless. Even if she woke up in a few days, it would be too late. Corneille — they were sure it was he — would be long gone. Not to Richmond, that was certain. Lizzie Snook had said the couple were going abroad. That could be anywhere. It might be a fairy story.

They heard her moan. Her eyes opened and closed again, but she was muttering something. Gaunt leaned over, the better to hear. 'No ... no... Jank ... wer ... Jack ... ank...'

'Anchor?' asked Stemp. 'Ship? Lizzie said she was going abroad.'

'There's an Anchor Street by the East India Docks.' Gaunt thought of Ned Carver. 'Or the Anchor Pub in Grog Court. It's just up the street.'

The girl seemed to drift off again. They waited, hoping she would say something more. Ada moaned and muttered again, 'ring ... werks, Ank...werks...'

A thought flashed into Gaunt's mind. 'Mr Dickens!'

'What? What about him?'

'Ankwerks — she means Antwerp — like Mrs Gamp.'

'Who —'

'Doesn't matter.' Gaunt was on his feet. 'We need to get to Inspector Bold — now.'

42: DOWN WITH THE TIDE

Dickens was thinking of the law and fog, both impenetrable. His article on red tape and its coils was nearly done; the fog was not, it seemed. It was early morning at Wellington Street, and fog, grey-green as yet, hovered uncertainly at the window. Indecision. He ought to finish his piece. He had come to the office early for that purpose. But he couldn't help thinking about Corneille. When the fog thickened as the day dwindled, it would be as brown as tobacco smoke, wreathing the city in darkness. So, in such shadow, a man could hide, slipping like a dark ghost through the streets.

Paris — next week, please God, out of this, and into bright and sparkling Paris with his friend, John Leech. Perhaps that's where Corneille would go — become the suave Frenchman like L'Estrange. He must know people there. Perhaps some charming girl like Marie-Louise would take him in. He wondered about the girl Stemp had seen. Corneille would hardly take a servant girl to Paris — no, he would have used her, and he would abandon her. But, what about the papers, now safely lodged with Judge Tallis? Perhaps Corneille knew they were out of his reach.

A knock on the door. Sergeant Rogers in a hurry. 'Cab at the door, Mr Dickens. Superintendent's off to Blackwall. No time to spare —' he grinned at Dickens — 'if you want to come.'

Two minutes later, Dickens was in the cab. 'Blackwall?'

Jones explained, 'The railway from Fenchurch Street. John and Stemp found the Richmond girl, beaten up. She's in the workhouse hospital — unconscious. But she did mutter something about someone called Jack.'

'Good Lord — Corneille!'

'They're assuming so. The girl's name is Ada Pitt. Her aunt is Lilian Twigg and her friend is Lizzie Snook.'

'Ah, Lilian Snook.'

'Constable Jack Straw at Wapping knew of a Lizzie Snook. Stemp and John traced her, found out she'd been to visit Ada Pitt at some lodgings off Nightingale Lane. Ada Pitt's fancy man was a Jack Dawkins, according to Lizzie Snook. They found her at the lodgings, but no Jack, of course. However, she did say something else —' Jones grinned at Dickens — 'something only John could understand — and you.'

'Me!'

'Ankwerks.'

'Mrs Gamp!'

'Exactly, and Johnno who is your best fan, apart from me, of course, remembered Mrs Gamp and deciphered "Antwerp".'

'Did he, by God? You think he's fled.'

'There's a chance he might have taken the Antwerp packet. It's Thursday, but it will have gone — it's after 9.00 now. We're to make haste to Bugsby's Reach, where Bold is to stop the steamer at Hookness.'

On the train, Jones explained that Stemp had been sent to St Katherine's Wharf from where the Antwerp Steamer sailed. He might get aboard, but he might not. Still, Bold intended to use one of the long wooden lighters, loaned from Jack Straw's brother. It would block the way of the steamer, which would have to stop. A lighter or a barge should always give way to a steamer, but this lighter wouldn't. If Stemp were aboard, then the hope was that he would apprehend the fugitive. If not, Bold and Gaunt would board.

'Assuming he is on board,' Dickens said.

'I know — it's not certain, but it's a throw of the dice. Bold thinks, and I do too, that Corneille knew things were going wrong. Ada had told her friend, Lizzie Snook, about going to Richmond, and when Lizzie went to the lodgings she gave her name and she mentioned Richmond so, assuming Corneille was there — Ada wouldn't let Lizzie Snook in — he would have realised that someone knew about him and that would be dangerous.'

'He'd wonder what else Ada had told.'

'Lizzie Snook said the name Jack Dawkins,' Rogers said.

'Lor', that would have given him a fright.'

'I imagine he forced Ada to reveal what she had said and beat her up because she admitted she'd talked about Richmond and had told his name, or at least part of it,' said Jones.

'I wonder if he meant to kill her.'

'Maybe, and she might yet die. We'll want him for that as well.'

'Will we be in time?'

'Hope so. There'll be a cab waiting at Blackwall to take us to Bow Creek. The steamer leaves at high water and goes down on the ebb tide, but Bold reckons that in the fog, the steamer will be slow — three or four knots, maybe. An hour and a half, perhaps.'

The cab was waiting at Blackwall. It took them away from the station and down to the road that led to the creek. They passed The Orchard House, an old inn, once a moated manor house. It had seen better days, though its drinking house and skittle ground were popular with the labourers who worked at the nearby Wigram and Black shipyards and the Thames Plate Glass works to the north of the inn. There were a cement works and some distilleries and a few lines of cottages.

Then buildings and cottages became sparser, and the road stopped suddenly before the spit of empty land that ended at Bow Creek, where the River Lea entered the Thames. Dickens and Jones and Rogers found themselves on the headland, surrounded by swirling fog. Then voices came at them and they made their way in that direction. They scrambled down a slope onto a strip of muddy foreshore to the river's edge, where they made out the shape of the police launch on the water.

'Superintendent Jones,' shouted Jones.

They had to enter the water where the boat bobbed on the rolling tide. In the distance, they heard the sound of the steamer's funnel. She was coming, though they couldn't see her yet. The oarsmen pulled hard in the choppy water down Bugsby's Reach towards desolate Hookness. There was nothing to see of the untenanted marshes which lay flat and grey beyond the riverbank. Sky, water and shore were all grey mist, but they could feel the cold wind and the sting of water on their faces. Dickens thought of the night they had been rowed down to Limehouse to find that Kit was missing. Now, he hoped, they were rowing to meet the murderer. Behind them the steamer's funnel sounded again. Dickens thought he heard the noise of the paddles. He looked back — nothing yet.

Then there were lights ahead, showing dully in the fog. The wooden lighter lay at anchor in mid-channel. It must have been thirty feet long and half as wide. As they neared, they could see a stolid looking man in a tarred cape standing in the bow holding a very long pole steady in the water. Bold standing, peering into the mist. Gaunt and three other policemen stood by, and there was a boy at the rudder. There was another police launch beyond her with three more men in her. Their rowers pulled into line. Bold had purloined as many lanterns as he could find. The steamer must see them. She must stop.

Dickens could hear the deep throb of the engines. She was coming out of the mist like a ghost ship. Mid-stream to get the benefit of the tide. He saw the black smoke plume upwards from the tall stack to mingle with the fog. Her lights were on — one on the masthead like a cyclops eye, one on the bow sprit and one on the paddle box. One of the policemen on the lighter waved a flaming torch, the kind used by linkboys, made of burning pitch and tow. Another fired a pistol. The shot rang out, echoing across the water. Her steam whistle sounded again. She had seen them.

Bold was on his feet, brass trumpet at his mouth. His voice sounded unearthly and hollow. 'River Police. You must stop.'

They could see the captain standing on the paddle box. He shouted something — ordering the engineer to stop her. They heard the paddles go into reverse. The steamer still came on. Fred Straw took up his anchor. The steamer was slowing. They could hear shouting on board — passengers wondering at the change. The steamer stopped, her steam blowing off. Now Fred Straw steered the lighter towards the steamer to get alongside. They heard her bump the side. Their rowers pulled closer, and Dickens felt their boat lift on the wash. Looking up, they saw the captain leaning down towards them.

'I need to board — wanted man.'

'Right.'

A rope snaked down, which one of Bold's men caught and tied to a belaying point. The lighter was made fast and steadier now. Then a ladder came down, which the boy held firm. Bold and his four men scrambled up.

Dickens could see pale ovals of faces as the deck passengers crowded at the guard rail to see what was happening. The boat in which Dickens and Jones sat bobbed away on the swell. The rowers tried to turn it back so that Jones could get into the lighter, but as they turned, Dickens heard a great cry on board the steamer. He looked up. A man had launched himself off the stern.

'There, Sam, there! Someone's jumped.'

'Turn round — man in the water!' Jones shouted.

The rowers struggled to turn the boat again. Dickens and Jones scanned the water, but no head came bobbing up. There was another shout. Someone dived, the body turning into an arc then straight as an arrow cleaving the water where the first had gone in. The diver came up again, shook himself like a porpoise and plunged again. Dickens's rowers pulled nearer. The head popped up, disappeared again and then they saw that there were two together, but the second was struggling to free himself from the diver. They went down again, the water threshing about them. The police boat was by them now. The diver came up, his strong arm clasped about the other's neck. Jones and Rogers leaned out to drag the man by his coat. They hauled him in. One of the policemen hauled in the diver, who lay breathless at Dickens's feet.

Dickens looked at a smiling face. 'Mr Lomax — I fear you have missed your voyage to Antwerp.'

'Mr Dickens! Good Lord.'

Meanwhile, Jones contemplated the sodden body at his feet. There was blood on the face. He was alive, but unconscious.

'We have them,' he shouted to the man on the lighter. 'We'll come to you.'

They pulled back alongside the lighter. Rogers climbed aboard and he and Fred Straw received the unconscious man, assisted by Jones and Dickens with the help of the seemingly inexhaustible Tom Lomax.

Jones searched the pockets of the long black coat. A leather pouch contained the papers which told him that the unconscious man was, indeed, Jeremie Corneille.

Inspector Bold appeared at the steamer's rail. 'You have him?' he called down.

'We do,' Jones said.

'I thought he was drowning — perhaps he couldn't swim. I saw that your boat was too far away. I didn't think — but then Uncle Lovelock says I never do — I didn't think about if he were the wanted man.'

Tom Lomax was telling his story. Wrapped in a blanket and with a brandy in his hand, he shook his head over the man who had fought with him in the freezing water and whom he had hit as hard as he could to save his life. He and Dickens were seated beside a good fire in The Orchard House, where Tom Lomax's clothes were drying. Jones and Inspector Bold were in an upstairs room where the injured man had been taken to bed.

'But I tell you, Mr Dickens, he tried to push me off. He didn't want to be saved. I had to hit him —'

'As well you did — the man you saved — Jeremie Corneille — is a murderer.'

'Oh — good God! Then I...' Tom Lomax looked stricken. 'Will he — I mean, have I saved him for the gallows? Will he hang?'

'I should think so.'

Tom stared into the fire. Dickens waited. He could see the shadows darken the open, cheerful countenance. His heroic act — which the fellows would have cheered to the rafters — had fallen to pieces.

He turned his troubled eyes to Dickens. 'I wish now that I had left him.'

'Do not believe it. You should know what he has done. He has killed three, possibly four — one a young girl of such promise, and there is a poor servant girl in hospital fighting for her life.'

'A bad lot.'

'I am afraid so. He may hang. I do not say I wish it, Mr Lomax, but he had to be caught for the sake of those he killed and those who loved them, whose lives are irredeemably spoilt.'

'I see that it is just. I suppose the irony — it seems so horrible, somehow.'

'I know. Murder and its consequences are never straightforward, but it is of the innocent we must think. My friend, Superintendent Jones, will be much obliged to you for your timely courage. He must know the truth of the matter — that Mr Corneille is truly the guilty man— for the sake of those left behind.'

'Why would a man do such things?'

'In this case, Mr Lomax, greed, the desire to have at all costs, to sweep away any obstruction to his selfish desire.'

Tom Lomax looked back into the fire. It was hard for him, thought Dickens, such a very cheerful young man full of hope for his future. He looked at the attractive face, remembering the boy's good humour when they had met him at the solicitor's. Youth would prevail.

Jones came in. 'Mr Lomax, I hope that you are recovered.'

'I am, sir, the fire and the brandy are doing their work.'

'I am glad and much obliged to you.'

'Mr Dickens has explained something of the case.'

'Good — then you will know how important your action was. It was brave of you.'

'Thank you — I'm a strong swimmer. I thought he was drowning.'

'He intended to escape justice, but, thanks to you, he will not. Now, we must leave you for a while. I need to speak to Mr Dickens, after which we will arrange to get you home to —'

'Twickenham. But I shall not go home — I don't want to tell them what has happened. I shall go to a friend's, and then I should be able to make my journey to Antwerp on the Saturday boat.'

'I hope so,' said Dickens, 'you must continue with your plans. Try not to brood on what has happened.'

Tom Lomax smiled. 'I shall try. Thank you for explaining, Mr Dickens.'

Dickens and Jones went out into the hall. 'Something wrong there?' asked Jones.

'He was concerned that he had saved the man for the gallows — he is a good-hearted young man. I explained what Corneille had done and that you had to know the truth. He understands, I think, and he is of an optimistic nature. In his case, youth's a stuff that *will* endure.'

Jones gave him a look. 'Poet?'

'Shakespeare.'

'I'll allow that — in our case, age will need to endure.'

'Corneille? He's not dead!'

'No, he has recovered consciousness. He has confessed to the murders of Mr Best and Rosanna Chibb.'

'Not Captain Valentine?'

'He says the captain was dead when he went into the cabin in search of the papers.'

'What! Do you believe him?'

'I don't know, but there are two things to think about. First, I can't think why he would deny the captain's murder. He has confessed to the other two. What difference would it make to the outcome?'

'None, I suppose. What a turn up. You said there were two things.'

'Well, the second thing does bear investigation — he said he picked up a lady's handkerchief in the cabin. He thought it was Marie-Louise's because of the scent.'

'Fleurs de Bulgarie.'

'Yes, I imagine so. He thought he'd pocketed it by accident and had dropped it when he took out the knife from his pocket.'

'So he was going to kill the captain.'

'He says not — only to threaten, but he would say that. However, think about the scent.'

'Lor, Sam — Judith Black.'

'My thought too. Of course, it may be Marie-Louise's. He may be lying about the captain, but, as I said, why would he? I have to look into it. I have to be sure.'

'Where is the handkerchief now?'

'He gave it to Ada Pitt. He thought no more about it until I questioned him about Captain Valentine, just as he thought no more about the captain. He thought only of the papers.'

'So now?'

'We leave Inspector Bold to arrange the transfer of Corneille to the workhouse infirmary and to sort something out for Mr Lomax, and we go to the hospital where I'm hoping we might find it in Ada Pitt's clothes, or, if not, we shall search the lodgings at Walnut Tree Court. If we find it, we then find Marie-Louise, and if it's not hers, we think very carefully about Judith Black.'

'She won't admit it's hers.'

'Then we must find another way.'

43: FLEURS DE BULGARIE

Henry Meteyard was watching a stranger at the door of the shop. He was a young man who seemed to hesitate before coming in. Then Henry saw the clerical collar. Not a murderer then.

'I wonder if I might see Mr Kit Penney.'

'I am afraid he is not here — he is away from home at present.'

'Oh, that is a disappointment — I had something important to tell him. I have come from the workhouse hospital. It is about a patient — a Black man. He was attacked and badly injured. However, he has spoken some words — he mentioned Mr Penney. I thought he might mean the ship's chandler, but I could not be sure. It seemed worth trying.'

'Is his name Pilgrim?'

'I think it may be — he has used the word. I did not know that he meant his name. Do you know him?'

'I do. He was the servant of Captain Valentine.'

'Good gracious — the captain who was murdered. It is surely nothing to do with Pilgrim?'

'I think not, except that he disappeared on the night of the murder. The police have been searching for him. I ought to inform Inspector Bold of Wapping Police Station.'

The young man looked even more worried. 'I wonder, Mr — '

'Henry Meteyard. I am a barrister at Lincoln's Inn — I have been looking after Mr Penney's shop.'

'Mr Meteyard, I would be most obliged if you would come first to see Pilgrim. He is terribly agitated at times, and there is some burden on his mind, I think — something which brings him terror. He cries out in his dreams as if haunted. When awake, he is hardly coherent — but he seems to want Mr Penney. I fear that the appearance of a policeman might well distress him further. You could tell him you have come from Mr Penney.'

Henry thought. It would be no harm to see the poor fellow first. He might be able to reassure him that a message would be sent to Kit, then he would go to see Bold.

'Very well. You are?'

'George Sax, curate at St. Anne's. I visit the hospital frequently. Pilgrim's case is so unfortunate that I would dearly like to assist him. I will tell you all on the way.'

Henry went in for his coat and walked with George Sax towards Church Lane. Along the way, the curate explained. Pilgrim had been found in an alley near an old wharf. He was quite naked, his head gashed and a knife wound in his shoulder. Even his gold ring had been ripped from his ear. He had been left for dead, but a kindly old woman had found him. Her son had fetched a doctor, who had arranged for Pilgrim's removal to the workhouse infirmary. A fever had set in and, of course, he could tell them nothing about the attack.

'He seemed so forlorn, Mr Meteyard — it was his nakedness, so pitiable. Such a poor outcast. I have thought much of the words of the book of James: "If a brother or sister be naked and destitute of daily food." Faith is nothing without deeds. I watched over him, hoping he might tell us something.'

'He has said nothing of the attack?'

'No, just confused words which mean very little to me, but he is very afraid, I think — there is terror in his eyes. Can it be, I wonder, something to do with the murder of Captain Valentine?'

'He may have seen something, but it is not for me to ask. I will speak to him of Mr Penney only — I will try to reassure him that Mr Penney will come.'

'Henry! What brings you here?'

Dickens and Jones were going into the hospital as Henry and George Sax arrived.

'Mr Sax, here is Superintendent Jones of Bow Street and Mr Dickens. Mr Sax has been concerned about an injured Black man in the hospital. He must be Pilgrim for he has asked for Kit. I thought to see him before I went to Bold.'

George Sax looked anxiously at the imposing superintendent. His words tumbled out. 'I asked Mr Meteyard to come, Superintendent. I did not want the first person Pilgrim sees to be a policeman. Pilgrim has been badly frightened. He was attacked and left completely naked. He is hardly coherent yet. The doctor diagnoses congestion of the brain, but he spoke the word "Penney" over and over in his delirium. I thought of Mr Penney at the ship's chandler's — that perhaps he knew him. Mr Meteyard told me of Pilgrim's connection to the murdered captain, but he says that you do not suspect Pilgrim. That is true?'

'It is — you need not worry, Mr Sax. You know that Mr Penney is absent?'

'I do. I thought Mr Meteyard might reassure Pilgrim.'

'I do need to find out if he knows anything about Captain Valentine's murder, but I see that a policeman is not suitable. However, he may remember Mr Dickens. Charles, are you willing to try while I go to examine Ada Pitt's clothing?'

'I am. I will do my best not to frighten him.'

'Who is Ada Pitt?' asked Henry.

'It's a long story, Henry. Charles will tell you all after he has seen Pilgrim. Mr Sax, would you take Mr Dickens to see him?'

As they walked away, Dickens explained his connection to Kit Penney, and after George Sax had recovered from his astonishment at meeting Charles Dickens, he told him what he knew of Pilgrim's plight. Dickens thought about the clothes and earring that Scrap had seen on the shore — it was clear that Scrap's assailant had been Long Jodd. That he should strip poor Pilgrim naked seemed all of a piece with his coarse nature. Jodd had probably thought that he had killed Pilgrim. Pilgrim might well have died had it not been for the kindly old woman. But could Pilgrim tell them anything about the captain's murder?

'When was he found?'

'A week ago.'

Ah, before the murder of Carver. Perhaps Carver had been there, had believed Pilgrim dead, too. That would make him dangerous to Jodd, who would have no loyalty to Carver.

'Did no one think to tell the police?'

'There was nothing to tell until the poor man woke up. Pilgrim was in a dreadful state. The doctor thought he had been set upon hours before he was found. It is a wonder that he did not die of the cold. His first concern was to save Pilgrim's life. As it is, he may not live.'

They came to the bed where the man lay tossing restlessly. His eyes were closed, but if he were asleep then he was in the grip of some nightmare. His lips worked and his hands grasped the sheet in convulsions. Dickens leant over and whispered the word 'Pilgrim'. The eyes fluttered as if they might open. He heard indistinct sounds and bent closer. He saw the beads of sweat break out on the forehead. Pilgrim tossed and turned, cried out, though Dickens could not say what was the meaning of the words. He thought back to when his friend, John Leech, had nearly drowned.

Leech had been knocked over by a bad blow from a great wave. He had congestion of the brain, was bled, had leeches applied and ice to his head, but nothing availed. Dickens remembered the alarming restlessness of his friend, his wife's fear that he might die that night. Dickens had resolved to try mesmerism — he had some skill in it — to hypnotise Leech into sleep. It had worked. Leech had slept tranquilly for an hour and a half. When he woke, he was much improved. It surely would work again. Pilgrim showed the same agitation as Leech. He needed the healing effect of magnetic sleep. Only then would he be able to speak of any of his terrors. Dickens knew he could do it, but he wondered what the curate might think, let alone the doctor. Cunning was required then.

'Mr Sax, I will sit with him for a while. If he wakes, I will try him about Mr Penney. Shall I send word to St Anne's if Pilgrim comes round?'

'I should be most obliged. I ought to return to the church — it is very good of you, Mr Dickens. I am glad to leave him in such good hands.'

George Sax went meekly away. Dickens felt a little guilty at the gratitude of the man whom he had manipulated into leaving, but he had to try. If a doctor came, he would see kindly Mr Dickens trying to comfort his patient — he hoped. Not many doctors approved of mesmerism, but Dickens's old friend, Dr John Elliotson was a practitioner. He had lost his post at the university because of it. Still, no use worrying. He turned back to the man on the bed and focused all his concentration on the movements of his hands around Pilgrim's head. He brushed the eyebrows gently with his thumbs and concentrated his gaze so that if the eyes opened they would see the power of his own.

Jones came to the door of the ward. He saw that Dickens was intent on the sick man. He knew what he was doing. It was not the moment to interrupt. There had been no handkerchief in any of Ada Pitt's pockets — he had half thought there would not be, but the thought of Corneille's assertion that he had not killed Captain Valentine still troubled him. It seemed such a pointless lie, and if, in court, the assertion was repeated, he would be asked what investigation he had carried out. He must try the lodgings in Walnut Tree Court. He would take Henry Meteyard with him — very convenient to have the barrister as witness if the handkerchief were found. First, however, there was another patient to see. Corneille ought to have been brought here by now. He would be closely guarded by Stemp and John Gaunt. Rogers he would send to Highgate. It was time for Kit to come home.

At Walnut Tree Court, the haggard child blinked and sent them up the stairs to the one pair back. *Depressing*, Jones thought. He had seen so many like it — cramped, fusty, shabby, and meant for birds of passage, for those who came and went and left no mark other than the smell of drink and stains on the sheets.

There was nothing much in it except a ramshackle table, a couple of chairs and the bed. Only a corner cupboard, hanging askew, gave him any hope. Inside he saw the shawl with the missing piece of fringe and a box — the sort of box in which a servant would carry her meagre life from place to place.

The box contained two things only: a piece of lace and a handkerchief. The handkerchief carried the faint scent of rose and musk — Fleurs de Bulgarie.

44: A DARK BLUE THREAD

Dickens sat still. He watched Pilgrim. The tossing and turning seemed less frantic. A doctor came and saw that his patient was quieter. He recognised the visitor.

'Your presence seems to soothe him, Mr Dickens. You know the man?'

Dickens explained and the doctor went away, wondering about what power the novelist must have. Extraordinary man, he thought, to come all this way to sit with a poor Black sailor. It looked as though he would recover. Perhaps he should ask Dickens the secret — if there were one. So many died in this ugly, violent place. Sometimes it seemed hopeless. No sooner had you patched one up than another came for whom nothing could be done.

Pilgrim's eyes opened and Dickens leant over. His blue eyes looked intently into the brown eyes until the expression of fear faded. Then he said, 'Pilgrim — Mr Kit is coming. Never fear. All shall be well.'

The eyes closed again, and Pilgrim slept. Dickens saw the change. Pilgrim's breathing was deep and regular now, and his face lost its expression of anxiety, and became quiet and peaceful. Dickens sat and waited once more.

Dickens was still seated at Pilgrim's bedside when Jones returned. He had been to see Inspector Bold and had, on his way back to the hospital, thought much about how to proceed.

'I have it,' he whispered. 'Come away with me for a moment.'

Dickens left the bedside and they moved to a quiet corner. Jones showed him the handkerchief. There was the faint scent of Fleurs de Bulgarie. And there was more. Jones turned over the handkerchief and Dickens saw where someone had unpicked a bit of embroidery. There was the letter 'J', a shadow of itself, as if written on the air — except for one bit of dark blue thread clinging to the end of the letter.

'Judith.'

'I think so, but I doubt if it is enough. Telling, yes, but not strong evidence. How many names begin with "J"?'

'And how many ladies use Fleurs de Bulgarie?'

'Exactly. I need more. What about Pilgrim?'

'There is a change. He opened his eyes, and I told him that Mr Kit was coming. He seems to sleep peacefully now, and when he wakes —'

'How long?'

'I don't know. We cannot hurry him. Nature must do her work. In any case, Mrs Judith won't be going anywhere. She doesn't know that she is suspected.'

'True, Charles, true. I have had a thought, however, about Gaspard L'Estrange.'

Dickens looked blank, then understanding dawned. 'Of course, she dined with him — you want to know when.'

'Was it before or after the captain's death? And did he see a handkerchief like this one? I must go straightaway. I'll leave you with your patient and be back as soon as I can.'

Time crawled by. Dickens waited almost unaware of the noise and hurry of the ward. He thought about Judith Black, imagining the scene in the cabin where, perhaps, she had demanded that Louis Valentine sell his shares in *The Redemption*. The captain refused. He spoke of Grace Fox and her child for whom he must provide. That would be gall and wormwood. She had no child. No son for whom to build her business. What about the sick husband? Was that why there was no child? What had that meant to her, a woman of such proud temper? She would hate the pitiable object who could not do anything for himself or for her. It would be a slow, corroding, growing hate. Perhaps Mrs Skillett had been right about the death of James Black. If she had killed once, it would not be so difficult to do it again if you were impelled by that burning passion to have what you wanted. L'Estrange had wondered what fire burned beneath the ice. Rage and hatred for another man who denied her.

Two murderers, then. Each possessed of a single, overpowering desire. There was terror in that.

'Charles?' It was Kit. 'How is he? Sergeant Rogers told me all about it.'

'Peaceful. I hope he will wake soon. It will do him good to see you. Yours was the only name he uttered. The curate, George Sax, says that he was possessed by some terror. I wondered if he knows something about the captain's death.'

Kit stood by the bed. Pilgrim's eyes opened. 'My dear old friend,' said Kit. 'Here I am to take care of you, and here is Mr Dickens who has watched over you until I could come.'

Pilgrim wept and Kit held fast to his hand.

Dickens went out. It was too soon to question Pilgrim. The sick man needed food. He would go across to Sampson. Amelia would have hot soup, he was sure. Something good and nourishing, and, later, they might ask if Pilgrim could tell them anything at all about the night of the murder. Of course, he might not remember — it was possible that whatever dreadful memories he had could not be unlocked after his injury. John Leech had recovered well, but that was not always the case, and Pilgrim had known such terror — the murder of the man to whom he was devoted, his flight, and then the attack.

When he returned with Amelia's soup, Jones was waiting at the door of the ward.

'I didn't go in — I don't want to disturb him, but I saw that he is awake.'

'I know — he wept like a child when he saw Kit. I am afraid to ask about the captain. In any case, he might not remember. Let me just take this soup to Kit.'

'Did you find L'Estrange?' Dickens asked when he came back.

'I did. Mrs Black dined with him on the night of the murder. He recognised the handkerchief. He put her in a cab at eleven o'clock. I wondered what time she got home.'

'Mrs Skillett? Worth asking?'

Kit came to them. 'He is asleep again. I have not asked him anything, Superintendent Jones. I dare not. Charles, you saw how he wept. I fear for him still.'

'I understand, Mr Penney — we will leave you now. Ask only if you judge it right. Charles and I must be about some other matter. We will return later.'

'The shop first. We need Scrap.'

'What for?'

'To go to the shipyard to find out if she's there. I don't want to see her at the house until we've questioned Mrs Skillett and that parlour maid.'

'Can we trust Mrs Skillett?'

'I've thought about that — what she said about the husband.'

'It occurred to me, too. And then I thought that L'Estrange wondered about fire beneath the ice. I think she hated the two men who thwarted her — one by his weakness and the other by his love for another.'

'Elizabeth said "a woman scorned", but we were thinking that she couldn't have killed Peter Best, so I dismissed the idea. I should have listened to my wife.'

'But it seemed impossible when we had found Best.'

They waited near the gates of the Black shipyard while Scrap went in to ask if Mrs Black were there, for he had a message for her. She was down at the wharf. Scrap made as if to go the way the man pointed, looked back to see that his informant had gone, threaded his way through the knots of labouring men, and worked his way back to Dickens and Jones.

'Down at the wharf.'

'Good. Pekin Place it is.'

'Yer want me?' asked Scrap.

Jones thought. 'I do — follow us. See if you can find a back way to the house we're going to. Come and tell me if anyone comes out.' He was thinking of Mrs Skillett — he didn't want to miss her.

'Now, Charles, we've got to be clever about this. I want you to go to the house first. If Mrs Skillett is there, bring her to the churchyard. If not, then I want you to charm the maid into telling you where her mistress was on the night before they heard about the captain, and what time she came back. The rest I leave to your imagination.'

There was a young girl at the front door, sweeping the steps. Not the parlour maid, an altogether humbler creature in a drab dress and overlarge apron. She smiled at him — the nice policeman in plain clothes. Just the girl he wanted. He asked for Mrs Black, but, of course, she was down at the yard. He looked disappointed, told her that 'is chief had sent him specially to ask some questions about the capt'n. P'raps 'e might see Mrs Skillett? She was out, too.

'I wonder, Miss —' All deference to the young lady. She was about fifteen, with rather too much nose and not enough chin.

'Speck, sir, Joan Speck.'

Dickens kept a straight face. 'You see Joan,' confidential, smiling now, 'I can't very well go back to my chief empty-'anded —'

'Tartar, is 'e?' She obviously knew about tartars. Mrs Black, no doubt.

'A regular terror, so I wonders if you could give me a bit of wot we call information. See, as I said, it's about the murder of the poor capt'n.'

'Downright wicked, sir.'

'It is, Joan, and I wants you to think about your dear, kind mistress, the capt'n's friend. We needs to find the wicked man wot did this.'

'She ain't that kind, cross as two sticks sometimes, but, oh, sir, I ain't sayin' —'

''Course not, Joan — I can tell you're a kind girl. All I wants to know is if there was any strangers about any time on or before the day you got the news about the capt'n.'

Joan thought. Dickens waited patiently while she itemised a pedlar, a muffin man, a cat's meat man she'd never seen before, and an ugly old gypsy woman who'd offered to tell her fortune. At the last item, her eyes opened wide. 'Cor, sir, mighta bin 'im — the murderer — in disguise. Read about that in me penny paper.'

'Lor, Joan — you might be right. I'll tell the chief. You mighta solved the case. Wish I 'ad your brains.' Joan's eyes were wider still. Time to strike. 'An' — er — on the night before you got the news you was all at 'ome?'

'Cook, me an' Mrs Skillett was all 'ere. Mrs Skillett was in a rare takin'.'

'Why was that?'

'Mistress was that sharp with 'er before she went out.'

'Mrs Skillett went out?' Just a simple copper.

'No, sir, Mistress went out ter dine with a Frenchman. Stayed out late, too. Mrs Skillett said she was no better than she should be — mean old cat.'

Dickens looked shocked. 'Oh, my word, Joan, this is a respectable 'ousehold, I 'opes, for your sake.'

'It is, sir, but Mrs Skillett said that mistress was away until the early hours — past one o'clock, she said.'

'And no strangers at all about the 'ouse?'

'No, sir.'

'I'm much obliged to you, Joan. The chief'll be that pleased. 'Ere's two bob — for information received, we say. And don't say nothin' about it to Mrs Black — we don't wants 'em all of a fright. I'm sure I can rely on a clever girl like you. Disguised as a gypsy — blimey, I'd never o' though o' that.'

Joan beamed, pocketing the two bob. What a gent. Nice lookin', too. Old, though — thirty-odd, she'd bet. Dickens did not hear that back-handed compliment. He might have been less inclined to boast.

'How much?' asked Jones with a grin.

'Two bob.'

'Cheaper than Sly — how do you do it?'

'Youthful charm. I was jest a simple copper with a terror fer a chief. She was putty in my 'ands.'

'And?'

'Judith Black was out dining with a Frenchman on the night of the murder. She didn't get home until the early hours — past one o'clock, Joan said.'

'L'Estrange put her in the cab at eleven o'clock in Brook Street — just outside Mivart's. He'd have paid —'

'The cabbie will remember, Sam, bound to. It's a hell of a way to Blackwall — if that's where she went — it would take an hour. And did he wait?'

'She'd not want to look for another cab round Blackwall in the middle of the night — a woman dressed up for dinner. If she intended murder, she'd not ask him to wait — it would be mad —'

'Perhaps she didn't — she just wanted to have it out with him away from prying eyes and too sharp ears at the house. She went on impulse.'

'And the knife? Whose was it?'

'Not hers if it were impulse.'

'The Captain's? Is a knife missing? She'd have got rid of it, surely. Bold and Gaunt found Captain Valentine's knives in a leather pouch — no blood. They asked the midshipman and Charley Gammon about money missing or valuables, but concluded that neither of them would know about the captain's personal possessions. We'd best get Scrap and go to Wapping — just to ask if there was anything said about a missing knife —'

'No stone unturned.'

'Exactly, and then to Brook Street.'

45 THE OLD BAILEY

Eleven identical white handkerchiefs, each with the letter 'J' embroidered in dark blue silk thread. There should have been twelve according to Mrs Black's maid.

A cabman remembered the Frenchie who'd given him an 'alf sovereign and a crown more to take a lady — Frenchie'd called 'er Madame Judith — to Bow Lane near East India Docks. Dint wanter go, but the 'alf soveriegn'd cover the journey back. One way was four bob — decent profit. Blonde lady, he thought, 'ard ter say as she 'ad a bonnet. Extra crown when the lady changes 'er mind — ladies does, he supposed. Took 'er ter a ship called *The Redemption*. Waited until she come out — don't know 'ow long. 'Eard clock at midnight as they arrived — twenty minutes, p'raps.

A missing knife with a jewelled hilt of Indian silver belonging to the captain. Mrs Tallis had told them it was her gift to her brother. Not that they had seen her. Judge Tallis had asked the question for them. Had Louis Valentine used it that night to cut the string to tie up a parcel? Gaunt remembered the parcel — which contained a box. Inside the box was a very large, very beautiful shell — a present for a small boy. And the Reverend Posthumous Fox could still, years later, hear the distant sound of the sea. He thought always of the captain, and of his mother, long dead by then, of a broken heart.

Not that Dickens and Jones knew that then, but Dickens had seen the shell. His anger rose as they looked at the perfectly composed woman who was sitting before them, listening to Jones's recital of the evidence. Dickens was aware of that perfume, and he also saw the faint flush at her neck and something in the pale cheek beating like a clock, but she held the policeman's eyes.

'I know nothing of any knife.'

'You threw it away.'

'No, Superintendent, I never had any knife, and you cannot say I did.'

You could almost admire her composure, thought Jones. The evidence added up, but there was no proof. Her story was perfectly logical. She would be called as a witness at Corneille's trial. She would tell her tale. And there would be a murderer in the dock, a man who had admitted that he had killed twice. It might seem logical to Superintendent Jones that Corneille had no reason to deny the captain's murder. But, to the jury? Corneille had wanted those papers and had killed to get them. Mrs Judith Black, a wealthy shipyard owner, needed no papers. She might have quarrelled with the captain. But murder? A handkerchief? Scent? A missing knife?

Judith Black regarded the policeman coolly as if she read his thoughts. Her face didn't change. Dickens watched the red flush fade. The clock stopped.

'If that is all, Superintendent?'

'It is not, madam. You may anticipate my return.'

'I think not. Good day, Mr Dickens. I look forward to your next book. I am sure it will be an even more fantastic story than the Superintendent's.'

Mrs Skillett showed them out. Jones looked hard at her, but she dropped her eyes.

Judith Black had managed to insult them both. Jones was as angry as Dickens had ever seen him. They walked away.

'She'll get away with it. Corneille will hang for all three — not that I care about him. Corneille's like a gambler who stakes all, and losing, blows his brains out.'

'And she's made of steel — no more pity than the kitchen poker.'

Jones did smile at the comparison. 'Less, but it's no use my railing. We'll not break her.'

And they did not. The police gave their evidence. Silas Cly and Lavender, Lizzie Snook, Ada Pitt, Monsieur L'Estrange and Mademoiselle Marie-Louise du Bois all gave their evidence as to the different identities of Jeremie Corneille. Judge Tallis's appearance created an awed hush. Even Mr Justice Gazebee who was trying the case looked nervous. Sir Napier Moss and Mrs Madeleine Tallis brought a whiff of tropical breeze to the proceedings. There was no frail, tired Black sailor because he could not, probably never would, remember what happened on the night of the murder of Captain Valentine.

In the gallery the gentlemen and ladies of fashion craned forward to pick up every word. Sensation indeed. Extraordinary business about that sugar plantation — forged documents, suicide, syphilis, murder — by God, it was as good as a play! Pretty woman, the judge's wife, but, my word, not a patch on the witness, Mrs Black. Now, that's beauty. A lady shipyard owner, forsooth. Probably a handful. And the French mam'selle — sexy little piece. How distinguished was Judge Tallis. How attractive was Monsieur L'Estrange. How handsome was the prisoner. Such smouldering eyes. What a waste!

It was just as well that Mr Charles Dickens, the great novelist was absent. There was sensation enough for the newspapers. The accused admitted the murder of Peter Best, the agent from

St. Lucia, and the girl, Rosanna Chibb, but he denied the murder of Captain Valentine. The prosecution could not shift him on that point.

Superintendent Samuel Jones of Bow Street was asked if there were any material evidence pertaining to some other person. He told the story of Mrs Judith Black, who had been aboard *The Redemption* and had left her handkerchief behind.

Recalled to the stand, Mrs Black was quite prepared to admit that she had been aboard the ship. She had expected Captain Valentine, the widower of her beloved dead sister-in-law — here she faltered, distressed no doubt at the memory of that death — to come to see her. However, he did not. She had been to dine with Monsieur L'Estrange — *lucky beggar*, thought one old roue, eyeing her slender elegance through his opera glasses. On her way back she had decided, on impulse, to visit him. Yes, there had been a disagreement about the running of the business. Yes, the shares reverted to her at his death. But she had always been fond of him as had her husband, James, now, alas dead. The beauty faltered again, put her hand to her delicate brow. Would she faint? Shame! That policeman trying to frame her. Disgrace! No, she recovered herself. Captain Valentine had been alive when she left him.

The judge reminded the jury that Mrs Judith Black was not on trial. They must consider the evidence pertaining to the accused, Mr Jeremie Corneille, who had been on board *The Redemption* after Mrs Black, and if they were satisfied as to his guilt in all three murders, that verdict they must return.

The verdict was guilty on all three counts. Jeremie Corneille shrugged. 'She is a very beautiful woman,' he observed to Superintendent Jones later, 'and I don't care for myself — I gambled and I lost, but so has Marcus Valentine. Mrs Tallis will turn him out, I hope.' He laughed. 'Still, I can't help liking the idea that you've been outwitted.'

He would hang and Jones found that he didn't care, though he never liked to see a hanging. The vileness of the drunken, brawling spectators always sickened him.

Going out into Old Bailey, he glanced up towards black Newgate where Jeremie Corneille would lodge in the condemned cell before his execution. Then he saw the cab just ahead. Judith Black was getting into it. Mrs Skillett was waiting just behind her. He stepped forward.

'Mrs Skillett.'

She hesitated then stepped forward. Judith Black turned and stepped down from the cab. Mrs Skillett stood between them, looking from one to the other.

'Skillett, the cab is waiting.' Her voice was ice. She did not look at Jones.

It was the word 'Skillett' that did it. *Why, I'm no more to her than a frying pan.* She went towards the policeman.

46: MRS SKILLETT'S EVIDENCE

Charles Dickens was waiting. It was time Sam was back. He had promised to come to tell him the verdict. He paced up and down his office. Wills came in, hovered, and went away. A boy came up with a sealed envelope. It wasn't from Sam. He didn't open it. He gazed out of the window into Wellington Street. He went back to his desk. Then he heard the newsboys calling. The verdict was in.

Jones came in. He looked weary.

'You've been hours. I heard the news. Guilty of all three.'

'Yes, but I've been down to Bow Lane.'

'What — you've found out something?'

'I have. Mrs Skillett —'

'Don't tell me — found a blood-stained knife — with an Indian silver hilt.'

'No, but blood comes into it. Let me start at the beginning. I saw Mrs Black and Mrs Skillett outside the Old Bailey. Mrs Black was getting into a cab. Mrs Skillett was just behind her. And something came to me — how she looked away when we were leaving Mrs Black's. I took a chance and called out to her. Mrs Black called too. She called out, "Skillett". And I saw how the woman's face changed. It was as if she understood that she was nothing to Mrs Black, nothing more than a kitchen pot.'

'But she must have known that before.'

'Not quite — let me tell the tale. She ignored Mrs Black and came with me. I knew then that she knew something. And she did. You remember the little servant told you that on the night Mrs Black went out to dine, she had been particularly sharp with Mrs Skillett in front of the maid — something trivial, but

Mrs Skillett was furious. That's why she told us about James Black. She wanted to pay her back by telling us that Judith Black had rowed with the captain. However, after that evening, Mrs Black apologised to her, told her that she was upset about the captain — it was all a terrible strain. Mrs Black continued to be all sweetness and light — even gave her a present — a dress.'

'A significant dress?'

'Exactly. She said that Mrs Skillett could re-fashion it. It was very good black velvet which could be made into a best day dress. Mrs Skillett put it away. It wasn't until later that she started work on it. Then she noticed the mud on the hem and the stains on the front and back of the skirt —'

'Blood!'

'No, Charles. I think she had had more than dinner with Monsieur L'Estrange.' Dickens raised his eyes. 'Post-mortem evidence — I've seen such stains before. You don't want the details. It was a rape case — horrible.'

'I can imagine. So that's why L'Estrange said "fire and ice". I didn't think he already knew.'

'And I think that's why she went to the captain. She was excited, reckless and filled with a sense of her own power. She was liberated. She wanted to quarrel with him —'

'Perhaps she wanted something else. He turned her down — she would be enraged.'

'And the knife was there ready — Captain Valentine had cut that string.'

'But, the blood?'

'Well, Mrs Skillett thought she could clean up the dress. I don't think she knew what the other stains were, but she said there was a smell when she applied water. There is. I read about it in Taylor's *Medical Jurisprudence*. Anyhow, she set about taking off the bodice, and that's when she found the dried blood on one of the sleeves. She didn't know what it was, so she took the damp cloth to it — it came off red.'

'Why didn't she tell us? She must have been suspicious.'

'She said not — not until what she heard in court. I don't think that she would have told me if I hadn't stopped her and if Mrs Black hadn't called her "Skillett". I'd hardly been friendly to her — I'd seen her off about her insinuations about James Black.'

'And rightly so.'

'And remember, Mrs Black was being decent to her. She'd a comfortable home, decent wages — she's not a woman of high principle, so why rock the boat?'

'So when she told you about the dress?'

'I went to Bow Lane. Mrs Skillett gave me the dress.'

'And you saw the ice queen? I tremble at the thought.'

'I showed her the dress — she knew nothing about any blood. It must have been Skillett's. The same old line: I couldn't prove anything. I said she could make her case at Bow Street. Rogers was there and we took her to a cell. And there she is.'

'Is it enough?'

'It is.'

Judith Isabel Black was tried and found guilty of the murder of Captain Louis Valentine. It might have been manslaughter had she not lied in the witness box at the trial of Jeremie Corneille. She never admitted it. She did not hang. She was expecting a child.

'It surely can't be L'Estrange's,' Dickens said when Jones told him.

'Hardly, she wouldn't know yet.'

'Whose then? Joan Speck told me that Agnes Skillett had said Judith Black was no better than she should be. Perhaps Mrs Skillett knew something — by God, Sam, you don't think —'

'The captain — it had occurred to me. Perhaps there had been something between them. Maybe she told him that night and he didn't believe her — told her it must have been someone else's.'

'Perhaps it was — that doctor she was close to — the one who gave evidence at her husband's inquest — what was his name?'

'Stephens. Could be, if she was still involved with him. She had her sights on Captain Valentine, though.'

'Yes, and I can imagine her rage if he had told her he didn't believe her. So, what do you think will happen to her?'

'Hanging postponed — remember Charlotte Harris, the Bath poisoner? Last year.'

'I do — she was reprieved in the end. Public opinion turned in her favour — there were all those letters and the Quaker, Mary Howett, petitioned the Queen — appealed to the woman's and the mother's heart.'

'It worked. Charlotte Harris was transported. I wasn't sorry. I'm not keen on seeing a woman hanged, not even Mrs Manning.'

'Nor I — it's a barbarous thing. Perhaps Judith Black was a woman wronged after all.'

'We shall never know.'

'The mysteries of the human heart, eh, old 'un.'

47: THE END AND A BEGINNING

Scrap looked at Mr Dickens. *Needs cheerin' up. I knows jest the thing.*

'Read yer book,' he began casually enough, but he couldn't keep the pride from his voice, 'all of it, by meself — sixty-four chapters there is.' As if Dickens didn't know.

Dickens heard the pride. 'Oh, Scrap, that is good news — you have done well.'

'Lot o' chapters. Lot o' words, Mr D. 'Ow many d'yer think? Millions?'

'I don't really know — thousands, more like.'

'Oughter count 'em as yer go — make a note like, in the margin. Then yer could tell folk — impress 'em.'

Dickens didn't laugh. Scrap was a practical sort — he liked to know how things worked. 'I will, I will.'

'Liked it, though —' *Though what?* Dickens wondered — 'it ain't like the *Arabian Nights*. Real I serpose. Feel as if yer knows them folks — that Uriah. Baddun. But Mr Peggotty — shame fer 'im, 'an that storm. Could see that. Yers, I likes it real.'

'I am glad.'

'Started next one?'

'Not yet.'

'I woz thinkin' — murder. Yer could tell about a murder wot a woman done. Like Mrs Black. Mr Jones says she won't 'ang. He dint seem sorry, but I dunno. That captain. Yer said 'e woz a good man, an' that girl, Rosanna. An' there's all them others wot's left. T'ain't fair.'

'No, it isn't, but you know, Scrap, people who do bad things get their comeuppance — usually, in some way or other.'

'Steerforth — serpose 'e deserved 'is whatdyercallit — fate, that's it.'

Having dispensed his wisdom, Scrap departed to find Eleanor and Tom, leaving Dickens to gaze into Jones's fire and think about the closing chapters in this story of murder and its aftermath. He hadn't gone back to Vernon House, but he had been on the river with Shakespeare Tabor to take him to the doors of the Old Bailey for Corneille's trial. The steamer had sailed past Wapping Stairs and the site of the Globe Theatre on the south side. Dickens pointed out the sights until Shakespeare had, at last, spoken of Grace. Her grief, the little boy's bewilderment. Shakespeare had kept the beautiful shell. Perhaps the boy might — later. But Captain Pink had come home safely to knit them all together. That was something.

He thought about Mrs Tallis, who had told her husband that she wanted nothing to do with those papers. Marcus Valentine could have it all. She didn't care. She had thought about her father. Perhaps it was his fault. She remembered her mother's pain, his drinking, the parties and the children who looked like him. She remembered all too vividly how terrified she had been of the shadow of the man with the burning eyes and no nose. Henry Meteyard told Dickens how she had wept for her brother, and for her own growing blindness. 'She doesn't know the cause, I don't think,' Henry Meteyard had told him. 'Damnable,' he said. 'The judge knows — Mrs Tallis told him things about her father of which she had not spoken before. The judge is broken-hearted. He is resigning.'

And Mrs Black's child — to be born in a prison. What would happen there? An orphanage? Perhaps she had relatives who might take the child, though she might not want her family to know. Children were sometimes adopted — if the mother were prepared to give up the child. It might be that Judith Black would not want an illegitimate child. He could imagine that. He ought to do something — find out what she wanted. The child must be cared for.

Jones came in. 'What was the secret?'

'He's read the whole of *David Copperfield* — he's impressed. Sixty-four chapters, he told me.'

Jones laughed. 'He liked it, especially the part about David in the bottle factory. Said he could tell you knew all about it.' He looked down at Dickens quizzically.

Dickens looked back at the man who was honesty incarnate, and whom he would trust with a secret until death. 'I do. I did. I was that boy, except it was Warren's Blacking at Hungerford Stairs — pasting labels on blacking bottles.'

Jones's steady grey eyes looked at him with understanding. *I'll tell him all one day*, Dickens thought.

'Ah, I thought you had steeled yourself to go back there last year when that poor boy was found.'

'I would not have gone if it had not been a child — I couldn't help thinking of myself as a boy there, sometimes larking about on the boats, imagining a future — maybe across the sea. That dead boy had none. I hadn't been near the place for twenty-five years.'

'Scars on the heart?'

'We are all hurt in action, Sam, but we must fight on. Oh, the past, Sam, it casts a very long shadow. Corneille, Marcus Valentine, Mrs Tallis and the captain — even that old man, Adam Valentine, picked up on a Limehouse wharf. He didn't even have a name. What made him?'

They sat together, looking into the fire in the silence that two old friends can bear so easily.

'I must make way to my ancestral halls — they'll think I've gone abroad.'

'I meant to tell you. Bold's men have found Long Jodd. Dead — stabbed in the back in some brawl.'

'How fitting. A death written by a celestial penman in the book of fate.'

'That poet again?'

'No, I wrote it, or said it. I can't remember, but it ain't poetry, Samivel. Poetry's unnat'ral; no man ever talked poetry —'

"'Cept a beadle on boxin' day,' added Jones. He loved *Pickwick Papers* and Tony Weller.

'Or Warren's blackin', or some of them low fellows —' Dickens grinned at Jones — 'never let yourself down to talk poetry, my boy.'

Jones let him out and watched him walk off. He heard the strains of a song. *'I've done with the toil of the seas, ye sailors...'* Smiling, he shut the door as the song died away. Dickens, the voyager, on his own stormy seas. Elizabeth was in the hall. Calm waters.

Dickens walked on into the foggy night. He thought of Limehouse and the river and the marshes where he had found William Lambert. Fog on the marshes, creeping along the yard arms, hovering in the rigging of great ships, drooping on the gunwales of barges and small boats, mingling with the steamer captain's pipe smoke, turning the river to cloud. He thought about a bleak, solitary house; about a woman with rage in her heart; an unborn child whose history might remain a secret; and a man who had died unknown. "Ded". He remembered the word traced on the table in The Old Ship Tavern, and Scrap's idea: 'Yer could tell about a murder wot a woman's done.' *You could*, he thought, *indeed, you could.*

HISTORICAL NOTE

The setting for this story is Limehouse in the East End of London on the River Thames. Limehouse was part of the docklands area which stretched for about ten miles from St. Katharine's Dock, just east of the Tower of London, to the East India Docks at Blackwall. Dickens knew the area well and Limehouse and Wapping are described in the novels *Dombey and Son, Our Mutual Friend*, and *The Mystery of Edwin Drood*. He also wrote about the docklands in his journalism; in an essay in *The Uncommercial Traveller*, Dickens gives a wonderfully vivid impression of the teeming, violent life there in *Bound for the Great Salt Lake*.

The opening section begins with the phrase 'Down by the Docks' where there are the crowded lodging houses, the eating houses, and the public houses in which the vast number of sailors gather to sing and dance with the wild girls in their gaudy dresses, drink their grog, spend their pay, pawn their pewter watches and their clothes. This is where 'anyone drunk will quarrel with anybody sober and everyone else will have a hand in it.' Murder can happen in a moment.

Dickens loved the river and the sea. He was born on Feb 7th, 1812 in Portsmouth where his father, John Dickens, worked for the Naval Pay Office. When later, the family moved to Chatham, the navy and the sea were still very much part of his life.

Dickens's full name was Charles John Huffam Dickens — Huffam after his godfather, Christopher Huffam, who was a friend of his father's and a prosperous sailmaker and ship's chandler in Limehouse in the East End of London. Huffam had contracts with the navy, which is how he must have met John Dickens. When the Dickens family moved to London and John Dickens sank into debt, it was Dickens's mother's idea that she would open a school for young ladies. Her hope was that Mr Huffam's connections with the East India Trade might lead to well-off merchants sending their daughters to her school. None of them did and the school closed before it actually opened, and John Dickens went to the debtors' prison, the Marshalsea.

Dickens's father took him often to Huffam's fine house in Church Row by St Anne's Church, and it is recorded that the young Dickens often sang for his godfather's friends; a favourite song was *The Cat's Meat Man*. He spent time in Limehouse exploring the warehouses, the canal, the river shore and all the nooks and crannies of this place of narrow alleys and teeming shops full of sailor's gear and marine instruments — all these sights are recorded in *Dombey and Son*, for Captain Cuttle lives down there at Brig Place 'on the brink of a little canal', and Walter Gay who visits him dreams of 'being an Admiral of all the colours of the dolphin'. In *Our Mutual Friend*, 'Rogue Riderhood dwelt deep in Limehouse Hole, among the riggers, and the mast, oar and block makers, and the boat builders and the sail lofts.' The Huffams had grown-up children in Dickens's childhood time, so I invented Kit Penney to be his playmate acting out the adventures of Robinson Crusoe and exploring the marshes of the Isle of Dogs. I'm sure he might have found such a boy to keep him company.

Limehouse and Wapping stirred his imagination, as did his boyhood reading. My inspiration for Simic Kaprillian came from my reading of Dickens in which *The Arabian Nights* and *The Tales of the Genii* are often mentioned. Dickens loved all these tales of magic and spells and would have been fascinated by Kaprillian's offices and all his curiosities.

John Dickens was in failing health by 1851 and living with Dickens's mother, Elizabeth, at the house of a doctor in Keppel Street, paid for by Dickens, of course, who was also supporting his younger brother, Fred, who was always in debt like his father. His youngest brother, Augustus, was a burden too, finally abandoning his blind wife and running off to America, leaving Charles to look after his disabled wife and children. Dickens had an uneasy relationship with his mother. It was she who wanted to send Charles back to the blacking factory at Hungerford Stairs when the family came out of the Marshalsea Prison. She was being sensible, perhaps, thinking about the extra money her twelve-year-old son brought in, but Dickens couldn't forgive her. He felt that he would be left there forever, and he just wanted to go to school. Years later, he told his first biographer, John Forster, 'I never can forget that she was warm for my being sent back.'

Debt seemed to have plagued the Dickens family, and even the prosperous Christopher Huffam died insolvent in 1839, his business having failed. There is no record that Dickens kept up with the Huffams in Limehouse, but there is a letter from 1870 addressed to Loretta Huffam, Christopher's daughter. She seems to have been applying for charity. Of course, Dickens supported her application.

Judith Black who owns most of the Black shipyard in Blackwall is based on the true stories of various women in Helen Doe's book *Enterprising Women and Shipping in the Nineteenth Century* (The Boydell Press, 2009). Women were employed in various sea ports in the rope-making trade, sail cloth manufacture, the coopering business, ships' chandlers, marine stores, the clothes trade, even in the mast making business, and there were 34 female ship owners, according to Helen Doe's research, including several in King's Lynn from where Judith originates. Mary Ann Barnard of King's Lynn, on whom I based Judith's mother, owned two ships and was the managing owner in charge of all the accounts and shore-based business. In the novel, Judith learns from her mother how to run a shipping business. Spinsters, wives and widows invested money in ships too, buying shares. Helen Doe points out that women in maritime communities had to be independent, given that marrying a sailor meant separation for very long periods, and many were left widowed with young children and were expected to cope. Mrs Aurora Penney comes to mind here — she takes over her husband's marine business until Kit is old enough.

I was astonished by the variety of businesses run by women when I scoured the *London Post Office Trade Directory* (1841). Many milliners, dressmakers, and shopkeepers, of course, but these include pawnbrokers, booksellers — even bookbinders — stationers, newsagents, and a printer. There were tobacconists, a few butchers, plenty of bakers, even a candle wax and tallow chandler. There were a chair maker, a boot-tree maker, a shoemaker and a bootmaker, even a coach maker, and Mrs Eliza Speed owned a livery stables in Blackman Street. Several ironmongers are listed, two fish mongers and two cheese mongers. Some women were designated as merchants: quite a few coal merchants and a stone merchant. There was even a lady plumber, and, appropriately, in Newgate Street, Mrs Logan, a locksmith. Mrs Eliza Le Cocq was a glazier in Finsbury Square, and Mrs Susan Harris a whitesmith (polishing or burnishing iron and steel) in Bowling Square. Manufacturers included Mrs Mary Hayward, a brass manufacturer in Drury

Lane, Mrs Garrett manufacturing toys in Bateman Row, and Ann Rider and her son making patent hats in Red Cross Street.

And they were not all married women or widows; there were a good many Misses: for example, Miss Lucy Powell was a cupper — cupping involved the placing of a glass or cup on the skin for medical purposes. Sometimes the skin was pierced, and blood then cupped. The treatment was meant to ease pain, relieve blood pressure and to have various other health benefits. Miss Manley was a bootmaker; Miss Robinson a coppersmith in Seven Dials; Miss Treluddra owned a turnery and warehouse; and Miss Sarah Walker was an undertaker.

Many women owned and ran warehouse businesses: Mrs Brown had a large concern in Great Carter Lane, dealing in oil and colours for artists; there were warehouses for china, earthenware, linen, artificial flowers, Italian goods — all run by women. Mrs Hollingworth ran a furniture broking business at 3, 4 and 9 in Broker's Alley, Drury Lane dealing in second-hand furniture in what sounds like three shops. Charlotte Pollard and company were artificial florists in Golden Square. Elizabeth Butler was a wine merchant in Water Lane and Mrs Sadler a bottle dealer in Upper Bryanstone Street. Elizabeth Collings, Dickens's wine merchant, traded at number 30, Seething Lane.

Round the dock areas, women were running businesses too. Mrs Eliza Stevenson was a cooper (barrel maker) in Dock Street; many women ran pubs, including Mrs Brendel who had The Artichoke in Blackwall, and a lady ran The Angel off Radcliffe Highway — these were some of the roughest areas. As formidable, perhaps, as Dickens's Miss Abbey Potterson who runs The Grapes, called The Six Jolly Fellowship Porters in *Our Mutual Friend* and tells Rogue Riderhood that he's not welcome. Dickens says of Abbey 'that a man must have drunk himself mad drunk indeed if he thought that he could contest a point with her.' Mrs Gladwell was a mast maker in Limehouse, and so was Mrs Haynes at Pickle Herring Wharf. Mrs Martha Unite was a ropemaker. Many women were slopsellers, dealing in old clothes, especially for sailors, and Mrs Shipway worked at Dockhead as a tobacconist and pipe-maker — plenty of custom round there.

So Rosanna Chibb's ambitions are not so far-fetched after all. Granted I didn't find a female marine instrument maker, but I found plenty of lady jewellers, an ivory turner, a goldsmith in Clerkenwell, a gold beater in Warwick Square, a glass watch maker, and Mrs Keat, who was a watch and clockmaker in Banner Street.

Alas, I didn't find the occupation of Mrs Bastard who lived in Long Acre. What a legacy from her husband! Perhaps she lived a retired life.

A NOTE TO THE READER

Dear Reader,

Setting plays a very important part in these stories in creating the atmosphere and the sense of realism that I want my readers to experience. It's important to be historically accurate about the places I name, and I find old maps very useful in tracking Dickens through London from his home at number one Devonshire Terrace near Regent's Park, down to Wellington Street where the office of his journal, *Household Words* was situated, to Bow Street, of course, and to any place where a body or witnesses are to be found.

The setting for this novel is Limehouse on the River Thames in the docklands area. It starts at St. Katharine's Dock, just east of the Tower of London, where yachts are moored now and there is a Dickens pub and some of the old warehouses, including the Ivory House. The docklands ended at the East India Docks at Blackwall where Judith Black's shipyard is located, and the West India Docks on the Isle of Dogs where Dickens and Jones go to find William Lambert.

I went down to Limehouse on a freezing April day to have a look at the locations where I intended to send my detectives to investigate the murder of Captain Louis Valentine. *The Topographical Dictionary of London* (1831) gave me directions to Salmon's Place where Mr and Mrs Cly live in their curiously narrow lodging house — a house I saw somewhere when I was following Charles Dickens for an earlier book. I had to move the narrow house because the Clys have to live in Limehouse.

The topographical dictionary told me that Salmon's Place is 'about a furlong on the left-hand side of Salmon's Lane, going from the Commercial Road.' I got off the bus in Commercial

Road and looked at the windows above the grimy shop fronts. Dickens would have seen some of those. I found Salmon's Lane quite easily (now Salmon Lane) and I looked down every left turn, but Salmon's Place had gone, I guessed, or perhaps it had changed its name. I do know that Alfred Hitchcock lived in Salmon's Lane and thinking of *Psycho* when I was in a rather dark and narrow alleyway made me turn round sharpish. You'd think I'd have more courage — after all, I am writing about murder.

I walked back towards St. Anne's Church, the clock tower of which I could see from where I was standing. I came to a bridge across the canal, the very bridge where Dickens meets Captain Pye in the novel, and I looked down into the murky water and saw bubbles and thought about Dickens imagining a body rising to the surface.

It was very cold, so I walked back to St. Anne's Church, designed by Nicholas Hawksmoor and finished in 1724, and very fine it is. Dickens will stand here at the gate, looking in, and thinking about the unknown drowned ships' boys who are buried here. And he must have stood here in reality, on these very cobbles, for I got to the top of Newell Street, which was Church Lane where Dickens's godfather, Christopher Huffam, lived at number five, Church Row. The house is not here now, but I can imagine it; there's a very fine row of eighteenth-century houses still standing, one for sale at over a million pounds.

I walked down towards Three Colt Street. Dickens must have come this way, too, for it leads down to the river. I paused at Three Colt Street where Rosanna Chibb will live at Five Bells Place, which I found in the topographical dictionary. It's still there, though it is Five Bells Alley now, and there's the pub, The Five Bells and Blade Bone — bells summon up the ship's bells, heard from the river, and the ship *Redemption*. The words "blade bone" were added in 1845 — a butcher nearby, perhaps?

I turned right into Narrow Street and continued to The Grapes Public House which Dickens used as The Six Jolly Fellowship Porters in *Our Mutual Friend* and where Dickens and Jones will meet Inspector Bold to discuss murder. Dickens certainly drank here — there are his books on the shelves and pictures of him; it doesn't appear to have changed much. Dickens was right: 'It had outlasted, and clearly would yet outlast, many a better-trimmed building.' He must have walked across these wooden floors — like walking across the deck of a ship, and the river is just outside the window as Dickens described it.

There is not even one jolly fellowship porter, and Miss Abbey Potterson is not at the bar to serve Purl or Flip or Dog's Nose, but there is hot coffee and a hot meal of sole and chips and Dickens looking at me from the wall. He looks a bit sceptical, one eye slightly amused. I wonder what he's thinking — *Detective Dickens, forsooth*.

I hope that you are thinking that you enjoyed reading the novel, and I thank you for taking the time to do so. Reviews are really important to authors, and if you enjoyed the novel, it would be great if you could spare a little time to post a review on **Amazon** and **Goodreads.** Readers can connect with me online, on **Facebook (JCBriggsBooks)**, **Twitter (@JeanCBriggs)**, and you can find out more about the books and Charles Dickens via my website: **jcbriggsbooks.com,** where you will also find Mr Dickens's A-Z of murder — all cases of murder to which I found a Dickens connection.

Thank you!

Jean Briggs

Sapere Books is an exciting new publisher of brilliant fiction and popular history.

To find out more about our latest releases and our monthly bargain books visit our website:
saperebooks.com

Printed in Great Britain
by Amazon

17563787R00212